Dirty Like Me

JAINE DIAMOND

DREAM
WARP
PUBLISHING Ltd.

Dirty Like Me
Jaine Diamond

Copyright © 2016 Jaine Diamond

This book is a work of fiction. Names, characters, places and incidents are the product of the author's imagination or are used fictitiously. Any resemblance to actual events, locales, organizations or persons is coincidental.

Alternate edition cover and interior design by DreamWarp Publishing Ltd.

Published by DreamWarp Publishing Ltd.
www.jainediamond.com

BOOKS BY JAINE DIAMOND

CONTEMPORARY ROMANCE (Interconnected)

DIRTY SERIES

Dirty Like Me

Dirty Like Us

Dirty Like Brody

A Dirty Wedding Night

Dirty Like Seth

Dirty Like Dylan

Dirty Like Jude

Dirty Like Zane

PLAYERS SERIES

Hot Mess

Filthy Beautiful

Sweet Temptation

Lovely Madness

Flames and Flowers

VANCITY VILLAINS SERIES

Handsome Devil

Rebel Heir

Wicked Angel

Irresistible Rogue

EROTIC ROMANCE

DEEP DUET

DEEP

DEEPER

Dirty Like Me

CHAPTER ONE

Katie

I DIDN'T MEAN to crash the meeting.

I fully intended to knock before entering, like a civilized person. Max had other plans. For one thing he was a dog, and for another he knew we were dropping in on my best friend, Devi. Devi was a total babe, and Max totally dug hot babes. One glimpse of the door to her office, which was ajar, and he streaked past the front desk, big wet tail wagging, startling a couple of Devi's coworkers.

"On it!" I blurted, diving after him, but he'd already hip-checked the door open. By the time I caught up, my wayward black lab was shaking off his rain-wet fur in a flurry of excitement, spraying Devi and the three other people standing in her office. I made a mad grab for his collar.

I missed.

Hovering awkwardly on the threshold, I clutched the tin of miniature pies I'd been unpacking in the lobby and mouthed a *Sorry!* at my BFF.

"Hey, Katie!" Devi smiled brightly, tussling Max's ears with a friendly pat. "Max! Aren't you wet." She shot me a look that said something like, *Nice to see you, but what the hell?*

"Um… hi," I said. Devi was a talent agent; her agency repped models and actors, so I was used to running into beautiful people in her office. Though I didn't usually crash her meetings with my dog, wet and disheveled in my paint-stained jeans. "Sorry about my dog. Come on, Max." I gave Max the *get-your-furry-butt-over-here* look, a look he knew well but completely ignored, since Devi and her pretty female guest were now loving him up.

"No problem. We were just finishing up." Devi gestured for me to stay put, though I really just wanted to grab my delinquent dog and get the hell out of there. I felt ridiculously conspicuous in my white tank top, which I'd regretted wearing about two seconds after it started raining. As Devi wrapped things up with her guests, I took stock. Yep. Purple bra totally showing through my now-transparent tank.

Great.

Devi was shaking hands with the built dude in the short-sleeve button-down, and I noticed some tattoos on his muscular arm, but that was about it. My attention had already snapped to the other guy as some unconscious, primal part of me registered his hotness before the rest of me could catch up.

Plus, he was staring at me.

Or at least, my see-through shirt.

Devi strode to the door to see her guests out and I stepped aside, holding my tin of pies, trying to disappear into the wall. He was coming at me. Tall and broad-shouldered, his thick, dark hair in unkempt waves that gave him a decidedly just-fucked look, like some lucky bitch had just clawed through it. Totally worked on him. He wore a fitted black T-shirt, which I swore I could see his well-defined abs through, and ripped, dark jeans molded to his long, hard thighs…

My brain must have short-circuited, because my gaze got stuck on the package in the front of those jeans. When I looked up, his molasses-dark eyes were locked on mine. He stopped a foot in front of me and stared.

Fair enough, since he'd just caught me checking him out like a horny perv.

I cleared my throat, which was suddenly tight. "Pie?" I fumbled with the tin, lifting it between us, blocking his view of my bra. "They're cherry."

He glanced in the tin, where two dozen hand-crafted miniature pies were neatly arranged, my signature cherry filling peeking out through the crisscrossed pastry tops. Then his gaze lifted to mine again. He had the longest, darkest eyelashes I'd ever seen on a man. High cheekbones. Luscious, kissable lips. Strong jaw shadowed with dark stubble, like he hadn't shaved in days. And those beautiful dark eyes, smoldering at me and making me blush, big time.

"Maybe another time," he said, the deep, sexy rumble of his voice stirring parts of my anatomy that hadn't been stirred in a crazy long time. I noticed something tick against his teeth as he gave me a faint yet heart-stopping smile. A piercing?

No. Candy.

Cinnamon. His breath smelled like cinnamon.

I glanced over at Devi. She and the others were standing in the doorway, staring at us.

Max, ever the opportunist, snuffled into the hand of the hottest guy in the world as I stood there, dazed. I noticed the big, silver rings on his fingers as he stroked Max's velvety ears, and the tattoo on his wrist, a pair of dark wings wrapped around his strong forearm.

"Come on, Max." I pulled Max back so he could get by. "Sorry. He, um, likes you." Normally Max preferred the ladies, but I could hardly fault his taste.

The hottest guy on the planet said nothing. He didn't really get a chance before the ever-charming Devi intervened and herded all three of them out the door.

I set my tin of mini pies on Devi's desk, feeling kind of wind-blown, like I'd just stepped in out of a storm rather than a light Vancouver mist. Really, a girl should be warned before a guy that hot gave her the most thorough eye-fucking of her life.

Did I really offer him pie?

Cherry pie?

Ugh. So fucking smooth.

I tidied Max into an obedient ball on the rug beneath the desk and willed him to stay put as Devi returned, shutting the door behind herself.

"I know," she gushed. "So fucking hot, right?"

Um, yeah. But I knew better than to answer that honestly. The last time I casually inquired about a hot guy I glimpsed at my best friend's office, she took it upon herself to hook the two of us up on a blind date. And when a hot male model gets set up with someone he assumes will be some equally hot female model, but turns out to be just some regular girl, things do not go well. For the regular girl.

Luckily, Devi didn't even wait for my response. "Jesus, Katie." She strode over, a takeout coffee cup in each hand. "What the hell?"

"I know. Max just bolted for your office—"

"Not that." She gave me a no-contact air hug, then glanced down at my chest. "You look like a sexy drowned rat. Heard of an umbrella?"

"My hands were full."

Devi scowled. "Do not tell me you rode your skateboard in the rain. I hate it when you do that."

I rolled my eyes a little. My glamorous best friend had never understood my love affair with my skateboard. Of course, she drove a luxury SUV her parents bought for her and lived in her own suite in their giant house, so she didn't exactly relate to my thriftiness. In the case of my preferred mode of transportation, she just saw it as risky behavior. Unfortunately, my big sister agreed with her. "Becca already gave me the lecture when I stopped to pick up the coffees."

Devi set my cherry-vanilla latte on the desk with a little *harrumph* and eyed the mini pies with suspicion. "You've been baking."

"Just some pies." I flopped into one of the chairs facing the desk, which still had hot guy pheromones all over it. I sucked back a deep breath, savoring the lingering scents of cinnamon, leather, and the faint, intoxicating musk of a warm, clean male.

"Katie."

"What?" I glanced up; Devi was studying me accusingly.

"*Just* pie?"

"And some scones."

She raised a slender eyebrow.

"And a few cookies," I added.

"What flavor?"

"Chocolate chip."

"Uh-huh."

"And pecan butter ripple."

"I knew it. What's wrong?"

"Nothing."

"Bullshit. You look…" Devi looked at me sideways. "Horny."

"I am not horny," I lied. Who wouldn't be after getting eye-fucked like that? My head was still dangerously deprived of blood.

Devi sat down behind her desk. She looked gorgeous, as always, her dark hair smoothed out, flawless cappuccino skin set off with velvety red lipstick, sleeveless black top tricked out with a chunky necklace and leopard-print leggings, all of which she'd probably worn specifically for the meeting she'd just had. Fashion was just one of the many ways Devi built rapport with people.

I, on the other hand, considered myself coordinated if I managed to pull on matching shoes.

"Spill." She gathered up the slew of model photos that littered the surface of her desk, stuffing them into a file folder. "I've got like ten minutes before my next meeting. What's up?"

"Nothing. We just miss you." It was true; my best friend had been pulling a lot of overtime, which was great for her career but not so great for me.

"I miss you guys, too." She reached beneath the desk and pet Max. "But that's not the reason you busted in here."

"Again, sorry. Just wanted to talk to you. I figured this may be my only chance to do it face-to-face."

"Talk about…?"

I took a breath and sighed. "I think… I may be ready."

Devi lit up, then caught herself and cooled her reaction. "Oh?" She was trying really hard not to jump for joy. It was kind of cute.

"I know you've been telling me this for a long time. I just had to get there myself."

"For sure."

"For so long I just wasn't ready, you know? And then maybe I was, sort of, but I was scared. And then it just got easy to keep avoiding it. But now…"

"Now?" Devi fluttered her dark eyelashes hopefully.

I sipped my latte. "Are you sure you have time for this?"

"Hell, yes."

"Okay. I think I need to go on a date."

"Halle-fucking-lujah!"

"Alright. Ugh. I'm so bad at this." Just saying it out loud to Devi made me nervous. Especially when she got all sparkly about it.

"What? Dating?" Devi sipped her coffee, waving a manicured hand in the air. "You always say that, but you never date. How do you get good at anything unless you practice?" She waggled her eyebrows, making me grin.

When it came to dating, Devi was a total pro. I, on the other hand, was pretty much a born-again virgin, more or less by default.

"You're going to meet someone who blows your lid off, babe. You just have to put yourself out there." Devi's cell phone buzzed and she glanced at the screen. "Oh! I should take this." She picked up. "Hey, Maggie!"

I wandered over to the stack of magazines on the coffee table. These days, I was getting used to sharing Devi with her other life. Just one more hint from the universe that I needed to get a life of my own.

I sank onto the couch and flipped through a French Vogue. Max came to lay at my feet and I toed his soft fur with my sneaker. Devi was such a natural with people. She'd forgotten more hot men than I'd ever dreamed of meeting. The concept of *not* putting herself out there wouldn't even cross her mind. But for me, the whole idea of exposing myself to rejection and failure made my stomach churn.

Still, she was right. I wasn't about to meet guys sitting at home with my dog.

Not like I hadn't tried.

"Okay? Oh. Okay…"

I glanced up at the odd tone in Devi's voice. Bad news? Her eyes met mine, but I couldn't quite read the look in them.

"Mm-hmm. Right. Okay… no, no problem. I totally understand." I went back to my magazine while she finished up the conversation, which was brief and consisted of a lot of "Totally," and "No problem," and "Of course."

I looked up again when Devi hung up. She was staring at her

phone, like it might somehow explain to her what just happened. "Well. That was interesting."

"A client?"

"No. Maggie Omura. You just met her. Kind of."

"Oh." Right. The pretty dark-haired waif with the hot guy and the even hotter guy. "Max liked her. Didn't you, Max?" At the sound of his name, Max woofed contentedly.

Devi leaned back in her chair, assessing me. "You also just met Jesse Mayes, which you're playing it awfully cool about."

"Who?" I slurped whipped cream from the top of my coffee.

Devi sighed. "Honestly, Katie. Are you kidding me? Jesse Mayes?"

"What? That guy who just left?" I pretended to be enraptured with a deodorant ad in my magazine. "One of your models?"

"I wish. Jesse Mayes is only one of the hottest rock stars in the world and as an incredibly cool young person you should really know what I'm talking about."

I assumed she added the "incredibly cool young person" comment since last week we got into an argument when she said my apartment looked like an old lady lived in it. And after I'd rigidly defended my music collection (on vinyl), my home phone (on a cord), and my TV (which didn't exist), I realized she had a point, and maybe she was just scared of losing her best friend to spinsterhood at the age of twenty-four, which was probably a realistic fear.

I gave her my best stink eye anyway. "So?" Then I went back to my magazine, because in truth I had no idea who Jesse Mayes was. Other than the hottest guy in the known universe.

"So," she said, "I thought you liked Dirty."

"Dirty what?"

"The band. Dirty."

"Oh. Who doesn't?" I looked up again. "You mean, he's in

that band?" I knew music. Kind of prided myself on it. But people? People were Devi's domain.

"He's their lead guitarist. And he sings like a sexy beast."

That, I could believe.

"He just put out a solo album and they're shooting a music video in town. The woman they cast to star in it with him as his music video girlfriend bailed." Devi tipped her pretty nose in the air. "Not from our agency, of course."

"Of course," I said, but she'd lost me somewhere around *sexy beast*. I was now trying to recall every Dirty song I knew, and imagining how Jesse Mayes would look playing guitar, and singing under a spotlight all covered in sweat.

"Anyway." Devi sipped her coffee, eying me over the rim. "Long story short. I met Maggie at a party a while back. She works with Dirty as the assistant to their manager, you know, the dude with all the tattoos."

Uh-huh. Hottie number two.

"She's involved in a lot of their publicity and whatnot and naturally we've been in touch."

"Naturally."

"She called me up last night. They're looking to recast, but they're having some issues getting Mr. Rock Star to commit to what he wants. Maggie knew they'd be in the neighborhood today, so she took the opportunity to haul his ass in here and have him choose one of our girls."

"That'll be some lucky girl." I kept flipping through the magazine, but I didn't really see the pages. I was too busy trying to picture Jesse Mayes with his shirt off.

"Exactly. They just hired one of our models."

"Well that's good for you, right?"

"It's great for me. Katie, pay attention." Devi stood, came around her desk and took the Vogue from my hands. "They changed their minds. They just called to drop her."

"Oh. Well, that's shitty." Why was Devi all up in my face about it?

She dropped the Vogue on the coffee table with a resounding splat. "They dropped her because they want *you*."

CHAPTER TWO

Jesse

IF THERE WAS one thing I hated about being a rock star, it was shooting music videos.

They were tedious as hell, or more specifically, limbo. It was all hurry up and wait, all fucking day.

They were also total bullshit. I'd spent half the morning shooting take after take after take. Fake singing with my guitar, fake singing with my shirt off, fake singing with my guitar with my shirt off. And fake was a total fucking turn off.

I'd spent the rest of the morning on my phone in one of Brody's spare bedrooms while the wardrobe girls dressed me up like a damn doll. Maggie had even gotten in on it, popping up between a couple of wardrobe racks with a pair of jeans that looked exactly like every other pair I'd tried on.

Fuck it.

I dropped the jeans I was wearing, and this time let my underwear go along with them. I kicked the jeans off my feet, stood there buck naked and said, "Make this one count, ladies."

Maggie took it like the pro she was and handed over the jeans with a frown of disapproval. One of the wardrobe girls seemed to have swallowed her tongue and got busy looking anywhere but at my dick. The other one almost said something as I stepped into the jeans, commando, and zipped them up. Almost.

"Perfect." I turned to leave.

"Jesse!" Maggie called after me. "We still need a shirt."

"Whatever." I yanked on my T-shirt as I went. "I'll wear whatever."

I headed downstairs, into the fray, waving off the half-dozen people who wanted to talk to me along the way. Any one of them probably would've fetched me anything I wanted, but I was already tired of being poked, primped and waited on.

All I really wanted was to get this day fucking over with and get down to L.A..

There were way too many people crowded into Brody's place. Film crew, band management, security, wardrobe, makeup, and the many models that had been hired for the shoot were making the massive house feel like the bus we used on our first Dirty tour —totally overrun with hangers-on.

The house was strewn with lights, camera equipment, and all kinds of crap that was being used for the morning-after scene in the living room. It might've just been easier to actually throw a party and let everyone trash the house rather than make it look like the aftermath of a shaker. Zane had suggested it; no surprise Brody vetoed that one.

I passed the living room, where they were setting up for that scene, crew prepping a camera on the dolly track. Zane was in there, the only women in the room swarming around him like bees on a honeycomb, dabbing at him with makeup sponges and finger-styling his beach-blond hair while he ate a bowl of something with chopsticks.

Zane and Dylan, two of my bandmates in Dirty, were doing cameos in the video, the second single from my debut solo album. Since the album was called *Sunday Morning*, Brody had asked me what I'd be doing on an ideal Sunday morning. I said, "Fuck-ing," he ran with it, and the concept for the video was born. Zane and Dylan would be passed out in the living room in the after-math of a party along with a bunch of babes, which would take about two seconds to shoot since all they had to do was lie around. Meanwhile me and the model that was playing my girl-friend would be getting it on, which would probably take hours to shoot, since I had to fake-sing the entire song to her while we went at it and the camera probably had to catch it from a billion different angles.

I was bored already.

I stalked into the dining room, which was mostly empty. Just a bunch of hot chicks fussing over their reflections in the big wall mirror and making goo-goo eyes at Dylan, who was in the adjoining music room, kicked back behind the drum kit in his kilt, talking to Brody, eating a sushi cone and being characteristically laid-back, borderline oblivious, about the attention.

I was about to dive into the sushi myself when the lone girl on the other side of the table snagged my eye.

She looked different from the other girls loitering around the house. For one thing, she was short for a model. The other girls were also completely ignoring the food. This one was hovering over it, looking adorably confused in her oversized bathrobe.

"You alright?" I took one of the avocado rolls she'd been eying and popped it, whole, into my mouth.

She looked up at me, and her already big eyes went wide. They were a pretty blue-green, a nice contrast to her dark hair. She looked familiar, maybe. But then again, I'd spent the last month having hundreds of photos of models shoved in my face.

"Um… I'm just not sure what to eat? They gave me a straw for my drink, to protect the lipstick, and the robe to protect my clothes." She held up the water bottle she was holding, a straw poking out the top. "But I'm not sure how to eat without destroying this." She made a sweeping gesture to indicate her face.

"Eat what you want," I told her. "They'll retouch it."

She nibbled on her bottom lip, unsure.

"Eating your lip will probably do worse."

She let go of the lip and blushed a little. I could see the color on her cheeks even through the high-def makeup they'd lacquered onto her already flawless skin. She smiled a little. "Thanks for the pro tip."

"And you've got lipstick on your teeth," I said, popping a cherry tomato into my mouth.

"Shit." She ran her tongue over her front teeth.

"If you're really worried about it, have some of these." I put the bowl of cherry tomatoes in front of her. "They don't even need to touch your lips." I winked at her and she blushed again.

This girl was too cute. Unfortunately she was fangirling at me big time.

Then again... I hadn't fucked a groupie in a hell of a long time.

"Hey, Jesse." Maggie walked in. "They're ready for your next shot. Then it's time for your scene with Katie."

"Who?"

"Katie." Maggie looked from me to the girl in the robe and waved a thumb at the girl. "Your girlfriend du jour. You met her at the agent's office."

I looked her over again, slowly—what I could see of her in the bathrobe. "What happened to the blonde?"

Maggie looked annoyed. "You didn't want the blonde, remember?" I did remember. I just liked messing with Maggie. "You said she was, quote, 'forgettable,' as soon as we left the office."

"Because I had no idea which one you chose." It was true. I'd pretty much been writing song lyrics in my head the entire time she and Brody perused the models on offer.

Maggie's eyes narrowed. "I knew it." She made a gesture toward the girl in the robe again, who was standing there like a fawn caught in the headlights of a Mack truck. "Good thing we picked someone else. Katie. Remember?"

I stared at the girl, and finally it came to me.

Girl in the wet shirt.

She'd looked different then. No makeup. Damp hair. Kind of flushed.

Unintentionally sexy.

Now she looked awkward-sexy.

Maggie made a noise of exasperation. "Don't mind him," she said to Katie. "He's been in a bad mood. For like a year."

"I remember." I held Katie's gaze, ignoring Maggie. "Cherry pie."

Her cheeks turned pink again. Damn, she was cute.

This shoot just got a hell of a lot more interesting.

"There's pie?" Zane walked in, and it took all of two seconds for his gaze to find Katie. And stay there.

Great.

"Who're you?" he demanded.

"Um, Katie," she said.

Zane, being Zane, went all the way around the very long table, took her hand, and kissed it. "Sweet to meet you, Katie. I'm Zane." He gave her his ultra-intense, ice-blue-eyed Viking stare down; the one that generally got him any pussy he wanted.

"Cool," Katie said. She stared at Zane, because that's what women did.

"Alright," Maggie said, rounding the table and hauling Katie away. Maggie was one of the few women I'd ever met who was immune to Zane's bullshit. "Don't mind Zane. He's like that with everyone."

Not everyone. Just women he wanted to fuck.

When the girls were gone, Zane looked over at me. He froze on the receiving end of the look I gave him. "What?"

I turned to leave, just as one of the wardrobe girls came in with a shirt for me.

"Not that one," I said, and walked out.

CHAPTER THREE

Katie

I'D NEVER FELT SO out of my element in my life.

The thing was, I'd been sitting on the sidelines of my own life for so long that I'd kind of forgotten what my element *was*.

Which was how I'd ended up here. I'd let my best friend convince me, Katie Bloom, regular girl with not one shred of modeling or acting experience, that I could play super-cool girl-friend-of-a-rock-star in Jesse Mayes' hot new music video.

What the fuck was I thinking?

Today was the first time in my life I had legit palm sweat.

I rubbed my palms on the plush robe, my hands tucked into the pockets as I followed Maggie through the massive house she said belonged to Jesse's manager, Brody, the guy with the tattoos from Devi's office. I'd met him for real this time, and he had this intensely sexy business-meets-rock-'n'-roll thing going on that made me all tongue-tied. I was relieved when the incredibly nice Maggie rescued me from that conversation. Same, when she did it again with Zane. Because what the hell would I say to Zane Traynor, the most charismatic frontman to rock a pair of leather pants since Jim Morrison?

Yeah, I'd hit up Google since getting hired for this thing.

A lot.

Dirty's lead singer had the body of a love god and a voice he'd clearly sold his soul to the devil for, and yes he was gorgeous, but I only stared at him because it was that or get sucked into eye contact with Jesse Mayes again.

And that was a serious threat to my sanity.

When the man looked at me, things happened to my body that I could only describe as temporary but all-consuming hormonal insanity. It was dizzying, thrilling and terrifying, and I needed to get my shit together before we shot this scene. I was supposed to be all cool and girlfriend-like, hanging out by his side at a party or whatever, not swooning like a pent-up virgin who might combust if he bumped shoulders with me.

It didn't help that he'd brought all his larger-than-life friends to the shoot.

Sure, I'd seen pictures of all the members of Dirty on the web. But since this shoot was for Jesse's solo album, I didn't expect Zane or Dirty's drummer, Dylan Cope, to be here.

What the hell *did* I expect?

Maybe some kind of sterile sound stage with an efficient, all-business film crew calling the shots?

This felt more like a party, people crammed into every room of Brody's architectural marvel of a house, which was in North Vancouver, up the mountainside in Canyon Heights, and probably cost high seven figures.

The film crew looked a lot like what I'd always thought roadies would look like, the roadies looked like criminals, the security guys looked like straight-up bikers, and the management team, which consisted of Brody, Maggie, and various underlings, looked like rock stars.

Jesse, Zane, and Dylan? They looked like something out of a Greek goddess's masturbation fantasy.

I'd never met people like this in real life.

When I'd first arrived, Maggie had mercifully plucked me from a roomful of women who looked like they'd come straight from backstage at a Victoria's Secret fashion show. I must have looked as out of place as I felt in my Rolling Stones T-shirt, paint-splattered jeans and purple kicks; apparently *all* my jeans had paint on them, which was something I'd only realized that morning.

Honestly, what the hell was I doing here?

For the second time today, Maggie deposited me in one of the upstairs bedrooms that had been taken over by the wardrobe team, promising to fetch me in ten minutes.

Ten minutes until my scene with Jesse Mayes.

My palms were sweating again.

The wardrobe girls freed me from the robe and stood me on a little platform to stare at me. Which wouldn't have been all that weird, given their profession, if I wasn't totally naked except for a bra and panties. It was definitely not my comfort zone, but since there were only a couple of models and the wardrobe girls in the room, and they did this all the time, I tried to convince myself it was no big deal.

Not terrifying in the slightest.

They had me do a quick change in the adjoining washroom, keeping the champagne satin and black lace bra, but switching out the matching panties for a pair of skimpy black lace boy shorts, which showed a hell of a lot of cheek. Luckily, I had decent cheeks.

"Oh, so perfect," one of the wardrobe girls gushed when she saw me, and I told myself it was kind of cute and not at all weird that they cared so much what I'd be wearing under my clothes, since no one was going to see it.

Then one of the makeup girls walked in with a makeup palette, her little tool belt filled with brushes and sponges, and started painting over a bruise on my thigh with her magic makeup that made it look like I had no pores.

And that's when it hit me.

These *were* my clothes.

Like, all of them.

Because apparently I was about to be filmed in Jesse Mayes' music video wearing nothing but panties and a bra.

"Is there time for me to use the washroom before I go down?" I asked anyone who would listen, hot panic rising like bile in my throat.

"Sure," the makeup girl said. "Just try not to smudge the makeup."

I dashed into the bathroom and shut the door, just in time for the first heave. I grabbed onto the beautiful marble sink and wretched, as quietly as I could, my stomach clenching as I dry-heaved. Thank God nothing came up. Kind of glad now that I never actually got to eat any of that sushi.

I swallowed, heaved, swallowed again, and focused on getting control of my breath. Aerosmith was rocking "Sweet Emotion" on the sound system in the next room, so at least I knew no one could hear me.

I squeezed my eyes shut and breathed, long, slow and deep. Then I dug through the pockets of my discarded jeans and found my phone. I called Devi with fumbling hands, a toxic blend of nerves, anger and humiliation broiling in my gut.

"Is he as hot as you remembered?" she answered, and I could hear the self-satisfied smile in her voice.

"Hotter. Devi. What the *fuck*."

"Huh? Are you okay?" Alarmed. She sounded alarmed now and I would've felt bad if I wasn't still swallowing down the bile.

"Did you *know* they want me to do this thing in panties and a bra?"

"Oh," my best friend said. "That."

"Yes, *that*," I hissed. I would've straight-up yelled at her for the first time in our lives if I wasn't afraid all the pretty people in the next room might hear me. I tugged at the skimpy lace of the boy shorts which now felt several sizes smaller than when I first put them on, trying, and failing, to cover more of my ass.

"Katie, Jesus. Seriously, are you okay? You sound all frothy."

"Yes, because I'm foaming at the mouth. You never told me I'd be doing this thing naked."

"One. Panties and a bra does not equal naked. You wear less at the beach. That sexy-ass string bikini of yours?"

"That's different."

"How is it different?"

Ugh. I hated it when she out-argued me. Which she did all the time. Hence, me standing here in sexy underwear that wasn't even mine. "I don't know. It just is."

"It's not. And two. I didn't get around to telling you they'd changed the plan because I knew you'd freak out and bail and I really, really think you should do this."

"What do you mean, they changed the plan?"

"That party scene thing? They called yesterday to say they'd altered it a bit, so your scene with Jesse will now be a one-on-one thing. Like, just the two of you."

Just the two of us?

What was she talking about?

"Devi, what the hell did you sign me up for?"

"Nothing. It's just a love scene."

Cold. I suddenly felt shivering cold. But the contents of my stomach… a churning ball of hot lava. "What do you mean, a love scene?"

Like, sex?

Simulated sex, on camera?

With Jesse Mayes? Hottest guy in the universe?

Hot panic. Bile rising…

I swallowed hard.

"All you have to do is fake make out with Jesse," Devi said, like it was the simplest thing in the world. "He's gorgeous, right? And you were all worried you'd have to dance on cue or strut around or something. This way, you don't even have to perform."

Right. Because pretending to make out with a super hot rock star while a camera crew filmed it was a daily occurrence for me. Totally natural.

"Not to mention I got you more money. You know, for doing it in your skivvies."

Slowly. In through the nose, out through the mouth.

"Katie?"

"I'm breathing."

"Where the hell are you?"

"In the bathroom."

"Okay... so breathe and then get your ass out there. We went over this. We drank wine. Remember? You're gonna rock this."

Rock this. Right. Despite Devi's confidence in me, I was pretty sure Jesse Mayes was the one who was going to rock this.

I was very possibly going to throw up.

For the first time since I started dry-heaving, I caught my reflection in the mirror: the reflection of the girl who was about to fake make out with Jesse Mayes.

Half-naked.

I blinked and stared, trying to imagine that girl in a music video.

She had a lot more makeup on than usual, but okay... it's not like there was nothing there to work with. Face kind of heart-shaped. Symmetrical features. Slender, arched eyebrows and decently high cheekbones. Full lips. Largish blue-green eyes framed by dark lashes. Pale Irish skin with a few micro-freckles dusted across a decently cute nose.

I looked over my figure in the lingerie, which was much sexier than I'd realized, now that I was seeing it through the eyes of the girl who was about to wear it in front of Jesse Mayes. I'd always been kind of petite, nothing like the other women they'd hired for this, but at least I had curves. I used to be a tomboy, actually. A skater kid, I dressed like the boys I hung out with and looked like them too. It was hard not to still see that girl in the mirror. I was kind of a late bloomer, but I *had* bloomed.

And someone liked what they saw, enough to hire me for this, right?

"Katie?" Devi sounded worried now. I didn't like being the one to make her sound that way.

I tried to wrap my head around the idea of walking out there, in *this*, in front of Jesse Mayes, and all his hot friends, and the camera crew and the security guys and all those other models —*real* models... and I just couldn't. I couldn't. My palms were still sweating as I clung to the sink.

"Shit, Devi," I said in a small, parched voice. "He doesn't even know who I am."

"Should he?"

"Um, yeah? I thought he picked me. But he didn't even know I was hired."

"So? You *were* hired. I know you feel all weird about it because you've never done this before, but who the fuck cares? Trust me, babe. This is the kind of thing some girls, beautiful girls, bust their asses trying to get their whole careers and never do. This is Jesse Fucking Mayes."

"Yeah. I'm aware."

Both Devi and Google had filled me in on the extent of the man's fame, informing me that Jesse Fucking Mayes was nothing less than a rock god, a sex god, and a total heartbreaker.

Not to mention that his current girlfriend was none other than Elle, the super hot female bass player of Dirty.

Even if I could muster the nerve to walk out there in this lingerie, I, Katie Bloom, was not built for that kind of pressure.

"You know we rep an actress who just shot a love scene with Leonardo?" Devi went on. "And an actual Victoria's Secret model. They passed on all of them. They want *you*."

"Uh-huh." That part, to be honest, still didn't compute. But it did make me feel more nauseous. "Why the *hell* did I agree to do this? You know I hate being in the spotlight." I shut my eyes, fighting back the spins.

Devi fell silent. She knew, alright.

She'd been there, standing by my side at the altar while the minister looked on with grave sympathy and the minutes ticked by. While everyone stood looking at me in my white dress; everyone but the one person who was supposed to be there.

The one who'd just walked out.

I wanted to disappear then, but I couldn't. I couldn't escape that horrible moment that just stretched on and on.

I was still reliving it, almost two years later.

"And that's exactly why you need to do this," my best friend said.

"Why, exactly?"

"You know why. Look, Katie, I've been there with you. Through all of it. I've watched you mope around for the last two years of your life—"

"One year and ten months. Let's not exaggerate."

Someone knocked on the bathroom door. "Katie?"

It was Maggie, here to take me to shoot my scene. I pictured Jesse Mayes out there, waiting... *Shit*, would he be half-naked too?

"Just a minute!" I called as sweetly as I could, even as the bile rose up again. I tried to choke it down, but it was winning.

"Okay," Devi pressed. "I've watched my best friend in the entire world feel bad about herself for a year and ten months, all over some asshole who didn't deserve her anyway—"

"Devi—"

"Wait. He never deserved you in the first place, and we both know it. I know you know it, deep down, that he was a total dick and the way he hurt you was despicable."

I threw up. Quietly.

Just a bit, in Jesse Mayes' tattooed manager's beautiful marble sink.

"But the fact that you're still letting it run your life," Devi said, oblivious to my vomiting, "...Katie, that's on you."

This.

This was exactly why Devi was, and would always be, my best friend.

She loved me when I needed love. And she *tough* loved me when I needed a kick in the ass. Unfailingly.

"You're right," I croaked. I swished some water around my mouth and spat in the sink, rinsing the vomit down the drain.

"You need to grab this moment by the balls. Take your fucking life back, babe."

Devi was always trying to get me to grab something by the balls. Usually life. Sometimes a man.

I'd never been more grateful for it.

"Okay," I said.

She *was* right, and I knew it.

I couldn't let what happened to me almost two years ago on that shitty day, the day that was supposed to be the best day of my life but turned out to be the worst, *ruin* my life.

And if I didn't take drastic action, that was exactly what was going to happen.

"I'm doing this."

I dabbed at my mouth with a tissue, making sure there was no trace of vomit on my made-up face as I studied myself in the mirror.

"Fucking right."

"And by the way," I told her, "I love you."

I hung up and rinsed my mouth with some of the mouthwash that had been left, thanks to some small miracle, on the little tray of guest toiletries.

Then I took a deep breath, opened the door, and went to make out with a rock star.

CHAPTER FOUR

Jesse

I SAT on the king-sized bed as the crew worked around me in somewhat-organized chaos, but it wasn't the chaos that bothered me. I was no stranger to chaos. I just tuned it out and played bits of a new song on one of my old acoustics, which seemed to me a better way to process whatever shit was going on in my head than the methods used by my bandmates.

When Dylan had shit to deal with, he tended to vanish into the ether.

Elle got confrontational.

Zane fucked his feelings away. Which was at least better than binge drinking at them like he used to.

I played guitar. I made music. I wrote songs until I felt better about whatever the fuck was bothering me.

Lately, I'd been writing a lot. It was either that or do that brooding shit that drove everyone around me crazy. I'd already been obsessing over what the next few weeks of my life were gonna look like and the cold war I was pretty much expecting as soon as I arrived in L.A., but I was impatient as fuck to get down there anyway. And as much as I hated the process, this shoot needed my attention first.

This video had to do well. The song had to do well. The album had to do better than well.

I couldn't let Zane fuck it up just by being Zane.

I'd told him to stay the fuck out of this room while we shot this scene. I didn't tell him why, but the man wasn't stupid. It was either tell him to fuck off or have him hanging around, throwing his fuck-me stares at Katie.

I saw that wide-eyed look she gave him. And I knew how things went from there. I'd seen enough chicks lose their shit over him to know when a girl was Zane-struck.

I could also see why Maggie and Brody picked Katie for this scene. She was super fucking cute. Yeah, I could snap my fingers and replace her with any girl in the house. But I didn't *want* any of the other girls in the house.

Anyone could see this girl was different.

And since I wasn't making out all afternoon with a super cute chick who was gone for Zane, I'd just have to make her forget about him.

I could see her standing at the bottom of the stairs talking to Maggie, but she hadn't yet stepped into the room. She had her back to me, just her dark hair and white robe visible through the banks of lights set up around the bed.

We were shooting the scene in Brody's walk-out basement, the legendary party room. I couldn't possibly count, or even remember, all the times I'd been drunk, high or laid in this room. I'd never seen it like this, though. No kegs, no carousing, no half-naked babes. The pool table and other furniture had been pushed against the walls and covered with protective blankets.

More lights were set up in the backyard, beaming in through the wall of windows. Long, billowing curtains had been hung and fans were set up to blow them inward, the light glowing through them. The set was simple but gorgeous. Liv, the director, had shot several Dirty videos over the years and I knew she'd make this thing look hot.

With that cutie in this bed with me, it was guaranteed.

Even if she would've preferred Zane.

I watched as she turned to follow Maggie into the room. The second Katie stepped over the threshold, Brody cranked the music, right on cue. The Rolling Stones' "Start Me Up" revved through the room.

Katie stopped dead, almost tripping. A couple of crew guys dove in to catch her, and she blushed as she waved them off. There were electrical cords running everywhere, taped down to the floor, and she lifted her robe, stepping gingerly over them in her purple shoes, flashing her bare leg.

Without even meaning to, the girl was making an entrance.

The song was perfect, the lyrics greased with lust and pretty much summing up the impression she was making on most of the guys in the room.

I watched her cross to the bed.

Katie Bloom. Age twenty-four. Lived on East 7th in Vancouver. After I saw her in the dining room I had Jude get all the intel he could. Apparently she'd arrived on a skateboard, wearing a Stones T-shirt and bearing cookies for the crew, which never made it past security since Jude's guys devoured them on sight. Other than a thing for baked goods, I had fuck all to go on other than an apparent interest in classic rock.

I strummed idly along on my guitar as she came to a stop at the very foot of the bed, pretty much the farthest point from where I sat near the headboard. Maggie introduced her to Liv, and Liv, a calm fixture amidst the hurried chaos of her crew, announced that we were about ready to start shooting.

"We'll start with some wide shots and gradually move in," she told Katie. "We're looking for passionate morning sex, like you've barely slept and been at it all night but you can't get enough. You've been briefed on all of this?"

"Uh-huh," Katie said, her voice small. I barely caught it over the music. "Maggie kinda filled me in."

She looked over at me, just barely. Her gaze completely missed my face, sweeping down over my bare chest and my arms as I played the guitar. I'd been offered a robe, but it was warm with all the lights and people in the room, so I wasn't wearing anything but the black boxer briefs the wardrobe girls gave me.

"Jesse will guide you through it," Liv was saying. "Just follow his lead. We'll start slow and go with the pace that feels right for you two." She said some other stuff about where the camera would be and whatever else. I wasn't listening.

I was watching Katie.

She looked kinda pale, but a makeup girl had materialized to touch up her face. As she did her thing, Katie looked pretty much anywhere but at me.

Maybe this girl wasn't so different after all.

I'd definitely met a hell of a lot of girls who'd bust their asses to get backstage, then act like they were too cool to be there.

But fuck, she was cute.

When Liv turned away, she met my eyes. Finally.

One of the hair girls stepped in to tousle up her already killer sex hair. Paired with her doe-eyed fawn-in-headlights look, it was starting to make my dick throb.

Fucking Zane.

As soon as we were more or less alone, Katie smiled at me a little. "I don't suppose you have another piece of gum?"

"I might." I chewed my cinnamon-flavored gum exaggeratedly. "Maybe this is my last piece. We could share."

She glanced at my mouth and blushed. "I don't think so. I, uh, just threw up."

Say what?

She turned toward me, carefully, like if she turned too fast the whole room was gonna spin out from under her. She even put a hand out and held onto the bed to steady herself.

I set my guitar aside.

Then I sent someone to get Jude to get the gum from my jacket, which was locked in Brody's office.

"I rinsed my mouth out," Katie explained, "but I feel like I could use a little more... you know..." She trailed off, her eyes huge.

I leaned forward, scoping her out. "Are you fucking high?"

Her eyes lit with surprise, bright and clear. "No."

I looked her over more carefully. "But you're sick?" Shit. I was planning to lay down some new rough tracks in L.A. within the next few days, and I couldn't do that if I was puking my guts out.

"No," she said. "Nothing like that."

I scanned her again, but the robe wasn't giving anything away. "You're not pregnant, are you?" *Worse* than being sick or fuck-struck for Zane. If I had to film a love scene with this chick while she was knocked up with some other dude's kid, it would totally buzzkill this entire thing.

"Definitely not." She blushed again, which was good. She could use some more color in her face. "Just... nervous."

And maybe I was an asshole, but that made me smile. Ear-to-fucking-ear.

One of Jude's guys appeared with the gum and Katie shoved a stick in her mouth. "Thank you."

Then one of Liv's minions called things to order and Liv strode over to us again.

"We're going to run through the song a few times," she said, "covering everything from different angles, then we'll push in for the closeups."

Katie nodded, chewing furiously.

Liv turned to me. "Feel free to go with what feels natural, like we talked about, and I'll let you know when we need to change it up."

"Got it."

"Let's lose the robe and the gum," Liv called out as she took her position near the monitor where she'd be watching what the camera captured.

Brody killed the music. Someone cleared my guitar away and handed over a couple of tissues for our gum. A wardrobe girl appeared to take Katie's robe.

Katie kicked off her shoes, took a little breath and unwrapped, shrugging the robe off her shoulders. The wardrobe girl took it, adjusted one of Katie's bra straps, and got out of the way.

Katie and I were alone by the bed, the lights shining over us. Everyone was looking at us.

At *her*.

The girl was petite perfection. Creamy smooth skin. Slim, curvy bod with a tiny waist and fat, natural tits. And those sweet, round hips...

I almost fucking drooled. I was a total hip man. Hips and ass. Give me something to grip while I fucked a girl.

"Okay, Katie, we'll get started with you on top," Liv called over. "We'll run through the song once to get everyone warmed up."

"Okay," Katie said. She looked at me, glanced at my crotch, but just stood there.

"Well, babe," I said. "You heard the woman." I leaned back on my hands to give her full access to my lap. "Hop on."

She rolled her eyes a bit. I caught that much before she averted her gaze and climbed onto the bed. She crawled awkwardly over my legs and finally looked up at me from under her dark hair.

I leaned forward, my lips brushing her cheek as I whispered in her ear, "Probably wanna get closer, if we're gonna fuck." I grabbed those pretty hips and she gasped as I yanked her toward me, forcing her to sit in my lap. Her crotch was still inches from mine, but it was a start. And she could go ahead and complain about the unprofessional way I was manhandling her to whoever would listen. I didn't care. Totally worth it to see that startled look on her face and that slow blush creeping down her chest, her breasts heaving as she breathed.

We stared at each other. This close, I could practically taste her. She smelled like candy and fucking sunshine. Like cinnamon gum and homemade cherry pie.

Then Liv announced that we were rolling and the song started playing.

The song.

The best song I'd ever written. *Co*-written.

"Dirty Like Me."

A classic Dirty song from our first album, I'd recorded a new, stripped-down version for my solo album, almost ten years after that original recording. The timing seemed right, and since the song was a fan favorite I hoped it would help sell the new album. The new songs.

Besides, I loved this song. The song, and Katie Bloom in my lap, kinda made this whole shoot worth it.

The camera had us in profile so I held Katie by the hips, leaned in close and ran the tip of my nose down her neck, just barely brushing her skin. She smelled even better up close. She tipped her head back, giving me access, and put her arms loosely around my neck, sitting up straighter so I could graze my lips down over her throat, her collarbone. As the lyrics kicked in I sang them to her softly, letting my breath tickle her skin as I almost-kissed her.

We weren't actually supposed to kiss. That was Liv's whole approach to the video, and I trusted her vision.

No actual kissing. Just a big fucking tease.

Right around the time Katie started wriggling around in my lap in response to my touch, I started second-guessing that whole plan.

"Slide your hands down, Jesse," Liv called out, so I did. I slid my hands down over Katie's round ass and squeezed her tight, plump cheeks through her lace panties.

Then Liv called, "Cut."

I let go of Katie's ass and after a small delay she let her arms drop from my shoulders.

Liv explained that we were gonna do the whole thing again from a different angle and had us turn slightly, so we were in the same position, but the camera could now see more of Katie's face.

I didn't take my eyes off Katie's.

"What?" I demanded when she didn't blink.

"Nothing," she said, her voice all soft and breathless. "I just… kinda love this song."

Yeah. What chick didn't?

You asked me, lyrically, it was the best song ever written. I could say that, since I didn't write the lyrics.

Of course, *she* probably loved it because she was used to Zane singing it.

She tried to break the gaze, but I grabbed her chin and held her. Just before we got rolling again, I leaned in and whispered in her ear. "Careful what you wish for, sweetheart."

She blinked her big blue-green eyes at me. As we started shooting, she whispered in my ear. "What the hell does that mean?"

"Cut," Liv called out. "Katie, we can see your lips moving. Save the talking for between takes, please. Let's start that one again, from the top."

The song started again and we followed Liv's directions as we pretended to make out. As Katie got more comfortable her hands strayed over my back. Her fingernails dug into my skin, sending little pricks of pleasure straight to my dick. And every time I squeezed her ass and made her gasp, or brushed my lips across her skin and made her shiver, my balls tightened. My nipples hardened. Goosebumps started tingling across my skin.

Fuck me.

"It means," I said, pulling her close in the next break, "you shouldn't have thrown your hat in the ring unless you were ready to ride with the big bulls."

"That's a weirdly mixed metaphor," she said in a disapproving schoolteacher tone, which was hot as fuck on her. All she needed was a pair of glasses and I'd spring wood.

As soon as we started shooting again, my hands went back to her ass to resume groping exactly where they'd left off. I squeezed her so hard her panties came down an inch and she flashed a scowl at me.

I winked.

"Cut," Liv called. "Katie, we're on you now, so watch your facial expressions, okay? We wanna see the heat. You're madly in love, this is the best morning of your life. And Jesse?"

"Yeah, boss."

"Stop fucking around, whatever you're doing."

I grinned. "Yes, ma'am."

Katie narrowed her pretty eyes at me.

I didn't stop. I kept on doing anything and everything I thought I could get away with to make Katie Bloom uncomfortable, and possibly aroused.

Call me immature, but yeah, I was that brat at school who pulled the hair of the girl I had a crush on.

Some things never changed.

I pretended to get my thumb caught in her panties and flashed a full ass cheek at the camera. I accidentally bit her earlobe while I was whisper-singing in her ear. I yanked so hard on her bra strap while we were pawing each other that her pretty pink nipple popped right out.

That actually was an accident, but no way she was gonna believe it. No one actually saw it but me, since her back was to camera when it happened, so I just went ahead and fixed it, slipping the stretchy lace over the perfect pink bud before she could react.

When I looked into her eyes again there was a definite spark there. A spark of outrage, maybe.

At least I had her full attention.

The next few takes became a kind of groping argument, a silent battle over who could irritate the other into more discomfort, or in my case, increasing horniness.

To my frustration, she was quickly winning.

At least our little wrestling match must've been reading well on camera, because Liv was fucking loving it. She kept saying things like, "More!" and "Yes, like that. Grab him *harder*, Katie. Think of all the girls who want to be where you are right now and make it count. *Rip him to shreds.*"

Jesus.

At one point, when Katie pulled my hair and bit my neck, Liv actually applauded.

I was starting to gain a new appreciation for music video shoots.

But while I was getting horny, I was pretty sure Katie was just getting mad. Because in-between the next few increasingly-sweaty takes we carried on a stilted argument, which went something like…

Her (with a dirty look): "I didn't throw anything in a ring, you know. I didn't even want to be here."

Me (trying to ignore my inconvenient semi): "Uh-huh."

Her: "I'm only here because my best friend is an incredible

talent agent and so good at her job that she convinced me to do this."

Me: "What?"

Her: "I'm not even a model."

Her: "I've never done anything like this before."

Her: "So if you don't like what I'm doing or you want me gone, you can go ahead and fire me."

Her: "Wait. Does that mean my agent won't get paid?"

Me: "You seriously didn't want this job?"

Her (panicking a little): "Forget what I said. Can my agent still get paid if I waive my fee and we call it even?"

Me: "You're only here because she made you do it?"

Her: "Yes. I mean... no. Um."

Her (floundering): "I mean... you seem... popular... and everything..."

Me: "Cut."

Liv threw me a black look. She hated it when I called "Cut" on her set. Which I usually did a lot, but fuck it. We weren't even shooting when I said it, but I was that fucking distracted by Katie Bloom's rambling.

"I need a word with Katie," I growled. "Talk amongst your fucking selves."

As the crew made themselves busy, I pulled Katie closer to me, shifting her hips up my thighs until we were almost groin-to-groin. Brody cranked the music. This time it was AC/DC, "You Shook Me All Night Long," because Brody was a fucking smart-ass— and he knew no dude could hear this song at the same time he had a half-naked chick this hot in his lap and not get aroused as fuck.

"Do you even know who I am?" I demanded, my nose an inch from Katie's.

She swallowed. "You're Jesse Mayes."

"Right. What does that mean to you?"

Blank. Big blue-greens blinking at me. "Um... what do you mean?"

"Do. You. Know. Who. I. Am."

"Um... yeah," she said, her voice getting smaller. "You're Jesse Fucking Mayes. You play lead guitar for Dirty and you just put out a solo album." She looked embarrassed, guarded, and maybe a little annoyed. "Is there something else I *should* know?"

I stared at her, totally fucking bewildered. Maybe because it'd been so long since I'd had a chick in my lap who *wasn't* full-out, tits-up star-struck. Actually, not sure I'd *ever* had a chick in my lap who wasn't star-struck, since I was already a musician by the time I started getting chicks in my lap.

Hell, even Elle had stars in her eyes when we fucked, and she was probably more famous than I was.

"I thought you were fucking *struck*, sweetheart," I said, trying like hell to figure her out. "That look you gave Zane, seen it like a million times."

"Struck?" She looked at me kinda blankly again. "What do you mean, struck?"

"You know, dumbstruck. Star-struck. *Cock-struck.*"

Her cheeks flushed pink and she wriggled a little in my lap like she was trying to put more distance between us. No fucking chance. My fingers dug into her sweet hips, holding her there. "Um... no," she said.

And fuck me, but I believed her.

She was breathing heavier though, and that blush I was starting to like one fuck of a lot was creeping down her chest. She looked flustered as hell.

And I was suddenly *stiff.*

What the fuck was happening?

"No?" My hands twitched, tightening, gripping her hips harder. Probably bruising her.

"Sorry." She swallowed. "That I'm not... *cock-struck.*"

I licked my lips like a fucking puppy. This girl was giving whole new meaning to the term. Because *my* cock was struck. I was hard as fuck. Luckily the girl was still looking in my eyes and hadn't noticed the hard-on a mere breath away from the lace covering her clit.

"Um… I'm confused, though," she said. "Is it Zane's cock or yours that I'm supposed to be cock-struck for?" Then her teeth caught on her plump pink bottom lip and I almost fucking groaned aloud.

Was I fucking stupid? Was I just jaded as fuck? Because it never even occurred to me that the girl wasn't angling for at least one of us.

"Dylan?" I said, swallowing hard.

"Um… I dig the kilt and all, but no." She leaned in, wrapping her arms around my neck, breathing her hot little breaths in my ear. "Before last week," she whispered all breathless, like she was asking me to eat her pussy, "I didn't know a one of you existed."

Fuck. Did she have any idea how much she was turning me on?

"Jesse," Liv called out. "Can we get rolling?"

"Yeah," I said, never taking my eyes off Katie's. The tiniest smile twitched at the corners of her pink mouth. I had no idea what I was seeing in those big blue-greens. I'd thought I had this girl all figured out.

I'd thought wrong. So fucking wrong it made my dick throb.

Apparently I liked being fucking wrong.

"Good, Katie?" Liv asked. "Let's see some more of that heat."

Katie smiled over her shoulder, to camera, and said, "Yes, ma'am," as sweet as could be.

Then she turned to me and whispered in my ear, "Maybe if I channel 'cock-struck' it'll make her happy."

And as soon as we were filming again, she lifted her hips and shoved her pussy against me like she suddenly couldn't stand a fucking thing between us… other than my dick, which she'd sat herself directly on. My incredibly *hard* dick, which she clearly wasn't expecting.

Her eyes went huge and her mouth popped open, but she didn't back off.

Which was fine with me.

Then "Dirty Like Me" kicked in and right on cue I opened my mouth… and choked.

Nothing came out.

For the first time in ten fucking years, I forgot the lyrics.

I *forgot* the lyrics.

Katie Bloom stared at me, her plump pink lips parted in surprise, and I couldn't fucking help it.

I leaned in and kissed her. Hard.

CHAPTER FIVE

Katie

HIS MOLASSES-DARK GAZE melted over me, his lips parting as he drew a shaky breath. I could feel the tension of his restraint in his hard, muscular body hovering over mine. His skin was getting slippery. A bead of sweat rolled slowly down his temple; I wondered if the camera caught it.

I clung to him, my fingernails digging into his muscled back as his hips pressed me to the bed. He moved against me, thrusting his hard length against the softness of my inner thigh, nothing but the soft cotton of his underwear between us. Then he did it again. Harder. Slower. My breath caught as the tip of his cock brushed my clit through the lace of my panties. Rihanna's "Rude Boy" started playing.

My eyes opened with a jolt.

Next to me, my dog nuzzled into the crook of my knee.

Fuck me.

I was doing it again. Reliving every steamy, breathless, lip-biting moment of my fake make out with Jesse Mayes at his video shoot, in my dreams.

I let out a hard sigh and rubbed my eyes. At least this time I didn't come in my sleep.

My dog continued to molest my knee with his sloppy tongue to the tune of "Rude Boy."

"Ugh. Max." I rolled over, tussling Max's ears and giving him a gentle shove off the bed.

My best friend's ringtone stopped abruptly.

I groped around on my bedside table for my glasses, then my phone. Devi had texted me when I missed her call. It said simply, *Number One, Baby!*

Devi had been tirelessly tracking absolutely everything to do with the "Dirty Like Me" video since its release two weeks ago. If anything even remotely related to my appearance in that video was mentioned in some random, dusty corner of the internet, Devi had a Google Alert for it.

And no, the video wasn't "Number One." Not exactly. But…

I opened the text that had come in last night from Maggie, who'd also been keeping me updated, on a more casual but factually accurate basis. Her text included a YouTube link and a more specific report.

Just surpassed November Rain.

My heart did a weird sledgehammer thing, which it'd been doing a lot lately.

I flopped on my back and stared at the big crack in my bedroom ceiling, the one that occasionally leaked and my landlord kept promising to fix. I swore it was kind of wiggling around. The whole room was vibrating, like a tiny freight train was doing circles around my skull, which was pretty much how I always felt after drinking red wine.

It seemed premature, to me, to be celebrating when we weren't actually "Number One," but Devi had all the excuse she needed to break out several pitchers of sangria last night.

"*Slash*," my drunken best friend kept saying. "You beat *Slash*."

She was totally pumped about the fact that, according to

Maggie, Guns N' Roses' "November Rain" was the most-watched rock video on YouTube, like, ever—until a certain video starring Jesse Mayes and, um, me, came along.

Now, "Dirty Like Me" held that honor.

I texted Devi back. *Work now. Talk later.*

Her response buzzed before I could put the phone down. *Meet you there! You're a star!!!!!*

That was followed by about fifty happy face emojis with stars in their eyes.

I groaned and tossed my phone aside. Then I stretched my achy, probably-still-a-little-drunk body and sat up.

Unlike Devi, who was dreaming up all the fabulous modeling jobs I should now try out for, I was in denial about this whole thing. It was just too much to wrap my head around the fact that I was now holding company with the likes of Rihanna and Adele—other women whose videos were watched as much as mine was, and oh yeah, were so famous they went by only one name. Kinda like Jesse Mayes' real girlfriend, Elle.

Not that I was that famous, but still.

Fucking weird.

At least all those women had actual talent. Not only did I not particularly want to be famous, I very particularly did not want to be famous for doing absolutely nothing but putting on some lacy underwear and getting groped by a rock star. Which I now kinda was.

While I contemplated this, Max whined and snuffled my foot.

"Yeah, Max. I know. Pee and food."

I gave myself three more seconds to be weirded out by all of it, then dragged my ass off the bed. Because even though I was some kind of music video sensation out there in internet land, in real life I was still a regular girl with bills to pay, no boyfriend—rock star or otherwise—and a job to do. A crappy job, but still.

And a dog to take outside to pee.

It was a gorgeous mid-summer morning, trees heavy with blossoms and the air sweet with the scent of freshly-mowed grass. The sun was already blazing out of a flawless blue sky. Max jogged alongside my skateboard as I rolled to work, tongue lolling contentedly out the side of his mouth.

Really, my life was pretty good.

By that I meant *my* life, not the life of that girl in the video who got to roll around in bed with Jesse Mayes. Because clearly that life didn't exist, as evidenced by the fact that once we were finished shooting it, I never saw him again.

That didn't mean my life hadn't changed at all.

I was still the same person, but now I had little kids coming up to me asking for my autograph, jealous chicks giving me catty stare downs, and random guys hitting on me a lot more than they used to. I'd even gone on a few dates. They weren't exactly earth-shattering or anything, but really, one could hardly expect regular, mortal dudes to compare with Jesse Fucking Mayes. Which was okay. Once the overwhelming memories of my hours in bed with him eventually dissipated, and the crazy, sexy dreams stopped, I was sure to find someone super cool who'd rock my world, right?

Or so I'd been telling myself to get over the feeling that the most thrilling thing I'd ever done, and may ever do, was over. And it wasn't happening again.

Forget about it, I told myself, part of my new daily mantra. *It was cool. It was crazy. It was brief.*

It's done.

Welcome to reality. It's not so bad.

My sister's place was a beautifully maintained heritage house in Mount Pleasant, less than five minutes from my apartment, where Nudge Coffee Bar occupied the front rooms. If I thought I could get away with it, I would've rolled right on past and taken

Max for a longer cruise around the neighborhood, but I was already running late, thanks to my red wine hangover. So I turned my skateboard and rolled on up the sidewalk toward the house.

I noticed the big dude out front right away. Kinda hard to miss. Over six feet, muscles bulging from his sleeveless black shirt. He was wearing dark shades and leaning on a black luxury car parked in the no-parking zone, and for a dude with a giant tattoo of a gnarly tree running up one arm he kinda had the vibe of a Secret Service agent. Or maybe a bodyguard...

Holy shit.

I rolled to a halt.

A rock star was sitting on the stairs to the front porch of my sister's house. Which would explain all the vibrating my cell phone was doing in my ass pocket on the way here. Kinda regretted ignoring that now.

He was wearing shades so I wasn't sure he'd seen me yet. He had a takeout coffee cup in hand and I started rapidly calculating the odds that he'd just happened by for coffee. Then his head tilted in my direction and a dazzling smile broke out on his face. He stood and started walking over to me.

Shit.

I looked away for a sec to get my bearings. I was in the right place, right? I was awake, right? This wasn't just another horny dream where we were about to go at it on the hood of his car while his bodyguard watched and then I woke up in a sweaty heap, alone with my dog?

I popped my skateboard up into my hand and let Max's leash out enough so he could bounce over to Jesse Mayes, which he was dying to do. I watched as Jesse Mayes patted my dog, then slipped his shades up onto his head where they sat in his thick, dark curls.

He stopped in front of me. "Katie Bloom." He was still smiling when he said my name.

"Jesse Mayes," I said as coolly as I could while my heart drummed like a Dylan Cope drum solo. His eyes dropped to my chest and for a split second I thought he could actually hear it. Then I remembered it was supposed to be hot as fuck today, so I was wearing a skimpy white halter-style bikini top and the tiniest jean shorts I owned.

Even though he'd seen me in less, I felt utterly naked as he looked me over. His smile faded, replaced with the same dark, unreadable look he'd given me most of the time we were shooting that video.

"Um... I thought rock stars didn't get out of bed before noon or whatever," I said. Because it was really fucking early in the morning to be standing face-to-face with Jesse Mayes, unprepared. And it was definitely too early for him to be looking so good.

"You've been in bed with a rock star?" he asked, straight-faced.

"Just the once."

At that, he grinned again. "You got a minute?"

For you? Um, yeah. Pretty sure I could find the time.

"Uh-huh. Want to come around back? I need to drop Max off."

"Lead the way."

We headed around the back of the house, Jesse's bodyguard remaining out front, but it was Max who actually led the way, bounding down the side lane and through the backyard gate. The fence was overgrown with trees and the entire yard was a maze of sometimes competing shrubs and gardens; my sister and her husband had dueling green thumbs. The yard said comfy chaos, and I loved it. It was one of my favorite places in the world.

And now Jesse Mayes was standing in it.

Trippy.

My niece and nephew came screaming in our direction.

"Katie!" Owen screeched, hurling himself at my leg.

"You're late," Sadie announced.

Great. Owen and Sadie were four and six years old, respectively, and had zero concept of time. Which meant my sister had been looking for me.

I bent and kissed Owen on his blond head, tussling his unruly hair. "Go tell your mom I'll be in in a few minutes, please."

"Yeah!" Owen dashed into the house, happy to have a job to do.

"I'm going to talk to, um, my friend," I informed Sadie, who was standing by, playing with the hem of her sundress and staring at Jesse. "Can you go play with Max?"

"Okay," she said, and steered Max over to the play area in the corner of the yard.

I watched them go, giving myself an extra few seconds to take a breath. Sadie watched Jesse over her shoulder the entire way, reminding me of the young girls who came up to me now and then demanding to know what Jesse Mayes was like. I usually told them he was super nice, because it was adorable when they got all giggly and starry-eyed. But the truth was I had no idea whether or not the guy was nice.

All I knew was that he'd paid me a hell of a lot of money so he could grope me, kiss me, and thrust his hard cock against me until I almost saw stars; then he'd tossed me to one of his big biker-looking security guards, who drove me home.

And now here he was, and I was pretty sure he was checking out my ass in my jean shorts... because they were that small, and honestly, if I was a cocky rock star, that's what I'd be doing.

I turned to face him and smiled. Like it was no big deal that he was standing here on the cobbled path between Becca's rose bushes and Jack's hydrangeas, looking at my ass.

"Cute kids," he said.

"My niece and nephew."

I blinked up at him, wishing I'd put on some makeup to cover up the sangria-induced circles under my eyes, instead of just planning to whip on some lip gloss and mascara once I got to work. Because the man was nothing short of dazzling, the sunlight catching in his eyelashes and glinting off his rings, blinding me as it bounced off the white T-shirt stretched over his hard pecs.

"Did you enjoy the pie?" he asked, all innocence, showing a flash of perfect white teeth.

Right. The pie.

Even though I hadn't seen him since the video shoot, I had heard from him. Once.

Sort of.

The morning after the shoot, he'd sent me a pie. Which was kind of cruel, since it just got my hopes up that I might actually see him again, or that sending me pies might be some kind of regular thing. It wasn't. There was only the one, sent to my apartment from Stella's Pies. A delivery guy had shown up with it, with a card that said, *I hear they're the best in town. J.*

The pie was cherry.

"It was good," I said.

"Just good?"

"Mine are better."

"I thought Stella's was the best."

"That's because you haven't tasted mine."

"I'd be happy to taste your pie, babe."

Whoa.

On the other side of the yard, Max barked as Owen came running back outside. I watched my dog frolic happily with the kids in their giant sandbox, which gave me an excuse to look distracted so I could recover from that comment.

"Well," I said, taking a chance, "maybe I can make you one sometime."

"I'd like that," he said. Which made my heart skip a few beats and gave me all kinds of wrong ideas.

"Look." He sat down on one of the stone benches in his ripped jeans, spreading his hard thighs, and gestured for me to sit across from him. "I want to apologize to you."

I didn't know quite how to take that. It was pretty much the last thing I expected him to say.

I sat down. "For what?"

"For kissing you at the video shoot," he said, "in that... situation."

I noticed he didn't say for kissing me, period.

"For making you uncomfortable. You know, being an asshole." A smile twitched at the corner of his gorgeous mouth. "Should I go on?"

"Or you could just stop doing things you need to apologize for."

"I'll work on that." He sipped his coffee. "Seriously, though. Sorry about that whole cock-struck thing. I honestly thought you were just there to meet Zane."

That, I didn't understand. Zane was gorgeous and all, but Jesse? Shit.

I studied him for any hint that he was kidding, but it wasn't there. "That happen to you a lot?"

He smiled, an incredibly genuine smile. "More than I like to admit."

Wow. Who knew cockiness blended with just the right dash of humility was so... hot.

I didn't know what to say. When I'd left the video shoot I definitely hadn't expected a morning-after pie, much less an apology in my sister's backyard.

"Okay," I said. "If it makes you feel better. I forgive you. But really, being kissed by you was hardly a low moment in my life." I felt my cheeks heating even as I said the words, but I said them anyway, in keeping with my promise to Devi to keep grabbing life by the balls. "It's cool of you, but you really didn't need to come here just to apologize."

"I'm not here just to apologize," he said. "I'm here to ask you to come on tour with me."

CHAPTER SIX

Katie

JESSE MAYES WANTED me to go on tour with him.

Um.

What?

Apparently I was wrong before. *That* was the last thing I expected him to say.

"As my girlfriend," he added.

Wrong again. *That* was the last thing I expected him to say.

"You know, like in the video."

I blinked at him. Repeatedly. "Um… in the video we were *acting*."

"Yeah."

I stared at him. For a while.

Then I started to get annoyed. What the hell did he think I was, some kind of rent-a-babe?

"Yeah," I said, a little edge to my voice. "And *you* were… *you know*…"

His mouth curled in a devious grin. "Hard."

Jesus. He didn't even try to make excuses or act the slightest degree embarrassed about it. Kind of made me feel sorry for his real girlfriend. Even though she was gorgeous, talented and filthy rich. I mean, her boyfriend was in bed with me, with a giant erection, and he wasn't even pretending to care.

And now this?

"But you *have* a girlfriend."

"Nope," he said. "Broke up."

Okay. Totally new information.

My hungover brain scrambled to make sense of it.

"But you were together when we shot the video?"

"Actually, we broke up over a month before the shoot. Just didn't go public with it yet."

Shit.

Which meant when we shot the video he *wasn't* being a dirty, cheating bastard when he kissed me.

I figured he'd only done it because his giant ego was bruised when he thought I was into Zane. And I'd only kissed him back because with his tongue in my mouth I'd kind of forgotten, momentarily, that he wasn't single.

I definitely would've felt a lot less dirty and conflicted over the whole thing, though, if I'd known he was.

He stared at me, grinning, as I contemplated this. I stared back, blushing like an idiot. Just trying to calm myself the fuck down and listen to what the man was saying. Because he wasn't asking me to *be* his girlfriend. He was asking me to be his girlfriend *like in the video*. Which meant...

"But... you were paying me to... um... do all that stuff."

"Right."

"So you want to *hire* me to be your *fake* girlfriend?"

"Yeah, on tour." When I just stared at him, he added, "A tour is what musicians do, usually after putting out a new album. You know, they schedule shows at various venues and people buy tickets to those shows and then the musicians show up and play their songs."

I frowned at him. "I know what a tour is."

"You looked a little confused."

Try a lot confused. "I think I need more information."

"Sure. I'm doing a six-week North American tour in support of my new album. Mostly in the U.S., a couple of shows here in Canada. And Brody's phone has been ringing off the hook. Everyone wants the scoop on the new girl."

"New girl?"

"The girl in the video," he said. "That's you."

Right.

"So apparently I have you to thank for the video being such a success."

"Um... you're welcome?"

He sipped his coffee. "Because, according to the gossip, we might be an item."

Yeah, I'd heard "the gossip" too. Thanks to Devi. Though I'd chosen to ignore it, since it wasn't true.

"I watched the video last night," he said, and I felt the heat rise in my cheeks again. The mere thought of Jesse Mayes watching that video... all those close-up shots of embarrassing things like my fingernails digging into his skin and my bottom lip shaking as I breathed... "You looked like you were enjoying yourself."

I blushed harder, but I couldn't exactly argue with that.

"So did you," I countered.

"I was."

God.

"So what do you say?"

I cleared my throat. "You want to *pay* me to pretend to be your girlfriend for six weeks?"

"Yes."

"Like, twenty-four seven?"

"Yes."

"Your girlfriend."

"Yes."

"Like I did in that video?"

"Exactly like that."

Um. "Why?"

"Because this is my first solo album and it means a lot to me. The song's doing well, and that's got a lot to do with you. Even if you're too modest to admit it, I can tell you it's a fact. But since the breakup…" He glanced over at the kids and rubbed a hand on the back of his neck, which I took to be Jesse Mayes in thought or possibly even nervous, which was hella cute. "Elle's solo album did incredibly well. It's sold more than the last two Dirty albums combined. Between the album and her other side projects, movies, cosmetics… she's killing it. And there are a lot of people who think this album will only sell if she's somehow attached. Some of those people are at the record company."

"But… you're the talent. I mean, not that Elle isn't talented… but you write the songs, right?"

He looked at me like I was adorably naïve. "It's not about talent, Katie. It's about what sells. And if they're right, they won't back another solo album from me." He leaned in, resting his elbows on his knees. "When Elle and I were dating, we were everywhere. We were visible. Everyone wanted to know every little detail of our relationship. Now that's over. We haven't exactly confirmed or denied, but there's only so long we can avoid the question. Only so long I can expect Elle to pretend she's still with me and not let her get on with her life, just to help my career. I need to let her off the hook, officially. I'm doing it tomorrow."

"But I would've thought your female fans would love you going single."

His lips quirked. "You might think so, right? But even so, I need some help staying in the minds of the fans. There's a saying, you're only as big as your last album. Or these days you could say your last single. Well, Dirty's last album came out almost two years ago. The tour is long over. And I've never done a solo album before. But you, sweetheart, you come out of nowhere, and you sell." His dark eyes blazed into me. "Or at least you and me together, *we* sell."

"Oh." I bit my lip. "So... basically... you want me to help you make money?"

"If you feel better about it, think of it this way. There are a lot of people counting on me to make money so they get paid. Brody and Maggie have been working their asses off, and every crew member we work with on the road makes a living because of me."

Okay. I liked Brody—after all, he'd hired me for the video—and I'd do about anything for Maggie. That girl had been nothing short of awesome to me. Though I was careful never to ask her about Jesse when we chatted, because A, I didn't want her to think that was the only reason I was keeping in touch with her, and B, I didn't want *me* to think keeping in touch with her would somehow mean I might see him again.

And yet here he was in my sister's backyard, offering me a job. A fucking weird job, but still.

"This is a special tour, Katie. I'm paying for a lot of it myself because it's that important to me. It's what I get up this early in the morning for." He grinned and sipped his coffee.

"What do Brody and Maggie think of this... proposal?"

"They don't know yet," he said. "What do *you* think?"

"I really don't know."

"Really?" The mildly stunned look on his face made me wonder how many times this guy had actually heard the word *no* from a woman's mouth... and that alone kind of made me want to say it. "Why not?"

"Well, for one, I have a job."

He held up his coffee cup. "This?"

"Yes, this. This is my sister's place and I work here four days a week."

"Yeah? How much you make here in a day?"

I crossed my arms over my chest. "You know, that's pretty rude to ask." Mostly because the answer was embarrassing. But thankfully we were interrupted by a timely door slam and a pair of high heels clipping across the patio.

I turned to find my best friend staring down at us.

"Hi," Devi said, smiling her charming smile at Jesse Mayes, then at me. "Owen said you were out here." Her tone said, *He neglected to mention you were with the hottest guy in the world.*

"We were just talking," I blurted, like we'd been caught making out behind the school or something.

"Actually," Jesse said, "I was just asking Katie to come on tour with me."

Devi looked at him, the charming smile stuck on her face. "On tour?"

"Yeah. Like a job offer," I said.

Devi's demeanor shifted. It was subtle, but I knew her well enough to sense my best friend going into full-on hurricane mode.

Shit.

"Oh. You mean you have a proposal for my client." She swept down from the patio and walked over to us. Even after last night, she was impeccably polished. The woman had never met a pitcher of sangria that could dull the shine on her armor.

"I do." Jesse got to his feet. "I was just about to offer Katie fifty grand to come on tour with me for six weeks. Which I'd guess is more than she'd pull in here in a year."

Holy shit.

I hopped to my feet. Not only was that embarrassing, it was true. And totally generous.

But Devi laughed, her white teeth flashing against her beautiful brown skin like a set of tiny, polished daggers. "Sweetheart," she said. "You paid her forty grand for one day's work for the video shoot and now you're asking her to walk away from her life for six weeks for fifty?"

Jesse smiled, his dark eyes sparking in the sun like coal briquettes. Great. *Two* negotiation junkies. "What did you have in mind? Seventy-five?"

"You've got to be kidding me."

I cringed, but Jesse seemed to enjoy the battle. "One hundred?"

"Double that and we can talk."

I made a little involuntary noise of distress in the back of my throat, but Devi just winked at me as if to say, *Don't worry your pretty self, I've got this.*

"Two hundred." Jesse rolled the words around in his mouth like he was seeing how they tasted. Though it sounded more like a statement than a question.

"Plus travel and accommodation, obviously," my BFF said.

I coughed, trying to clear my throat. Apparently I had some kind of allergy to other people having a high-stakes salary negotiation over me.

"Obviously," Jesse said.

Then the two of them looked at me, like I'd suddenly just joined them.

"Uh, do I get a say in this?"

They waited in silence. *Shit.* I was kind of hoping they just wouldn't let me get a word in, since I wasn't even sure what the hell to say.

I turned to Jesse. "While I thank you for the generous offer and for thinking of me for the… um, opportunity… my answer at this time is going to have to be a no."

"Give me a moment with my client." Devi hooked her arm through mine and yanked me through the garden like a Muppet on a hook. Once we reached the farthest corner of the yard, she whirled on me. "Katie. Two hundred grand. Six weeks. Don't be an idiot."

"You don't even know what he wants me to do!"

"Let me guess. More of the same? Make him look good and make him mad cash in the process?"

"Well… yeah. Except I don't think he actually needs my help to look good, and incidentally 'whore for a rock star' isn't exactly something I've been dying to add to my resume."

"Your resume could use all the help it can get." I frowned at her and she waved her manicured hand in the air like it was no biggie. "Just tell him sex isn't on the table. You pose for pictures, show up where he needs you to show up, look good on his arm. Done."

"Right. You think he's not gonna want to bang me as part of the deal?"

"If he does and you don't want to, you say *no*. You're a big girl. We write up a contract and if he sexually harasses you, you walk away. What have you got to lose? *Nothing*," she answered for me. "And what do you have to gain?"

"Let me guess…"

"Two hundred motherfucking *grand*. That's enough to jump-start your life, Katie. You can get a *real* art studio. You can be an artist without having to starve for it. This is every artist's *dream*. Just think of him as a crazy, wealthy patron."

I sighed. "When you put it like that…"

She took me by the shoulders and gave me her serious face. "Look. That man out there is already living his dream, Katie. He's making his money from it. A lot of money. *Two hundred grand* plus travel and accommodations. He didn't even bat his crazy-long eyelashes when I demanded a quarter million for your services, babe. He's got money. You've got something he wants. Let him hire you. Six weeks is nothing, a blink of an eye. Then you get on with your life, with some big juicy bank backing *your* dream."

I knew she was right about at least one thing. It's not like I couldn't use that kind of money.

I'd already spent every penny of the forty-thousand dollars Devi had gotten me for doing the video—minus her agency fee, and after setting aside what I'd have to pay in taxes—on repaying my student loans. Which meant that the expensive art school education I'd received but hadn't yet put to use was now at least *almost* paid off.

Though the best thing I'd gotten out of the entire experience was the kick-start to my creativity. I'd been painting regularly again, which was totally priceless.

I looked over at my niece and nephew playing with my dog. I could smell coffee wafting out through the windows and hear the clank of dishes and the din of voices and laughter in the distance.

I tried to tell myself, like I always did, that this wasn't so bad. What other job would let me bring my dog to work? And I got to hang out with my niece and nephew on my lunch break. And Jack, my awesome brother-in-law, had cleaned out a big space in the basement for my canvases and art supplies so I could set up a temporary studio space.

It wasn't much, but it was what I had.

Which was kind of pathetic, actually.

Because *really* what I had was a pile of debt, an unused degree, a job I only kept because I loved my sister and I was avoiding getting on with my life, and the remnants of a shattered dream.

My best friend stared me down with her steady brown eyes. "You made me a promise to grab life by the balls," she said. "Well, there's a giant set of balls over on that bench, waiting for you."

"Ew," I said. "Fine. I'll give him a big sweet maybe."

"Yes!" Devi kissed me on the cheek, adjusted my bikini top to show a little more cleavage and marched me back over to Jesse Mayes.

"Way to make me not feel like a whore," I grumbled at her, but she just smiled.

Jesse looked up at me as we approached, the sun catching in his eyes. The man was even gorgeous when he was squinting.

"You look angelic," he said, getting to his feet. "All silhouetted by the sun like that."

"Um, flattery is always welcome, but it won't help your case. I could really use some time to think about this."

"Take your time," he said. "The tour doesn't start 'til Sunday." He sipped his coffee. "This really is great coffee."

"Sunday? Like... *this* Sunday?" I sputtered. "The day after tomorrow?"

He grinned. "Yep."

"Um... you couldn't give me a little more notice?"

"Just got back into town a few days ago. I've been down in L.A.. And, well..." He shrugged. "Things move fast in my world. Speaking of which. We're having a VIP party in town, tomorrow night, just a small private show to kick off the tour. Come as my date. Give it a chance. If you decide I'm a creep or you can't hack the three-ring circus, I'll understand."

Devi elbowed me slightly, when I just stood there like an idiot.

"Um, okay?" I managed.

"She'll need a plus one," Devi put in.

"You can meet us there," Jesse told her, then nodded at me. "I'll pick you up. Eight o'clock." Then he sipped his coffee, did a little finger-to-eyebrow salute thing, turned and walked out of my sister's yard.

I looked at Devi, my jaw dangling open.

Seriously. What the fuck just happened?

I had a date with Jesse Mayes?

And a job offer?

My best friend beamed at me and did a sexy little celebratory dance in her incredibly high heels. I couldn't help grinning at her. Because *shit*. "You're fucking insane."

She beamed. "Which is why you love me."

"*Two hundred grand?*"

"Will buy a hell of a lot of paint brushes, babe."

CHAPTER SEVEN

Katie

AT EIGHT O'CLOCK THE next evening, I found an illegally-parked black Ferrari in front of my apartment building.

Jesse Mayes leaned against a tree wearing sinfully fitted jeans, a loose, scoop neck T-shirt, a blazer and shades, presumably watching me try to navigate the front steps in my high heels and not slip on my own drool. His mouth quirked in a sexy smile as I drew near. My heart did a strange little lurch when he said, "Hi."

"Um… hi. Where's your driver guy?" Were we going to this thing alone?

"Sometimes I like to drive myself, sweetheart." He slid his shades onto his head and nailed me with those dark eyes, his expression unreadable as he looked me over. He reached to open the car door for me. "Why? You got a thing for Jude?"

"Um… the big dude with the tree tattoo? No." Feeling the need to explain, I added, "Not really my type."

"What, dark and dangerous?"

Of course, dark and dangerous could just as easily describe Jesse, though he was a different kind of dangerous; the kind that fucked you silly and broke your heart in the process. His hired muscle, on the other hand, looked straight out of a scene from *Sons of Anarchy*.

"Nice dress," he added, before I could formulate a response. "Leather and lace," he mused, then stood back and held the door for me.

"Thank you." I turned and got my ass in the car, settling into the low seat as gracefully as I could. I tried not to give him an eyeful of my panties as that smoldering gaze flirted with the hem of my short red lace dress and drifted down my bare legs. Then he shut the door and I exhaled.

Time for my little pep talk. The one I'd prepared in my head since I'd agreed to this fake date, this bizarre little trial run to determine if there were going to be more fake dates. Six weeks' worth of them.

I reminded myself that I didn't have to be here. If Jesse Mayes turned out to be a total dick, I really didn't need two hundred grand that bad. My integrity was not for sale, at any price. This was just one night. Then I could walk away. Tell my future grand-children that I once went on a date with a rock star. Even they didn't need to know it was fake.

The sun was in Jesse's eyes when he got in the car but he didn't put his shades back on, probably so he could eye-fuck me every chance he got, like he was doing now. "You look hot in red."

"You don't have to say that."

The Ferrari roared to life and we pulled out into the street. "Can't a guy hit on his own girlfriend?" he asked, all filthy innocence.

"I'm not your girlfriend."

"You are tonight, sweetheart. What I'm paying you for, right?"

"Paying me?"

"That's the deal. Two hundred grand for the next six weeks."

"Yeah, *if* I come on tour." Ugh. Hearing him say it out loud, it felt all kinds of wrong. I still balked at what seemed an exorbitant price for my "services," but if he was willing to pay it, as Devi put it, I'd be crazy to turn it down. Still… "Let's just call tonight a freebie. Consider it a try-before-you-buy." The thought of him paying me for tonight's date made me feel like an escort, and I couldn't stomach it.

"Thought I already had one of those." He tossed me a heated look that brought back every steamy moment of our pseudo make out session at the video shoot.

"Yes, but this time I'll be vertical."

He laughed, an amazing, sexy laugh that set off tingles in some pretty intimate places. He definitely hadn't laughed like that at the video shoot. Tonight he seemed in a better mood. "If that's the way you want it."

"I do," I said primly.

"But I'm paying for drinks, the hotel, and anything else that comes up."

"Hotel?"

"We've got rooms near the venue. We'll be out late."

I studied him sidelong as he drove.

Right. Out late.

Did he really think I'd be that easy? Were other girls that easy? *Really?* He just snapped his fingers and panties dropped?

Hell, no.

We took the sharp turn onto Main Street and I clung to my seat. The Ferrari had balls; I'd never been in such a powerful car. It sent my heart racing the way it went from zero to whiplash at the merest caress of Jesse's booted toe. But he looked hella sexy driving it, totally at ease, his hands loose on the wheel.

He wore a lot more jewelry than any man I'd ever known; rings, bracelets, layered necklaces. It was sexy and kind of badass, like everything else about him. His blazer was a matte velvet, so dark brown it was almost black, very close to his eye color. And the denim molded to his thighs was distressed; in fact, I could see slices of skin through the rips…

I glanced up… and met his gaze.

Great. He'd caught me ogling his thigh-meat. I felt the blush creep over my body as his jaw flexed; he was chewing gum again.

"So, um… you like cinnamon." Way to make conversation. "I mean, I just noticed…" I could smell the gum. It went rather well with the smells of new Ferrari and male rock god, but I wasn't about to tell him that.

"My oral fixation?"

"Is that what you call it?"

"I do like to have something in my mouth at all times." A grin spread across his gorgeous face and he chewed his gum exaggeratedly. "I quit smoking last year. Chewing gum helps, but I don't like mint."

And now I couldn't stop staring at his mouth.

"So, who's going to be at this thing?" I changed the subject, trying to sound breezy even as I white-knuckled the leather seat. Luckily traffic was pretty backed up so we couldn't go very fast.

"Just the band," he said as we slid up to a red light. "Some media. And a bunch of people Brody invited that you don't need to worry about. We'll be in the VIP room."

"The new band?" I kind of hoped and prayed that's what he meant. The thought of spending the night with the members of his new solo project band, whoever they were, seemed far less daunting than hanging out with the members of Dirty. According to Devi's intel, only Jesse still lived in Vancouver, where Dirty got their start; the other band members lived in L.A., but I had no idea what to expect tonight.

"Both of them, actually," he said.

Well, shit.

Would Elle be there?

"Do they know about this?" I asked. "Us?"

"Only what we tell them."

"You haven't told them?"

"That I'm paying you to pretend to be my girlfriend? Not so much."

"So... they think we're really together?"

"They will when I show up with you."

Holy shit. This was getting real.

Jesse's gaze had fixed on something up ahead, and I followed his line of sight. It was a bus shelter. One wall held a glass-encased ad featuring a gorgeous brunette model wearing jeans, sunglasses, lipstick and not much else.

"So," I asked as traffic got moving again, "why me? I mean, you could have anyone. You could have her." I indicated the model as we drove past.

"That's my sister," he said, his tone a little gruff.

"Your *sister*?" I rubbernecked to get a better look. Of course Jesse Mayes would have a model for a sister. But too late; the Ferrari had already left the shelter in its rearview. "Will she be there tonight?"

"She's in L.A.."

"What's her name?"

His lips quirked a little. "Jessa."

"Excuse me?" I couldn't help a laugh. "Jesse and Jessa?"

Again, the hint of a smile. "Uh-huh. I guess my mom felt bad that our dad left while she was pregnant. So she let me name the baby. I wanted to name her Jesse, but Mom said I had to pick something else, since that was already my name. I picked Jessa. I was four." He glanced at me. "Guess you should know all that, since we're a couple."

I tried to pretend I didn't like the sound of that, but I couldn't deny the little warm spot that story ignited in my chest and the several miles warmer I felt toward him after hearing it.

God, I was such a sap. I just had to remind myself, and keep reminding myself, that this was all fake. All of it.

No matter what happened between us... or seemed to happen.

Anything he said to me, he was saying out of obligation. Protecting the lie he'd invented himself, for his public image, for the sole purpose of selling albums and concert tickets.

And I didn't like the idea of pretending to be something I wasn't, but for the tune of two hundred grand and a chance to get my life on track, I'd promised Devi—and myself—I'd try.

"Right," I said. "Well, since we're a couple. My sister's name is Becca, short for Rebecca. She's ten years older than me."

"That's a gap."

"Yeah, I was sort of the 'oops' baby my parents had in their late thirties."

"Any other family?"

"Becca is married to Jack. Happily. They've been together since they were teens. You met their kids, Sadie and Owen. Becca and Jack own Nudge Coffee, you know, where I work."

"Right. And why do they call it Nudge?"

"Apparently, Jack came up to Becca in the crowd at a concert and gave her a nudge. And I guess the rest is history."

"And what else do you do besides work at Nudge and bake tiny pies?"

Sadly, that was pretty much it lately. "I hang out with Devi a lot. We've been best friends since sixth grade. You should probably know that too. She's my in-case-of-emergency phone call, my one-call-from-jail call. You know, all that stuff."

Jesse cocked an eyebrow in my direction. "You planning on going to jail tonight, cherry pie?"

"One never knows when hanging out with a rock star."

There it was again, that sexy, throaty laugh.

"Do you have a best friend?" I asked.

"Yeah. Jude."

The big, biker-looking dude with the tree tat? I'd just assumed the man was an employee. "Oh. I would've guessed it was someone in the band."

"Brody and Zane are close too, but Jude is the closest thing to a brother I've ever had. All four of us grew up together. Those are my boys."

"I didn't know that." As soon as it was out of my mouth, I regretted it. It begged the question of what I *did* know, and the only way I *could* know anything about Jesse Mayes was by creeping on him online.

He didn't miss it. "How about you tell me what you do know, and I'll tell you if it's true or not."

I sighed. "Okay, full disclosure? I didn't know anything about you until I was cast in the video. When we met in Devi's office, I really didn't know who you were."

"Really?"

"Really. But when I got hired, I looked you up. I was kind of hoping you'd turn out to be a loser with a sordid track record of yo-yo rehab stints, baby-daddy paternity lawsuits and scary mug shots."

He looked perplexed, but amused. "Why?"

"So I'd have an excuse to steer clear."

He absorbed that a moment. "And how did that turn out for you?"

"Not so well. For a rock star your reputation is oddly lacking in scandal and controversy. I think the most alarming thing I came across was the stalker incident. A bunch of girls broke into your house?"

"Two girls, actually."

"What did you do?"

"Called security, gave them each a kiss and sent them on their way."

"Really?" For once, I was kind of glad traffic heading onto the viaduct into downtown was at a crawl. Getting to know my fake date was becoming pretty interesting.

"I got a restraining order against them, on recommendation of Brody and our lawyers," he said. "They seemed harmless enough, maybe a little cuckoo. I get a lot of overzealous fans."

"So what's the difference between overzealous fan and stalker, if breaking into your home doesn't qualify?"

"It qualifies. But I had a serious stalker once, back in our early days. A guy who dressed like me and managed to wrangle his way backstage at a few shows, stole one of my guitars and snuck onto the tour bus. The girls who broke into my house swam in my pool. This guy slept in my bunk, wore my dirty clothes and jerked off in my guitar case. I'd call that a different shade of crazy."

"Wow. Restraining order?"

"You better believe it."

"Poor fella. Maybe all he wanted was a kiss."

Jesse grinned. "What else has the internet told you about me?"

Ugh. I hated having to admit I'd been reading up on him. "Not much other than the obvious. You know, rock god, guitar legend in the making, blah blah blah. Oh. And you've dated a lot of famous women. Models. Actresses."

"That's true."

I was kind of hoping he'd deny that one. Not that it should matter to me—fake girlfriend that I was. But I didn't exactly relish being compared to his usual "type."

"But not many actual girlfriends," I said, digging a little.

"Also true."

"One, actually." Because according to Wikipedia, Elle was the only woman who held that distinction.

"Two," he said. "I had a girlfriend in high school. Then we went on our first tour and fame took its course. Relationships got sticky."

Sticky how, I wasn't sure, though obviously the long distance thing probably sucked. And I could imagine dating a guy who suddenly rocketed into the spotlight would be a lot to take, especially when he was being pawed by rabid female fans every night. But I wasn't sure I wanted the details on that; I was nervous enough about walking into this party on Jesse Mayes' arm and being the object of jealousy and judgment. I'd had a taste of that since the video came out, and it was pretty hard to swallow.

"So, you just don't do the girlfriend thing?"

"No."

I was surprised by the blunt answer. And maybe, way deep down, just a tiny bit disappointed, which was beyond stupid.

"You'll probably hear a lot of things," he said. "But here's the truth. Elle is family to me. But she wasn't any more right for me than any of the other women I've dated these last ten years. We stuck it out a while, probably longer than we should have, because of the band. We were in the middle of the tour when we realized things weren't right."

"How long were you together?"

"About a year. But the last few months of that was a prolonged breakup."

"Okay," I said. "Thank you for filling me in."

"That it?" he asked. "The internet trail go cold there?" Clearly, he knew it hadn't.

"Not exactly." I met his gaze. "You get horny on stage."

He grinned and kind of rolled his eyes. "I wish I could say that's a lie."

"It embarrasses you?"

"If I said yes, would you believe me?"

"I don't know yet." After the way he'd pretended to fuck me senseless in front of a camera crew, all the while with a raging hard-on, it was hard to imagine anything would embarrass the man.

"Anything else?"

"Um… yes. It also seemed evident that you have a reputation as…" I tried to put it as diplomatically as I could, and not give his ego too much of a stroke. "A talented lover."

To my surprise, he didn't laugh or gloat. He didn't say a thing about it.

"What about you?" he asked. "What would your ex-lovers say about you?"

"I don't know. Maybe you could ask him sometime."

"Seriously?"

"Unfortunately, yes."

"How is that?"

"How is what?"

"How is it you've only had one lover?"

"I'm a slow learner?"

He smiled at my lame joke. "Seemed to know what you were doing when you kissed me at the video shoot."

"You mean, when *you* kissed *me*." I tried not to smile too big at that comment. "And thanks for saying that. I was feeling a little out of practice." I glanced at him. "Like, um… two years out of practice."

Jesse looked over at me, his mouth open, like he meant to say something. Then he shut it. Then he opened it again.

"Well, fuck," he said.

Yeah. Pretty sure I'd just blown his mind. Though maybe not in a good way.

"So…" He cleared his throat. "What else should I know about Katie Bloom?"

"Um… I don't know. I've never had a stalker. I've never been on stage, so I don't know if it would make me horny."

"What's your favorite food?"

"Pizza."

"Everyone likes pizza. What kind?"

"Double cheese. Triple if I can get it."

"That's it? No toppings?"

"Cheese is a topping."

"Any weird allergies?"

"Nope."

"Strange quirks?"

"You mean like stage horniness?" I threw him a sidelong look. "Hmm... I never wear matching socks."

"Never?"

"Never. I mismatch them as soon as I buy them."

"Weirdo."

"I have a lucky leather jacket." I indicated the one I was wearing.

"And it's lucky because...?"

"Because good things always happen when I wear it. I wear it sparingly."

He looked at me like I was dead crazy. "Why wouldn't you wear it all the time?"

I gave him the same look right back. "Because what if I wear all the goodness out?"

He laughed at that logic. "Okay... Favorite sexual position?"

I had to think about that. "Missionary?"

"Really?" His tone was entirely disbelieving. We were now stuck in a slow crawl into Gastown, so I wasn't getting out of this anytime soon.

"Yes."

"Really."

"Yes."

"What do you like about it?"

"Well... I like having a man on top of me. You know, being able to feel him... his weight and his strength..." I opted to shut my mouth there, since Jesse's eyes were blazing into me. I shifted in my seat; I was beginning to sweat in my leather and lace. "How about you?"

"Favorite food, T-bone steak, rare," he said. "I'm allergic to cats. I sometimes talk in my sleep."

"Really? What do you say?"

"I don't know. You're my girlfriend. You tell me."

"I think I heard you mumble something about getting my name tattooed on your ass."

"Sounds like something I would say."

I laughed. "Favorite sexual position?"

"My face. Between your legs."

My laughter choked off as heat flushed my cheeks. Right. Oral fixation. "Um…" I swallowed. "Isn't that more of a foreplay position?"

He didn't answer that, just chewed his gum and smiled. The roar of the Ferrari echoed off the close buildings as we made our way through the narrow streets.

"So, what do I tell people?" I asked, looking to steer the conversation away from sex. "I mean, they're gonna ask. You know, me, with you." Maybe all prettied up with makeup and lingerie and fancy lighting in a glossy music video I was a match for him on some level, but the truth of the matter was that Jesse Mayes was way the hell out of my league. He had to know it.

Everyone else would.

"Just tell them I fuck your brains out every night and you've never been happier," he said, unconcerned. "What more do they need to know?"

"But shouldn't we have a few details worked out? Corroborate our stories? Like what do you like most about me? Assuming that what I like most about you is that you fuck my brains out every night."

He grinned. "I like fucking your brains out every night."

I blushed; it was getting bloody hot in my leather jacket, but I was afraid to take it off and get eye-fucked all over again when he got a glimpse of the plunging neckline of my dress.

"Tell me what else I should like about you," he said.

"I don't know. I like animals. You've met my dog, Max. I'm fairly neat and organized. I'm a good baker."

"You just described my grandma."

I blushed again, this time from embarrassment rather than rising horniness. Why I didn't mention my painting, I wasn't sure. Maybe I didn't want to sound like a pathetic wannabe. Too many times I'd seen the spark of interest in someone's eyes, only to see it snuffed out again when they discovered I'd never actually *done* anything with my artistic aspirations. "Um... and I fuck like an animal?"

"That's more like it."

"And what else do I like about you, other than the frequent sex?"

"You like my big ego," he said easily. "You find it charming. You like my big dick. And I'm a phenomenal lay."

Sweet Jesus. "Is that all?"

"What more do you need?"

"How did we get together?"

"I sent you a dick pic after the video shoot and the rest is history."

"Seriously?"

"Why not? Not everyone can fall in love over a nudge. Some girls need a little dick."

"I thought it was a big dick. See? We need to get our story straight."

He laughed. I liked making him laugh. Which was not a good sign.

"What about L.A.?" I asked. "I thought you were out of town since the shoot."

"Not a problem. We've got sexting, phone sex, and there's always Skype. And I've been back in town for six days."

We'd stopped at another red light, at the edge of Coal Harbour, and I tossed him a skeptical look.

"Trust me," he said. "We could do a lot of damage in six days."

Well, then. "Okay… so as of right now, we've been doing it for six days straight?"

"Every spare moment."

As the light turned green and his gaze left me, I tried to hold back my smile. This fake relationship was starting to sound like a hell of a lot of fun.

"And is there anything to this relationship besides sex?"

"Of course. Just wrote a new song about you that I'm gonna sing on tour. It's called 'New Girl.'"

I assumed he was joking and laughed, but he didn't. He looked darkly serious as we turned into the drive of an incredibly posh hotel near the water.

"No one really cares who I'm fucking, Katie," he said. As we parked at the valet stand, his dark eyes locked on mine. "Not for more than five minutes. Jesse Mayes in love, that's the story."

CHAPTER EIGHT

Katie

WHEN WE ARRIVED, the club was already packed.

About a thousand bouncers were waiting to escort Jesse and his entourage into the venue. Jude and another one of Jesse's personal security guys, Flynn, had met us at the hotel, and along the way we'd managed to accrue a number of other big, leather-clad dudes with tattoos. I had no idea if they were Jesse's buddies or his bodyguards or both. He'd given me his hand and I clung to it with both of mine and didn't ask questions, just tried to take everything in.

The club was in an old but renovated building, original, hundred-year-old stone outside, glass and steel inside. We went in through the lobby of an adjoining building, through the bar's staff entrance. I could make out Hugo's "99 Problems" thumping through the glass wall that looked into the bar and I could tell it was pretty dark, people crowded at least three deep up to the two long bars. Over the stage an illuminated backdrop featured the image from the cover of Jesse's solo album, *Sunday Morning*: a pair of men's dirty leather boots, discarded on the floor next to what was obviously a woman's bed.

There were a bunch of people waiting to talk to Jesse in the narrow staff hallway. He spoke with a few of them, briefly, but didn't introduce me. I hung back with Flynn, who seemed to be hovering near me, but Jesse never let go of my hand. So far, he was a pretty classy date. I just hoped I didn't disappoint him. I had no idea what to do or say to all these people, so I just smiled —enough that I looked like I was happy to be here, but not so much that I looked like a weirdo. As soon as Jesse was done talking, Jude gave the nod and the bouncers whisked us up a flight of stairs into the VIP room. Which was cool, because I'd never been a VIP before.

It took several seconds for my eyes to adjust to the darkness. There were candles burning in glass bowls on low tables with cushy blood-red seats grouped around them. A web of tiny lights like stars filled the ceiling. The room was surrounded on three sides by a low wall with a railing that overlooked the club floor below and had an incredible view of the stage. Two giant screens, one to each end of the room, played the video for the first single off *Sunday Morning*, "Come Lately," which was mostly footage of Jesse playing the song in an empty field while his hair blew around his face and he played his guitar so hard sweat ran down his body... which, if you asked me, was all you really needed to put in a video.

I tore my gaze away from the giant image of Jesse to follow his lead through the dark room. We headed straight for a giant party booth in the middle with a bunch of tables clustered inside it. There were a lot of people there already. Men, mostly. I recognized Jesse's bandmates, Zane and Dylan, right away, and his hot manager, Brody, who rose to meet us when he saw us coming.

I scanned the group but I didn't see Elle.

"Hey, brother," Brody greeted Jesse, but his eyes were on me. A smile spread across his face. I wondered if he knew yet about the proposal Jesse had made me, which was kind of embarrassing,

but I'd just have to deal with it. "Katie. Nice to see you again."
He took my hand, though Jesse never let go of the other one.

"You, too," I said.

Dylan greeted us next. He towered over me, sweeping his
dark auburn hair back out of his green eyes as Jesse introduced
us. Then the big drummer gave me a huge grin and pulled me in
for a quick hug. Thank God he was wearing jeans this time. When
I'd met him at the video shoot he was wearing his kilt, and he'd
put one booted foot up on the couch while talking to me, showing
so much muscular thigh I'd almost choked to death on my water.

Zane was next, greeting Jesse and giving me a thorough once-
over. He noted my hand in Jesse's and his blond eyebrows rose.

"Where the fuck do I know you from?" he said, and his tone
was so dripping with innuendo, I swore for all he thought he
might've fucked me on some distant, drunken night he couldn't
remember.

Dylan leaned in and said something in his ear I couldn't hear.
The music had gone up a notch and The Black Keys were
thumping out the opening lines of "Your Touch." Zane's ice-blue
eyes crinkled as he burst out laughing.

"You're fucking kidding me. The girl from the video?" He
pulled Jesse in for a one-armed, chest-to-chest bro hug, then
tossed his head back, flashing his white teeth, and roared again.
"Shiiiiit, brother."

I was blushing by this point, but lucky for me the dim lighting
in the room probably hid the fact. Which was good, because I'd
be doing it a lot.

Jesse slapped Zane on the cheek. Zane never stopped grinning. At me. Then he tossed his arm around Maggie, who'd materialized, to my delight. Maggie rolled her eyes, shrugged him off,
sort of, and hugged me. "Katie!" She looked at my hand in
Jesse's, then at Jesse, her expression curious, then accusing.
"What the fuck did you do?"

"Nothing," Jesse said, and winked at me.

Right. Nothing. Except sent me an alleged dick pic.

Shit. Were we really going with that story?

I watched, helpless, as Jesse started getting sucked away into the growing crowd of people wanting his attention. Twenty-four hours ago, if someone told me I'd feel *less* nervous with Jesse Mayes at my side, I'd say they were high as fuck. But right now I didn't want to let him go. He did a really sweet thing, though, and looked me in the eye, told me he'd be back, and kissed my hand before he let go.

Luckily, Maggie was there to scoop me up.

I fucking loved this woman.

She looked hot tonight too, her little black dress showing off her flawless light-brown skin, her sleek, dark hair loose around her pretty face. Which was probably why Zane kept putting his arm around her. She kept dodging it, though this seemed like a long-established game between them. I wondered how she kept her sanity around all these hot men. Did she sleep with any of them?

Were she and Zane lovers?

I really couldn't tell. But she pretty much ignored him as she introduced me around in a whirlwind to what she called "the VVIPs."

Besides Dylan and Zane there was Dylan's buddy, Ashley, who told me to call him Ash. He had this punk-meets-surfer-dude thing going on with his inky black hair, serious blue eyes and many piercings. And he was crazy hot.

What was it with these guys and their friends?

Did one need to be a perfect ten—minimum—to even hang with this crowd?

I was introduced to the members of Jesse's solo band next, and my nerves settled a little. These, at last, were dudes from my planet. While none of them could be called unattractive by any stretch, they probably weren't responsible for causing whiplash in the streets, and that was probably a good thing.

I was told that Rafael played rhythm guitar and various other instruments; he also co-wrote a couple of songs with Jesse on the album. Letty was the bass player and Pepper was on drums. Pepper and Ash were in some alt-rock band I'd never heard of called the Penny Pushers, who often toured with Dirty as their opening band. And as it turned out, after chatting with the members of Jesse's solo project band, and laughing with them, and enjoying the first pint of beer that Pepper handed me, I decided they were pretty fucking awesome on their own. What was it about rock 'n' roll musicians that was so... yummy?

The carefree, bad boy vibe?

The tight jeans and leather?

Yeah. That.

And as I soaked in the vibe, I realized it wasn't just the way they looked, or dressed, or the in-your-face sex appeal, but the sheer, potent electricity of raw male energy. It was this unapologetic way they had of taking up space, sitting with their thighs spread wide, throwing their heads back to laugh out loud, showing their teeth. They wore big, chunky rings and had tattoos, and Zane even wore a smudge of eyeliner, which made his arctic eyes look even bluer.

Not to mention they were all talking at once. Once in a while Maggie rolled her eyes and told one or all of them to shut up, but it barely made a dent.

After a while, Jesse collected me and took me around to pose for some photos with him. He introduced me to pretty much everyone he talked to, either as Katie or in some cases as "my girlfriend, Katie," which I couldn't say I minded, though everyone was starting to become one big, beautiful rock 'n' roll blur. Maybe it was the beer. More likely it was my nerves. I just hoped I wasn't getting quizzed on all these names later.

I just had to *look* like I knew what I was doing, right? Because if anyone asked me for a sound bite, I was pretty sure I'd choke. I was already dizzy with the sheer overwhelmingness of the growing crowd.

And then, in the middle of it all, I found a little respite—a tiny old lady I hadn't even noticed at first.

She was calmly drinking a beer out of a pint glass when Maggie deposited me next to her on one of the plush chairs, introducing her to me simply as "Grandma Dolly."

"This is my friend, Katie," Maggie said, which was super nice of her. "She's here with Jesse tonight."

"Isn't that nice," Dolly said in a kindly way and squeezed my hand. She looked like she might blow away if you breathed on her too hard and her skin was soft, like wrinkled velvet, but there was strength in her grip. She wore cornflower blue slacks and a sweater with a sparkly music note on it, bejeweled with blue rhinestones. Her hair was white and set in waves close to her head, the same way she'd probably worn it for decades.

She was adorable.

"You're Jesse's grandma?" I asked her.

"Ah, my Jesse. He's a special one," she said, her pale blue eyes soft. "He's not really mine though, dear. Zane is my grandson. I met Jesse when he was eight, when the boys were in school together."

Just then Jesse came over to greet her, and Dolly held up her glass in toast. I tipped the rim of my beer glass against hers. "To Jesse and his wonderful new album," she said in her scratchy little voice. Everyone else around our table—Zane, Dylan and Ash, Maggie, and now Brody and Jude, who'd come over with Jesse—fell silent to listen and raised their glasses and bottles, following Dolly's lead. "It's lovely, dear. Zane played it for me this afternoon."

"Thanks, Dolly," Jesse said.

"I knew you had more love songs in you," I heard her say as he bent close to kiss her forehead.

Once Jesse had turned away to talk to Jude, I leaned closer and told her, "He seems very fond of you."

She nodded and patted my hand. "He and his sister spent a lot of time at my home when they were young, and once their mother died, I took Jessa in."

"I didn't know that." Jesse had mentioned his father leaving, but I didn't know his mom had died. "When did that happen?"

"Oh, Jesse was about twenty or so. Jessa was only sixteen. But they spent so much time at my house even before their mother got sick that I felt like they were my own flesh and blood. Still do." She glanced over at Jesse fondly. "Such a shame that Jessa won't be here tonight."

"They must've been cute kids."

"Oh, yes. You wouldn't believe the condition they showed up in some days, though. Dirty. Hadn't eaten all day. I used to make extra food in case they showed up for dinner, and more often than not, as the years went by, they did. Jesse did what he could to care for Jessa, but he was just a child, too. He had a job from the time he was thirteen, to help out, but I didn't like Jessa being left alone at home, so I told him, you bring her on over anytime you need. You go to work, you bring her. And so he did."

Wow.

I glanced over at Jesse. He was deep in conversation with Jude and Brody and if I pictured him as a boy with no dad and a sick mom, taking his little sister over to Zane's grandma's house so she could be fed, I definitely saw him differently.

Maybe I was an idiot, but I could've sworn it was the first time I really saw him as a human being.

"That's incredible, Dolly." I smiled at her, kinda wishing I'd known my own grandma. Both of mine were long gone when I was born. "They were so lucky to have you."

"Well, I did what I could. Mind you, we didn't have a whole lot more, but my grandkids always lived better than that." Her kindly gaze lifted to Zane, who was standing over us, just in time to see him squeezing the ass of a hot blonde chick in a tight metallic dress.

Dolly shook her head a little. "What a handful they were."

Maggie nudged me as she leaned over, picking up on the conversation. "Imagine these guys as horny teenagers and you get the idea."

"You wouldn't believe the half of it, young lady," Dolly said. "The songs they came up with in my garage. Oh, the racket they made. This one with his screechy little voice."

"My ears are twitching." Zane dropped into the love seat across from us, the blonde glued to his side.

"Oh, you've always been this band's dirty mouth," Dolly said to him, her tone teasing but proud.

"That's a fact," Brody put in, joining the conversation.

"And its pretty face," Zane said with a giant grin.

"And I've always said, Elle is the heart of you all," Dolly said matter-of-factly. "Isn't it strange to all be together without her."

"That it is," Zane agreed.

I met Jesse's gaze. I wasn't sure how to take Dolly's assessment, though I was privately relieved that Elle wasn't here. He sipped his beer, his eyes on mine.

"But my Jesse," Dolly said. "You've always been the soul of Dirty."

"Thanks, Dolly," Jesse said.

"I'll drink to that." Brody raised his glass. "To Jesse, and a killer new album. With soul."

We all cheered to Jesse once again, and swigged our beers.

"So what does that make me, Doll?" Dylan asked. The big drummer waggled his eyebrows. "The brains of the band?"

"I think you mean brawn," Maggie said.

"Aw, honey," Dolly said, and took a sip of her beer. "Everyone knows you're its balls."

Dylan choked on his beer. The other guys whooped with laughter.

Zane laughed so hard he fell off the love seat, nearly taking the blonde with him.

It was getting louder in the club as the anticipation of Jesse's set built and the crowd thickened. Arctic Monkeys' "R U Mine?" was blasting and I was somewhere near the bottom of my third beer when Devi arrived. She dropped into a seat next to me, which Brody vacated for her, and Dylan was quick to hand her a beer. This song always gave me serious lady sweats, so it didn't help when I spotted Jesse returning through the crowd with Jude... in leather pants.

Ung. I pretty much bit my tongue to keep it from falling out of my mouth.

I'd had just enough time to fill Devi in on the events of the evening so far, up to and including the fact that the hot babes—of the female variety—had been multiplying at a staggering rate since I'd arrived. The chick-to-dude ratio in the VIP room was now a solid three-to-one. Zane, Dylan and Ash had women all over them. I was kind of relieved Jesse had vanished to take care of some business; I wasn't sure how excited I was to watch random chicks climbing all over my fake date.

I sipped my beer as I watched him work his way toward me, getting pawed all along the way. He was still wearing the velvet blazer over the soft drapey tee with the scoop neck that showed off his sexy collarbone. And yeah. Black leather pants.

I tried really fucking hard not to stare, but no man had ever looked so good in leather pants.

Ever.

He was also wearing his sunglasses, indoors, in a dark club... and somehow managed not to look like a douche doing it.

He walked over to me, nodded a greeting at Devi and crouched down next to my chair. "How's it going, beautiful?" He pushed the shades onto his head to rest atop his silken curls.

"Good," I said, managing not to choke on my tongue. Barely. Shit, the man was beautiful up close. The twinkly lights were sparkling in his eyes, his long lashes casting shadows. "Your friends are nice."

He laughed heartily at that. "Must be on their best behavior. Trying to impress my new girl."

My heart beat a little faster at that. I liked how it sounded coming out of his mouth. A little too much. "I told Maggie about the, um, dick pic." It was true. She'd asked how we hooked up, and I told her. She'd laughed and rolled her eyes, but at least she seemed to buy it. Bad enough I lied to her; at least the lie went over. "I think she believed me."

"See?" Jesse grinned. "No problem."

"Right. Except everyone's being so cool to me, I feel like an asshole lying to them."

His eyes narrowed a bit, twitching in a sexy almost-smile. "You're not an asshole, Katie Bloom." He leaned in. "Gotta get my ass backstage." Then he kissed me on the mouth, just like that.

I held my breath; his lips lingered longer than I expected them to. Then he slowly drew away.

"Wish me luck," he said.

"You don't need it," I said, breathless. The man needed no help from me.

He grinned and walked away. I watched as he and the other guys in his solo band headed off, Jude and a bunch of bouncers escorting them. When I lost sight of him, I returned my attention to Devi.

My best friend was wearing the biggest, slyest shit-eating grin I'd ever seen on her face.

"What?" I said, sounding a lot more pissy than I meant to.

Her eyebrows went up. Way up. "Nothing." Her grin morphed into a sexy expression as she said, "*You're not an asshole, Katie Bloom*," in a low voice.

I sipped my beer, ignoring her.

"What was that about?" she pressed.

I sighed. "We're telling his friends he sent me a dick pic and that's how we got together. He was just trying to make me feel better about it."

"Sick." Devi leaned in. "Let me see it."

"There's no dick pic, you perv. It's just a joke."

Several songs later and halfway through another beer, I was getting antsy for the show to begin. My heart rate still hadn't returned to normal after that unexpected kiss and I was pretty much on the edge of my seat to see Jesse play live. I'd listened to his solo album about a hundred times since agreeing to this "date" and Dolly was right; the music of Jesse Mayes was lovely. It was also gritty, bluesy, dirty, dark and twisted, not to mention sexy, and addictive as all hell.

I probably could've gotten up and done some dancing to work off my nervous energy; a bunch of girls had started up an impromptu dance floor in the corner of the VIP room overlooking the one below. But I had a killer view of center stage, so I wasn't giving up my seat for any-fucking-thing. Some guy was chatting up Devi next to me but I didn't feel like I could hold a conversation, so I just people-watched. My leg was vibrating as I tapped my foot with anticipation, so it took me a delayed moment to realize my cell phone had buzzed in the pocket of my leather jacket. Twice.

I dug it out and swiped the screen, opening the messaging app, to find a dick pic staring me in the face.

Um…

I tucked the phone under the table, checked that no one was paying attention and took a furtive peek. Against my better judgment, I tapped the message, enlarging it.

Yep. I'd just received a photo of a cock, standing tall and proud, and wrapped in a man's hand wearing a couple of big silver rings.

I swallowed.

I scrolled to the next message, which said simply, *Now you don't have to lie.*

"Katie!"

I jumped a good inch off my seat and banged my hand on the underside of the table. "Jesus!" I closed the app and tucked my phone away. Devi was standing over her seat, staring me down.

"What the hell are you doing under there? I said your name like eight times."

"Nothing. Checking my messages. What's up?"

"I was saying, these gentlemen are buying us drinks." She introduced me to the two guys standing next to her, but I honestly forgot their names as soon as she said them.

"Katie, right?" one of the guys said. "Nice to meet you."

"You too." I shook the offered hand but didn't stand up. Devi was making eyes at me. I knew that look, but no way was I picking up some random dude while I was here as Jesse's date.

"One sec," she said to the guys and leaned over to shout-whisper in my ear. "They're going to a party after this. We should totally go."

I shout-whispered back. "I'm already on a date!"

"A fake one!"

"Shh!" I glanced around, but Led Zeppelin's "Black Dog" was rocking the house, way too loud for anyone to hear a word of what we were saying. "It's supposed to be real. Brush them off!"

"Uh-uh. I'm hooking up." She then smiled, handed over one of the cosmos that had just arrived—her favorite drink—and stood to join the guys again.

The one who'd shaken my hand leaned in across her empty chair. "Mind if I join you?"

"Oh. Um, actually I'm here with someone."

"Oh yeah?" He smiled a genuine, friendly smile. He had twinkly blue eyes and seemed nice enough. "Who's this guy who would leave you here by yourself?"

"Uh, Jesse Mayes?" There was really no way to say that without sounding like a bitch. I realized it as soon as it came out of my mouth.

The guy's smile faltered, just as an arm reached between us. A super-muscular arm with a black full-sleeve tattoo of a tree with long, gnarly roots. A large fist with a big silver skull ring on the middle finger set a drink on the table. It was a champagne glass filled with shimmering bubbly, a swirl of red liqueur at the bottom.

I looked up into Jude's face. "From Jesse," he said with a little more growl than was necessary. Fortunately, the growl didn't seem to be for me.

I glanced at the blue-eyed guy, who'd leaned back, out of my space. Any trace of a smile was gone. He glanced from Jude to me, then nodded at me. "Take care, Katie." He leaned in to say something to his friend, who was engrossed in conversation with Devi. Then he was gone.

Wow.

Dude repellent, maximum strength.

"Thanks," I said to Jude, a little dubiously. I sipped the drink, which was amazing.

He nodded, and I caught the barest hint of a curl to one corner of his mouth. He handed an identical champagne cocktail to Devi, then headed back to his lookout spot by the railing.

And as I sat there sipping the drink Jesse had sent me, all I could think of was that dick pic. I fought against the temptation to pull out my phone and take another look.

Because apparently I, Katie Bloom, was a huge perv.

Fortunately the image was imprinted on my brain. That rock-hard cock straining in Jesse's hand, the thick shaft filling his strong fist... and, yeah. It was fucking big.

I swallowed and sipped my drink, glancing guiltily around, but no one seemed to notice as I crossed my legs so I could squeeze my thighs together, the flesh between my legs throbbing with need. God, it had been too long. The mere thought of Jesse taking his cock out, wrapping his own hand around it...

Where the hell did he take that photo? The washroom?

Did he think about *me* when he was getting that hard?

Did he jerk off?

"What the *fuck*," I heard Devi say, jolting me from my dirty thoughts.

I blinked the lust haze away as she settled into her seat next to me. The guy she'd been talking to was gone, probably to get her more drinks or something. Her red lips were parted in stunned horror. I turned to look at what she was staring at, but she grabbed my arm to stop me. "Don't," she hissed. "Look like you're having fun." Then she pasted on a brilliant Devi-smile and laughed.

"I am having fun."

"Just do it!" she said through her smile.

"Okay. This party is freaking amazing. I swear I just saw that guy from *The Walking Dead* over there."

"That wasn't him," Devi said distractedly, still smiling. "Met him at a party once. He's a lot shorter." She kept snatching furtive looks across the room and it was making me uneasy. She sipped her drink and tossed her hair as she smiled bigger, like I'd just said something amazing. "I can't fucking believe it."

"What the fuck is going on? Who's over there?" I turned to look in the direction Devi was looking, over Dolly's head.

Devi's hand tightened on my arm. "Slowly!" she said. "And don't make it obvious."

"Okay." I glanced around our table and the table next to us, pretending to peruse the faces of our companions. Then I glanced beyond, following the line of Devi's furtive gaze, where Brody was standing talking to some guy—

"Don't stare!" Devi said, and I spun back to her.

Because oh.

My.

God.

It was Josh.

My ex-fiancé, Josh.

CHAPTER NINE

Katie

I SIPPED my champagne cocktail and stared at him, trying to pretend I wasn't staring at him.

Joshua Breckenridge, Jr.

It was him. Dressed in a bespoke suit, because that's what he wore at all fucking times, even to a rock 'n' roll party.

I slumped in my chair, trying to instantaneously vanish.

"Do *not*," Devi hissed at me. "Sit up fucking straight."

I sat up. "What the hell is he doing here?"

"I don't know." Devi set her drink down on the table. "Don't worry, babe. I'm all over it."

With that, she stood and sashayed her little butt straight over to Maggie. If anyone could get the goods, Devi would.

I finished my champagne and started into the cosmo, and Devi returned in record time. "He owns the fucking bar," she said, sitting down. "Or daddy does. Whatever. Apparently they put in a bid to host this party and made Jesse's management an offer they couldn't refuse. How much do you want to bet he saw you in that video?" She flicked her chin at the big screens, which were now playing the "Dirty Like Me" video on a loop. Me and Jesse, larger than life. Going at it.

"Oh, God."

"Don't sweat it." Devi squared her shoulders, a dark glint in her pretty eyes. "I'll run interference all fucking night if that's what it takes. He's not getting near you."

"I'll be okay." I was feeling kind of faint, actually. I drank some more, my thoughts starting to swim.

This couldn't be happening.

I had no desire to see Josh. I hadn't seen him in two years, since the moment he walked out on me at the altar. I knew I'd run into him again someday, somewhere... but here? Now?

As if this night wasn't strange enough. This was probably the absolute worst place and time for this little reunion to happen.

I glanced over again. He was facing me, but didn't seem to be looking at me. He had to know I was here, though. He had to have seen me.

It kinda pissed me off, actually, that he was acting like he hadn't.

And it fucking depressed me that he looked so good.

Not Jesse Mayes good, but good.

"The guy thinks he owns the fucking world," Devi said. "Well, screw him. You don't belong to him."

I clinked my glass to hers when she toasted me but sat in silence, letting that sink in.

She was right. I didn't belong to Josh Breckenridge, Jr., but the truth was, I never had. Not if he was willing to walk out on me the way he did. And he was. He was so, so willing.

"Just leave it," I told her. "He's not coming over here. Not with all these guys around." If I knew one thing about Josh, he wouldn't risk getting shot down in front of all these VVIPs.

"He'd better not," Devi huffed, settling back in her chair. "What a fucking creep. Do you think he wants you back?"

Jesus. The thought hadn't even crossed my mind.

"No," I said.

I tried to smile when I noticed Jude glancing over. Then I took a deep breath and tried to relax.

I had my cosmo, my lucky leather jacket, and I had Devi. I had frickin' *security*.

All I really had to do was forget Josh's existence, which I'd become fairly good at, and enjoy the music of Jesse Fucking Mayes while he performed in those hot leather pants.

I had no idea what Josh's game was, but no way he would approach me with the likes of Jude standing watch.

My ex-fiancé was many things; brave wasn't one of them.

One kick-ass rock show, many champagne cocktails and three encores later, darkness finally fell as Jesse left the stage.

I was so blown away I just stood there applauding for at least five minutes with my jaw hanging open.

I definitely wasn't the only one.

The show had started with a couple of on-air DJ's from a local morning show introducing Jesse and warming up the crowd with some jokes. They said some really nice things about Jesse and all the cool things he'd done for the local music scene and the community, like investing in a local music school, starting up a music camp for at-risk youth, and co-producing an album for an up-and-coming local band.

Then Zane and some local record producer came out and said more nice things about Jesse—when the crowd would stop screaming enough to let Zane speak. He laughed through most of it and told everyone to calm the fuck down, which just made the crowd go wilder.

By the time Jesse, Raf, Letty and Pepper took the stage, it was to a storm of applause. They kicked off the show with a slightly sped-up version of the first single off *Sunday Morning*, "Come Lately," which heated up the club, fast.

The rest of the show was like a slow descent into a simmering make out session.

They played about half the songs from the new album and a bunch of Dirty songs, Jesse Mayes style, which pretty much meant stripped down, slowed down and completely panty-peeling. I already knew a lot of Dirty's songs, and I'd been listening to them on repeat since we shot the video. I could definitely say I was now hooked on the band. Hard not to be when you combined Zane's dead-sexy voice, raw, throaty and powerful, and the band's lusty, aggressive, drive-you-to-the-edge-of-an-orgasm sound, with some of the most heartrending, brilliantly poetic lyrics I'd ever heard. By the time the show climaxed with Jesse's orgasm-inducing version of "Dirty Like Me," there was no way there was a dry pair of panties in the place.

For the first encore, Dylan took over for Pepper on drums for a high-octane performance of one of Dirty's greatest hits, "Down With You," which completely blew the doors off the house. Then Zane joined Jesse on stage for an unplugged version of Dirty's "Runaround." The final song of the night was a stripped-down acoustic version of one of my favorite songs off Jesse's new album, "Breaking Bitter," featuring Jesse and a guitar alone on stage.

The thunder of the crowd kept on rolling as I stood there cheering, my hands sore from applauding, my throat getting hoarse from all the screaming. If I didn't feel like I could call myself a legit fan of Jesse Mayes' music before this night, there was no question I was one now. The man had thoroughly convinced me of his genius. I already knew his recorded music was amazing, but his live show was epic.

I had goose bumps.

I was sweating.

I was horny as hell.

I suddenly understood why chicks threw their underwear at dudes on stage. There was, in fact, at least one pair of panties that someone had tossed at Jesse at some point in the night, and Raf had hung on his mic stand. It was still dangling there in the single light that shone on stage, frilly and pink. The sight of it pretty much summed up Jesse's effect on the crowd.

I was pretty sure everyone was hoping he'd just keep coming back out on stage to blow our minds again and again. But the club DJ signaled the definite end of the show, dropping The Killers' "Somebody Told Me." Devi headed down to the dance floor with some guy who'd glued himself to her side during Jesse's set. The rest of Jesse's group was staggered throughout the VIP room, talking, drinking, and generally making noise.

I excused myself from the table where I still sat with Dolly, figuring it was a good time to use the washroom. Jude had disappeared toward the end of Jesse's set, no doubt to meet up with him backstage. I nodded at Flynn, thinking I should acknowledge him, since the man had watched my every move all night. It was clear to me by now, though no one had said so, that he'd been told to watch over me.

I headed down the hall off the VIP area where I saw the washroom sign, quickly. I wanted to be back at the table when Jesse arrived so I could congratulate him on the incredible show and be on hand if he needed me for any photo ops or whatever.

At the mirror over the sink, I took inventory; I figured I looked kinda killer in my red lace dress, which flattered my dark hair and my blue-green eyes—though they were kinda hazy from all the champagne. I was washing my hands, but my mind was on what I'd say to Jesse as I tried to put words to my thoughts about the show. So I didn't quite register the door of the washroom opening behind me... until I glimpsed Josh in the mirror.

That's right. My ex-fiancé, tall, blond and entitled, strolled into the ladies' room.

Then he shut the door and flipped the lock.

"Hey, gorgeous," he said. He sauntered over to one of the open cubicles in his expensive suit, stood with his back to me and undid his pants, and pissed in the toilet.

I stared, dumbfounded. "What the hell are you doing?"

I looked around; no urinals. I was definitely in the ladies' room.

"Taking a piss," he said. "And a moment of your time."

As he shook himself off, I grabbed a paper towel to dry my hands, bent on getting the hell out of there. By the time I grabbed my purse and bolted for the door, he'd intercepted my path. His belt was still undone, but at least he'd put his dick away.

"Come on, babe," he said, taking me by the shoulders. "You gotta talk to me sometime."

I shrugged his hands off, avoiding his pale blue eyes; his hair was longer than it used to be and kept flopping into them. It was a good look on him. "Do I?" I crossed my arms over my chest, clutching my purse to my ribs.

"You won't return my calls. What do you expect me to do?"

"I don't know. Maybe not accost me in a bathroom?"

True, I hadn't returned the calls he'd made to me after he walked out on our wedding. But the last one of those was over a year ago. And this was hardly the way to attempt a reunion.

He smoothed the blond strands out of his eyes and smirked at me. "Just want to remind you how good we are together, sweetheart."

"*Were*," I corrected, "and we were never that good."

"No? I guess I remember it differently."

"I guess you do. I remember being humiliated in front of everyone I love." I tried to look at his face, but I couldn't quite meet his eyes. I focused on his mouth, on that arrogant smirk.

"Maybe you got a kick out of that, but I gotta tell you, it wasn't so fun for me." The anger was rising, but I swallowed it down. I would *not* lose my cool in front of him.

"I apologized for that like a hundred times."

"Right. To my voicemail."

"Because you wouldn't return my calls."

"What do you want me to say, Josh?" Finally, I drew myself up and looked him right in those pale blue eyes. The man looking back at me was the same Josh I remembered. Two years older, but for all I knew, two years more an asshole. "Call me old-fashioned, but I guess I figure when you walk out on your bride, apologizing is something better done face-to-face."

"Hey, I'm here now." He cocked his head, his tone softening, like that meant something. His fingers brushed a lock of my hair off my shoulder; the move sent a shiver down my spine. He shifted closer, his head bent to me, putting us pretty much nose-to-nose. "And like I tried to tell you, I regret what I did."

"Do you?"

"Yeah, baby."

"Uh-huh. And was that before or after you slept with one of my best friends?"

It was true. Not only had I lost my fiancé in the ordeal, I'd lost a friend. Several of them, actually; as it turned out, some people weren't the friends I thought they were. When the line was drawn, Josh or me, a hell of a lot of them chose the beautiful rich boy.

Go figure.

"I should thank you, actually, for helping me to see who my real friends were, and who truly loved me. News flash, Josh: you weren't one of them."

I moved to get around him, but he blocked the door. "Aw, babe. Why've you gotta be like that? We could be so good together again."

"I don't think so."

"You've just gotta give me a chance to make it up to you."

Man. Some things really hadn't changed. Still the entitled brat who thought he had a right to any fucking thing he wanted.

"No, actually. I don't."

I shoved past him and lunged for the door, threw back the lock and stormed into the hall, putting distance between us before I did something I'd feel bad about later, like slap that stupid spoiled smirk right off his face.

"Katherine, wait." He followed me into the hall, grabbed me by my arm and yanked me around to face him. "If you just give me a chance to show you..." And with that, he planted a kiss on me.

I gasped, stunned. He thrust his tongue into my open mouth. I didn't even realize his hands had migrated to my waist until his fingers dug in, hard, and he crushed himself against me. I felt his belt buckle, still undone, and his erection, jabbing against my stomach in the red lace dress.

And it made me really fucking angry.

Because Josh Breckenridge, Jr. had forfeited any right to kiss me, or press his dick up against me, ever again, when he walked out on me.

I wrenched myself from his grasp and spun away, wiping my mouth with the back of my hand.

Josh was quick to put himself in my path, again. I had to stop short to avoid running into him.

"Come on, Kath," he panted, "just think about it. We've got so much history."

"Yeah, Josh," I said, also panting, a torrent of emotions threatening to overwhelm me. "And that's just what it is. History."

I stalked past him, heart pounding, shoving his hand away as he made a grab for me again—and found Jesse Mayes standing in the hall, staring at us.

His hair was damp and clinging to his neck. He was still

wearing his leather pants, but he'd changed his shirt to a distressed gray T-shirt that showed off the long, muscled lines of his tanned arms, the veins running up his forearms.

I swallowed, not knowing what to say. I looked from him to Josh, who'd come up behind me.

Jesse took a long look at me, and then at Josh, who wasn't exactly being discreet about the fact that he was doing up his belt.

Fucking *great.*

Jesse flexed his right hand, then made a fist. His gaze locked on me. "You alright?"

"She's great," Josh answered for me. "Aren't you, babe?"

I cringed. In all the years I'd known him, Josh had never had a sweet or sexy nickname for me. And now it was all *baby* this and *gorgeous* that. When we were together he called me Kath. Short for Katherine. Which I always hated. No one called me Katherine. Even my parents called me Katie.

I cringed even more when he swaggered on over to Jesse, offering up the same hand he'd just used to shake the piss off his dick for a manly handshake. "Joshua," he said.

I think I fell totally in love with Jesse Mayes for a split second as he stood there, completely unimpressed, looked at that hand, and made no move whatsoever to shake it.

"Katherine and I were just reminiscing about some good old times." Undaunted, Josh slipped his hand into his pocket. "And discussing some plans for the near future."

I heard a door open and glanced back. Brody stepped out of the men's room behind us. He saw us, saw Jesse, and stopped.

Which meant Josh was now flanked by two men who could very easily pound the shit out of him if they wanted to. At the moment, I didn't much mind if they did.

"Not too near, I hope," Jesse said, looking at me again. "Since Katie's coming on tour with me as of tomorrow."

Josh turned, slowly, to face me. He tried to look all nonchalant but I saw the tension in his neck, the hardening of his jaw as he ground his teeth. "On tour? What the fuck for?"

"Oh, you know…" I walked over to Jesse. He reached for my hand and I let him take it, let him lace his fingers through mine. "Keeping my man company on the road." I looked up into Jesse's dark eyes, and he gave me the slightest grin in return, a look of deep approval on his face. "Nice to see you again, Josh," I said pleasantly. Then I turned away, my heart thudding.

I fucking hated confrontations.

Though as far as uncomfortable run-ins with exes went, this one probably went down in the record books for awesome endings… as I walked away hand-in-hand with a rock star.

CHAPTER TEN

Katie

"I KNOW it's barely past midnight and this is all very Cinderella of me…" I held up my shoes, which I'd taken off like an hour ago, in emphasis. "But I'm not feeling so hot. I think I need to crash."

We were sitting on one of the couches in the VIP room between Brody and Maggie, and Jesse had his arm draped around me. The champagne was keeping me pretty sparkly, but I was definitely wilting at the edges. I'd taken pretty much all the photo ops and handshakes and smiling I could for one night. But really, I was feeling kind of sick to my stomach from the post-Josh adrenalin dump.

Jesse smoothed my hair away from my eye as his gaze searched my face; I felt his pulse beating against me in his finger-tips, hot and slow. My eyes met his, and I felt guilty. I was crazy to run away from him, right? He was beautiful, and he'd been a perfect gentleman so far. But despite my efforts to tune him out, I kept catching glimpses of Josh watching me from across the room. I had to get the fuck out of here.

"Actually, it's past one," Jesse said. "I've got an after party to hit, though. You should come."

True. I should've gone with him. If Devi hadn't left with some guy a while ago, after I'd sworn up and down that I was fine without her running interference, she'd tell me that right now. But I was spent. Emotionally tapped out over the run-in with my ex and the barrage of ugly feelings unearthed by his smirking face. I wasn't proud of it, but there it was. I kinda just wanted to go bury my head somewhere and feel shitty, but I wasn't about to tell Jesse that.

Instead, I gave him what I hoped was my prettiest, most apologetic smile and said, "I'm so sorry it didn't work out. I can pay you back for the hotel room and everything—"

"Katie." He dug in his pocket, took my hand and pressed a hotel room key card into it. "You were amazing tonight."

I shook my head in protest. "Really. I can just get a cab. It's no problem."

"The hotel's a few blocks away," he said, gently but firmly. "You're exhausted, sweetheart."

"I should probably just head home…" I knew I sounded unsure. Tempted.

I couldn't help it if I really, *really* liked it when he called me *sweetheart.*

He leaned in closer, his lips brushing my ear as he said, "You know, Katie, my girlfriend would probably stay, and let me buy her breakfast in the morning."

Also true.

I blinked up at him, trying to come up with a rational argument, but the idea of a luxury hotel room for the night was alluring. Max was at my sister's for the night anyway, so it's not like I had to rush home to my crappy apartment to feed my dog.

I tucked the key card into my purse. "Okay."

"Go get some rest," he said, and kissed me on the cheek. "Flynn will walk you over."

I made it to the glitzy bar in the hotel just in time for last call. It seemed like as good a place as any to bury my head for a while.

I'd considered going right up to my room and passing out. Maybe taking a hot bath first to soak the more shitty aspects of the night off my skin. But as Flynn walked me over to the hotel and the night's music rang in my skull, it was impossible to get Jesse out of my head. His songs. His voice. The way he looked up on that stage. The way everything else just seemed to melt away when he sang, like he was singing right to me.

The feel of his warm, guitar-string-callused hand in mine.

And Josh, sizing him up.

That arrogant asshole. Only he could do something so taste-less. Turning up out of nowhere, injecting himself back into my life and trying to ruin this for me.

But then I did something even more tasteless. I lied right to Jesse's face.

I said I was going on tour with him, right there in front of Josh, and Brody.

The buzz from the bubbly I'd drank at the party was starting to wear off, and I wasn't ready for it. Somehow I managed to convince Flynn to leave me at the elevator, and when he was gone, I made a beeline for the hotel bar. As I walked in, I just hoped my sexy red dress was dressy enough. The place was drip-ping with chandeliers. I'd only been in a more opulent bar once; the one Josh's dad had booked for our wedding reception.

The wedding reception that never happened.

I went straight to the bar and shrugged off my lucky leather jacket. There were a couple of men in suits at the far end, but the room was emptying out. Wait staff were clearing tables and flirting with lingering customers. Some crazy-sexy slow song was playing and it made me want to go straight back to that party and slither into Jesse Mayes' lap.

Maybe I should just fuck him and get it over with. It couldn't possibly make my life any worse.

"What can I get you, hon?" The female bartender came over. "Last call—you've got about twenty minutes."

"Southern Comfort and amaretto on the rocks, please. Lots of cherries. Make it a double. Actually, since it's last call, make it two doubles. And two for him." I gestured at the empty bar stool next to me as if I was expecting a date any second. Drinking eight shots of liquor myself in the next twenty minutes probably wasn't the best idea, but at least it would help erase this lingering awful taste Josh, Jr. had left in my mouth. And not just with his tongue.

The bartender went to make my drinks. I caught a glimpse of myself in the mirrored wall behind the liquor-lined shelves; at least I didn't look like the mess I felt. I caught the eye of one of the suits at the far end of the bar. His gaze lingered, but I looked away.

The bartender returned, setting the drinks on the bar on a couple of cocktail napkins—two in front of me, and two in front of my non-existent date. "Thanks." I started digging my wallet out of my purse.

"No need, hon," the bartender said. "The gentleman at the end of the bar took care of it."

I glanced over. The two guys in the suits were looking at me. The younger one, about thirty or so, handsome, maybe a little drunk, raised his glass.

I turned back to the bartender. "Thanks."

"Cheers."

She walked away and I picked up my first drink, considering. Maybe it was rude not to thank the stranger who'd paid for my drinks, but I really didn't want him coming over. I sipped at it, letting the sweet tang of the liqueurs linger on my tongue, the warmth flooding my chest. I closed my eyes and instantly saw him, burned into the black: Jesse, up on stage, rimmed in multi-colored lights.

"Feel like company?"

I opened my eyes but didn't turn around. I could see him in the mirror, the guy from the end of the bar, standing behind me with a drink in hand.

"I'm here with my boyfriend," I managed, my tongue finding the words before my brain caught up. "But thanks for the drinks. You really didn't have to."

"My pleasure. Having a rough night?"

Was it that obvious?

"Nothing my boyfriend can't fix." I didn't feel up to faking niceties. I didn't want to owe him anything just because he'd bought me a drink. Or four drinks.

"I don't see him here."

But suddenly I did. Over my shoulder in the mirror, approaching from the lobby, his long-legged stride eating the distance between us.

"Jesse…!" I spun around, lost my balance and tumbled off my barstool. Jesse closed the distance, his hand on my arm faster than I could recover, faster than the suit could react.

"Hey, sweetheart," he said, guiding me back onto my stool. "Miss me?" His mouth quirked in a faint smile. Then he glanced aside at the hovering stranger.

"Always," I said, doing my best impression of the smitten girlfriend. It wasn't hard. Pathetic thing was, I had missed him. It had barely been half an hour since he'd kissed me goodbye.

The suit eyed him, then glanced at me. Clearly he was outmatched here, no matter if he knew who Jesse Mayes was or not. He lifted his drink and shrugged. "You two have a good night, huh?" He wandered back to his end of the bar, throwing a lingering look my way.

Jesse watched the man go. He'd changed into a slouchy gray knit hat that covered most of his hair, a gray cashmere sweater and jeans. Moments ago, I wouldn't have believed he could look any better than he did in those low-slung black leather pants. But he looked so good right now, I felt the strongest pull to sink into his arms, let him wrap me in cashmere and his warmth.

Which was definitely the liquor at work.

I looked away. And there was Jude in the mirror, standing just inside the bar, leaning on a tall table, looking slightly pissed off. Hopefully not at me. Or Flynn.

Jesse slid onto the stool next to me, eying the untouched drinks on the napkin before him. The soft sleeve of his sweater brushed my arm, setting off sparks on my skin.

"Expecting someone?" he asked in that low, sexy voice, now a little rough from singing his heart out.

I took a fortifying sip of my drink and summoned my most casual tone. "Just thirsty."

"Uh-huh."

"You can drink them, though."

"I will." He plucked the plastic sword loaded with cherries off the rim of one of the glasses and set it aside, then raised an eyebrow at me. His dark eyes never left mine as he took up the drink and sipped. His lips quirked a bit at the taste.

"So what's this?" I reached to finger the wool of his hat and the curl of soft, dark hair poking out beneath. "Disguise?"

"Something like that. Fool you?"

"Nope. You've still got that face, you know…" I trailed off, running out of words as his eyes seemed to darken a shade in the flickering candlelight. Which was when I realized my fingers were still touching his hair.

I dropped my hand.

"You didn't know who I was when we met."

I laughed, which came out as a kind of snort, which tended to happen when I was buzzed. "But anyone with half a clue does."

"But not you."

"Not me. Ask Devi. I'm clueless."

I grinned, raised my drink to toast that statement, and drank.

Jesse watched me, his dark, unreadable eyes twinkling in the candlelight. "I thought you were going to sleep."

"I thought you were going to an after party."

"Yeah, well. Too many people crammed into Dylan's suite right now, and enough booze flowing that no one will notice I'm gone."

"I doubt that." It would take a lot more booze than one could fit in a hotel room to forget Jesse Mayes.

"And I got a little worried when you didn't answer your phone."

"You were gonna wake me up?"

"You looked a little rough when you left the party. I wanted to make sure you were okay."

His gaze left me as he sipped his drink. I would've given pretty much anything to know what that smoldering, far-off look in his eyes meant. Then those eyes returned to me, and I felt the answering heat deep in my belly, an unstoppable visceral response to that look.

The man had a pull, like an incredibly sexy magnet, and I could feel myself getting drawn in. I had no way to know if he was turning it on intentionally, or if it was just *him*. I tried to resist, but what I really wanted to do was give in. Toss my arms around his neck and crush my lips to his. Taste him again, that ever-present hint of cinnamon.

Stupid.

Reckless.

Not gonna happen.

"Luckily, I saw you from the lobby." His gaze slid down over my body, briefly. "That red dress is like a beacon." He glanced at the suits at the end of the bar.

"Well, what good is an arm ornament if she doesn't sparkle?" I finished my first drink and set the glass aside with a small bang. I sucked the cherries off my plastic sword and cringed at my own words; God, that sounded cynical.

Jesse just sipped his drink, studying me. "Wanna talk about it?"

"About what?"

"Whatever's eating you. If you're going to be my girlfriend, I should know what, or who, put that look on your face."

I finished my cherries and started into my second drink. I didn't want to talk about it, but the liquor was obliterating my better sense. "Just someone I wasn't keen to run into. Ever again."

"Let me guess. Blond guy with the chip on his shoulder and too much of daddy's money to burn."

"That would be him."

We drank in silence a moment. Jesse finished his first drink and set the empty glass next to mine. "What happened between you two?"

"It wasn't so much what happened as what he did."

Jesse's jaw flexed as he considered that. "What did he do?"

"He left me." I flooded my nerves with another swallow of liquor. "At the altar."

"Damn."

"Like, literally at the altar. I was standing up there in a white dress I couldn't afford with everyone looking at me, and he bailed. He waited until that exact moment." I glanced away, afraid I'd do something ridiculous like start crying if I had to look into Jesse's eyes any longer. "I mean, he couldn't have just told me beforehand?"

"He could have. But then maybe you wouldn't be sitting here

right now feeling bad about it. And maybe that's not what he wanted."

"I'm not feeling bad about that. I'm feeling bad about all the time I wasted on him before that. So many years. You know how many?"

"I don't."

"Five." I looked him in the eye again, feeling loose-lipped and reckless with liquor. "You know how many times we had sex in those five years?"

Jesse's perfect mouth quirked in the hint of a smile. "You kept count, sugar?"

"No, but it was lots. Lots of times. Lots of times that he was *this* close to me." Jesse's gorgeous face had filled my vision, and in the back of my mind I wondered where the rest of the world had gone. "Lots of times he told me he loved me," I breathed, my gaze dropping to his lips, "and one time he even said 'Marry me, Katie.' He never once said to me, 'Katie, I don't love you. You are not the woman I want to spend the rest of my life with.'"

Jesse's gaze dropped to my lips, and I realized how close I was to him. Leaning on the bar, our shoulders literally rubbing, we were close enough to kiss.

"I'm not defending him," he said. He licked his lips in the same casually seductive way he'd done at the video shoot, which made me wonder if he even noticed he did it. "Just pointing out it takes courage to say a thing like that. And a man who would leave you at the altar, babe, he doesn't have that kind of courage."

"Yeah."

I turned away and took a breath. Time to get my shit together before I fell on Jesse Mayes' dick and ended up just one of the many horny drunk chicks he'd probably fucked and forgotten. I needed a libido killer, and Josh would do just fine. Jesse was right. My ex was not a man of courage. Or integrity. Why hadn't I just seen that sooner?

It's not as if there weren't any warning signs.

"It's not all his fault, though. The truth is that he started walking out on me long before that. And I just let it happen. I never said a thing to him, either. I just kept pretending it wasn't happening." Maybe I was ashamed of that most of all. Not the fool he'd made of me, but the fool I'd been long before that humiliating day in his parents' church.

"Why?"

"Because." I forced myself to look at Jesse again, wishing he might somehow understand without me having to admit it. "Because I thought he was the king shit. I thought…"

"You thought…?"

"I thought I'd never do better than him."

Oh, God. It sounded horrendous coming out of my mouth. Mostly because it was true.

"Let me tell you, Katie Bloom, you can do a hell of a lot better."

I avoided Jesse's gaze. Why did he have to go saying things like that and being all decent and cool? Why couldn't he just be a stupid, slutty rock star who was impossible to take seriously?

Why did he have to go and become real?

"I know," I said softly, trying not to get choked up. "I mean, I know that now."

"Do you?"

I knew there were tears forming in my eyes because my vision was swimming. I covered it by slamming back the last of my drink. "He doesn't," I said. "I guess that's the thing that still bothers me, you know? I got over the sting of his very public rejection. I got over the humiliation. I even let go of the anger I felt at him, at myself. I thought I did. I learned to live with the fact that we'd both made mistakes. But seeing him tonight… the way he looked at me…" I trailed off in search of the words. I scanned Jesse's gorgeous face, his famous face, and for a second I saw what Josh must have seen. "At first I thought it just pissed him off when he saw me in that video because he couldn't stand seeing me happy. But that wasn't it. He just couldn't stand seeing me with you." I blinked back the tears and focused hard on those mysterious dark eyes. "He doesn't think I'm worth it. He doesn't think I'm good enough for all of this." I gestured grandly and a little drunkenly at the exquisite bar. *For you*, I could have added, but I didn't.

"And you think he's right?"

"I don't know." *Don't say it*, some small part of me that sounded a hell of a lot like Devi whispered, deep down in some tiny back room of my heart. *Don't show him. He doesn't need to know how broken you are.* "Maybe I fear he's right."

I really should've called it a night. Like, immediately. Gone up to my room and drunk dialed my best friend. The only person who could be trusted to witness me like this and not judge.

By now Jesse Mayes was probably trying to figure out how to rescind the entire offer, kick me the hell off his pant leg and high-tail it out of here.

But he didn't move.

He sipped his second drink, slowly, savoring it. Then he put the empty glass down, stared at the melting ice a moment, and turned to me.

"I'm going to tell you something now and you're going to wait until I finish so you don't take it personally."

"Sure." I picked up my own glass and busied myself crunching on the ice, avoiding that magnetic stare.

"The guys in the band, both bands, actually, and Brody, even Maggie, don't think this is a good idea. Me and you. Bringing you on tour."

I glanced at him. "And this is supposed to help convince me?"

He cocked his head a little, flashing his charming grin. "I didn't know I was still convincing you."

I started polishing off my second swordful of cherries.

"If you want out, Katie, I'm not going to hold it against you," he said. "I'm not gonna twist your arm. I'll give you tonight to think things over. It's only fair. There was a lot of pressure on you tonight. All these new people, your ex-fiancé showing up. The media. And you're looking like you could use some time to sleep it all off." I noticed he politely omitted my current state of intoxication from that assessment. "So. Here's what we do." He leaned in a little, his shoulder nudging mine. "I'm taking you up to bed."

Heat raced through my blood. I looked up into his eyes. Maybe he hadn't meant that as dangerously as it sounded, but I really couldn't tell. The man was impossible to read, unless he was overtly flirting, which he didn't seem to be doing just now. Still, the butterflies in my stomach did a drunken twirl.

"You're going to sleep," he went on. "And in the morning, you can let me know what you decide. No pressure. You come with me on tour, or you don't and we forget about all of this. You go back to your life, and I never bother you again."

One thing I knew: I did not want that. But it was dangerous to want what I was beginning to want when I looked in Jesse Mayes' eyes.

"But first..." He took my plastic sword and empty glass and set them aside, holding my gaze. "I want you to know *why* the guys don't think bringing you on tour is a good idea, and why I'll do it anyway. I've never brought a girl on tour with me before, Katie. Other than Elle, but we're in a band together, and even then it didn't work out so well. My friends aren't used to me getting serious about anyone so fast, and they don't see how it will help the tour. They think the only way the media or the fans or the record company will give a damn about the girl I'm dating is if she's some starlet or supermodel. Someone more famous, more glamorous than Elle."

I cringed, inwardly. He really didn't need to spell out for me all the ways I didn't measure up to his ex-girlfriend. Clearly I was nowhere near as glamorous. Or as talented. Certainly not as famous, even with our steamy video burning up the charts.

"They don't think anyone will care if I show up on tour with an ordinary girl," he said. "And by ordinary, I mean not famous. But here's the thing, Katie. I think they're wrong about that. And for the record, I don't think there's an ordinary thing about you. The world got a glimpse of that in the video. It's what your ex saw. It's why that video has been viewed online over *seven hundred million times* already."

My stomach did an uncomfortable flip, because I still couldn't quite digest that fact. "You don't have to say that." No matter what he said, I knew it was *him* and the incredible song that had people watching that video.

The bartender came for our glasses and Jesse told her, "I'll take the bill."

"No chance, sweetheart," she replied. "Gentleman at the end of the bar took care of it."

Jesse looked kinda pissed at that. He acted like he was oblivious to the woman practically drooling as she said goodnight, before finally walking away when he only stared me down.

I wondered if he got that a lot. I wondered if the bartender was drooling because she knew who he was, or if that didn't even matter when you looked like he did. When you exuded that kind of effortless, feral sexuality. The kind that told a woman, without words, what he could do to her.

The kinds of things he pretended to do to me in that video.

Jesse sighed and rubbed his hand over his face. He looked tired, something I hadn't picked up on before. My own drunkenness and hurt feelings had gotten in the way of seeing what this night meant to him, and what it had taken out of him. Suddenly I felt ashamed of my selfishness, my petty drama over my ex.

Josh wasn't worth this. I should never have let him get to me or get in the way of whatever time I might have with Jesse Mayes, even if our relationship wasn't real.

"I'm sorry," I said. "This isn't your problem."

"It isn't yours either." His eyes locked on mine again. "Look. I don't know what he saw all those years. Those five years you were together, and all those times he fucked you and told you he loved you. Or that day when he left you at the altar. But he wasn't seeing you." His gaze searched my face, heating my skin. "You're more than that, Katie. You're more than the girl he abandoned, and you're more than the girl in bed with me in that video. If you come on tour with me, you'll have a chance to show the world, including him, who you are, if that's what you want."

"But that's not really me, either," I said. "Your fake girlfriend."

"No one knows that. They don't know you yet. You can be whoever or whatever you want to be, starting tomorrow morning, and the world will believe you. Your ex believed it. That's why he hosted this party. To see for himself. That video gave him a glimpse of what he's missed out on, and now he's got regrets."

And that's when it struck me, as I stared at his beautiful face in the flickering candlelight. That all the time I was worrying if I was going on a date with some rich, entitled asshole who might turn into a creep at any second, I should've been preparing for a different scenario. Because what if Jesse Mayes turned out to be nice?

No; fuck nice. I could handle nice.

What if Jesse Mayes turned out to be *awesome?*

I swallowed as his dark gaze skimmed my lips. "I don't know about that, Jesse."

"I do." He stood and offered his hand to me. "Don't live with regrets, Katie Bloom."

CHAPTER ELEVEN

Katie

I WOKE NEAR DAWN, hungover as all fuck.

Correction: still a little drunk.

Morning light was beginning to bleed around the edges of the blackout curtains as I blinked my crusty eyelids open. The clock by my head said it was six seventeen. The light of the digital display stabbed at my brain and I closed my eyes, groaned, and rolled over, intending to go right back to sleep. Which was when I realized I wasn't alone.

I was in bed with Jesse Mayes.

Naked.

I rubbed my eyes until I could see straight. Until I was sure of what I was seeing.

Jesse lay sprawled beside me on his back, his gorgeous form skimmed with the faint window light. His face was turned away from me, one arm bent so his hand lay across his muscular chest, the white sheet tangled low around his bare hips.

I clutched the sheet to my chest, carefully running my free hand over my body beneath.

Yep. Definitely naked.

I peeked under the sheet, slowly, moving an inch an hour as I lifted it from his hip, until I could make out his cock. The cock he sent me a dick pic of last night. Not quite as enthusiastic this time, but he did have a decent morning semi going on.

I dropped the sheet like it'd scorched me.

What the *fuck*??

My skull crackled as I looked around, squinting into the near-dark. I remembered leaving the hotel bar with him. And some kind of argument over the bed?

God, did I do a strip tease for him?

The rest of the night came back in disjointed flashes as I scrambled to piece it together.

We'd ended up at the after party in Dylan's hotel suite. I remembered having a drink in my hand, and various people refilling it, so I must've had several. I could still taste the salt and lime. Margaritas; that's what Dylan's buddy Ash kept making. Which would explain my raw tongue and the battery acid churning in my gut.

I *hated* margaritas.

I remembered Brody announcing that the guys needed to sleep because they all had shit to do in the morning, and Jude kicking people out. But the party kept going. I also vaguely remembered sitting there in the midst of the rowdy energy, the rapid-fire conversation, the raucous laughter, and thinking that this would be what life would be like on tour—if I went.

I worked my way to sitting, careful not to disturb the bed or the sheet around Jesse's hips. The hand on his chest twitched but he didn't wake. I could remember his hands on my body at various points last night... On my back. On my waist. On my thigh as he sat next to me on the couch.

I let the sheet go. I wasn't a religious person, but I did a little prayer that Jesse Mayes wouldn't wake up in the next few seconds to the sight of my bare white ass dashing to the bathroom. Or up in the air as I searched the floor for my clothes.

I found them, one piece at a time. My red dress, flung on the coffee table. My panties just under the bed. My bra on the couch. My lucky leather jacket over near the door.

It was a big suite, like Dylan's, but I barely remembered walking into it last night.

My hotel room.

Jesse's hotel room, apparently.

It didn't quite dawn on me until we were inside it that my room *was* his room, and vice versa.

I don't get my own room? I'd whirled on him and asked that, incredulous, when it became clear he was heading for the bedroom.

You're my girlfriend, we share a room. You get a separate room and that shit gets out.

Okay. That did make sense.

Whatever. But I get my own bed. There were two of them, thank God.

But somehow we'd both ended up in the same one.

Got two beds. Which one you use is up to you.

Fuck.

And ugh.

Fugh.

Because it was up to me, wasn't it?

I slunk off into the bathroom after a failed search for one of my shoes. Shutting the door and turning on the light, I winced as an invisible ax cracked my skull. I gave myself a few moments to adjust, blinking, and held onto the counter for balance. I was bloody dizzy. And dehydrated. I really must've been wasted to drink tequila in any amount. Especially after all the beer, champagne and assorted cocktails I'd already put back throughout the night.

Tequila had never been my friend.

I ran the water in the sink, just a trickle so it wouldn't make noise, splashed some on my face and downed several glasses of it.

I pulled on my panties, shakily, stopping to grip the counter at intervals.

God. What a mess.

What the hell did I think I was doing? Clearly I was in way over my head here. I'd spent the better part of the last two years in a virtual cave; I could barely handle a night out with Devi and a few pitchers of sangria, much less Jesse Mayes and his rock star friends.

As I stood with my eyes closed, I felt his arm around me. A memory of last night, his hard body warm against mine, his hot lips brushing my ear. *You choose who you are out there, Katie. Who you want to be for them. You give what you want to give.* And then his lips on my neck. *Who you are in here… you choose that, too.*

Yeah, I chose.

I chose to be a lippy flirt.

I opened my eyes and took in my reflection, naked but for my black panties, and cringed as the memory came. Walking over to the bed closest to him, all bravado and boozy courage.

You're sleeping over here, then I am too. I'm gonna fake girlfriend the shit out of this joint.

Up to you, babe.

Then he proceeded to undress. That part I remembered.

Vividly.

Because I got an eyeful of naked Jesse Mayes.

Apparently he had no qualms about stripping down in front of me. Not surprising, really, for a guy who'd texted me a picture of his dick only hours before. A guy who grinded me to near-orgasm while a camera crew recorded every simulated thrust and very real gasp.

The guy had no shame.

I busied myself finger-combing my hair and wiping the raccoon makeup from under my eyes. Thank God I'd had the sense to remove my disposable contacts before I passed out, but I really could've come more prepared. A toothbrush and some powder foundation would do wonders right now.

Was that a bloody *hickey* on my neck?

Jesus…

More fragments of the night came back. Like telling him to put his dick back in his pants, when the ship had already sailed on that, since his jeans were on the floor. Did the man not wear underwear? And I must've been blatantly checking him out, because I could recall every detail of his gorgeous body. The long, lean lines of his torso. The muscles that bunched in his chest, his rippling abs, his thick biceps and long, muscular thighs as he pulled back the covers, tossed them on the floor, and flopped onto the bed.

Always sleep naked, sugar.

He'd reclined there, the sheet haphazardly over a leg, like he'd meant to cover up but didn't, his superb cock on full display, half-hard. He tossed his right arm over his eyes, showing off the sexy tattoo on his forearm, and appeared to be going to sleep.

But apparently I didn't want him to sleep. Hence my bull-headed response.

Fine. If you're sleeping naked, I am too.

And hence my clothes ending up all over the room.

I scowled at my reflection in the bathroom mirror and stood up straight, hoping I at least looked hot while I was making an ass of myself. I put on my bra and squeezed myself back into the red dress; anyone who saw me this morning would know it was the same dress I'd worn last night. This was not a Sunday morning dress. It was a Saturday night dress.

A walk of shame dress.

The kind of dress a stupid girl stripped off in front of a rock star, apparently.

Because I had.

Stripped.

In front of Jesse Mayes.

I'd turned it into a show when he started clapping and hooting, doing a clumsy drunken dance and flinging my clothes around. I cringed as I suddenly recalled what had happened to my lost shoe.

I'd tossed it in the air, where it got lodged in the ceiling light fixture.

Wonderful.

He'd howled at that smooth move.

When I peeled off my panties, though, the laughter died and his expression darkened.

You get in this bed like that and neither of us is sleeping, cherry pie.

I got in the bed.

Put your panties back on.

What's the matter? You said you'd be happy to taste my pie.

He'd growled and rolled away, onto the very edge of the bed, as far as he could get without falling on the floor, and covered his head with a pillow.

I'd closed my eyes then, thinking I'd prove I could sleep even if he couldn't, but that was a mistake.

Ugh. Is your side of the bed spinning?

The bed shook as Jesse got up in an agitated huff and stalked to the other bed. He tore the blankets off that one, got in under the sheet, and buried his head in the pillow.

I got up, went over to his bed and got in.

Fuck, Katie. I'm not sleeping with you naked unless we're gonna fuck, and we're not gonna fuck while you're this drunk. Especially the first time.

First time? Like there would be other times? *First time?* For some reason that struck me as hilarious, and the last memory I had was of my naked, drunken self, laughing my ass off.

And waking up in the morning with an ax in my skull.

Fuck. Fuck. *Fuck.*

Did we have sex?

No. No fucking way. I'd know.

Wouldn't I?

Yes. Absolutely. No way I'd forget that.

Right?

I scanned myself in the mirror. Reasonably presentable.

For a walk of shame.

My hair looked a little ridiculous and desperately in need of a brush, but because it never let me down, my lucky leather jacket coughed up a hair elastic buried in the lining of a pocket. I managed to work my hair into a decent braid. "Get your shit together," I whispered at my reflection. Then I squared my shoulders and prepared for what was sure to be a humiliating journey home.

When I cracked the bathroom door, Jesse's body was still flung across the bed. He hadn't moved. I could hear the slow, deep, throaty rhythm of his breaths.

I glimpsed the dark form on the ceiling that was my shoe, wedged into the light fixture. Clearly, that was a lost cause. No way I could rescue it without standing on Jesse's face.

I grabbed my purse and slipped out, barefoot.

I saw no one in the hall or the elevator, thank God. I went down to the lobby and spoke to a guy at the front desk. "Is there anything you can do for a patron on the occasion that she got super drunk last night and lost a shoe?"

"Oh, dear." He poured me a glass of cucumber water, which I accepted gratefully and downed in seconds. "I'd be happy to have the concierge send someone out to purchase some shoes for you up the street. Once the stores open, of course."

Right. Like I could afford shoes from anywhere in this neighborhood.

"I don't have time for that. Is there nothing in-house? The gift shop?"

"I don't think so. However, we do have flip-flops for the spa patrons. I could sell you a pair of those." He looked something up on his computer. "I'd have to charge you sixty dollars." He looked at me and said, "They're pink," like that somehow sweetened the deal.

Sixty bucks? For a pair of disposable flip-flops? Christ. But it was that or get home barefoot.

"Size seven please."

"They're one size fits all."

Sure they were. "Great. Can you point me in the direction of an open drug store?"

I paid the man, waited while he sent some underling to collect the flip-flops, then hit the road in my red lace dress, oversized pink flip-flops, and black leather jacket.

I walked the five blocks to the twenty-four hour drugstore where I picked up a bottle of Tylenol, a gift bag and a gift card that was blank inside. Somewhat fittingly, it had a little drum on it. It was green and silver. Possibly leftover from Christmas.

Then I bought every pack of cinnamon flavored gum they had. And every cinnamon Tic Tac.

I ducked into two convenience stores on my way back to the hotel and bought their entire stock of cinnamon gum, too.

In the hotel lobby, I stuffed the gum and Tic Tacs in the gift bag, threw back a couple of Tylenol with some cucumber water, and signed the card.

Have an amazing tour. K.

On second thought, I tossed the bottle of Tylenol in the bag.

I left the gift bag with the front desk for "the guy in 709" since I assumed the room wasn't under Jesse's real name.

I grabbed a cab and stopped by my sister's place to pick up Max. Then I went home, had a long, hot shower and passed out in my own bed, spooning my dog.

CHAPTER TWELVE

Jesse

JUDE LEANED back against the Bentley, settling in with his breakfast burrito as I punched the number to Katie's apartment into the ancient intercom system. After several staticky beeps there was a click and a scratchy little voice. "Hello?"

"Had breakfast yet?"

Static-filled silence. "Pardon me?"

"Have you had breakfast?" I enunciated. Through the static, I heard a scratchy little voice say a very bad word, which made me grin. "Wanna buzz me in?"

Silence followed by some staticky fumbling and a loud buzzer.

I found Katie's place on the second floor. The door was ajar and a red-rimmed eyeball sized me up through the gap from behind a pair of cute, turquoise-framed glasses.

"Please tell me you brought coffee."

"Nope. But Jude will get some." Katie opened the door wider; I was already texting Jude as I stepped inside. "Nudge open today?"

"Yes, but you don't have to do that." She shut the door behind me. Her dog sat at her feet, wagging his tail. "I'm sure your best friend doesn't really want to be your errand boy."

"The amount I pay him to be my errand boy, I don't give a shit. What do you drink?"

She sighed. "A cherry-vanilla latte. Actually, make it iced, with extra—" She caught my look and gave me a little eye roll. "Just tell them it's for Katie."

I texted the order to Jude, then tucked away my phone and rubbed the dog's head. He licked me, decided I was cool and wandered off into the kitchen.

"Max really likes you," she said. "He's usually kind of, um, indifferent toward guys."

She hugged herself as I scanned her outfit. Pink pajama pants with hearts all over them, a green tank top and mismatched socks. Not a woman expecting company.

She followed me into the tiny kitchen and poked her nose in the bag I set on the counter. "Oh, God. Juice!" She moaned orgasmically as she dug the carton out of the bag.

I grinned. "Playing hooky today?"

"Nope. Threw up an hour ago." She swatted Max out of the way and pulled a couple of lidless mason jars from a cupboard, then sloshed the orange juice into the jars and handed one to me. "Cheers," she said, bumping her jar to mine and throwing the juice back.

I took a swig and watched her throat work as she chugged. There was a conspicuous hickey on one side of her neck which I vaguely remembered putting there when she pretty much dared me to. Apparently the girl got mouthy when she got drunk, and since I wasn't known for backing down from a dare—a good dare —it was a dangerous combo. A fucking fun combo.

I unpacked the groceries and watched Katie down a second helping of juice. Despite how wrecked she was, she did hungover well. Kind of adorably disheveled, her hair piled into a messy knot-bun thing, loose strands sticking to her face. She did look a little pale, but other than that, cute as ever.

She was also braless, which didn't hurt. I could make out the exact shape of the perfect handful of her breasts, her nipples hard against the thin cotton. My dick definitely liked that. The pajama pants sat low, showing a slice of creamy skin, the sexy indent of her hips and the lacy edge of her white panties—

She smushed a little burp against the back of her hand and shot me a regretful look. "'Scuse me. I feel so gross. How much did I drink last night?"

I might've laughed if she wasn't in such a sorry state. "I cut you off around four a.m., so you do the math."

"Ugh."

"You haven't eaten?"

"Kind of afraid to."

"Sit your ass down." I started searching the kitchen for what I needed. The cupboards were old and worn and the dishes mismatched but in order, everything in tidy stacks and rows.

"Make yourself at home," she grumbled, but pulled a stool up to the little bar and sat. Max curled up at her feet.

"If I was gonna do that, sweetheart, I'd be naked." I turned up the heat under a pan and unwrapped the bacon. "Lucky for you, I'm cooking bacon."

"Which means?"

"The clothes stay on."

"That is lucky," she said dryly.

Maybe she was clueless on this, but her surliness did fuck all to diminish the cute. If anything it kinda spurred me on. Which definitely wasn't my usual mode with women. Since pretty much puberty, and definitely since fame hit, I'd become pretty comfortable with women pursuing *me*.

In fact, Katie might've been the first woman to cross my path in years who wasn't gunning for what she'd already decided I might be worth to her—namely my dick, the contents of my bank account, and/or one of my friends. I was pretty much ready to sales pitch this chick on why she should take my money.

"Kill me now," she moaned. "Dehydration hurts." I watched her rub her little nose. In the morning light coming through the window, it had a smattering of tiny freckles on it like gold dust. "I feel like I snorted a fucking desert last night." She poured herself another glass of juice.

"Drinking your body weight in booze can do that."

She gave me a nasty, dirty look, which was beyond refreshing.

Yeah. Katie Bloom was all kinds of interesting.

Mainly because she didn't seem to give one fuck who I was or what I did for a living. That much was clear from day one, at the video shoot. And damn if I didn't like that about her even more now than I did then. Which was a lot. Enough to kiss her and send her a cherry pie afterward like some idiot with a crush.

Enough to know I should probably forget about her. Which I'd managed to do for a while.

But the success of the "Dirty Like Me" video was too much to ignore. It was just more proof that the girl was something special… beyond just a cute face and a great set of tits.

I finished putting the bacon on to cook and dug the last item out of the bag, tossing it at her. "I brought your shoe."

She caught it and fumbled, but recovered. "Oh. Sorry I left it in the light fixture. What a tool." She was blushing again; it was good to see some color coming back to her cheeks.

"No worries. I've never had a girl do the Cinderella dash on me. Kind of made me feel like Prince Charming." In truth, I'd been more than a little disappointed to wake up and find her gone.

"You really didn't have to bring it. I left the other shoe there anyway."

"I'll have Maggie track it down."

"Please don't. These things were designed by a woman-hating

sadist." She tossed the shoe on the couch behind her, watching as I sautéed the onions and mushrooms I'd already diced up at home. "What the heck are you making?"

"You've never seen an omelet in the works before?"

"Just surprised Jesse Mayes knows how to make one."

I ignored that and cracked a bunch of eggs into the bowl, mixed in a splash of cream and the rest of the diced veggies, and poured the whole thing into the sauté pan over medium-low heat.

"Keep an eye on the bacon." I handed her a fork and helped myself to a tour of the living room. Katie didn't even have to get up to join me, just turned around on her stool.

It was a small place, something like the first apartment I ever had, shared with Jude, Brody and Zane just after high school, when we were busting our asses to get club gigs. Just before we inked our record deal. This place was a hell of a lot cleaner, though. Smelled better, too. And the living room wasn't crowded with unmade futons and music gear. It was just as old, just as plain, but well-kept. There was nothing on the walls. There was, however, an album collection that filled a couple of bookcases and took up one whole wall.

I perused the vinyl, noting the overwhelming array of classic rock. "You like any music from after you were born, sweetheart?"

"Sure. Just don't collect it on vinyl. I grew up on classic rock and it's pretty much in my soul. That started out as my dad's collection."

"That's cool." I thumbed through the albums, all neatly alphabetized by band. "My mom had about three albums when I was a kid. Sugar Ray, Snow and Limp Bizkit."

Katie laughed. "And one wonders where his love of music came from…"

I thumbed from Deep Purple through The Doors, the egotistical ass in me unable to resist checking to see if she had any Dirty vinyl. She didn't. I fired up her turntable and put on *Waiting for the Sun*, dropping the needle on "Hello, I Love You." When I looked up, Katie was watching me and hugging herself.

"So where did Jesse Mayes learn to make a proper omelet?" She twisted her bottom lip between her teeth, a sweetly unsure expression on her face. "I would've thought you had a celebrity chef on retainer or something."

Right. So that was it.

She was freaked out about the whole celebrity thing. And since she didn't give a fuck about *my* celebrity in particular, my best guess was that she was freaked out about where she fit into it all. And how it was going to fuck with her life.

Couldn't say I blamed her for that.

"I sometimes cooked for me and my sister when our mom was working, which was always," I said as I went to check the omelet. "Believe me, I tried to get her to cook, but she was like six, so unless we wanted to live off toast and maybe mac 'n' cheese, I had to do most of the cooking." I poked the bacon, separating some strips that had stuck together. "How crispy do you like it?"

"If by crispy you mean burnt, then yes, please. And by the way. Please don't think I don't appreciate the food. But are you ever gonna tell me what you're doing here? And don't say making me breakfast."

"I'm here to get your answer about the tour."

"I gave you my answer."

I locked onto her blue-green eyes. "You gave me a year's worth of cinnamon gum and told me to fuck off."

"I did not tell you to fuck off."

"I read between the lines." I opened the container of cheese I'd pre-shredded and dumped it over the omelet, turning down the heat. "Assuming you like triple cheese on your omelet, same as your pizza?"

"You assume correctly."

"Man," I muttered. "Chicks must hate you."

"Excuse me?"

"You eat like a very large man and have the body of a twelve-year-old boy." I tossed some grated cheddar into my mouth. "With awesome tits." I looked her over, slowly, enjoying the way it made her fidget. "And hips," I added. "And an incredible ass."

She shook her head as if to clear it of nonsense. "I have no idea what to say to that."

"Say you'll come on tour."

She bit her lip again. Then she pushed her glasses up her nose, which was too fucking cute. "Honestly, Jesse, I don't know if I can say that."

Damn. Really not the answer I came for.

But this was far from over.

"Because you don't want to," I said as I started flipping the bacon, "or because you're afraid to?"

Katie crossed her arms and glowered at me. "You said if I chose not to go on tour you'd leave me alone."

"That was before you snuck out in the night like a bandit."

"It was morning, the sun was coming up, and I didn't *steal* anything."

"It's cool. If you're afraid you won't be able to resist screwing my brains out when we've been lip-locked for the cameras all day, just say so."

"I'm sure I can find it in myself to resist the urge."

I wasn't so sure about that, but if that was the way she wanted to play it…

The thing was, I'd watched the video. A lot. And I'd come to a pretty interesting conclusion. It wasn't that Katie was great at faking. It's that she wasn't faking at all. Every gasp I'd elicited from her, every squirm, every time her nails dug into my flesh or she bit her lip or her breath caught, every time her pupils dilated so huge I could've sworn she was high, she was rushing on *me*. Hard.

It wouldn't exactly be a stretch to pretend I was hot for her too. Even in her mismatched pajamas and bed hair she was making me hard.

So maybe we'd actually be faking *not* wanting each other. I'd do my best if that's what she wanted. And if I never got to touch her when no one else was around, maybe it wouldn't be my first choice, but I could live with it.

I still wanted her on the tour. The tour was too important to fuck up, even over a cutie like Katie Bloom.

She chewed on her plump pink bottom lip. "Can you answer one question for me?"

"Anything."

"Why me?"

"Because the fans like you," I said. Then I added, "And I trust you."

"You don't even know me."

"I know enough."

She looked at me over her glasses like a disagreeable librarian. A really fucking hot librarian. "You know what I like on my pizza."

"Marriages have been built on less."

"And divorces have followed."

"I know you're on the pill," I said, just as the phone rang. Katie's mouth popped open. "You told me last night. Said you couldn't stay at the hotel because you usually take it first thing in the morning and didn't have any with you."

Katie buried her face in her hands. "Oh my God."

"All coming back now, huh?"

I plated the food as she got the phone and buzzed Jude up. Then I went to the door, grabbed Katie's coffee from him, and waved him away. Jude just grinned an ear-to-ear grin, which he never fucking did.

I shut the door before he could say a thing and returned to the kitchen, where Katie was gingerly eating her omelet. "This is really good," she said. Then her eyes narrowed as they met mine. "So what else did you learn about me while I was all drunk and vulnerable?"

I pulled up a stool and joined her at the bar. "Not much. Just that you like to snuggle." She blushed something fierce and I decided to let her off the hook. "Already found out everything I need to know anyway."

"Such as?"

"Your standard stuff. Criminal record, background check, known associates."

Katie started to laugh, but then gathered I was serious. "Really?"

"I've had you looked into."

"Come again?"

"I've had Jude run a security check on you. On your ex-fiancé too." Unfortunately the guy was clean, criminally speaking. I flexed my fingers, playing with my rings, distracted by the thought of that asshole hovering over Katie at the club, doing up his fucking belt.

I attacked my omelet, irritated as fuck that I didn't clock the dude when I had the chance.

Katie was staring at me. "Why would you do that?"

"Because there are things I need to know before I get involved with you. That might sound cynical, but it's my reality."

"You could've just asked me. I'll tell you whatever you want to know."

"Not the way it works," I said. "If we do this, we do it my way."

She made a cute *harrumph* noise that made her sound like an uptight old lady. "Who says we're doing this?"

"If we weren't, I wouldn't still be here." I stared her down for a few seconds, then cut the flirting and leveled with her. "Look,

Katie. It's a lot of money. And I don't see you having any problem telling me to go fuck myself if you don't want me here, but you haven't done that yet. Which tells me I've already won you over, or at the very least, I'm about to."

"Maybe I just want the eggs," she said. "And this beautiful burnt bacon." She munched her bacon and smiled.

Damn. The girl was cute even when she was busting my balls. Cuter, even.

"Don't think so, babe," I said. "But nice try." I didn't love this part, but I pulled the folded letter envelope from my back pocket and handed it to her. "While you're deciding to say yes… I didn't want to lay this on you last night, with everything else, but we should go over it."

Katie opened the unsealed envelope and peeked at the papers inside.

"It's a contract. An NDA," I said. "Brody insisted."

She examined the papers in her hand, scanning over the legal contract.

"It's a Non-Disclosure Agreement. It means—"

"I know what an NDA is," she said, leafing through to the last page, where the signature lines were. "I'm not signing this." She handed it back to me.

Damn. The girl had backbone. "Brody won't like that."

She ate her omelet in silence, in careful little bites, like she was still afraid she might hurl.

"You realize I'm being asked to go on a six-week tour in a foreign country with a man I barely know, pretending to be his lover, surrounded by other men—giant men, incidentally," she added, eying me, "who all work for him. I need to know that I have some protection. If this thing goes bad, if you turn out to be the world's biggest creep, I need to know I can say that to whoever I need to say that to."

She had one hell of a point.

I folded the envelope and tucked it away. "I can live with that."

"What about Brody?"

"I'll talk to him." Brody would just have to accept it. Had no choice, because I was bringing Katie on the fucking tour. "Maybe we should define creep, though. What if I get handsy and you don't like it?"

"Then I'll throw a drink in your face like a civilized bitch."

I felt the grin twitch at the corners of my mouth. "Sounds fair. But I do have a couple of conditions. We don't need it in ink. A verbal agreement is fine with me. I'll take you at your word."

"Okay…?"

"You'd be coming on the tour to act as my girlfriend, so if that illusion falls apart because you're involved with someone else—"

"I'm not involved with someone else."

"Good. But if you were to get involved, and the media got wind of it—"

"I'm not getting involved with anyone. If I do this I'm pretending to be your girlfriend for six weeks. That's the deal. I won't do anything to make you look bad."

"Which brings me to my other condition. You can't tell anyone the relationship is fake."

"Pretty much assumed that. With the exception of Devi, who already knows."

I didn't love that, but so be it. "Alright," I agreed. "But no one else."

"Understood." She was slowing down on her omelet and set her fork down. "I have some terms of my own, you know." She leaned her elbows on the bar and looked incredibly businesslike for a woman in pajamas and no bra.

"I'd expect no less."

"Devi wanted to write up a contract of our own, but I don't think it's necessary. I think we need a little trust between us if we're going to do this. So." She fixed her blue-greens on me. "One. *You* can't tell anyone the relationship is fake."

"Agreed," I said. "With the exception of Jude, who knows every fucking thing I do, for security reasons."

"Fine."

"And Brody, who already knows." Brody was also pissed that I'd gone to Katie with my "indecent proposal," his words, before consulting him. Maggie wasn't gonna love it either. "Which means Maggie, too."

Katie frowned.

"My public image is their domain. I can't keep Maggie in the dark."

"Fine. Number two. You can't see anyone else."

"Okay."

"I have to be the only one," she insisted, as if I'd put up an argument. "If I'm gonna do this, let everyone believe we're a couple and play the adoring girlfriend for all the world to see, I'm trusting you not to humiliate me—"

"Understood."

I got it. Really. She was left at the altar. Two years ago. And hadn't kissed a single dude since. Except me, a guy who was paying her for a fake relationship.

This girl was on recovery road from something that had scarred her deep, and going on this tour, trusting me, was a major leap of faith.

"Oh..." she said, like she'd been ready for a debate. "Um. Okay. So, then... if we do this, we both commit to keeping up the illusion. Which means..."

"Which means?"

She rolled her eyes. "You know what it means. It means no fucking around. No getting your roadies or whoever to sneak groupies to you behind my back. No hooking up with old flames in every port. No messing around with Elle."

"Is that all?"

"You get the idea. No going all slutty rock star behind my back."

"Not a problem."

From the look on her face, she really had to suspend disbelief on that one. Which rubbed me the wrong way and then some. But it wasn't like she was the first woman to ever doubt my ability to keep my dick in my pants.

I leaned toward her on the bar. "You got one thing wrong, though. As my woman, my crew is there to look out for you, too. Especially Jude and his team. And I take that shit seriously."

"Okay." She still looked unconvinced. "Number three. And I take this shit seriously."

"Lay it on me."

"I need you to promise me it's only a business deal," she said. "That none of it's real." Her expression was steadfast as she held my gaze. "You don't do girlfriends, and I don't do rock stars who don't do girlfriends."

Was that it?

She was afraid I was gonna put pressure on her to make this thing more than what I'd sold her it would be?

"It's not real," I said.

Which didn't mean we couldn't fuck like animals... but no need to negotiate *that* right this minute.

"And it's just for the tour," she said. "Six weeks."

"Six weeks."

She stared at me for a long, long moment. "Okay," she said.

"Okay?"

She nodded and relaxed. "You have a deal, Jesse Mayes."

Really?

That was all she needed to hear, all this time? That I wasn't gonna pull a Romeo on her and get down on one knee or some shit at the end of all this?

"Then you'll do it? You'll come on tour?"

"Yeah. I'll come on tour." She lifted her Nudge coffee cup.

I toasted her with my juice. "Fuck, yeah."

She sipped her drink. "I still don't get why you bothered with all of this, though. Wouldn't it have been easier to just pay some model to hang out on your arm for six weeks?"

I cocked my head, closing one eye to scrutinize her. "You mean like that super hot model who starred in my last music video?"

She blushed. "I was thinking someone with a little more experience as an arm ornament."

"Ah, but she's a quick learner," I said. "And speaking of quick..." I got to my feet. My cell had been vibrating in my pocket non-stop; if I didn't get moving Brody was gonna have Jude knock the door down and drag me out of here. "You leave tomorrow. Maggie will be in touch about your travel. Keep your phone on."

"Okay. What about you?"

"Flying to Montreal today." I tossed my plate in the sink, startling Max from his slumber. "You'll have to do the dishes yourself, sweetheart."

"Fuck that," she grumbled. "I'm going back to bed."

I took one last look at her in her pj's as she toed Max's fur, her chin resting on her hand. "Probably a good idea."

"So that's it, huh?" She looked up at me, a hint of a smile on her lips. "No rest for the wicked?

"Welcome to the fast lane, babe." I planted a kiss on her cheek and walked out the door, a big-ass grin on my face.

CHAPTER THIRTEEN

Katie

THE NEXT DAY, the day I joined Jesse on tour, was not much like I thought it would be.

For one thing, I didn't see my new "boyfriend" all day. Then again, I'd never dated a rock star before. Much less fake-dated one.

I was picked up at my apartment, flown to Montreal with Maggie and Flynn, and driven to a hotel. I was told Jesse had flown out yesterday with Brody, Jude, the rest of his new solo band and key crew. At the hotel, I was given a key card to the room I'd share with Jesse.

His things were flung across one of the beds, but he was gone. And yes, the sight of all his stuff in *our* room gave me a little thrill. But I tamped that shit down, stat.

Maggie had told me he'd be busy doing promotional inter-views, then sound check at the venue before the show. And despite my best efforts not to get caught up in the incredibly weird, exciting, and/or overwhelming of all of this, I was looking forward to seeing him again.

A lot.

I mean, it was okay to *like* the guy, right? After all, he'd made me bacon and eggs, and in my books, that was fucking A. And there was no denying the man was incredibly easy on the eyes.

When I woke up that morning it all felt too good to be true, and for a split second as I blinked my way out of sleep I had an infinitesimal panic attack that it wasn't real. Like maybe the entire weekend, everything that had happened from the moment Jesse showed up on my sister's front steps, was another fucked-up dream. I'd fallen off my skateboard and whacked my head to shit, and was lying in a hospital bed right now, hallucinating this whole thing.

Two hundred thousand dollars to spend six weeks on the arm of a ridiculously gorgeous rock star?

Really?

But when I found the text waiting on my cell phone, it hit me all over again.

This was happening.

Good morning beautiful, it said. *Pack light. Maggie will take you shopping in Montreal.*

That was it.

I called my parents from the hotel room, to let them know I'd arrived safe. I'd told them I was working as Jesse's "assistant," but given the fact that I'd never expressed an interest in working in the music industry before *and* the fact that they'd seen the two of us going at it in the "Dirty Like Me" video, I kinda doubted they believed me. I called my sister, who definitely didn't believe me, and who was taking care of Max; I heard my dog woofing happily in the background and already missed him like crazy.

I got off the phone feeling weirdly alone.

I allowed myself a few seconds to linger in the hotel room, and run my fingers over the clothes in Jesse's open travel case. But I wasn't gonna be a weirdo and snoop.

I wasn't going to swim in his pool without an invite, so to speak.

I tore a page out of the sketchbook I'd brought and drew a little caricature of myself, adoring hearts shooting out of my eyes as I gazed at a little caricature of Jesse Mayes, who was holding a guitar in the air. It was a damn fine sketch. I signed it with the words, *I'm here!*

Then I left it on the bed for him, in case he came back to the hotel before I saw him.

I spent the afternoon with Maggie—and Flynn, by default—on Rue Ste-Catherine.

While it was incredibly weird to me that Flynn escorted us everywhere but didn't actually talk to us, I had to admit being babysat by an ex-military tough guy, who looked something like James Bond in a motorcycle jacket, had its perks. He carried our bags, opened doors, and drove us around when we got tired of walking. He even got us seats in a busy restaurant for a late lunch when we needed a break.

By late-afternoon, though, Maggie had several new outfits and I'd picked out only one item for myself—a pair of jeans from a sale rack.

"It's on your new boyfriend," she told me. "Don't be shy. Trust me, he can afford it."

That didn't help.

I still wasn't keen on feeling like an escort, and being asked to dress differently than I normally did, which was at least being implied by this shopping spree, made me want to revolt. I'd thought shopping would be fun, but bottom line, every time I tried on some item Maggie handed me and stepped out of the fitting room for her perusal, I felt like a whore.

"Hon," Maggie said when we walked out of the umpteenth store empty-handed. "This isn't a criticism. No one's telling you how to dress. I just want you to think about the image you put out there. You've seen Jesse, right? In photos? On stage? And how does he look? What does he wear? He's oiled up, his pants are undone, his shirt is off."

"Uh-huh." Yeah. I'd noticed that. Kinda hard not to.

"Well, it's not an accident," she said, as we stepped into yet another amazing boutique. "A lot of work goes into that image. You're his girlfriend now. Your image is as important as his."

By now, I knew that Maggie knew the relationship was fake, but she was cool enough not to mention it. Actually, everything about Maggie was cool. The girl was gorgeous, the kind of gorgeous you might not even notice at first glance, but by the second or third, you were riveted. She managed to pair a giant infinity scarf over an asymmetrical T-shirt with rolled-up boyfriend jeans and stiletto-heeled boots, and she walked in those boots like they didn't have four-inch heels. She was a tiny thing, probably just over five feet out of those boots, but she had the kind of presence that told you she didn't put up with bullshit. From anyone.

Which was undoubtedly how she'd survived so long co-managing the hottest band of rock 'n' roll bad boys around.

"It must be interesting, you know, being the only woman on the team," I said as I browsed through a rack of beautiful but exorbitantly-priced leggings. "I mean, besides Elle. You must see just about everything." Yeah, I was digging, but I was acutely aware that this might be my only chance to get the dirt from Maggie. She and Brody were flying home to Vancouver tomorrow. Apparently they had their hands full managing Dirty, even when the band wasn't touring or promoting a new album, so they couldn't also handle the day-to-day of Jesse's tour. They'd hired a tour manager and a bunch of other people for that.

"Just about," Maggie said. "Didn't see you coming, though."

I glanced over the racks of clothes that stood between us.

"I guess I shouldn't be surprised," she said. She held up a pair of red skinny jeans, and even though I didn't mind them, I wrinkled my nose without meaning to. I couldn't help it; I had an aversion to this whole process. She put them back on the rack and kept searching. "In my eyes, Jesse is the most mysterious guy in the bunch," she explained. "Hard to get a lock on, even in the years I've known him."

"And how many years is that?"

"Like six or so. I came on after *Love Struck*, so I kind of missed all the debut album madness." She came over to me with several dresses and began holding them up to me, one at a time. "I can tell you this. He's not a bad guy. He's also not a saint. If I had to pick one word to sum up Jesse Mayes, it would be... unpredictable." She waved over a sales associate and handed her some dresses. "She'd love to try these on," Maggie said, shooting me a look.

"And this," I relented, handing the sales girl a skirt.

"Take you, for example." I followed as Maggie continued browsing. "This whole girlfriend-for-hire thing." She glanced my way like she was checking if it was okay with me that she called it what it was.

I smiled awkwardly.

"Never would've expected it," she went on. "But that's Jesse. You never know what he's going to do next." She pulled a sexy black mini dress from the rack and held it up to me at arm's length. "You had a spark, though, you and Jesse. Brody and I both saw it. You know, when you offered him that cherry pie?"

"Oh. That."

"Yeah, that," Maggie laughed. "That's why we wanted you for the video. That spark. Didn't know it would ignite on screen like it did, but damn, it was hot." She flipped through the dresses, throwing a few more over her arm. "You have this quality... How did Zane put it? 'The girl next door I really want to fuck.'" She rolled her eyes a little.

I blushed, not sure if I should feel flattered, but I laughed too. "And is he exactly what he seems?"

Maggie's gray eyes clouded over. "Zane? Oh, he's everything you see in the media and then some." Her tone was breezy, if not a little condemning, but it was the first time I got the feeling she was filtering her comments. "He's a lot of other things too, none of which are good news. He's pretty much a nightmare for any woman." She plucked one more dress from the rack and turned to me. "Really," she said, "the only useful thing I can tell you about Zane Traynor is keep your distance."

Interesting. But not a problem since he wasn't coming on this tour.

Maggie off-loaded her pile of dresses to the sales girl and kept foraging. I followed, managing to pick out a pair of rocked-out jeans that were ripped to hell and cost a fortune.

"What about the new guys?"

"Friends of Jesse's," she said, "cherry-picked from other bands. They're all in a really different place than the guys in Dirty, though, and I think that's why he chose them. They're all married, for one, and Raf has two kids. Letty's wife is pregnant. So it'll be a way different vibe than it is on a Dirty tour."

"Which is?"

"Total madness," she said, and laughed. "Lucky for you, you won't have to deal with it."

"Right." Because once this tour was done, I was history.

Day one and I was already starting to feel a little regretful about that, even though I'd agreed to it. Hell, I'd made *him* agree to it. But I just wanted things to be clear. I didn't need my naïve self thinking this was more than it was, or weaving some kind of fantasy that it was going to continue beyond the tour.

The very last thing I needed was another broken heart.

I was here to do a job, and that was all. On that note, I tried to put more effort into the shopping thing. Maggie was just doing her job and we were running out of time. We were supposed to be at the concert venue in like an hour. And when I held up a sexy-as-sin champagne-pink dress and Maggie said, "Nuh. Jesse's not into pink," I was finally struck with inspiration.

When I held up a sweater and Maggie said, "Jesse prefers red," I took it in blue.

When I held up a skirt and she mentioned, "Jesse hates plaid," I took all the plaid I could find.

Soon, I had a pile of items that Maggie had attempted to veto on behalf of Jesse's preferences.

Outside the fitting rooms, I was squeezed into the champagne-pink dress, which was super hot, low-cut and showed miles of leg, when I realized she was on to me. "Oh yeah," she said, shaking her head. "Jesse would hate that."

I narrowed my eyes at her. "Whose side are you on?"

"Whatever side makes Jesse happy. You would not like working for that guy when he's in a funk."

I checked out my champagne-pink ass in the mirror.

"Just get the damn dress, Katie," she said. "You look terrible."

I grinned. I knew the dress looked good. It felt good. To hell with Jesse Mayes if he liked it or not. Despite what he might think, I wasn't wearing it for him.

The last time I wore a dress for a man it was white, and that didn't turn out so well for me. I sure as fuck wasn't going down that road again—bending over backwards to be what I wasn't to try to please a guy. *Any* guy.

"I'm proud of you," Maggie said, eying me in the mirror. "I kinda feel like you're the little bird under my wing. I wish I was coming on tour to keep you safe."

I looked at her, slightly alarmed.

"I'm kidding. But seriously, it's cool you're standing on your own. A lot of girls would milk this for all it's worth, all the time doing their damnedest to get their hooks into him. But not you. You understand this isn't fucking Cinderella, right? The kingdom isn't actually up for grabs." She handed me a pair of ankle boots to pair with the dress. "You're looking at this as a job, and how best to rock it while maintaining who you are. I totally dig that about you."

"Thanks." I wasn't sure I relished the compliment. Jesse and I had a deal, yes. But it didn't exactly feel super-awesome being reminded by someone who knew him well, someone I liked and he obviously respected, that I was nothing but the hired help.

Maggie stood back to check me out. "Don't look now... but I'd say you look about ready for life in the spotlight."

"Great," I said. The thought still made my stomach turn, actually.

She stared me down in the mirror. "It fucks people up, you know."

"Uh-huh." I turned to face her. "Honestly? I'm pretty freaked out that I have no idea what I'm about to be dealing with. I've never done anything like this before."

"Gone on tour, or dated a rock star?" She handed me my lucky leather jacket. "Or pretended to be in love with someone you aren't?"

"All of the above." I slipped the jacket on and turned to the mirror again. My jacket looked totally kick-ass with the pretty, sexy dress and the killer boots. And it also made me feel like myself... only a lot more glamorous.

Maggie stood beside me so we were both in the reflection. "You'll be amazing," she said. "Like you were in the video. Just stay out of the way when you're not needed, and pretend the fuck out of being his dream girl when you are."

I eyed my reflection skeptically. I looked good. But Jesse Mayes' dream girl?

Shit.

"He chose you, right?" Maggie said, picking up on my unease. "My best advice? Just be yourself." She reached under the collar of my jacket to adjust the shoulders of the champagne-pink dress, sliding them outward, deepening the cleavage-revealing V of the neckline. "While wearing this."

CHAPTER FOURTEEN

Katie

WHEN WE GOT BACK to the hotel, Jesse had come and gone. Maggie said he and his entourage had gone ahead to the venue. He'd taken the time to dirty up my drawing though, making the little caricature Jesse's eyes bug out of his head in the direction of the little caricature Katie, and adding a lump to the crotch of his pants.

I laughed but tossed the sketch into my sketchbook so it wouldn't get left behind.

There was also a little bag on the bed with my name on it.

Inside, wrapped in tissue, was an incredibly gorgeous bra and panties. Silky black with lace around the edges. The bra had sparkly little rhinestones set in the lace, which made it both pretty and badass. It had skimpy demi cups, and when I tried it on, not only did it fit perfectly, it did monumental things to my cleavage.

I put on the panties too, because why not?

Once I'd gotten over the thousands of dollars Maggie had dropped on clothes for me this afternoon, I'd decided to accept the fact that things that seemed outlandish in my world—the normal world—were normal here, in Jesse's world, and I might as well get used to it.

So I wore the beautiful, super-sexy and no doubt expensive underwear, bought for me by a rock star—or more likely, one of the members of his entourage—under the super-sexy champagne-pink dress, also paid for by said rock star, put on my expensive boots and lucky old jacket, touched up my makeup, and met Maggie in the lobby.

Flynn drove us to the venue in a rental car and when we parked in back, inside a security gate and alongside the opening band's tour buses, my heart started to thump like *I* was about to take the stage.

Which, in a way, I was.

We sailed through security at the door, thanks to Flynn, and Maggie navigated the bowels of the arena like she'd been there a dozen times, which maybe she had. We ended up at a dressing room door, which was open, and joined Raf, Letty and Pepper inside. They were just pouring shots from a bottle of bourbon.

I'd glimpsed Jude in the hallway, but didn't see Jesse until he came up behind me and slipped his strong arms around my waist.

I looked up, my gaze locking with his in the wall mirror.

"Hey, beautiful," he whispered in my ear.

"Hey, handsome," I returned. The thunder of the crowd rocked the building, but I swore I could hear the thunder of my heart right over it.

The opening band had finished their set, and the crowd sounded mad with lust to see Jesse Mayes in the flesh. Not that I could blame them. From where I was standing his flesh was looking pretty fucking delicious in a pair of low-waisted brown leather pants with a lace-up crotch, and a sleeveless shirt that showed off his fantastic arms.

His hands slid down and gripped my hips. He turned me toward him so abruptly I grabbed his shoulders to steady myself, and he landed one on me before I could think.

The kiss was long, hard, deep and hungry. I had no idea where it came from, but soon I'd forgotten everything but that kiss, the room dissolving to nothing but Jesse and I, locked together in a slow, hot, mind-melting make out.

When we broke apart, everyone was staring at us, but kind of pretending not to.

Someone cleared his throat.

"Jesse?" Pepper was holding out a shot of bourbon to Jesse. Raf and Letty were each holding a shot of their own. Jesse took the shot and handed it to me. Raf took the cue and handed one to Maggie, then poured another for Jesse.

We all did our shots, Jesse kissed me again, quickly, and then they were gone, all four guys heading out the door to take the stage.

When I turned to Maggie she was staring at me, a small grin hooking the corner of her mouth. The bourbon—and that kiss—had left me feeling all warm and fuzzy, and yes, horny. I shook it off as she took my hand. "Come on, *beautiful*," she said, imitating Jesse's husky voice as she pulled me into the hall, where Flynn was waiting.

We hurried to follow the band toward the stage, hanging back to keep out of the way as Jesse, Raf and Letty strapped on their guitars. Jesse exchanged a few words with the guitar tech that I couldn't hear and they both laughed; his spirits were incredibly high, which was intoxicating to be around, and it wasn't just that kiss. The man had electric energy that seemed to set off sparks in the air and was more than electrifying; it was magnetizing.

I wanted to get closer but I stuck to Maggie like glue.

As of tomorrow, I'd be doing this alone. Tonight, I was in no rush to leave her side.

While she chatted with Jude and Brody, I just stood there watching Jesse. Some local radio personality was on stage, pumping up the crowd, announcing the imminent appearance of Jesse Mayes in French and then English. The crowd went ballistic at the sound of his name, and then the guys were heading on stage.

Jesse turned, his gaze sweeping the small crowd that had formed. When he found me, he walked over, everyone moving aside for him. He took my face in one hand, brushed his lips against mine, and said, "See you after I do this thing."

Then he turned and sauntered on stage. The curtain dropped, Pepper hoofed out a beat on the bass drum, the crowd's insanity fired up another octave and the band kicked into "Come Lately."

My heart was thundering so hard I could feel it over the insane vibrations of the music through the concrete under my feet.

Maggie bumped shoulders with me, and when I glanced over at her she smiled. "Time to see your man in action."

She drew me through the small crowd; I didn't even know who all these people were or what they were doing. Some wore press passes, and some were obviously crew, or members of the opening band. Whoever they all were, none of them bat an eye when Maggie and I, flanked by Brody and Jude, made our way into the side stage area to watch the show.

Which was incredible.

Jesse blew me away.

It was nothing like the VIP show in Vancouver, which was small, intimate, and largely unplugged.

This was huge, concrete-rattling, blow-your-hair-back, electric rock madness, and Jesse was totally in his element. The man was electric backstage, but on stage, he was on fire. This was so clearly his passion. I could feel it in his music.

His voice filled the venue, somehow carrying over his guitar and Raf's. Pepper was a madman on the drums but he and Letty and Raf didn't bother trying to upstage Jesse, and even I could tell that at times they could barely keep up. The man's fingers flew over his fretboard, so fast and hard I thought for sure I was actually going to see sparks fly. He crunched out raunchy Dirty covers and played the most melodic and moving songs from his solo album, his voice one with the music, haunting and raw.

I fucking loved his music.

I got so lost in it, I forgot about everything else going on around me. I stopped feeling conspicuous or caring if anyone thought I should be here or questioned who the fuck I was. I forgot about Maggie and Brody and Jude.

I got so lost in it that it startled me when Jesse announced they were playing the last song.

Then the band ripped into "Try Me On," the heaviest track from *Sunday Morning*, and Maggie leaned over. "Let's go see it from the other side," she said.

It was oddly otherworldly walking through the outer area, the public area, of the arena while the band played the final notes of "Try Me On." The music was muffled, my head felt like I was underwater and I made a mental note to get some earplugs before the next show. When the song ended, the thunder of the crowd was also muffled, thudding like an erratic heartbeat.

People began to trickle out of the many entrances from the arena bowl, and soon the trickle became a never-ending throng. Inside, thousands of people were still chanting Jesse's name, demanding an encore.

The corridors filled, and Maggie took my hand as we made our way through the crowd. Flynn followed at a distance, as usual. I glanced back at him, his dark head visible in the crowd. All of Jesse's security guys were tall; now I could see why.

Curious, I leaned into Maggie conspiratorially. "Hey. Can we give him the slip?"

"No," Maggie said, and leveled me with a no-bullshit look. "And you're not gonna try."

The crowd had thickened to near-impassable, and suddenly everyone was in a mad rush, heading back inside the arena bowl. I could hear Jesse's voice; he was talking on stage, but I couldn't make out what he was saying. I was trying not to get sucked into the stampede, and pretty much flattened myself against the wall. I tried to avoid eye contact with the people passing us by. Was that an effective way to avoid being recognized?

Just how famous was I by now?

Maggie laughed, pulling me toward a set of stairs that led under the arena, blocked off with a chain rope. We went over the rope, Flynn close behind. I heard the band rip into "Dirty Like Me." The crowd hit a new level of off-the-hook, and I just hoped we'd get our asses backstage before the show let out.

Down the stairs was the same as up, with less people milling about. The music was even more muffled but I could still make out the slow, grinding thump of "Dirty Like Me." I really would've liked to see Jesse play this song, but Maggie had run into Jude and was chatting with him. I wandered over to a big double door with a security guy sitting in front of it; every time it opened the music swelled. I listened to Jesse's voice, getting swept up in the song.

"Hey, sweetheart."

I turned. A couple of roadies in crew shirts had approached and stood staring at me. The guy in front had a big grin on his face. The other one, who looked pretty shifty, peered at me over his buddy's shoulder, a cap with a worn old Slayer patch pulled low on his head.

"Hey," I said.

"You wanna blow my friend, I'll get you backstage."

Um… *right.*

Before I could respond to that generous offer, a shadow fell over us and the guy's eyes went wide. I turned to find Jude standing over me, Maggie at his heels.

"Come on, Katie." Maggie reached around Jude, grabbed my arm and yanked me toward the double door. When I glanced back, Flynn and Jude were talking to the roadies. The security guy opened the door for us and Maggie whisked me through. "Don't wander off like that, 'kay? And put this on." She handed me a backstage pass like the one she was now wearing.

"Why's everyone all twitchy about me being alone?" I asked as I followed her backstage, but my heart was still pounding. The frenzy of the thunderous crowd, which was going berserk in the aftermath of Jesse's head-spinning, heart-stopping version of "Dirty Like Me," wasn't helping. "It's freaking me out."

We stopped at the back of the side stage area, just out of the way as the guys started coming off stage; I saw Pepper toss his drum sticks into the crowd.

"I guess it's hard to understand the level of madness that comes along with fame until you've experienced it," Maggie said. "Crazy shit happens at rock shows."

"Uh-huh. Like some dude asking me to blow his friend."

"What dude?"

I whirled around. Jesse, all dripping with sweat and stage lust, swept me up in his arms, holding me against him so tight I felt the thunder of his pulse pounding through his body and his semi against my groin. Evidently, he *did* get horny on stage.

He kissed me, long and hard, until my knees almost gave out. He tasted like the salt of sweat. When he relaxed his hold on me enough that I could look into his eyes, they were narrowed. "What dude?"

"Um, one of your roadies asked me for a blow job?" I didn't know why it came out like a question except that my head was still spinning from that kiss.

"What roadie?" He did not look amused. Though that kind of thing must've happened all the time in his world. It was fucking weird to me, but as this day had made even clearer to me, I wasn't from Jesse's world.

"Uh, the guy with the crazy hair?" I looked to Maggie for help, but she just raised an eyebrow, staying out of this one. "You know... the kinda bow-legged one." I looked up into Jesse's eyes, which were blackening by the second.

Pepper and Raf walked up and Pepper slapped Jesse on the back. "Great show, man."

Jesse ignored them, still locked onto me. "A blow job?"

Pepper and Raf took their cue from Jesse's tone and made themselves scarce. I would've liked to join them, but Jesse still had me in his arms and his grip wasn't letting up.

"Um... actually, he asked me to blow his creepy friend. Lame, right?" Damn. He looked pissed.

I didn't even do anything wrong.

"Uh-huh. What creepy friend?" Okay. Definitely pissed. And also sexy, even when pissed.

It was starting to dawn on me, however, that I wasn't the one he was pissed at.

"Oh. The, uh, mute one in the Slayer cap."

I glanced at Maggie again, who for once had nothing helpful, clever or managerial to say.

Not a good sign.

"Last one?" Raf called over, switching out his guitar.

"In a minute." Jesse wiped the sweat from his face with a towel someone tossed him. "Wait here," he told me. He tossed the towel aside, kissed me again, and stalked back toward the stage.

The guitar tech handed him one of his guitars and he slung it on. I followed as far as I could and stood with Brody at the side of the stage, watching.

A single white light shone on Jesse as he walked on stage. The thunder of the crowd was deafening as he took his place, center stage. It died down slightly when he gripped the mic in his fist, and gradually hushed as he began to speak.

"This one's for Katie," he said, and the crowd erupted again as the band kicked into a song I'd never heard before.

By the time they reached the chorus, I figured it out.

It was the new song. My song.

The one he said he was going to play for me on tour. I'd really thought he was joking. Flirting.

But the song was real. And it was awesome. Sweet. Sexy. Catchy as all hell.

By the end of it I was humming along with the chorus. If Brody wasn't standing right next to me, I would've sang it out loud.

There's a new girl, and she's just my kind...

Found a new girl now, and I'm gonna make her mine.

CHAPTER FIFTEEN

Katie

I COULD TOTALLY SEE how it could overwhelm a guy, like completely hijack his hormones, when a bunch of pretty French-speaking chicks in very little clothing swarmed around him, begging for his autograph and firing questions at him with their cute accents.

For a moment as Jesse and his entourage, including *moi*, entered the crowded, thumping afterhours club, I found myself mentally preparing to get ditched. I could easily envision Jesse getting swept away in the tide of adoring fans and the promise of fast, easy sex, completely forgetting everything he'd promised me in my kitchen.

I stayed back and out of the fray with Flynn, pretending I was caught up in Pepper's story about the last time he was at this club, with his other band, and he got kicked out for taking off his pants. It was probably a hilarious story; everyone was laughing but me. I just couldn't take my eyes off Jesse, and the girls circling like sharks over a bit of bloody meat.

I knew the way I was feeling was irrational, because the man wasn't actually mine. Maybe it was *because* he wasn't mine, would never be mine, but I felt a wicked stab of envy toward those girls. I couldn't even be one of them, outright throwing myself at him in hopes of getting noticed. I couldn't afford to throw myself at him. I was his contracted *employee*. If I did that and he told me to take a cold shower and get over it, I'd be humiliated.

Worse, if he took me to bed once or twice, then lost interest, I'd be crushed.

Yeah, that was the sad truth of it. I could handle this whole pretending thing, knowing he didn't actually want me. As long as he kept believing I didn't actually want him either.

But there was no way I *ever* wanted to be his groupie du jour.

As I watched him with those girls, it all became so clear.

The guy had just sang an amazing love song about me in front of thousands of people, but the fact of the matter was that the song wasn't for me. It was for *them*.

His fans.

Not long after Jesse was engulfed by the mob, Jude plowed in and scooped him out, a couple of bouncers sending the flustered girls scattering. They hung back, waiting for an opening to dart back in, but more bouncers had appeared and quickly formed a wall around Jesse and the rest of us. The girls were starting to sniff out the other guys, mainly Pepper and Raf, who were pretty famous themselves, if not Jesse Mayes famous. It was kind of exciting, not to mention impressive, the way the club staff worked with Jesse's crew, really fucking fast, to get us all into the club without any of the musicians losing a shirt.

Just when I thought he might've actually forgotten me, Jesse turned, worked his way over to me and gripped my hand. I held on tight as we followed Jude and a couple of bouncers into a raised area behind one of the bars.

My stomach fluttered with nerves, but to my surprise, I kinda *liked* how people looked at me when I was with Jesse. I saw a hell of a lot of envy, sure, and some catty spite, but there was also something I didn't anticipate: appreciation.

Men and even women were checking me out, their gazes moving over my body in the champagne-pink dress. Jesse Mayes' new girl... out with him in public. I guess it *was* a big deal, if you knew who Jesse Mayes was, and right now, it seemed like the entire late-night scene of Montreal did. Everyone within eyesight seemed to be watching us.

But it was late, the party had been going awhile, the music was loud, and by the time our group dropped into the dark booths awaiting us, most of the clubgoers had gone back to dancing, drinking, talking, and making out in the dark.

Jesse had chosen a funky little couch for us to sit on, just the two of us. It had a low half-back and only one arm, on his side, so when he leaned back and pulled me along, I went with him. I relaxed against him, crossing my legs, my side flush against his. His arm was wrapped over the back of the seat behind me and he was warm. No; he was hot, and he smelled so fucking good.

Cinnamon. Leather. Jesse Mayes. These were fast becoming my three favorite scents in the world.

He'd changed into jeans after the show, a distressed white T-shirt, so soft and thin I could make out his nipples beneath the cotton when he moved, and a leather motorcycle jacket, which he'd discarded when we sat down. I would've been happy to watch the way his clothes shifted and stretched over his muscles as he talked and laughed with the guys, but it was probably a better idea to focus on something other than his hot body pressed to mine. So I gazed around the club, trying to just absorb the scene and relax.

Jude put a drink in my hand and took a spot in the corner where he stood watching over us with a couple of bouncers. I lifted the drink in thanks. He nodded, then continued his visual sweep of the room. He never strayed far from Jesse, always watching his back. The man didn't seem to smile all that much but I'd caught the two of them laughing their asses off a few times over some private joke, and seeing their effortless, close connection made me miss Devi something fierce.

I brought the drink to my lips for a taste. It was a SoCo and amaretto on the rocks. With extra cherries.

Jesse had remembered my drink from the bar in Vancouver.

He'd been talking to Brody but when I glanced up, he was watching me. He shifted closer, leaning into me. "How you doing?"

"Great," I said. "Devi would love this place. I wouldn't have thought it was your scene, though."

"Why not?" He sipped his own drink, which by the looks of it was whiskey of some kind. "Good music. Good energy. Beautiful women." His gaze slipped down from my face, to the low-cut V of my dress.

I felt the answering rush of heat through my body. "A rock star who likes electronic music?"

His dark eyes flickered up to mine. "Also like to look at beautiful women."

There was that word again.

Beautiful.

I'd tried to let it roll off the first few times, but since he kept using it, I had to wonder. I watched his gaze sweep down to the hemline of my dress, which had crept up my thigh when I crossed my legs. Seriously. Jesse Mayes thought I, Katie Bloom, former skater kid and glasses-wearing wannabe artist, was beautiful?

It wasn't like he was the first guy to ever say it, but come on. *Jesse Mayes?* The man was beauty incarnate. Did he not own a mirror? How could anyone look at that face on a daily basis and use the word beautiful to describe *me*?

It must've been the plunging neckline of my sexy dress messing with his whiskey-addled mind.

He set down his drink and placed his hand on my bare knee, his fingers cool from gripping the glass. Sipping my drink, I glanced around at the faces of the band and crew. I kinda felt like we were on a tiny stage here on the couch, like everyone was waiting for some kind of performance to begin. But to my relief, they weren't actually watching us.

Jesse, though, was definitely watching me.

"Um, tell me something," I said, looking to distract myself from the hand on my knee and the smoldering look in Jesse's eyes that at this late hour, in this crazy club lighting, looked a hell of a lot like lust. "Did I get someone fired tonight?"

He stared at me, smoothing his thumb back and forth across my thigh. "Like who?"

"You know who. The roadie who asked me for a blowjob."

"No, Katie. You didn't get anyone fired."

"But you *did* fire him?" I pressed, reading between the lines of that response.

His hand left my knee as he picked up his drink. "Doesn't matter," he said.

"Then you're not gonna tell me?"

"Don't worry about it, Katie. They won't bother you again."

They? Oh, man. He fired them both.

I'd been wondering since Jesse came off stage. After the show wrapped up, he'd showered and we'd set out with some of the crew to hit the club. There were a ton of people still working at the venue when we rolled out, tearing down the stage, but I didn't see either of those roadies who propositioned me anywhere.

"Promised you my crew would look out for you while we're on the road. You feel safe going to those guys for help, sugar?"

"Well, no."

His jaw clenched, the same way it did backstage when I told him what that roadie said to me. He downed his drink, set the glass aside and reached for me, cupping my face. Then he leaned in and brushed his lips against mine. I didn't move. I was pretty sure I stopped breathing. His lips were hot, velvety and tasted of bourbon. His mouth lingered over mine when he said, "Assholes had to go. Not your fault." His lips dragged against mine again, hot, soft. His bottom lip caught on mine and for an instant the wet of the inside of his lip touched mine.

My pulse rammed through my body as he drew back, my breath coming shallow and fast as I licked the taste of Jesse Mayes from my lips. "Um, I just thought... maybe you could give them another chance."

I watched as he took another round of drinks, delivered by a pretty cocktail waitress. She smiled at Jesse, her white teeth gleaming against her tan skin, but he didn't seem to notice. He never took his eyes off me.

I took the drink he offered and reminded myself that I wasn't getting drunk tonight, for good reason. My pulse was already slamming between my legs, Jesse's nearness and that fierce, protective look on his face doing crazy things to my brain.

"I mean, they didn't *do* anything," I went on. "They just propositioned me. That must happen all the time at rock concerts."

"Don't give a fuck," he said. "They propositioned *you*."

Right. And I was Jesse Mayes' girl... as far as everyone knew.

I watched in what felt like surreal slow-motion as his hand went to my knee again, this time smoothing right on upward. I could feel the guitar string calluses on his fingers, the slight roughness making me shiver. His gaze flicked to mine as his hand continued up beneath the hem of my dress. He gripped my thigh, his fingers digging into me as he drew my knee up onto his lap. His gaze caught on my lips and I almost choked on my nerves. Then he leaned in and kissed me again.

This time, it wasn't just a brush of his lips against mine. He nudged my mouth open and lapped his tongue against mine in a long, firm stroke, then sucked my bottom lip into his mouth before breaking away.

I knew I was blushing but at least in the near-dark it would be hard to see. What wouldn't be so hard to see were my eyes practically rolling back in my head when he pressed a kiss to my throat, just under my jaw. Then he lounged back, retrieving his drink from the table for a sip. He was still watching me, assessing me with his now-hooded molten eyes.

I sipped my drink, the booze and Jesse Mayes making me feel warm all over.

Too warm.

How the hell did I think I was getting through six weeks of *this*?

I would've squeezed my thighs together in an effort to get a little more comfortable and contain my rising excitement, but my knee was still drawn up over Jesse's thigh. Right about now, I could understand why Devi advised me to pack my vibrator. I'd laughed, but didn't pack it. Now, I don't know what the fuck I was thinking. If this was my life for the next six weeks, I'd definitely need *something* to take the edge off.

I sipped my drink again, trying to get my breathing under control, trying to keep from going all lust-faced with desire. According to Devi, I got "sex face" anytime I thought about getting it on, and right now, I couldn't think about much else.

"So… what is it we're doing here, exactly?" I asked when Jesse remained silent. "You know, me, you, hanging in a club?"

"We're making out." His mouth twitched in amusement. Then he licked his bottom lip, slowly, and said, "You taste like sunshine."

I burst out laughing, partly because I was nervous, but partly because WTF? "What the hell does sunshine taste like?"

He grinned slowly. "Like Katie Bloom and that girlie shit you drink."

I couldn't remove the stupid grin from my face if I tried.

"What we're doing," he said, and sipped his bourbon, "is being seen." Then his gaze left me as he looked out over the dance floor.

Right.

Being seen.

When Brody nudged Jesse's shoulder and started talking in his ear, I breathed a small sigh of relief as he turned away. The guy was intense. The way he touched me, the way he *looked* at me, turned me into a flustered mess.

I pressed my cocktail glass to my chest and rolled it between my breasts, trying to calm the fuck down, but my heartbeat practically rattled the ice in the glass. The guy was making my head spin. But I was prepared for this. I *knew* it was all for show. I couldn't let it floor me every time he touched me.

No matter how good it felt.

No matter how much I really wanted him to *keep* touching me.

Because every time he touched me, it was in public, and it was for a reason. And the reason wasn't to make me feel good. It wasn't even because he wanted to touch me.

It was to be *seen* touching me.

The lines of "New Girl" repeated in my head. He'd made a very public declaration of love to me tonight with that song, and now here we were, officially together, in public. Our relationship was out there. Our *lie*. And everything we did from this night on was meant to back it up. I was here for one reason: to help him sell that lie, to make it look real. I was being paid a hell of a lot of money to make it look real.

Jesse was playing his part, and he was playing it well.

What else said *I own this piece of ass* like sticking his hand up my dress in the middle of a crowded club, or firing his staff because they hit on me? Or making me pant like a bitch in heat every time he kissed me?

He was staking his claim over me, publicly, and I needed to get used to it, fast. This was only the beginning. I'd signed on for *six weeks* of this.

And it meant absolutely nothing.

I took a swig of my drink, the voice of reason in the back of my head reminding me to slow the fuck down.

Jesse was still talking to Brody. He squeezed my thigh a little when I shifted, but he didn't let go. In fact, his grip had migrated subtly northward, which was messing with my brain. I had no idea if he was jacking me up on purpose. Did he have any idea how much he was turning me on? Or did he just think I was a really great actor, like he was?

Like I'd been in the video?

Except I wasn't really acting in the video. I was just being hot for Jesse Mayes, for real. I'd let things go as far as he took them, more or less. And now the question I'd been asking myself since I'd agreed to come on tour with him circled in my brain. I felt it beating in the rhythm of his pulse, in his hand on my thigh.

How far would I let this go? How far would I go for two hundred grand?

How far would I go for Jesse Mayes?

This far, I told myself, glancing at his hold on my thigh, the edge of his sexy wrist tattoo disappearing beneath my dress. *This far and no fucking farther.*

I took a peek at my phone, looking for some respite, and found a text from Devi. It was about the hundredth time she'd checked on me today. So far I'd answered each text by sending her a pic of whatever was going on around me, but I decided not to send her a pic of Jesse's hand on my thigh. Instead, I panic-texted her back. *What the fuck was I thinking?*

Seconds later, her response came in. *OMG are you okay??*

I'm sitting in a club with Jesse, I texted her. *His hand is up my dress.*

Devi's response was again immediate. *I repeat, are you okay??*

Ask me tomorrow.

Get out your vibrator and calm the F down. You can't sleep with him on day 1.

Sage advice from a woman who'd never owned a vibrator because "Why would I get it on with a hunk of plastic when I can get it on with a hunk?"

Didn't bring it. I sent that text and stashed my phone away; Jesse had turned back to me.

"Hi," I said.

He said nothing. His gaze swept down over my face, my dress, his hella long, dark eyelashes masking his eyes. And just when I thought I was in danger of getting good and groped, he withdrew his hand from under my dress and skimmed it up my waist instead. His knuckles brushed my breast. My nipple hardened, tingling inside my bra as he lay his hand on my neck.

"Can I kiss you?" he asked. Which was kind of sweet but strange, since he'd already kissed me, without asking.

I nodded a little, unable to wrangle any words.

My lips parted just before he crushed his lips to mine, and then I knew why he'd asked.

This was nothing like those other kisses.

He shifted closer to me, tipping my head back to meet him, and delved deep. His hand slid into my hair, holding me to him as he devoured me. Slowly.

The club music vibrated through us but the club was gone. There was nothing but me and Jesse in the thudding dark, melting into one another.

I kept up with the slow, mind-melting pace of his deep kisses. I even remembered to breathe each time he pulled away to kiss my face or my neck. I sipped my drink while he kissed my ear, just chilling with my fake boyfriend, having a slow, easy make out in a club like it was no big deal, even as the shivers ran up and down my spine. My breasts ached and swelled. My clit pulsed and begged for attention. I just kept telling myself that we were *being seen*, that it wasn't real, as much as my body protested the fact.

His hand gripped my hair harder and he found my mouth again, kissing me even slower, but deeper still. I swore my heartbeat slowed to match his rhythm, beating deep in my chest, between my legs. My fingers shook as I spread my hand on his chest. My fingernails dug into the hot, soft cotton of his shirt. I swirled my tongue against his until I felt the low vibration of his moan or growl, but I couldn't hear it in the noise of the club. I let my teeth drag against his lip. I sucked on his tongue. I did everything I'd ever wanted to do to a man's mouth with my own since I'd hit puberty.

Because—fuck it. What if the world ended tomorrow and this was my only chance?

I wasn't willing to take that risk.

When we broke apart, he was panting softly. His gaze slid down my dress again. Then he said, "Crazy lighting in this place, kinda looks like you're naked."

I was still recovering from his kisses, but managed to get my head together enough to say, "I thought you didn't like pink."

His dark eyebrows drew together. "You wore this because you thought I wouldn't like it?"

"Well... you can buy my time and my faked affection, Mr. Mayes," I said, still trying to get a hold of my breathing. "But what I put on my body is up to me."

His eyes smoldered, darker than I'd ever seen them.

He leaned in and whispered in my ear, so close and so slowly that his breath made me shiver. "I like you in pink."

CHAPTER SIXTEEN

Jesse

I WAS PRETTY sure I could get used to this.

All the perks of having a girlfriend, without actually *having* a girlfriend.

Well, maybe not *all* the perks. I had no idea if that particular perk was gonna end up part of the deal. That was up to Katie, because my dick had been good to go pretty much from the first moment I'd met her, standing there in her rain-wet clothes, offering me cherry pie.

And now, wearing that slinky pink dress, the one that made her look fucking naked as she slithered around in my lap, her soft breasts pressed to my chest, her plump pink lips sliding against mine, that little tongue of hers flicking out to taste me... Christ. I was stiff as a fucking rod. I didn't care who was looking. I would've sucked on her from head to toe, licked that fucking dress right off her if she'd let me.

By the time we hit the next club and walked into the dimly-lit VIP room, Katie holding my hand as she looked around, I was still trying to adjust my wood in my jeans. I really had to stop looking at her ass every time the girl got walking.

A couple of dudes at the glowing bar in the corner had turned almost completely around on their stools to look at her in her clingy, skimpy flesh-dress. I tugged her closer, tightening my grip. Couldn't have her wandering away in that thing.

"Can we sit over there?" she asked, pointing at an unoccupied love seat.

"You can sit anywhere you want, darlin'," Jude answered. Jude had a way of calling women *darlin'* that tended to make panties drop, and I didn't mind that he used it on her. He liked Katie. I liked that he liked her. Jude fucking hated most of the women I dated. He hadn't said so, but I was pretty sure he thought Katie was adorable, which she was.

The only thing he had said about her, or about my relationship with her, was, "You sure about this, brother?"

"She'll be good for us," I said, as vaguely as fucking possible. And she *was* good for us, already. She was helping us sell music. She was keeping us entertained. She was already making this tour more interesting than it would've been without her. No question about that.

But as much as I liked Jude liking her, and it kinda made the egotistical prick in me get a pride hard-on when he looked at her the way he did when she showed up in that dress tonight, I didn't want him liking her *that* much.

Right about now, I was really fucking glad I'd made her agree not to mess around with anyone else. The last thing I needed was for Katie to fall for Jude or anyone else on my crew. I didn't need that complication.

Fuck it. That was bullshit. The truth was I didn't want to share the girl.

She may be my fake girlfriend, but she was *my* fucking fake girlfriend.

I pulled her flush against me and she smiled up at me. Then I laid one on her, kissing her long and deep, giving those fuckers at the bar an eyeful. She stretched up on her toes as I drew her tighter against me. When I let her go, she stumbled back a little in her high heels, but I held her, steadying her.

Jude was speaking with the hostess. The room was scattered with low couches, most of which were occupied, but she led us straight to the love seat Katie had pointed out, facing the wall of windows overlooking the dance floor below. I didn't really care where we sat. Just wanted a break from the madness outside.

Jude ordered us a bottle and he and Flynn got scarce as Katie and I sank into the low love seat together. The waitress brought over an ice bucket on a stand and a bottle of champagne with two glasses. I poured us both some champagne and noticed Jude turning away a couple of women who wanted to come over. He wouldn't let anyone get close. I flung my arm up on the back of the seat and relaxed as Katie sank against me. I definitely didn't mind having her to myself for a while.

My hand found her bare shoulder, where the dress had slipped off and she hadn't fixed it. I smoothed my thumb over her bra strap and leaned in closer. I let my lips graze her ear when I said, "You wore the lingerie."

She looked at me over her shoulder, narrowing her eyes slightly. Then she lifted her champagne in toast. "To your new tour."

I lifted my glass, touching the rim to hers. "And my new girl."

My thumb was still stroking her shoulder, playing with the strap of her bra. She rolled her eyes a little. "I like the rhinestones," she admitted, sipping her champagne. "They're pretty."

"They're diamonds."

Katie choked on her bubbly. "What?" She coughed and sputtered and reached to set her glass on the table by our knees.

I lounged back on the love seat, a smile tugging at the corner of my mouth. "I said, they're di—"

"I heard you." She was already wrestling beneath her dress, taking the bra off, apparently. "I can't wear diamonds."

I just watched the show, amused and a little perplexed, drinking my champagne as she stripped the bra off without removing the dress and yanked it free through an arm hole. "Why the hell not?"

She tossed the bra at me. "Because the diamond industry is, like, totally evil."

I lifted the bra off my chest and brought it to my face. It smelled like her, like cherries and cream. Her mouth fell open as she watched me smelling it.

"The entire diamond industry?"

"You'll have to take it back," she insisted.

I dropped the bra on the couch beside me. "I don't think they take back lingerie that's been worn."

"Well, we'll donate it to charity." She smoothed her dress. "Do you normally buy diamond-encrusted gifts for women the minute you start dating them?"

My gaze slid over the perfection of her tits, braless in the soft dress. Then I adjusted my dick in my jeans, spreading my legs as I eased further back in the seat. At this rate, the girl was gonna keep me perpetually hard. I looked up into her blue-green eyes, wondering how drunk she was. How much of this was Katie Bloom and how much of it was for show.

"You, Katie Bloom, are definitely nothing like the women I normally date."

"I'll take that as a compliment," she said, glancing at my hand on my crotch.

"You should."

"Well, I have my integrity," she announced. "And I don't care if my values are misguided or not. They're mine."

She crossed her legs and my gaze dropped to the hem of her dress. My cock throbbed at the sudden image: me, balls deep in Katie Bloom, my hips rammed up between those creamy, smooth thighs. "What about the panties?"

Her eyes narrowed at me again. "They don't have any diamonds on them. And they're staying on."

She sank into the love seat again, pleased with herself, and leaned into my side. My arm returned to the back of the seat, fingertips smoothing over her bare shoulder again. She glanced up at me.

Then she turned into me and kissed me.

It took me by surprise, but I wasn't an idiot. I kissed her back.

When she pushed her body against me, I growled into her mouth, my dick straining in my jeans. My hand moved into her hair and I held her against me as my tongue found hers. We pressed into each other, my other hand stealing to her soft breast, squeezing her gently through the dress. She melted into my hands and I had the overwhelming urge to spread her legs and do exactly what I was doing to her mouth to her sweet, soft pussy.

I dug my fingers into her thigh, probably bruising her, groaning as she swept her soft tongue against mine. My thumb skimmed her hard nipple. Then she pulled away and drew a breath, and I let her go.

She reached for her glass and glanced around but no one was paying much attention. We weren't the only ones making out.

She dropped her hand to my thigh and left it there, close to the bulge in the crotch of my jeans. Dangerously fucking close. My heartbeat rammed in my chest, in my dick. If she moved her fingers one more fucking inch, I swore I was gonna blow.

"So... how come you never date ordinary girls?" She cleared her throat a little and took a shaky swig of champagne. "And by ordinary I mean not famous," she added, using the line I'd used to describe her that night in the hotel bar.

As she met my gaze she looked horny as hell, her pink lips swollen from kissing me. I wanted to kiss her again. I wanted to push her back on the love seat, rip off those black lace panties and spread her thighs, and lick her all the way to a screaming, shuddering orgasm. I wanted to suck her off until she came so many times she forgot how to breathe. I wanted to screw her with my tongue until she forgot her fucking name.

Instead, I took a deep breath and exhaled.

"I have no idea," I said.

CHAPTER SEVENTEEN

Katie

SOMEHOW WE MADE it back to the hotel before the sun came up.

We went up to our room, Jesse, me, and the thudding music of every bar we'd been in tonight all muddled together, pounding in my brain. I had a cool dubbed-out remix of Baby Bash's "Suga Suga" in there, still making me dance. I danced right into the hotel room as Jesse shut the door, but despite the cacophony in my head, the room was empty. We were alone for the first time all day.

Just the two of us.

It was the end of the first night of the tour, an incredibly long night. What felt like a whole lot of nights in one.

An *incredible* night.

Jesse stumbled over to the beds in the near-dark and tossed his stuff off onto the floor. I turned on a light, wondering how the hell I was going to keep up with this pace as I stumbled taking off my new boots. It reminded me of the first night we'd spent together, in that other hotel room. Except this time I wasn't planning on doing anything stupid, like stripping in front of him. Which was exactly why I'd paced myself throughout the night.

Mostly.

I'd done my best to make sure that this time Jesse was drunker than I was. This was no easy feat. The man could hold his alcohol. But luckily for me, everyone and their damn dog wanted to buy him a drink, so inebriation was a definite eventuality. The real kicker was when we'd crossed paths with a bachelorette party of eight drunken women, who'd insisted on sending us three bottles of champagne. Jude had flatly refused to help us drink them, apparently feeling responsible for our drunk asses and realizing, correctly, that he was the last sober line of defense between Jesse and a stampede of horny drunk chicks. So Jesse had ended up ordering Flynn, on threat of dismissal, to drink with us.

I was pretty sure Flynn was short-pouring his own refills though, just like I was, making sure they were ten percent champagne, ninety percent bubbles.

We never said it out loud but at some point in the night Flynn, Jude and I had definitely colluded to get Jesse trashed.

I watched him stagger a little as he sat down on the bed and yanked off his boots. I then shrugged off my lucky leather jacket, tossed it aside, and did something stupid.

I decided to help Jesse Mayes get undressed.

I couldn't help it. Seeing him all cute and wobbly and drunk, I felt this ridiculous but overwhelming protective urge, maybe because he'd been so protective of me with the whole roadie-blowjob thing. Maybe it was stupid and misguided, but I really wanted to look after him. I felt like it was my duty as fake girlfriend.

And I got down on my knees to do it.

"Don't worry, babe," he told me. "I don't always get wasted after a show. Wouldn't wanna disappoint you with whiskey dick."

I laughed and struggled to undo his jeans, which had an incredibly stubborn zipper. Or else I was just that drunk. He let me do it, leaning back on his hands to enjoy the show as I fumbled.

When I glanced up, his dark eyes were hooded, though not with drink. Clearly he was enjoying the fuck out of this.

"You are not that drunk," I accused.

"Am I?" A grin spread across his face.

I squinted at him, but admittedly my judgment was more than a little impaired. There were two of his sexy faces smiling down at me.

Shit. In the silent stillness of the hotel room, I was way more drunk than I'd thought.

I sat back on my heels. "I thought you were totally wasted. You drank like five million drinks."

"Nope. Like watching you down on your knees, trying to figure out how to get my pants off though."

After that, I let him figure it out himself. Which didn't take long, because by the time I'd stepped out of the bathroom with my makeup removed, teeth brushed and pj's on, he was in bed.

I'd splurged on the matching camisole and pj pants yesterday, just for the tour. They were flattering but didn't exactly scream *I want to get boned*. Normally I slept naked, but I figured that was a dangerous habit to keep up in Jesse's presence.

I turned off the light, but Jesse had switched on a lamp by the bed. I knew he could still see me. I also knew he was naked because every inch of skin that I could see was bare, and the one area that was just barely covered with the corner of the sheet had a definite tent-like shape.

He followed my gaze to his blatant erection, then grinned a cocky grin. "Just wanted to make sure I could. In case you wanted to."

"Wanted to what?" I crossed my arms over my chest and stared down at him.

He waggled his eyebrows, making me laugh.

He was teasing me. I knew that much. This was all a game to him. A game he played well and probably often.

I saw the way those women looked at him tonight—all of them. If I'd had any doubt before, there was no doubting it now. Jesse Mayes could get it anywhere, any way, and with pretty much whomever he wanted. And yet he'd promised not to get it *at all* while I was around. Which meant I couldn't really blame the guy for giving me a hard time.

I let myself take a good look at his almost-naked perfection, once, those unsettling questions rolling again through my mind.

How far would I go for two hundred grand?

Not *that* far.

How far would I go for Jesse Mayes?

Undecided.

I took a breath and shored up my courage. No matter how unsure I was, I had to set my limit with him, now, or I was fucked. Literally.

So I told him as breezily as I could, "Not tonight, handsome." Then I climbed into the empty bed, pulling the covers up tight around my chin.

"G'night, beautiful." His voice was low and gravelly from use as he turned off the lamp by his bed.

"Good night, Jesse."

I breathed quietly in the dark, my toes still tapping to "Suga Suga"… more or less waiting to see if he was gonna make a move.

He didn't.

I glanced over and I could just make out his arm, tossed over his face, his wrist over his eyes, and it was so fucking sexy. I could stare at him all night, the faint light from the window skimming the long curves of his smooth, golden skin…

He shifted, sinking deeper into the bed and exhaling. His hand went to his crotch. I watched as he cupped his cock and adjusted himself. He pulled the sheet up over himself. Then he breathed deeply and went still.

Sadly, truly pathetically, I felt bad. Bad that Jesse Mayes had to waste a perfectly good erection on my behalf.

I also felt hornier than I'd ever felt in my life.

The things I wanted to do to him, right now, in the dark, made me blush... and at the same time, made my clit throb, my pussy clenching with need as I resisted the urge to climb into bed with him. Maybe I *did* need a vibrator. How the hell else would I make it through the next six weeks without molesting Jesse in his sleep?

Hopefully I was just drunk enough that I would soon pass out and forget how good it felt to be in his arms tonight... the feel of his kisses all over my face, my neck...

I like you in pink.

I groaned, quietly, jamming my mouth with the pillow to silence myself. I rolled over, turning my back to him, and wondered if I'd made a gigantic mistake agreeing that this whole thing was just for show.

Because I wanted him. I couldn't help wanting him.

I'd had his body against mine, his hands on me, his tongue in my mouth... and worse, I'd seen that look in his eyes. The one that said *I want to fuck you.* It was a look I hadn't experienced up close in far too long.

I listened to the soft rumble of his low, deep breaths as he drifted into sleep. And yes, I wanted him.

I could admit that much to myself here in the dark.

I'd never wanted anyone more.

CHAPTER EIGHTEEN

Katie

THE NEXT DAY we said goodbye to Maggie and Brody. They flew home to Vancouver, and I was sorry to see them go. I liked them both, and since the two of them were the business end of this whole thing, I figured I was safe with them around. Safe from what, I wasn't sure.

Having my underpants charmed off by Jesse Mayes?

Um, too late. I'd already stumbled over that line with my strip tease and now dangled precariously on the precipice over the danger zone. I feared, as the minutes ticked by, that there was very little keeping me from diving pussy-first off that cliff.

As if reading my hormones, Maggie's parting words to me were, "If you value your sanity keep it in your pants. He won't." Then she hugged me, kissed me, and left me standing on the curb in my overpriced new clothes with Flynn, my ever-present, muscular shadow.

Then I flew with the band from Montreal to Toronto—first class; the tour trucks had made the drive last night to set up for tonight's show. When we landed, we were whisked to a TV studio where Jesse did an interview with a live audience, in which he answered a bunch of questions about his new girl—me. Which was surreal, for me, though he handled it with incredible professionalism. Somehow he kept it light and mysterious, giving up little detail about *our* personal life while confirming that yes, he and Elle were a thing of the past, and yes, he was head-over-heels for one Katie Bloom.

Crazy.

I watched from backstage as he signed autographs and generally got pawed by a hell of a lot of adoring women, which he handled with incredible ease. He seemed pleased with how they were taking the news. According to Devi, #JessesGirl was trending on social media, which was a good thing, I guessed, since Maggie had also told me that a big-ass spike in song downloads was reflecting the fans' excitement about Jesse's new love.

Though it didn't keep them from throwing themselves at him.

On the way into a signing and meet and greet at a record store, I saw a chick, in broad daylight, peel up her shirt, shoving her perfect, braless boobs in Jesse's face and asking him to sign them. Which he did with a big black permanent marker. The girl couldn't have looked any more pleased if he'd just planted his lovechild in her womb.

I tried to pretend it didn't bother me. Because as the girlfriend of a sexy-as-fuck rock star, you probably had to get used to that sort of thing. Fast.

When I failed at pretending it didn't bother me, I went ahead and let it bother me, so I could process it and let it go. But I failed at that, too.

That night, after another massive, sold-out show, there was no clubbing, which was probably a good thing. The last thing I needed was another night of slow, steamy making out in public to really fuck with my head and leave me with a raging case of "blue clit," as Devi so aptly called it when I texted her to recap the previous night's events.

While Jesse went to sound check in the early evening, I'd let Devi convince me to take her shopping—keeping her on speed-text while I picked out a vibrator.

So at least I'd gotten that taken care of.

After the show, we piled onto Jesse's tour buses and drove for the Canada/U.S. border, heading to Buffalo. Jesse and I were sharing one of the enormous buses with Jude and Raf, the tour manager, Mick, and Kenny, our driver. Flynn, Letty, Pepper, and a bunch of crew guys were on another bus that had a ton of bunk beds. Ours had four bunks for the guys and a big bedroom in the back, which belonged to Jesse.

And now, me.

Since we were crossing the border, everyone was on their best behavior. No boozing or partying. The bus was pretty quiet, most of the guys playing cards in the lounge. Apparently we had at least two hours before we hit the border, and I was exhausted. I sat in the lounge drawing in my sketchbook, but everyone kept telling me to just go to sleep. I had no idea if Jesse had put them up to it, but Jesse himself had disappeared into the back and I could hear him playing an acoustic guitar through the open door. I waited as long as I could before I wandered back there, too tired to put off sleep any longer.

The tour bus bedroom was nicer than the one in my apartment. Decorated in shades of cream and white with mahogany leather furniture and clean, modern lines, it had recessed lighting, plush carpeting, and a big closet with all kinds of built-in drawers that I'd already put some of my stuff into. There was one big bed in the middle. Jesse was sitting on it, curled around an acoustic guitar, cradling the neck of it in the crook of his arm like some swooning lover as his dark gaze swept over me. He smiled. That freaking gorgeous mouth… that scruff of week-old stubble… those whorls of thick, dark hair… God, he was beautiful. In a too-easy-to-fuck-you-over kind of way.

I washed up and changed in the washroom and by the time I came out, the lights were dim. Jesse was already in bed.

Naked.

I approached the bed in my pj's. "So you seriously always sleep naked?" I asked in my most prudish tone.

"Always."

He'd already tossed his arm over his eyes, his tattooed wrist turned out so that the tender flesh of the inner wrist was exposed. Damn. I couldn't get over how sexy it was when he did that. I just wanted to kiss that wrist and lick the long, curved lines of his tattoo—a set of wings that wrapped around his forearm and met behind the back of a small figure on his inner wrist. An angel?

His muscled torso was bare, the sheet around his hips, and as usual, he'd kicked the blankets on the floor. I'd already figured out that the man ran hot; if I wasn't here he probably wouldn't even bother with the sheet.

I grabbed a blanket, switched off the light and slid into bed, pulling the sheet over myself and tucking myself in under the blanket.

My heart thudded as I felt him move. He shifted closer to me, the bed dipping, making me tip slightly backward… and up against Jesse. The entire length of his hard, hot body, under the sheet with me.

I took a breath, quietly, and ignored him.

His hand snaked beneath the sheet; he placed it on the curve of my waist, his grip gently tightening, and drew me closer against him.

The son of a bitch was spooning me. Naked.

"Let's play a game," he whispered, his hot breath tickling my ear, his voice low in the dark. "Actually… let's make it a wager."

"Mmm," I murmured noncommittally, pretending I was half-asleep. It was really my only line of defense. My heart slammed in my chest, my pulse pumping between my legs. It was getting really hot in here, really fucking fast.

Unfortunately I hadn't yet had the opportunity to take my new vibrator for a test drive, so all the horniness from last night had only been compounded by hanging out with him on and off all day, watching him up on stage tonight, and enduring his many kisses… when he went on stage, when he came off stage, when we posed for photo ops throughout the day. I just kept taking the kisses, the hugs, the familiar gropes. It was all just for show, just part of the act.

Of course, we didn't exactly have an audience in the bedroom at the back of the tour bus in the dark, but still. I knew he was up to something.

When he ran the warm, wet tip of his tongue up the back of my neck, I was sure of it, but I still shivered, hard. He groaned in response and pushed in closer, so I had to push back or end up flattened beneath him. He ran the tip of his nose up the nape of my neck, through my hair, making me shiver again. Then he whispered in my ear, "Bet you give in before I do."

Evil.

The man was pure evil.

His fingers dug into my waist, holding me still as he shifted himself… fitting his very large, very hard cock right into the notch at the top of my ass, at the base of my spine… setting off sparks in that killer erogenous zone that was hardwired to my clit. I gasped and bit down, tasting cotton as I ate pillow once again. It was like the guy had some sort of manual. *Press these buttons to drive Katie crazy.*

I felt the tickle of his hot breath against the back of my neck as he laughed.

I stiffened, pulling away from him.

Fuck *this*.

The man thought he could play me like an instrument?

I tossed the covers aside and stumbled out of bed in the dark. Yes, I was hot for him. Did that mean I was just gonna spread my legs and let him have at it?

Not so much.

I started peeling off my clothes. First the stretchy camisole, then the pj pants, and last, my panties. At the moment, despite the incessant ache between my legs that told me all I really wanted was for Jesse Mayes to shove his big, gorgeous cock inside me, as deep as he could get it, and pound me stupid, I didn't really *care* how much I wanted him. There was no fucking way I was ending up just another conquest in his long line of broken hearts. Worse, some kind of one-hit wonder that he fucks right out of his system. Yes, he was hard for me this minute. What did guys call it? *Available pussy.* Well, I was definitely available. But if I gave it up, what happened tomorrow?

I'd seen the groupies at his shows, angling to get backstage. *Maybe* he wouldn't fuck any of them until our deal was done, but that didn't mean I'd be able to hold his interest any longer than any of his previous lovers had, which, apparently, wasn't very long.

If the illustrious Elle barely got a year, I'd be lucky to get a week.

I went around the other side of the bed and slipped in behind Jesse. I grabbed his hip and shoved my naked body up against his backside, exactly the way he'd done to me.

Two could play at this fucked-up little game.

He started to turn toward me, but I bit his earlobe. Hard.

"Ow! Fuck," he complained.

I soothed the hurt by licking his ear, and then his neck, the way he'd done to me. "If you lose this stupid wager," I said in my sweetest voice, nuzzling the hair at the nape of his neck, just like he'd done to me, and shoving my pussy up against his ass, "you play your next show *naked*."

"No fucking way," he said, swallowing. His voice was low, rough, his breaths coming faster as I slithered against him. "I've done it with Dirty. When I was younger and stupider. I'm not doing it in my solo show."

I relaxed away from him an inch, my breasts still touching his back. I made sure he felt my hard, swollen nipples dragging against him. Yes, I was torturing myself, but as long as I was torturing him too, I didn't care. I ran a fingertip down his spine and stroked that lovely notch at the top of his ass, which made him buck against me. The groan he let out gave me goose bumps.

"Then I guess you're not doing me," I said, sounding a hell of a lot more sure than I felt.

"Katie…" He blew out his breath through gritted teeth as I stroked him again.

"Jesse," I whispered.

He rolled back, almost crushing me, but I slipped out of the way. He lay on his back, looking at me in the near-dark as the bus rumbled along. His eyes were in shadow, his dark eyebrows drawn together. His bicep flexed, his hand shifting under the sheet as he adjusted himself.

I hoped he had the hard-on from hell.

"*You* lose," he growled, "and you give me a *private* show. Naked."

I stretched, leisurely, arching my back, and pretended to yawn a little. "Not gonna lose," I mumbled as I cuddled into my pillow and went to sleep. Or at least, pretended to go to sleep. As I lay there aching in the dark, I really didn't know who I was torturing more.

Jesse groaned and grumbled. I opened one eye to peek at him. He was still on his back, and I watched as he gave his cock a single pump, then said, "Fuck," and threw his arm over his eyes in defeat.

And when he said, "You're gonna kill me, Katie Bloom," I smiled.

CHAPTER NINETEEN

Katie

BY THE TIME we arrived in New York City a few days later, I'd more or less wrapped my head around the whole crazy rock 'n' roll routine.

Each night was pretty much the same. Concert. Rabid fans. After party. After-after party. Fake make out.

Followed by a raging case of blue clit.

Even on the nights when there was no show, there were always so many events to go to, to "be seen," that it felt like Jesse was always performing in some way. It was pretty inspiring, actually, to be around someone who was living his passion twenty-four-seven. And of course it was thrilling to be on the receiving end of some of that potent, seductive energy.

Somehow, I was even managing to hold my own in the insane battle of will otherwise known as our fucked-up little bet. Though I didn't feel as confident about actually winning the bet as I pretended to be. I just knew I couldn't lose.

But Jesse wasn't showing any real signs of giving in either.

It was our third day in NYC, following two sold-out shows, and I was wandering SoHo with Flynn after lunch, dipping in and out of shops looking for the perfect gifts for Devi and my sister, when Jesse called me.

Jesse had never called me before.

Normally Flynn just coordinated my "schedule" with Jude, and took me where I needed to be, which was wherever Jesse wanted me to be. Days were a little calmer than the nights, but no less packed. Usually Jesse sprang out of bed mid-morning, long before I was coherent, went for a run or a workout with Jude, then spent some time with his guitar. By then I was up and we had breakfast more or less together, though sometimes the other guys were also in and out, and Jesse was often on the phone, so it wasn't exactly quality time. In the afternoons he was scheduled up the ass with interviews, meetings and appearances, some of which I accompanied him to—mainly the ones where any kind of camera was involved. There were none of those today, and no show, and no one had yet told me what we'd be doing tonight. I hadn't really expected to see Jesse until the evening.

But here I was, standing in the street listening to the slow, sexy classic guitar riff at the beginning of Heart's "Magic Man," completely confused as to why it seemed to be coming from my purse... when I remembered that Devi had programmed it into my phone as Jesse's ringtone before I left Vancouver. I'd forgotten to change it.

Flynn raised an eyebrow as I dug my cell from my purse. Blushing, I turned away and answered. "Hey, Jesse."

"Hey, beautiful. Meet me for an early dinner at five? Flynn knows where."

"Okay. Sounds good."

"Perfect."

He hung up. I grinned at my phone a moment, then tucked it away and continued shopping.

For the rest of the afternoon I pretty much floated around,

light on my feet, with this stupid-happy feeling percolating in my chest.

I was having dinner with Jesse.

I never had dinner with Jesse. His dinners were always on the go or over a meeting, while I ate with myself, Flynn or whoever happened to be around when I was hungry.

I met him at five at a cool little bistro-bar, where he obviously knew the owner. We were shown to a private table at the back, behind a partial wall. Jude and Flynn had the nearest table, which was far enough away that we were on our own.

Jesse hugged me and gave me a quick kiss. Just on the cheek, but no one could really see us where we were. Then he pulled out my chair for me and said, "You look hot."

Which I did. Literally. I'd caught some sun in Central Park and I was shimmering with sweat. I'd come straight from my shopping spree and it was a hella hot day, so I was wearing a new sundress.

Jesse, as usual, looked amazing in a short-sleeve white button-up shirt and well-worn gray jeans, his sunglasses pushed up into his thick, dark hair.

I tossed my tote bag on the chair between us, my sketchbook sticking out of it. Jesse ordered for us and as soon as the waiter departed with our order, he asked, "What is that?"

"My sketchbook."

His eyebrows went up. "You draw?"

"Sometimes," I said, buttering myself a bread roll. In fact, in the first week of the tour I'd drawn more than I had in the last year; I'd already sketched everyone on our tour bus and was starting on the guys on the other bus. But for whatever reason, I didn't feel like saying so. "So, you come to this place whenever you're in New York?"

"Usually." He eyed my sketchbook again. "I've seen you with

it at sound check. I thought you were writing. Like keeping a journal."

I shrugged. "I just like to draw."

Our drinks came and I dove into my SoCo and amaretto. Before I knew what was happening, Jesse plucked the sketchbook from my bag and started flipping through it. I slammed down my drink, a little harder than I meant to, and snatched the book from his hands.

His dark eyebrows furled. "What was that? Raf?"

"I dunno." I closed the book on the sketch of Raf. "Lots of people in there." I stuffed the book back in my bag and gave him my most serious stink eye.

"It's really fucking good."

"Just something to keep my hands busy. Baking on a tour bus seems unlikely." I sipped my drink again, keeping an eye on him this time, but he made no further attempt to molest my privacy. "You have your oral fixation, right? Well, I've got a thing with my hands."

He sipped his bourbon, which I'd come to learn was his drink of choice, eying me over the rim of his glass. "I've got something you can do with your hands."

Sweet Jesus. We didn't even have our appetizers yet and the man was already flirting. No, not flirting. *Daring.* Because of our stupid bet. And quite obviously he was doing his damnedest to make me lose it.

But all I had to do was remind myself of that "private show" he was expecting if I lost, and I rallied my resistance.

"No need," I said coolly. "Busy enough sketching Raf."

Jesse's eyes narrowed a little. Raf was an interesting-looking dude. He wasn't the sex god Jesse was, but he had an easy smile, attractive caramel-macchiato skin and a crazy Sideshow Bob hairdo that got him plenty of attention. It wasn't like I could make

Jesse Mayes jealous, but I suspected his giant ego wouldn't appreciate me paying Raf a compliment, even indirectly.

Evidently, I was right. He eyed my sketchbook again, like it was killing him not getting to look inside it.

"And Dylan," I said. Because fuck yes, I'd drawn him too, all six-foot-forever of him, kilt and all. "And Zane," I added. Mostly to be cruel, but it was true, the sex Viking of rock was in there too.

Jesse's eyes narrowed further. "Heartless," he said, and I grinned.

For the rest of dinner the sketchbook was there between us, taunting him. I managed to steer the conversation toward other things, briefly, and got him talking about his day. Apparently his sister was in town and he was supposed to meet up with her, but she'd bailed on him, so he'd ended up running errands with Jude and later having a meeting with someone from his record company. I would've been happy to hear more, because his life sounded pretty fucking interesting to me. For one thing, I'd never been in a meeting with a record company exec. For another, I definitely didn't have a sister who was a supermodel. Becca was pretty and all, but shit. I'd stalked Jesse's sister on Google after he told me her name, and as it turned out, Jessa Mayes was drop-dead gorgeous and had modeled for more fashion labels than I'd ever heard of.

But all I got out of Jesse on that topic were one-word answers. Any chance he got, he brought up my sketchbook again, asking how long I'd been drawing and what kinds of things I drew. I answered his questions as vaguely as I could. I never felt comfortable talking about my art. Maybe because I had so little to show for my aspirations. But I was definitely enjoying watching Jesse try to sort it out.

All along, I knew what he was really asking. He wanted to know if I'd ever drawn *him*.

I didn't think he'd actually come out with it, but by the end of dinner, as he stared me down while I finished the last few bites of my pie, *I* almost broke. Instead, I channeled all my sexual frustration into licking the last bit of fruit filling from my fork. Slowly. It was blueberry. I would've ordered cherry if they had any, but he got the point. By now, I knew the guy must've been bursting at the seams from lack of sex. I knew I was.

"You gonna tell me if I'm in your book, cherry pie?" he pretty much growled.

Of course he was, but I wasn't about to offer up that information. His ego was bloated enough.

"Why? You were wondering?" I slid my fork back in my mouth for one last lick. The way he watched my tongue defile the utensil pretty much said it all.

"You know I was."

I set the fork down on my empty plate and shrugged. "Seeing as you already get your ego stroked multiple times a day by your adoring fans, I really didn't think you'd also need me to stroke you."

Damn. I was getting pretty good at this flirting thing. The smoldering glint in Jesse's dark eyes told me so. I was pretty sure that last comeback was wood-worthy.

I sat back in my seat, content in the knowledge that if his cock was throbbing half as hard as my clit was, I'd done my job.

Lucky for me, I had a couple of hours to burn, alone, back at the hotel after this. Well, not *alone*. With my new vibrating friend.

Jesse, poor guy, had another appointment.

And since I was only his *fake* girlfriend, it really wasn't my problem.

CHAPTER TWENTY

Katie

AFTER DINNER, Flynn drove me back to the hotel in his rental car. All the way there I wondered if I'd taken things too far. Was I being a bitch? I thought we were having fun, but the burning look Jesse gave me as he got into the other car with Jude was worrying me. He never even said goodbye.

I was trying to decide if I should text him to say sorry, when Flynn parked us in front of the hotel and came around to open my door. I didn't know Jesse well enough to know how to navigate this sort of faux pas. I didn't even know for sure if I'd pissed him off or if this was all just part of his game. Maybe he thought I was a cock tease and he regretted hiring me, but for all I knew, he just wanted to make me sweat.

I got out of the car, then almost fell back in when Jesse loomed outside the door.

I glanced over at the other car, where Jude had pulled in behind us. Jesse grabbed my hand, pulling me with him. "Hang out," he ordered Flynn. That was it. No mention of what we were doing or when he'd be back as he yanked me toward the hotel.

I hurried to keep up with his long-legged stride. He stalked through the lobby so fast that if any fangirls had been hanging around, they might not even recognize his blur.

"Um, don't you have an appointment?" As far as I knew he was supposed to be doing a radio interview with Raf in like half an hour. But he punched the elevator button and said nothing while we waited for it to arrive. His jaw was granite, but I couldn't tell for sure if he was mad or what.

Was I about to get fired?

My heart raced. I'd never been fired from anything before. Plus, I was really starting to enjoy the perks of this job.

The elevator arrived and the very biggest perk of this job yanked me onto the elevator with him. An elderly couple joined us, but as soon as they got off on the fifth floor and the door shut, I started to apologize. "Jesse, I—"

He turned to me, wrapped his hand around the back of my head and kissed me. Hard.

And holy *hell*, the man could kiss.

I could barely keep up with the demands of his mouth. Every time he kissed me it was different; this time it was fast, hungry and dominant, his tongue plundering my mouth. My knees buckled a little and I clung to his shirt collar as he fisted my hair.

Jesse Mayes was kissing me. He was kissing *me*. In an elevator.

Where no one could see us.

"No one's... um... *here*," I managed between tongue-gropings, feeling light-headed as the elevator settled.

"Don't care," he said, and crushed his mouth to mine again.

The elevator door opened and he ripped himself away, yanking me down the hall. I staggered along behind him. What the hell was going on?

He pulled me into our room, slammed me up against the door and kissed me again. And I let him. I kissed him back, harder, faster.

Then an ugly thought leapt from the dizzying pool of my thoughts.

The bet.

The motherfucking *bet*.

He was trying to make me lose the bet.

I wrenched my mouth away from his, panting for breath. "Wait," I gasped.

"Tired of waiting," he panted, kissing my neck.

"It's only been like a week."

"Try two goddamn months," he mumbled against my skin. "Never waited this long for a girl. Any fucking girl."

"Two months?" I asked, confused. "Since we met?"

"Since we shot the video and I started thinking about doing this." He gripped me under my knees, hitched my bare thighs up around his hips and thrust against me. I wrapped my legs tight around him and he growled into my neck, dry-humping me against the door like he wanted to fuck me right through it. "Fuck, Katie," he groaned.

I almost lost it right there. It was the tone of his voice, like he was starving for me. But I tried like hell to keep my head. Because I had no idea if I could trust my instincts on this, or if my wires were just short-circuiting from hormonal overload.

I looked up at the ceiling. It had been a long, agonizing week, and I needed to come so badly I was afraid I'd explode all over him if he looked at me wrong. I still hadn't tried out my new vibrator. Because I was an idiot, apparently. I'd gotten myself off in the shower a couple of times, quickly, but that was just barely keeping me sane. It was nowhere near satisfying the desire I had for the man currently wrapped between my legs to fuck the living hell out of me. And if he kept grinding up against me like this... *fuck*. I felt like a live wire about to go off in a shower of sparks.

"What about the bet?" I panted, shoving at his chest to hold him off as he sucked on my neck. "How do we know when someone loses the stupid bet?"

"Whoever comes first?"

I laughed nervously. "Uh-uh." I bit my lip as he ran his tongue up my throat and nibbled my ear. The man's oral fixation was turning me into a panting, quivering mess. "Whoever touches the other person's goodies first."

He looked at me. "Goodies?" Incidentally, his fingertips were mere inches from mine, since his hands were digging into my ass as he gripped me tight against him.

"You know what I mean. *Dick. Pussy.* No touching."

I could've sworn I saw flames leap to life in the dark depths of his eyes as he swiped his tongue over his lip. "I like it when you say dirty words." Then he kissed his way down my throat as I clutched at his muscular back, trying not to dissolve in a puddle of ecstasy.

"What's the matter, Jesse?" I pretty much purred, pretending like hell that this wasn't driving me insane. Maybe I *was* a good actress. "You wanna touch my pussy?"

He growled and picked me up, hauling me to the bed. I screamed as he swung me around and laughed, again nervously, as he tossed me on my back on the bed.

Jesse wasn't laughing as he followed me onto the bed on his knees. "Those are fighting words, woman." He hooked his arms under my legs and yanked me toward him, so my dress bunched up around my waist and my crotch ended up in his lap. Then he lowered himself onto me, ramming the hard bulge in his jeans against me.

Before I could protest, he kissed me. Then he tore off his shirt, losing at least one button in the process. I heard it hit the wall as I gripped the bedspread beneath me, trying to resist putting my hands on his naked chest. But as he thrust against me, I couldn't stop myself from riding up and down a bit on the hard package in his jeans. His heat was soaking through the thin cotton of my panties, creating hot, maddening friction.

He yanked my sundress and bra down, baring my breasts. Then he leaned down and groaned, running his tongue over the peak of one nipple as I panted beneath him.

Fuck. Too much. Too fucking fast.

"This wasn't on your no-touch list..." He flicked my hard, throbbing nipple with his tongue and I gasped. *Fuck*—it totally wasn't. Major oversight. I grabbed his hair in fistfuls meaning to stop him.

He didn't stop.

He totally ignored my grip on his hair and my attempts to squirm away, and sucked my nipple into his mouth.

I cried out.

My heart was going full-throttle, like a runaway train. I tried to relax, giving in for just a sec so my heart wouldn't explode. I tried to collect my scrambled thoughts but words were totally failing me.

I tried to reason that he was trying to make me lose.

I knew he was, and I couldn't afford to lose to him. If I did that, I'd be setting myself up for a world of hurt. A world in which Jesse Mayes could use me up and toss me away like yesterday's lay.

I definitely *wanted* to let him tear off my clothes and fuck the hell out of me, repeatedly, but I couldn't. Not like this. Not when I didn't know if it was just about the bet or just about him wanting something he couldn't have, or about anything at all other than him just wanting *me*.

"Wait," I said, but I sounded all breathy and turned on and I might as well have screamed, *More, please!* He growled something against my skin as he licked his way to the other nipple. He nipped my taut flesh with his teeth and the pleasure shot straight to my clit. I was throbbing, gasping, desperate for more...

Which was okay, I told myself. It was okay because I had my secret weapon. I had my shiny new vibrator and I was more than ready to take it for a test run. I'd even charged it up yesterday while Jesse was at the gym. And I had nothing else to do for the next couple of hours.

Jesse, on the other hand, had an appointment to get to.

"Wait. Stop," I panted, a little more vehemently, and he lifted his head. His lust-hazed eyes locked on mine. I was so caught up in fighting my own response I hadn't quite clocked his; the man was panting like a very large, very horny animal.

There was a knock on the door. "Jesse? Katie, you in there?"

Raf. Probably wondering where the fuck Jesse was.

"Coming!" I called out.

Jesse glared at me. I just smiled, shakily, and once he untangled himself and lifted his big, hard body off mine, I tucked my breasts away. Then I got up and dashed over to the door to let Raf in before Jesse could stop me.

I didn't hear a thing the two of them said. I just smiled and watched Raf's lips move, and nodded at what I thought were the appropriate places. I did not look at Jesse. Or his crotch. Though I was dying to know how he was managing to disguise and/or tame his hard-on.

From the corner of my eye I saw him put on a new shirt. He kissed me goodbye and gave me a regretful, heated look, then they were gone.

I leaned against the closed door for several minutes just listening to my heartbeat slam in my ears, recalling in excruciating, throbbing detail how Jesse had rammed me up against this door only minutes before. I stared at the tousled bed where we'd just been making out like fiends.

Without an audience.

Shit.

I didn't even care about the stupid bet anymore, although I

didn't like letting the man win. I definitely didn't want to be his latest fuck-me-and-forget-me. But I seriously didn't know how much longer I could hold out and keep my sanity.

I was literally *shaking* with desire.

I dove to the bottom of my suitcase and unzipped the compartment where I'd stashed the vibrator and lube. I didn't even bother undressing. I just flopped on the bed, exactly where I'd been when Jesse was on top of me, and propped myself up on some pillows. I could still smell him on me. If I worked fast... yeah, if I concentrated, I could still feel him.

I pulled down my sundress and my bra, exactly like he had, and skimmed my fingers over my breast, imagining what he'd felt when he licked me there, when he sucked my nipple into his mouth. I jacked up my dress to get at my panties and wiggled them down a bit.

I cradled the palm-length vibrator in my hand. It was a glossy, iridescent pink, shaped like a small, flattened cigar with a slight curve at one end. I set it to buzz on one of its many settings; the buzz was steady but not obnoxiously loud. And as much as I would've preferred to come all over Jesse, I was incredibly relieved that I was finally going to do this.

Repeatedly.

I just couldn't fucking take it anymore.

I squeezed some lube onto the vibrator. It was cherry-flavored and smelled fucking amazing. I thought about how Jesse called me *cherry pie* and bit my lip.

When I ran the vibe down between my legs, I pretty much imagined it was his hand. Or his dick. Or his dick in his hand. Caressing me, up, down, around. Buzzing object aside, it wasn't hard to imagine. I'd only been fantasizing about it since the day I met him.

The vibrator sent a pleasurable buzz through my core and I relaxed into the sensation. When I ran the slippery, curved end over my clit and imagined it was Jesse's tongue, the rush was so intense I was afraid I'd come in two seconds, so I eased back off that line of thought. Might as well enjoy this for a bit.

I tried to just concentrate on my breathing and not picture Jesse, but when I did that all I could picture was Jesse. I felt his hungry kisses on my neck, his strong hands on my ass, his body hard and pumping heat into mine. I heard the tap of the key card and the click of the door handle but my reaction was delayed. As the door swung open, I jumped, yanking out a pillow from behind my head. By the time Jesse strode into the middle of the room and the door swung shut behind him, I'd just managed to cover up with the pillow. More or less.

Jesse just stood there, staring at me.

The vibrator was still buzzing in my hand. It took a few tries but I managed to turn it off, then tossed it on the bed like a hot potato. Like he hadn't already noticed it.

It hit the bed and bounced onto the floor, landing at Jesse's feet.

He looked at it, then looked at me. His gaze swept down over my body, which was now wrapped around the pillow like a koala, and finally landed on the vibrator again. He picked it up and stared at it.

Then he switched it on.

Yep. I was about ready to die.

The vibrator buzzed in Jesse's fist. His gaze flicked from it to me. My face flushed hot and my brain scrambled for words. *Say something. Anything!*

"I… um…"

He switched the vibrator off. Then he swallowed, dragged his gaze over me again, and tossed the vibe on the bed.

"Fuck," he said.

He turned, rubbed the back of his neck, looked around like he'd forgotten what he was doing, and made an awkward grab for something on the floor. Then he turned back to me. "Forgot my…" He held up his cell phone, which must've fallen out of his pocket when we were going at it. He stared at me.

I bit my lip.

"Fuck," he said again. Then he adjusted himself in his jeans and walked out.

CHAPTER TWENTY-ONE

Jesse

I WAS SITTING in some club in Atlanta at a table covered in drinks, my boys gathered around, talking shit and drinking. It was Friday night, after the show. Half-naked dancers were grinding up on poles between the tables. The dance floor was packed, a mass of bodies pumping in the dark.

Flynn was trying really fucking hard to keep his professional distance from some hot little blonde who was begging him to dance with her. Mick had some wasted redhead in his lap. Letty's wife had come up from Florida and the two of them were going at it, his hand spread possessively on the round bulge of her pregnant belly.

Next to me was an empty seat. Come to fucking think of it, it had been empty a while.

Which was when it really hit me.

It had started sometime after New York. After I'd walked in on Katie getting her sweet rocks off with a cherry-flavored vibrator.

But fuck if I knew *why* it started.

Before that, I knew she was hot for me. But *damn*. Never did I think I'd walk in on the woman pleasuring herself between dinner and drinks. If only I'd had the time to do something about it right then. But she hadn't exactly asked me to join in. She just sat there looking super fucking embarrassed, while I stood there feeling like an ass for barging in. Like maybe I should've knocked? On the door of my own hotel room?

I flushed hot like a fucking school kid, my dick getting hard as I remembered it. I could still see her, lying back on the bed, her cheeks flushed pink, dark hair clinging to her neck, still damp with sweat from our make out session, her bare tits saluting me as she grappled with a pillow trying to cover up, clinging to the thing like a fucking life preserver.

She tossed the vibrator away like it was on fire, and fuck yeah, I picked it up. I had the little pink thing in my hand as I stood there staring at her, blood thundering to my dick. I clicked it on. The vibration was strong, and I could smell her on it. Cherry-vanilla sunshine and pure sex.

I had a hard-on bordering on painful by the time I dragged my mind out of the memory, all the pent-up lust from every make out session we'd had since the start of the tour aching in each throb of blood through my veins. I'd wanted to fuck her senseless every fucking day.

But I still hadn't done it.

Mainly because the girl was playing it that way. Every night when I came to bed, she was already asleep. And I never got another fucking chance.

The east coast was a mad cyclone of shows, interviews, appearances, signings. The tour was going fucking great and the album was selling better than I'd ever dreamed, but I could hardly keep my head straight. I was so booked up, half the time I didn't even know what time it was or what town we were in or which fucking end was up. Jude and Mick were pretty much keeping my shit together. Dirty had a massive following out east and I wanted to see every fucking face of every fucking fan while I was here.

That's what I'd told Brody when the team set out to book this thing.

But somewhere around DC, I started regretting the frantic pace... right about the time it sunk through my hard skull that Katie was getting distant. For some reason, her head didn't seem to be in the game anymore.

Her body was another thing. She did her job and she did it well. She played her part to a fucking T, and she looked amazing doing it. To all appearances she was still crazy about me, my devoted girlfriend, hanging out backstage, on my arm at every event, tongue wrestling me in every dark nightclub we hit up. Anytime I wanted it—in public—she was there, warm and ready. But she was holding something back... holding herself back, and I had no idea why.

The girl was doing everything I'd contracted her to do, and you'd think that would be enough for me. Apparently, it so fucking wasn't.

I looked around the table, but my so-called girlfriend was nowhere to be seen.

Correction. She could definitely be seen. She could be seen by every person in the fucking place, standing up at the raised bar, her short skirt riding up her creamy white thighs as she leaned over to get the bartender's attention. She was standing between Pepper, who was busy talking to some dude on his other side, and some random dipshit with a mohawk who was checking out her ass. As I watched, mohawk leaned in and accidentally-on-purpose bumped shoulders with her, struck up a conversation and bought her a drink.

I cranked back several fingers of bourbon, letting the liquor heat my blood.

I watched as haircut made some kind of brilliant fucking joke. I knew it was brilliant because Katie laughed. An honest-to-fuck Katie laugh, her head tipped back, her perfect little white teeth showing, her cheeks all rosy and her eyes sparkling in fucking delight. The guy was a goddamn comedian or some shit, because I hadn't seen her laugh like that in days.

And I couldn't fucking take it.

I didn't absorb a word of what Mick or Raf or whoever was shouting on either side of me, or what anyone else at our table was saying, and our table was fucking *loud*. All I heard was that laugh. I heard it in my head, because I couldn't actually hear it over the noise of the club and the heavy, bassed-out version of The Weeknd's "Can't Feel My Face" slamming against the walls and making Katie's hips rock in that tiny skirt.

All I saw was Katie smiling up at that mohawked asshole while he smiled down at her thinking about how he was gonna get her on her back. And I could take him thinking he was gonna get her there. I could take him buying her a drink and hovering over her so close that his knuckles, wrapped around his beer, acciden-tally-but-fully-fucking-on-purpose brushed against her tit. I could even take it when he started introducing her to his friends like he knew her. Like he was here with her and I wasn't.

But I couldn't take that fucking laugh. That pure, unfettered Katie joy coming out of her perfect pink mouth.

He might as well have made her come right in front of me.

I slammed my glass down on the table, which Raf took to mean I needed a refill and sent another bourbon my way. I pounded it back and flexed my hand, taking a long look at the rings on my fist as Raf refilled me again.

Clearly, there were two moves I could make.

One, I could go over there and do something stupid like break this random asshole's face with a fistful of metal. And see it all over the internet in about five seconds.

Two, I could sit here like a pussy and let Jude deal with it.

My best friend made the choice for me. Good thing, because I was about three seconds from making a major fucking scene I'd regret. But Jude, as always, had my back before I even knew I needed him to.

I watched him stroll over and insert his wide body into the narrow space between Katie and mohawk. Katie beamed her sweet smile right on up at Jude, but big fucking surprise, mohawk's smile dropped right the fuck off his face like Jude had smacked it off. Then he backed the fuck out of there and turned his attention elsewhere. Not just a comedian, then; smart, too.

Jude ordered up some shots and Katie took the one he handed her. They toasted, shot back their booze, and headed back to our table, Katie apparently oblivious that some dude had just tried to get up her skirt and almost met with some broken teeth.

Jude deposited her in the chair next to me, where she'd barely spent five minutes in the hour since we'd arrived. Her smile vanished. A small frown appeared in its place when she looked at me, her eyebrows pinching together. She leaned in. "What's wrong?"

"Nothing," I said, sipping my drink. "Not a thing. Just watching my girl get a drink."

She stared at me a moment, the little frown twitching at the corners of her mouth. Then she leaned back, settling into her chair as she looked out over the dance floor, tapping her heels to the music.

I leaned closer to be sure she heard me. "That dude know you're here with me?"

She turned to me again, the frown deepening. "What dude?"

"Dude with the fucking mohawk."

"Oh." Her eyes widened a bit. I didn't know what the fuck that meant, but I didn't like it. "He had this cool pattern up the side." She made a swirly motion with her finger up the side of her head.

"Does he know you're here with me?"

"I am here with you," she said. Then she got up and wiggled

her sexy ass onto the edge of my seat. She pressed up against me and peered at me over her shoulder. "See? Look at me, doing my job."

She sipped her drink, her eyes never leaving mine, and there it was again. The distance, even though she was pressed so tight against me I could feel the heat of her bare thigh through my jeans.

I put my arm around her. She relaxed against me, her body wedged into my side, where she stayed for the rest of the night.

"The fuck is this?"

I tossed Katie's sketchbook at her feet. She'd just come out of the bathroom wrapped in a hotel bathrobe, her hair all glossy and wet. I stood there in my underwear, staring at her, half-hard at the mere smell of her all warm and moist from the shower.

She stared at the sketchbook, open to the most recent sketch—a dude with a mohawk and some twirly pattern shaved up the side of his head.

Then she looked at me, scanning me from head to toe with her big blue-green eyes, apparently unimpressed as shit with whatever she was seeing.

I was drunk. Pretty much because I was pissed off, for no real reason, and I was tired, and annoyed and fucking jealous, which was not a feeling I was well-acquainted with or fucking thrilled to be feeling at all. And yes, I fucking knew that drunk was not the way to approach a conversation that was sure to go down all wrong, unless I wanted to make it worse.

I didn't want to make it worse. But I did want to fight. Or fuck.

No. Actually, I really, really, really wanted to fuck.

I wanted to fuck Katie Bloom.

Instead I'd just snooped through her sketchbook, which she'd left out and had obviously been sketching in. While I took my shower. Alone. With the image of Katie laughing in my head... standing there at the bar talking to some stranger with a dumbass mohawk and smiling like I hadn't seen her smile in my direction in days.

Fuck.

If anyone could've seen it.

Rock star Jesse Mayes jerks off in the shower, again, because he promised a chick he's not even sleeping with that he wouldn't fuck anyone else.

Fucking idiot.

"That's my sketchbook," Katie said, still staring at me.

I flicked my chin at the dude on the page. "That guy know you're my girlfriend?"

Her eyes narrowed slightly. She was getting mad, I was pretty sure, which only made me fucking madder. "I'm not your girl-friend," she said.

"Wrong answer." I stalked over to her and got close, looking her in the eye. She looked annoyed, and worse, fucking concerned, like she was worried I'd trip in my drunk-ass state and break my head open. "The deal is you're fucking *mine* for the next four weeks. That means your ass belongs to *me*. That means you don't flirt with dudes in bars when my back is turned."

She looked taken aback, and worst thing yet: hurt.

"You're drunk, Jesse. Let's talk in the morning."

"Is this about me walking in on you getting busy with your little pink friend?"

She blinked at me, looking embarrassed all over again. "What the hell does this have to do with *that*?"

"That's what I'm asking. You've barely smiled at me since."

"Well, I'm *sorry* that I haven't smiled at you enough. I didn't know there was a daily quota I was supposed to hit."

"So are you pissed because we didn't fuck, or because we almost fucked?"

"What?"

"You told me to stop. What did you want me to do, keep going?"

"No," she huffed, but that looked like one hell of a lie.

"Well, something's been bothering you. You ever gonna tell me what it is?" I leaned closer, until my nose almost bumped hers. "Or is it because you were about to lose the bet?"

"That's not true."

"No? You weren't about to lose your shit if Raf hadn't knocked on the door?"

Her little nostrils flared, her cheeks turning pink for an entirely different reason than the one I usually liked. "*You* were the one who was about to lose your shit. *I* was in control."

"Right."

"You were the one who started flirting with me at dinner. *I* was more than happy to go back to the hotel alone and finish myself off with my little pink friend. *You* were the one who stalked me there and tongue-fucked my face in the elevator."

"Tongue-fucked you?" I laughed. "Sweetheart, I tongue-fuck you, I'm not doing it to your face."

She stared at me.

Then she took a deep breath and let it out through her teeth, slowly, like she was resisting the urge to strangle me. "I didn't flirt with that guy intentionally," she said calmly. "He was funny. I laughed."

"He wanted to fuck you."

Now she looked pissed again. "So? Half the women in the room wanted to fuck *you*. And the other half wanted to blow you when their boyfriends weren't looking. And it's like that in every room we're in."

I stood back, all thought grinding to a halt. Complete fucking traffic jam in my head.

I rubbed my hand through my hair, feeling really fucking tired. "That bother you?"

She wrapped her robed arms around herself. "Um, yeah, Jesse. It kinda makes me look like a chump."

"How?"

"Because you eat it up. You flirt, you hug, you sign breasts. And I just stand there."

I stared at her. She stared back, her mouth curved in an angry pout.

"Well… maybe I need to pay more attention." I blinked at those plump pink lips, feeling like a complete dick with a side of drunken asshole.

"Maybe you do."

She stared at me.

I stared back.

Then she turned and stalked back into the bathroom.

I kicked her sketchbook across the room, then slumped down on the bed. I stripped off my underwear, burrowed under the sheet, and waited for her to come back as I fought the spinning sensation, the waves of sleep and the echoes of "Can't Feel My Face" throbbing through my skull in an endless loop.

The next thing I registered was Katie, standing next to the bed in her bathrobe looking down at me, silhouetted in the light from the bathroom, which was way too fucking bright.

"Katie," I heard myself say.

My eyes were shut when she got into bed. I felt her warmth and smelled her cherry-vanilla smell. She laid her head on the pillow next to me and sighed.

And even in the dark, in the ringing silence, I felt the distance.

CHAPTER TWENTY-TWO

Katie

MY FAKE BOYFRIEND WAS HUNGOVER.

It was actually kind of cute. It also took the edge off my frustration over what happened last night.

I watched him drag his sexy ass out of bed, naked, and weave his way to the bathroom, stretching out his sculpted body as he went. I'd never seen him like this before, all groggy and stumbly. He tripped a little, mumbled and slammed the door and I just grinned. It was the first time since the start of the tour that I was out of bed before him.

He emerged a few minutes later. "Room service." He looked at me with one eye open, the other one squeezed shut like the light was killing him. "Omelet," he croaked. "Juice."

I gave him a kiss on the cheek. "I'm on it. Take a shower and don't break anything." Then I added sunnily, "You've got a show tonight."

Confused, he struggled to open the other eye and focus on me. "Just kidding!"

He groaned and tried to grope me but I dodged the clumsy attempt. He grumbled and disappeared into the bathroom.

After his shower he looked a hell of a lot better. At least he had both eyes open and he managed to get dressed. He didn't say much. He ate half his omelet, then Jude showed up and to my surprise, they went to the gym.

Which left me some time to evaluate as I finished my breakfast. In the morning light, things looked a little clearer than they had last night.

Despite my recent Sahara-sized romantic dry spell, I wasn't totally clueless. I knew Jesse had to be on edge over our, um... fucked-up situation. It couldn't be easy on a guy making out with a girl every night, then sleeping alone, or worse yet, right next to that same girl, and not being able to fuck her. Especially for a guy who wasn't used to having to wait—as he put it, for any fucking girl. It probably felt like he was being punished, when he hadn't even done anything wrong.

I kept using the excuse that I was tired from the crazy pace of life on the road so I could go to sleep before he got any ideas about groping me. Which was kind of true—I was always ready to fall into bed by the end of the night, but I was definitely avoiding another steamy make out in private, because there was no way in hell I could stop him if the man started licking my nipples again.

So far he'd been a gentleman about it, keeping his hands on his side of the bed and letting me sleep, which was just kind of making it worse. Maybe this would be easier if he got pushy and gave me a reason to tell him to fuck off. Then I'd have a convenient excuse to run away and avoid the whole problem.

I was pretty good at avoiding things. It was kind of my go-to survival mechanism.

But I didn't want to run away from Jesse. I wanted to stay, even though I was on the verge of going batshit with desire. He was totally right; I was upset that he hadn't fucked me yet. I was upset that if I gave in and fucked him, I'd regret it. I was upset that this couldn't just be easy, and I was upset with myself for making it so hard. I was annoyed as fuck that he was still getting his flirt on with his groupies night and day, right in front of me. I had epic blue clit, I had no idea how the guy felt about me other than, apparently, finding me fuckable, and I was terrified of letting myself get carried away over the man's awesomeness and ending up with my heart smashed all to hell.

And now he was upset because some dude in a bar bought me a drink?

Seriously. I couldn't even begin to get a read on the man. Though I could admit to myself that seeing him all bent out of shape about it did give me a little glimmer of hope that he actually *liked* having me around, and not just because of whatever I was doing for his career.

The problem was I still didn't know what he wanted, other than for me to do my job, and maybe do him on the side.

Was he thinking that through, though? Like what was going to happen *after* he fucked me?

And after the tour ended?

Shit.

I pushed my unfinished plate away. I couldn't even eat when I fast-forwarded to that. Because the truth was I had no idea how I was going to say goodbye to Jesse Mayes.

I spent the rest of the day shopping and sketching while Jesse went to a couple of interviews. I had dinner with some of the guys at the hotel, then everyone piled onto the buses and we spent the evening on the road. We were headed to Florida for a couple of shows, and things between Jesse and I seemed okay. He was pretty quiet, a little reserved, but he sat next to me and kept giving me his smoldering fuck-me eyes, so I was pretty sure things were about as normal as ever between us, if not still a little tense.

By now I'd realized that things were always going to be a little tense, unless we tore off each other's clothes and fucked for about a day and a half. Which I couldn't seem to stop thinking about doing. And every time Jesse did something remotely nice, like passed me a bottle of water or asked if I wanted something to eat or told Pepper to shut up when I was trying to get a word in, I wanted him just a little more.

Was it possible to overdose on desire? Like some kind of hormonal overload that makes you pass out or something? Because every time I thought I'd reached that place where I wanted Jesse Mayes more than it was possible to want anyone or anything, he managed to turn my crank just a little more.

What a lovely, fucked up kind of torture.

I texted Devi to tell her, *My vagina is in love, and we haven't even done it yet.*

And my best friend texted back, *That's one stupid vagina.*

Which made me laugh so hard I almost cried, and everyone looked at me and wanted to know what was so fucking funny. Especially Jesse.

But luckily the guys were kind of distracted.

Pepper had crashed our bus to jump on Jesse and Mick and Raf, literally, going on and on about his birthday. Apparently it was two nights ago but we hadn't celebrated sufficiently for his liking, and now that we had the night off, the man wanted to party.

The guys finally gave in and we rerouted both buses to Savannah, even though we were supposed to drive all the way to Tampa. The drinking started, posthaste, but I noticed Jesse stuck with water, and I opted to sip rather than partake of the shots the guys passed around. They were happily buzzed by the time we rolled into the club. All fifteen of us. That's thirteen half-drunk rock 'n' rollers, Jesse and me.

The herd immediately dispersed in search of women, except

for the married guys, who took to the VIP area with Jesse and I.
Pepper was a one-man gong show; apparently drumming his ass
off almost every night wasn't enough to let off all his steam. He
was so fucking happy we were celebrating his thirtieth, he was
making everyone else happy. Including Jesse. And it was so good
to see that sparkle in Jesse's eyes again, his teeth showing when
he grinned. He held my hand and I snuggled against him, because
I was damn good at my job. And also, because he was Jesse. And
when we were out, being seen, it was easy.

It was when we were alone and the lines weren't so clearly
drawn that things got hard.

Hours later, I stumbled off the dance floor, my legs kinda rubbery
from dancing so much. I collapsed next to Jesse and he wrapped
his arm around me, smiling.

"Having fun?"

I lifted my sweat-damp hair off my neck. "Oh, yeah. Pepper is
off the hook." Actually, I was pretty sure he was about to lose his
pants and get us all kicked out. "That guy makes me laugh." My
smile froze and I bit my lip a little, remembering the conversation
we'd had about me flirting with that dude last night.

"He's a one-man riot," Jesse agreed. "If Dylan wasn't ten
times the drummer he is, I'd want him for Dirty. But don't tell
him I said that." Then he winked, and I knew we were okay. No
drunken arguments tonight, no going to bed mad. I also noticed he
was still sipping a water. I hadn't seen him drink all night.

Which was cool. I appreciated that he had restraint. In all
areas.

He smoothed my hair off my cheek, his gaze drifting down
over my chest, which was still heaving in my ruffled tank top as
my breath worked its way back to normal.

"Kiss me," I said. Maybe I just wanted to see if he would do it on demand.

He did.

His lips met mine and we came together in a slow burn, my hand running up his chest to grip his soft T-shirt. "I'm sorry about last night," I breathed against his lips.

"Don't apologize," he said. Then he kissed me again, and he didn't stop kissing me for like half an hour, so there wasn't much else to say on the topic. I pretty much forgot whatever I was trying to apologize for anyway, or why, or anything else other than the feel of his lips on mine, his tongue in my mouth and his hand on my thigh, up under my skirt. His thumb grazed my panties, sending a thrill of pleasure through my clit, and I squirmed.

"Jesse—"

"Katie." He did it again, rubbing his thumb between my legs, and I parted my thighs just a little, wanting more. Then he leaned in to say something in my ear. "You see all these girls?"

I was panting with need by now and not particularly interested in looking at any girls, but we were definitely surrounded by them. "Uh-huh."

He kissed my neck, then my ear, and said, "I know I could take my pick of who to screw tonight." He withdrew his hand from my skirt, touched my chin and turned my face to his so we were nose-to-nose. "I'm not going to," he said, brushing his lips over mine.

"I know," I breathed. "We have a deal."

"Fuck the deal," he said, and kissed me again, deep.

I didn't know what that meant, exactly, but whatever it was my body really, really liked it. I let him kiss me, let him touch me, let him draw me closer and closer against him.

Then I started reciting the list in my head.

Night after night, as I'd lain in bed in the dark just inches from him, I'd made myself a list. A list of all the reasons I couldn't even begin to fucking think about falling for Jesse Mayes.

There were many. Not the least of which was that he'd *hired* me to be here—to *pretend* to be in love with him. He had never once asked me to feel anything real.

But I did. I could feel it igniting in my chest like a tiny, uncomfortable spark. Every time he walked in the room. Every time he looked at me. Every time he kissed me like he was starving and I was his last meal.

I told myself it wasn't his fault that he was a fabulous kisser, that his touch made my pulse race, my head spin and my toes curl. It wasn't his fault that my vagina was sending mixed signals to my brain and I was reacting erratically. Sometimes I was all over him. Sometimes I was distant. Sometimes I overcorrected and got weirdly cheerful.

Tonight I was so relieved we weren't fighting and so thrilled to be back in his arms that I was all over him, and I didn't even try to hold back.

So I really shouldn't have been surprised when, after the bar closed and we all piled back onto the buses, Jesse instantly corralled me in the back bedroom.

But *fuck*.

He shut the door, locked it, and turned to me like a raging bull.

I could feel the heat rolling off him. There was a hungry gleam in his dark eyes that made me swallow, hard. He tore off his shirt like he was burning up, tossed it aside and stood there, heaving, like he'd just run a few miles. And if he kept looking at me like that, my panties were gonna drop in about three-point-five seconds.

We smashed together. We kissed like we wanted to devour one another. His chest was slippery with sweat, pulse slamming in his hands as he gripped my head. I held onto him as he walked us to the bed and threw us down on it.

He tore off my skirt and panties in seconds, groaning with lust. Then he knelt between my legs and spread my thighs with his big hands.

"Um! What about the bet?" I gasped.

Jesse lowered himself between my legs, giving me the most smoldering look I'd ever seen. "Fuck the bet," he said, and went down on me.

At the first swipe of his tongue I sucked in a breath and collapsed back on the bed. My arms were shaking; I couldn't even hold myself up if I tried. All thought of resistance ground to a halt.

All *thought* ground to a halt.

The man kissed me there the same way he kissed my face.

Like he was starving for it.

He pinned my thighs to the bed, keeping me spread wide as he lavished me with his tongue. He sucked on my clit, caressed my opening and fucked his tongue into me as I writhed and gasped. He was panting as he did it, like this was driving him crazy with desire, and I totally couldn't take it. I wanted his hard dick inside me so bad, but I wasn't gonna last.

I squirmed, fighting the pleasure that was rising like a tsunami. "Fuck... Jesse..." Then he wrapped his warm lips around my pulsing clit and sucked and it was all over. I gasped. His gaze lifted, locking on mine. He licked my clit, slowly, and the wave crashed through me. I threw my head back and cried out as I started to come.

His hand reached up and covered my mouth, because the tour bus wasn't even moving yet and the guys were on the other side of a very thin door, talking, yelling, still drinking, and probably overhearing at least some of this. I wasn't known for being quiet when I came. Maybe I should've warned him?

Instead I bit down on the finger he shoved in my mouth, sucked on it and tried not to scream as the pleasure tore through me. I gripped his hair and kind of rode his face and just tried not to writhe all over the place like a lunatic. "Oh, God... oh... God..." I heard myself say a couple of times.

He licked me softly as I came down, the scattered fragments of my mind, which he'd just blown all over the place, gradually drifting back together again.

When my sanity had just about returned, he slipped a finger inside me. I was so sensitive that I bucked against him, moaning. I couldn't find words. He pushed another finger inside me and started stroking me in an aggressive rhythm to match what his tongue was still doing to me. I came again before I could even get a hold of what was happening. This time I grabbed his hand and smushed it over my mouth. The bus was finally moving, so at least it would be harder for everyone on the bus, and like two miles over, to hear me getting off.

This time as I drifted more or less back to my senses Jesse was stripping off his jeans. He reached for one of his travel bags and dug through it, tossing things around. Then he turned back to me, condom in hand, and sheathed his big dick so fast I bit my lip. He came to me and I spread my legs to take him, my entire body flushed with heat, desire still throbbing in my core.

He lowered himself over me until his eyes were inches from mine. His lips parted in a silent breath; I could feel the tension in his body as he struggled to go slow. He kissed me softly and I felt the head of his cock caress my clit, then nudge my opening.

"Fuck, I want to savor this..." He watched me bite my lip as he thrust into me, slowly. A wave of heat rushed through my body as he filled me. Then he thrust deeper, so deep it almost hurt, but it felt so fucking good at the same time.

I closed my eyes. I tried to relax, to calm the fuck down, to not go over again so fucking fast.

I was supposed to be resisting this...

Why, again? No idea.

Fuck. Jesse was fucking me.

Fuck.

"You okay?" he whispered, and kissed me again.

My eyes popped open and I nodded. I was more than okay. But I had told the guy that I hadn't done this in two years; he probably wanted to make sure he wasn't hurting me. I grabbed his ass and squeezed. "Don't stop," I urged him.

He fucked me slowly, grinding hard against me. Warm waves of pleasure rolled through my body. My clit hummed, the pleasure quickly coiling tighter like a spring about to release. My nipples were tight and hard and I couldn't believe how fast he was about to make me come again. Every drag and thrust of his dick was bringing me closer. I tried to fight it, to hold on, to last a little longer, but I couldn't.

"Fuck... Jesse... I'm gonna come again," I managed to whisper between thrusts as I fought to hold on. Which only made him fuck me harder, speeding up until I crashed over the edge.

"Fuck, yeah," he said as I cried out. He held me tight as I writhed beneath him, thrusting his tongue in my mouth to muffle my cries. He kissed me until I caught my breath, then lifted up, shifted one of my legs down between his and proceeded to fuck me like that. The pressure of my thighs pretty much closed around his dick as he fucked me, tight, was too crazy much. His hard body moving over mine...

"Fuck... Jesse... I can't... oh my God... yeah... ah... fuck me like that..." A whole string of nonsense was coming out of my mouth, and he was loving it. Every time I begged him to fuck me harder, he groaned or panted or kissed me deeper. When I panted, "You're so fucking big. You feel so fucking good..." I felt his cock strain inside me. He was sweating all over me. I had no idea how he was able to hold on for so long, but the man had stamina, that was for damn sure.

And just the thought of him trying not to come made me come again, the white-hot pleasure peaking through my body, a lightning bolt ripping through me. I clung to him as he kept on fucking me. But I honestly didn't think I could take any more. As much as I wanted him to just fuck me all night, every which way, I wanted him to come, hard. I wanted him to let go... to lose control.

His thrusts sped up, and it felt so good and so raw and so intense, he had me gasping again.

"Oh, God. Come, Jesse."

"Yeah? You want it, Katie?" His voice was all thick and husky and his entire body was hardening. He was riding the edge, and I wanted to yank him over to where I was. I wanted him to spin out of control and come crashing down with me.

"Yeah... please... give it to me..."

"Fuck... I want you." He kissed me, plunging his tongue into my mouth as he fucked me harder.

You have me.

I sucked on his tongue and drove my fingernails into his ass. The tension rolled through his body in a wave and his hips snapped against me. He groaned into my mouth and I held him tight, my thighs wrapped around him as he came. I felt him pulse deep inside me and it was so fucking hot I wanted to come again.

He collapsed against me, burying his face in my neck. I wrapped my arms around his back, my legs going limp around his ass. I wanted to hold him like this for-fucking-ever as he breathed against me. His warm weight on top of me. His smooth, slippery skin against mine. His salt-and-cinnamon taste in my mouth.

He kissed my throat and I kind of hoped he was about to start pawing me again as he propped himself up on a shaky elbow and looked at me.

"Condom..." he panted, "... bathroom."

Then he slipped himself out of me, flopped off the bed and stumbled to the bathroom to clean up.

And I lay there just feeling kind of stunned. Because oh my God. *That* was sex?

Uh-uh. I'd had sex. Lots of sex. With Josh. And it was never like that.

What the fuck was this man *doing* to me?

He'd just made me come, *repeatedly*, while sucking me and fingering me and fucking me, and I'd done pretty much nothing in return… except come all over him.

I lay there on my back, staring at the ceiling as the bus rolled along, swaying and bumping gently over the road, just trying to get my breathing under control.

It had all happened so *fast*.

My pulse pounded in my temples like my skull was about to explode. My clit throbbed. I was *still* fucking horny.

I kinda felt bad that he only got to have one orgasm.

He came back from the bathroom and tossed himself on the bed beside me, still breathing heavy. He lay there looking at me for a moment, then reached over and skimmed a finger down my throat, pausing briefly to feel my racing pulse. Then he dragged his fingertip down to one nipple and circled it. I twitched as the nipple peaked, ticklish in my overly-sensitized state. His eyes darkened dangerously.

Then he moved on down the bed. He spread my thighs and leaned in to go down on me again.

Oh, God…

Someone banged on the door, which made the entire doorframe shake. Jesse's mouth hovered an inch from my clit.

"Jesse! Jesse and Katie! Get your naked asses out here and have a shot with us."

It was a drunken Raf.

"It's my motherfucking birthday motherfuckers!" chimed in Pepper.

Jesse grinned at me. I grinned back. "The man has a point," he said. Then he feathered a fingertip over my clit.

"Uh-huh," I whispered, squirming at his touch.

"So what do you say we go get you that drink?" He gave my throbbing pussy a slow, thorough lick, making me groan, then his dark, hooded eyes met mine. "Then we'll come back here so I can fuck you some more."

CHAPTER TWENTY-THREE

Katie

I WOKE to the tune of "Foxy Lady." At least I thought that's what it was.

I cracked one eye open to find Jesse sitting next to me on the bed playing one of his acoustic guitars. His tattooed forearm was in my line of sight, the whole mattress rocking to the rhythm of his ardent strumming. My gaze traveled down to the bare thigh the guitar was resting on.

My other eye popped open. He was naked. Like buck-ass naked. When he sang the first line of the song, I recognized the lyrics. Definitely "Foxy Lady."

The bus was rolling along, faint morning light leaking in around the blinds. And Jesse's sexy, slightly raspy morning voice made every tiny hair on my body stand on end.

Wow.

His gaze met mine and he kept singing. I just lay there and enjoyed, snuggled in under the covers. After a while I closed my eyes, because listening to Jesse Mayes play an intimate serenade, in bed with me, was just as beautiful as watching him do it. Though some of the lyrics made me giggle.

When the song started to fade out, I opened my eyes and

struggled to sit up. "What's going on?" I croaked, my voice rough from too many nights in concert venues and bars, and too many shots of bourbon with the guys late last night, after Jesse and I had mad, rabid sex... and before we did it again.

And again.

We'd probably barely gotten an hour of sleep.

"Your naked show." He ended the song with a flourish. "You won the bet."

I rubbed my eyes. Obviously I was adjusting to life on the road with a bunch of rock 'n' roll lunatics, because I barely felt drunk, much less hungover. "This wasn't what we bet." The sheet slipped down and Jesse's gaze went with it. I was naked too.

"You said I had to play my next show naked."

"Very clever. But not what I had in mind." If this was the only naked show I was gonna get though, I was milking it for every drop. Which meant I was getting dressed, now, to make his nakedness as conspicuous as possible.

I got out of bed, taking the corner of the sheet with me. I held it against my chest with one arm, barely managing to keep my ass covered as I dug out some clothes.

Jesse tilted his head sideways, following the sheet with his gaze as it rode up over my ass cheek.

"So, you're saying... my performance left you unsatisfied?" he asked, his words dripping with innuendo.

I blushed as the sensations of last night came flooding back. I bit my lip, recalling the way he'd hooked my leg over his arm, spreading my thighs as he drove himself deep... God, I had never been fucked like that. So... intensely. Every time I thought I couldn't take any more, he gave more, which only made me want more. The man made me insatiable. I lost count of the orgasms somewhere in the double digits. At that point, it pretty much became a blur of bourbon and pleasure until I passed out from raw exhaustion and happiness.

"Your performance was, um... perfectly adequate," I said, refusing to give a more enthusiastic review of either last night or "Foxy Lady." His ego didn't need it.

"Adequate." He grinned. "Sounds... underwhelming."

"Yeah. That," I muttered, pulling on my clothes. Clearly, he didn't believe me. If the orgasms didn't tell him otherwise, maybe all the filthy things I'd whispered in his ear while he was giving them to me did the job.

Apparently bourbon loosened my tongue, much like every other type of alcohol I'd ever met.

I flopped onto the bed as he started into a new song, one I didn't recognize. I lay back on the pillows to listen as he started to sing. *"Katie I'm sorry for being a dick... can you forgive me for being a prick...?"*

I grinned.

"That's all I've got so far," he said, ending on a final strum.

"What're you sorry for?"

"For snooping in your sketchbook the other night while you were in the shower."

"Oh. That." I kicked his knee, gently, with my big toe. "You should be sorry."

"I'm not sorry for getting jealous."

Jealous? Jesse Mayes? Of some random dude in a bar?

A random dude I wasn't even interested in?

"You're in there too, you know," I said, nodding at the sketchbook, which was lying on the floor.

He eyed the sketchbook, then dove for it about a millisecond before I did. He snatched it up and settled back onto the bed, ditching the guitar. I tried to wrestle the sketchbook from him, never mind the fact that I was wrestling a very large and muscular, not to mention naked, man. A naked man who had me on my back in two seconds flat, pinned down by his large, muscular body, his cock stiffening against my thigh in the process. "Show me," he said, his voice all gravelly with lust.

"I thought you snooped."

"I just looked at the last sketch. The one of that dilhole from the bar." He ran his nose up the side of my neck, his hot breath caressing my throat. "Then everything turned red and I forgot to keep snooping."

"Amateur," I muttered, but clearly *I* was the amateur, because I was already starting to pant as his teeth nipped my neck, followed by his lips. "I forgive you," I said with a swallow. "As long as you don't do it again."

His lips grazed my earlobe. "Show me the one you did of me and we'll call it even."

I laughed. "What 'even'? I didn't do anything."

"You flirted with the dilhole."

I wriggled beneath him as his lips worked their way back down my neck. "I told you that was unintentional. We were just talking. I didn't even think I was flirting." My breath caught as he licked the little hollow at the base of my throat. "I, uh... wasn't interested in him."

"Katie." He moved lower, his mouth skimming my collarbone as he spoke. "You talk to a dude in a bar and let him buy you a drink, he thinks you're flirting." His stubble rasped against my skin, making my nipples harden. "You breathe in a guy's general direction and he's gonna hope like hell you're flirting."

"Well, that's his problem," I said, breathless.

"No, it's my problem."

I wriggled in his grasp again, but he pinned my wrists to the bed. "Um, can you let me up? I'm gonna pass out if I don't eat something before you have your way with me again."

A slow smile spread across his gorgeous face. "Not until you say we're even."

"We're even."

His dark eyes narrowed. But he eased off my wrists and rolled slightly to the side so I could sit up.

"Don't snoop," I said, righting my clothes, which were all askew.

"Show me the drawing of me."

"No."

His eyes narrowed further.

"And you want me to trust you, you don't snoop. Even though you know there are sketches of you in this book." I stressed the plural on *sketches*, picking up the sketchbook and flipping through it in a leisurely manner, but at an angle that he couldn't see anything.

"Fine." He looked like a dejected kid who'd been deprived of ice cream as he flopped back on the bed. "Katie, in all seriousness. It's really fucking good. You should be doing something with it." He tried to get a look in the book, but I shut it and hugged it to my chest.

"Tried. Didn't work out."

"So what? You're just gonna let that stop you?"

I shrugged. I was in no mood to discuss my professional ambitions, or lack thereof, this early in the morning, on incredibly little sleep, while suffering a major sex hangover. I was hungry, thirsty, and achy in all the right places, and thanks to Jesse, I was now horny again.

"Where do you think I'd be if I stopped in my tracks every time something didn't go exactly how I wanted it? Do you think I just woke up one morning and the fucking music fairy left a record deal under my pillow?"

"Maybe. Did you sleep with her?"

"Har har. Trust me, it wasn't that easy."

"I'm sure it wasn't."

"So?" He sat up and stared me down, waiting.

"So what?"

"So whatcha gonna do about it, babe?"

"About what?"

He tapped my shoulder, softly, with his fist. "About your mad talent, girl."

"I dunno."

"Katie. What the fuck."

"Can we not have this conversation while you're naked?"

"Why?" He slid his bent knee a little closer to me, spreading his thighs. "Too distracting?"

"No." I held up a hand, blocking my view of his semi. "But it's hard to, you know, take you seriously when you're naked." That wasn't it, exactly. More like it was hard to keep my mind on anything but his smooth, golden skin, his hard pecs, his sculpted thighs, and whatever was going on behind my raised hand.

"Fine. Let's smoke a joint and hash it out." He bounced off the bed.

"I don't want to hash it out, Jesse. I wanna go back to sleep, like a sane person."

But he was already stepping into his jeans, drawing them up over his sculpted ass as he headed for the door, completely ignoring my protests.

"Jesse...?"

CHAPTER TWENTY-FOUR

Jesse

HALF AN HOUR LATER, Katie was devouring a giant breakfast sandwich with two fried eggs and triple cheese. I'd already wolfed mine down. Raf had smoked us up while the other guys grabbed our breakfast and we were on the road again. We were about half an hour from our destination, which meant I had about fifteen minutes to get Katie to tell me what the fuck was going on with her art, and fifteen for a quickie.

I could work with that.

"That is the most amazing… most mellowest… yet potent weed I've ever…" Katie said between bites. She was sitting cross-legged in her cut-offs, her tits bare beneath her thin tank top, her smooth, pale skin looking slightly sun-kissed.

I mellowed out against the pillows in my jeans, idly playing my guitar. "Cool. Now tell me why you don't want to be an artist."

I serenaded her while she thought about that, bits of "Dirty Like Me" and Eric Clapton's "Layla" and I didn't even know what else, just some fragments that had been bouncing around in my head and might turn into a new song.

Finally, she said, "I didn't say that."

"But you're crazy talented and you obviously love doing it. You're always drawing in that book. So what's the problem?"

"I don't know."

"Bullshit. Haven't you ever dreamed of making a living off the thing you love doing?"

"Of course."

"So what happened to that dream?"

She shrugged. "Life happened. I used to draw like a fiend. And I painted all through my teens. Pretty much since I was about ten years old and I realized drawings and paintings weren't just things on walls or in books, they were something I could do."

Damn. She painted too? I'd pay money to see a Katie Bloom original. And not just because she had a sweet ass and perfect, lickable tits.

"And?" I prompted.

"And I hung out with a bunch of skater kids and some of them were into street art so I got into that."

"Street art? You mean graffiti?"

"Yeah. You really want to see my work, there are remnants of it all over Vancouver. I can tell you where to go."

"I will," I said.

She shook her head, brushing that off like it wasn't even worth pretending to believe. "I just kinda got lost along the way, you know? I think it started when I got arrested."

My hands stilled on the guitar. "You what?"

"I got arrested."

"Sweet Katie Bloom? Mug shots and everything?"

She scowled at me. "Don't tell me you've never been arrested, Mr. Badass Rock Star."

"I haven't."

"Bullshit."

"Scout's honor. Ask Jude, Brody, anyone."

"Oh. Well, I have. It's not fun. I was eighteen and I was dating

Josh, so his dad's lawyers were able to get the charges dropped, and eventually got the record purged. Which is why Jude never found it." She grinned a little sheepishly.

"What the hell did you do to get arrested?"

"Got caught in the vicinity of a wall I'd just painted on, with my paints. And then they found the weed."

"Shit. You were a badass."

"Not really. Just a kid." She finished the last of her sandwich and started into the iced vanilla latte with extra whipped cream that Jude had picked up for her. He'd even found her some cherries to put in it. "The whole experience was brutal. Josh's parents decided I was a misfit at that point. He defended me to them, more or less, but over time I could tell he'd lost respect for me. If he ever had it in the first place. He always acted like if he could just clean me up a little I'd be more acceptable."

"Seriously?"

"Yup. It came up in little ways, pretty much daily. It seems so stupid now that I didn't see it then, the way he would criticize my friends and the music I listened to, every little fucking thing. When we went to dinner with his parents, he'd veto my outfits and tell me to change into something more 'presentable.' When he jumped ship at the altar, I'm pretty sure they were elated."

"You ask me, you dodged a bullet." It was obvious to me that the douche didn't deserve her. But I was pretty sure she didn't believe that yet.

"Yeah, except… I'd just graduated from art school, and Josh's dad owned an art gallery. One of his many investments. We were planning to have my big debut there that winter. Not like he actually gave a shit about art, or me, but more like he was throwing me a bone to win points with his son. As soon as the wedding was off, Josh, Senior canceled the show."

"Oh, fuck."

"Oh, yeah. 'Cause that's what happens, apparently, when your fiancé ditches you and your first big art show is supposed to take place at his father's gallery. You get dumped twice over."

"Jesus." Douche Junior and Douche Senior.

"Uh-huh. Personally and professionally kicked to the curb." She slurped her drink. "Lost my studio space in that great purge as well. Also owned by—"

"Josh, Senior?"

"You got it. No way I could afford the rent on a studio of my own, so after that I moved my things into my sister's basement."

"That's shitty, Katie. But you know you can't let it stop you, right?" I wondered if she'd thought about using the money from this tour to start something up, but it was pretty obvious she didn't have the confidence to believe she could really make her way as an artist. Not yet.

"Yeah. Well." She shrugged. "You ask me why I don't want to do anything with my art. It's not that I don't. It's just that I don't know *what* to do anymore, or even where to start." She flipped idly through her sketchbook, not bothering to hide the pages from me anymore, but I didn't look. I didn't want to look again until she invited me to.

She caught me watching her and gave me a sweet smile. "I guess I kind of lost my mojo."

"Then we'll just have to get it back."

"Yeah," she said quietly.

She flipped through her book some more, but she didn't seem to be looking at the drawings.

"Hey, Jesse?"

She looked at me, her big blue-greens softening as she searched for the words. Pretty sure it was the pot, but it was a good look on her. She looked more relaxed than usual, less... on guard.

"I know you hired me and this is a business deal, but I just want to say... I don't know... thank you, I guess. For giving me something I never thought was possible."

I set my guitar aside. "Such as?"

"Such as... I don't know... I guess, I..." She blushed something fierce. "I just never knew that sex could, um... be like that."

I grinned, ear-to-fucking-ear. "Like what?" I moved closer to her on the bed, grabbing her by her hips and yanking her toward me.

"You know." The blush deepened. "So... volcanic."

I laughed and pulled her onto my lap, so she straddled me in her tiny cut-offs.

"I'm serious," she said, her eyebrows pinching together.

"I know you are." I yanked her closer against me so she could feel me getting hard for her. "But you say it like it's some fluke..." I brushed her hair out of her face. "You're fucking molten hot, Katie."

Then I rolled over, taking her with me, and started peeling off her clothes like I'd been dying to do all morning.

CHAPTER TWENTY-FIVE

Katie

JESSE'S HAND skimmed over my breast. My nipple peaked in response and I glanced around.

We were sitting in the very dark back corner of a packed club, after his Miami show. Actually, I was sitting across Jesse's lap. I'd worn a halter top with no bra and he'd been eye-fucking me and groping me like crazy ever since he got off stage.

Good to know that hadn't changed since we started having sex.

He rubbed his thumb over my taut nipple, then tugged the thin fabric of my shirt aside, baring the side of my breast—the side in front of his face. He nuzzled against me, his tongue flicking out to lick my nipple. I glanced around again but I didn't think anyone could see. Still, I turned into him a little more to block what he was doing from the rest of the room.

He took the opportunity to suck my nipple into his mouth. I let him suck on it for a few seconds, because really… *ung.* Then I wriggled free, grabbed his hair and tipped his head back, leaning in close to his face.

"What are you doing?"

"Helping you get your mojo back." His nimble fingers sought out my nipple and plucked at it gently.

"Uh…" I breathed as the pleasure throbbed through me. "Right now?"

"Yeah. Right now." He sucked my bottom lip into his mouth and bit it gently.

"Here?"

"Mmm…" he said between kisses. "Why not?"

Why not?

Maybe because today Devi had sent me a link to some pictures of me online. Unflattering pictures. I mean, I looked fine in them. I was smiling and dancing, but I was smiling and dancing with Pepper. And Letty. And a bunch of other guys who weren't Jesse. Because someone at the bar had taken photos of us when we were celebrating Pepper's birthday. And now they were online, making me look like a major flirt.

It wasn't like it was the first time there were pictures of me online. Since we'd started the tour, Jesse and I were all over the place. Devi sent links to me almost daily, though I tried not to click on all of them. It was too much for my brain to process, but the fact was there were probably hundreds, if not thousands of photos of us out there already.

But this was the first time there were pictures of me partying *without* Jesse, and I didn't like what they implied.

Jesse caught my chin and pulled my face to his. "Hey. You okay?"

"Yeah. Just… embarrassed."

"About what?"

"You know. Those pictures."

"Babe. You've got nothing to be embarrassed about."

"But when we agreed to this deal you said I couldn't get involved with anyone else. I wasn't supposed to do anything to make you look bad. Those pictures kinda implied—"

He wrapped his arms around me. "You didn't make me look bad, cherry pie. You could never make me look anything but good."

I rolled my eyes. "You're just saying that because you're all horny and there's no blood left in your head."

"That may be true, but I'm not just saying it. The fans love you. They love that I'm in love with a regular girl, not some celebrity." His lips quirked. "Brody's calling us the great Canadian love story."

I grinned. "Uh-huh." I mean, it was thrilling, really. I didn't mind being the "regular girl" in this particular love story, swept off my feet by the super-sexy hero. I just didn't like how the story was going to end. "Except that it's a lie. Which still feels weird to me. Being envied... and being judged for things that aren't even true."

He laid his hand on the side of my face and stroked his thumb over my bottom lip. "Don't let it bother you, Katie. None of it's real anyway."

My stomach fell at those words, but I just nodded.

"How could any of it be real?" he went on. "What the fuck does the world know about what's really going on in people's private lives?"

I shrugged. "Nothing, I guess."

"Not a fuck of a lot, anyway."

He kissed me, and I tried to let it go. "We just need some more," he mumbled between kisses.

"More?"

"More volcano sex."

I laughed.

"That's better. Don't make me fuck that sad look right off your face."

I laughed harder and kissed him. The man had a way of making everything feel better.

I even felt less ashamed of my floundering ambition since our pot-induced discussion about my art. In fact, sharing the details of how my life had gone so off-track with Jesse made it all seem kind of trivial and a hell of a lot less daunting, like a blip in the road, in the past, that I could finally put behind me.

He pulled back and looked at me with his dark, hooded, ready-to-fuck eyes. "You wore your glasses tonight," he said, and licked his lip.

"Um... yeah?" Seriously? He liked my glasses?

He slipped his hand up my skirt, in full view of Jude, who was sitting on the couch next to ours. "And your little white panties."

I bit my lip and met Jude's gaze. He looked away. I squirmed as Jesse brushed his thumb between my legs. I leaned in and told him, "You have no shame."

He pulled me closer. "Tell me, Katie Bloom. What do I have to be ashamed about?"

I didn't have an answer for that.

He stroked my clit and I tried to squeeze my thighs together a little to keep control. I was unraveling at his touch, but more embarrassed than usual to be doing it in public. It was unnerving. It was also dizzying, exhilarating, and hot as fuck.

"I've never known anyone like you," I said.

"It scares you."

My heart beat in my throat. I wrapped my arms around his neck as he pulled my panties aside. He slipped his finger along the soft, slick flesh of my pussy... then pushed inside me.

My mouth dropped open.

He kissed my bottom lip, lapped his tongue into my mouth, and then we were going at it. He fingered me as we made out, his thumb rubbing against my clit. The sweet friction built, fast, heat swelling in my core. I kissed him hard, holding on tight as the pleasure gripped my body.

"Oh, God." I pulled away a bit, panting for breath, dangling just on the edge. "Not here," I begged.

He stroked me softly, his finger still inside me. My head spun. I needed to come so badly, and I could. Jesse wanted me to. But I just wanted to savor this feeling, sitting in his lap with his hand between my legs, blood and breath and pure ecstasy coursing through my body.

I took a long, deep breath.

Free. I wasn't used to feeling this *free*.

It felt fucking good. Incredible.

It felt like life used to feel. Like who I used to be, who I was becoming before I fell for Josh and my life took a different path than the one I thought I wanted.

It made me wonder about that girl. Was she here now, sitting in Jesse Mayes' lap?

He withdrew his hand from my skirt and leaned over to talk to Jude, then got up and took my hand.

He led me out back, to an alley behind the club. Jude accompanied us to the door, but didn't follow us outside. No one was around. It was quiet, just some distant traffic noise and the muffled thud of the club as we walked into the shadows.

I glanced back, a little alarmed that Jude wasn't coming with us. "Um… what if someone tries to mug us?"

"Then I'll kill them."

"Well, shit." I did a little skip-step in my new pink studded Valentinos. "That's good. Because I really wanna keep these shoes."

He pressed my back up against the wall. "Good. Because I really wanna do you in those shoes." Then he got down on his knees in front of me.

I took a shaky breath as he pushed my skirt up over my hips. I widened my stance, trying not to fall over in my four-inch heels. "Fuck," he said, yanking my little white panties down my thighs. He skimmed his fingertip over my clit. "You, Katie Bloom, are every fucking wet dream I had when I was a kid."

Then he ate me out. I gasped into my hand to keep from making too much noise. I teetered in my high heels and he pressed me against the wall. He licked and sucked at my clit until I was dripping, aching, kind of wishing he would fuck me right here, but I didn't know if he had a condom.

While he feasted on me, he undid his jeans, took his cock out, and jacked himself off. And oh, God... it was way too fucking much. I could see him working his cock in his hand, his rings glinting in the shadows. His breaths got faster the more I squirmed with arousal. He moaned and I felt the vibrations in my clit. I came suddenly on his tongue, clutching his hair in fistfuls and gasping into the dark while he sucked on me.

Afterward he stood up in front of me, his hard length still in his fist.

"Didn't do much for you?" I teased, breathless, glancing down at his cock. He hadn't come yet.

He held my face with his other hand and kissed me hungrily. "This is what you do to me," he said. Then he groaned against my neck as he came, jerking himself on my pussy.

After we'd caught our breath, I rubbed his come into my skin like some kind of luxury lotion, because I really didn't know what else to do with it. He grinned and kissed me. Then I licked my fingers, because they were sticky, and again, because I didn't know what else to do. Also, because they tasted like Jesse. His pupils dilated as he watched me do it and he bit his lip. "Fuck, Katie," he said, then he kissed me again, deep.

"I really should've saved it, to sell it on eBay," I said, when we finally stopped making out again.

"Huh?"

I fixed my panties and raised an eyebrow at him as I smoothed my skirt. "The essence of Jesse Mayes. Would've made us a pretty penny."

He shook his head at me, but laughed. "You are one twisted bitch, Katie Bloom."

I grinned at that.

He pulled me roughly against him, kissing me again. "How do you feel?" he mumbled against my lips.

"Dirty," I said as he wrapped me in his arms.

Free, I should have said.

It was many days later, somewhere on the road to Nashville, that the tour bus pulled off the highway at a truck stop and I took a wander, alone with my phone.

"I'm crazy, right?" I asked my best friend.

As soon as I had Devi on the line, I'd filled her in on the state of things as vaguely as I could—Devi didn't need *every* dirty detail, as much as she might want them—while still making it clear I'd lost my mind.

Because the night before, Jesse and I had barely slept. Instead, we'd fucked for hours on end without any condom. I was on the pill, and he'd shown me the blood work he'd conveniently had done at the beginning of the tour, "Just in case," with a big shit-eating grin on his face. For my part, no one had touched me in the last two years; anyway, I'd taken every test ever invented, three times over, when I found out Josh had ricocheted into the bed of one of my best friends after our almost-wedding—because who knew who or what he might've been doing even sooner than that. Jesse and I had discussed it in a mature fashion, then gone at it like monkeys. Skin to skin.

So the glove, and all bets, were officially off.

And as the sensations of last night came flooding back, a

wave of arousal coursed through me. My stomach clenched and my breath caught. I bit my lip. I almost dropped my phone.

"Uh… hello…?" I heard Devi on the other end.

"Yeah." I closed my eyes for a sec and just breathed. All I saw in the dark was Jesse, kissing me, moving over me, holding me down… God. I could feel his cock pumping in my mouth and taste his salty, intoxicating taste. I swallowed, hard. The flesh between my legs still hummed from his touch, sore, almost, and ready to go… again. "I'm having unprotected sex with a sex symbol who's probably screwed his way coast to coast. Blood work or no, I'm crazy."

"You're falling for him."

Fuck.

Not what I wanted to hear.

"And that's crazy, right?"

"I don't know," my best friend said. "I think it's only natural, Katie. I mean you're with him all the time. You're sleeping together."

"I'm so screwed." I turned to look back at the bus from across the lot. Jesse was there, shirtless, stretching, looking like some sun god, all gorgeous and golden in his low-slung jeans.

"I thought that was the good news," Devi teased.

Jesse caught me looking and grinned. I turned away. "I can't think straight around him."

"Do you think he's screwing anyone else?"

"I don't think so. I mean, he could be. It's not like he couldn't get it anywhere he wanted, if he wanted."

"But you don't think he wants to?"

"I don't think so." I didn't. Despite the sheer volume of hot babes tossing themselves at his feet, I really didn't. Which was maybe part of my problem.

"Maybe he's falling for you, too."

"Don't start putting that shit in my head."

"Katie…"

"What?"

There was a long, strained silence as trucks whipped by on the highway and I braced myself for what I knew was coming.

"Do you seriously believe you can't be loved?" Devi asked. "Just because of what Josh did to you?"

The worry in my best friend's voice killed me a little.

"I don't know, Devi. I can't have this conversation right now, okay?" I felt dangerously close to crying and no way I could handle that. Not now. Not until I was home and miles away from Jesse Mayes and all this craziness was over with and I could think straight again.

"Okay."

"Okay."

Another silence.

"He fucks like a beast," I whispered.

"Holy hell."

"He's so hot I think I might melt."

When I turned around he was still there. No surprise, a couple of girls had materialized out of the ether with crap for him to sign. He was saying something that made them laugh and play with their hair.

"That's awesome, Katie."

I watched as Jesse smiled at whatever the girls said back to him. Then he looked over at me and smiled bigger.

"But you know, no matter how real this is or isn't, or how long it lasts, there's only one thing that really matters," my best friend said, from so far away. "Is he good to you?"

CHAPTER TWENTY-SIX

Jesse

"THE DAMAGE you did to my tongue will have me singing with a lisp," I informed Katie as I climbed into the driver's seat of the tour bus. I checked my swollen tongue in the mirror, and the angry red damage where the tooth had cut through.

"I didn't bite your tongue," she said, settling back in the passenger seat. "*You* bit your tongue."

True.

"Which was your fault," I said.

Also true.

We were on our way to Austin when I decided to commandeer the wheel of the bus. A few days back we'd passed that point, the one that came on every tour, when I got sick as fuck of life on the bus and started pacing, climbing the walls, and generally driving everyone else nuts. Travel time between tour stops didn't justify flying, so I had no choice but to endure the road. I'd taken over driving to change things up.

When we'd stopped for gas, Kenny got out to fuel up, Mick and Raf went for beer, Jude disappeared wherever, and I pulled Katie into my lap on the co-pilot seat. I then proceeded to dry-hump her like a horny mutt. I'd been trying to get up her skirt all morning, also to stave off my road boredom. I started to peel her tank top off, she protested something about windows, and I shoved my tongue down her throat to shut her up. She pulled my shirt off, distracted me by scraping her fingernails over my nipples, then wrenched her mouth free, licked my ear and whispered something that sounded distinctly like *I should fuck you up the ass*.

Which made me bite my tongue so hard it bled.

Unfortunately the guys had started piling back on the bus before I could make her pay for the bloody tongue, or explain that comment. My tongue was still throbbing, the coppery taste of blood still in my mouth.

"Practice," she said. "Sing something and I'll tell you if you lisp."

I started singing the chorus to "Dream Weaver," of all things. And I did lisp a little on the *v* and *th* sounds. It also hurt to try not to. Katie roared with laughter. Then I said, "Ow," and she shut her mouth.

"What's wrong?" Mick appeared, cracked open a cold beer, handed it to Katie and took away her empty; she'd already pounded one back while we'd waited for Jude and Kenny to return.

"Thanks!" She took a swig. "I made Jesse bleed," she said with fake-ass sympathy.

"Keep it up," Mick said, and disappeared into the back.

"Don't encourage her," I growled after him.

"Aw. Poor baby," Katie said sweetly, her big blue-greens gleaming with joy.

"You're lucky there's no show tonight."

"I've never seen you pout before," she said, still wide-eyed with glee. "It's adorable."

"Not pouting," I grumbled. "Bruising."

She laughed again as I steered the bus out onto the highway, humming the chorus to "Dream Weaver."

"Maybe you could just hum the whole show tomorrow," she suggested brightly.

"If you're gonna pull co-pilot, make yourself useful," I ordered.

"And how would I do that?" She glanced over her shoulder into the lounge, then leaned in and whispered, "I am not giving you a roadie."

"Why the fuck not?" I started to make a suggestive gesture with my tongue, but stopped when I tasted fresh blood. "Ow. Fuck." I shot her a look, daring her to laugh at my injury again.

She smiled prettily and drank her beer. "Don't worry, I'll be more entertaining when I'm inebriated. Help you pass the time. I'm going full-bore co-pilot on this."

"Uh-huh. And what do you do to pass the time on a road trip?"

"I dunno. Talk about boys? Last time I went on a road trip I was eighteen."

"Sounds fucking boring."

She hooked an eyebrow at me over her beer. "You saying boys are boring?"

"And hairy. And they stink. Trust me, I've been on plenty of road trips with dudes and they're highly overrated."

Katie laughed. "Okay. So what do you stinky boys do on the road? I mean, you know, besides all the hookers and blow or whatever."

"Hmm." I pretended to think about it. "I don't know. We've never run out of the hookers and blow before."

She rolled her eyes. "Uh-huh. We could play a road game."

"Sounds like some good clean PG fun."

"Though unless it's a drinking game…" She held up her beer and toasted the air. "I don't really see the point." She punctuated that with a swig of beer, then smiled. And I really wished she'd wrap those pretty pink lips, wet with beer, around my cock.

Maybe later. There were always more rest stops.

"You keep drinking, babe, we'll make it a drinking game. But the only road game I remember is Top Five. Got into a lot of fights over it."

"Oh yeah?"

"Oh yeah. Bad words were said. Drinks were thrown. It was ugly."

"Sounds awesome."

"It's not for the faint of heart."

"Teach me!"

"Okay. It's easy. I just give you a topic and you say the top five things in that category."

"Such as?"

"Top five bands."

"Oh, that's easy."

"That's what I said. But it's deceptively controversial, I warn you."

"Maybe for stubborn, overly-opinionated rock stars. I, on the other hand, am a civilized lady." She took another swig of her beer. She was already looking flushed, her cheeks pink; it didn't take much. The girl couldn't hold her booze worth a damn.

Which was fine with me. I happened to like drunk Katie.

My dick liked her too. Especially when she rolled the frosty beer bottle between her breasts, making her nipples harden against the cotton, the condensation dripping down inside her tank top...

Fuck.

Eyes on the fucking road.

"So go ahead, sweetheart. Top five bands."

"Like, of all time?"

"Yes."

"Okay. Number one. Dirty. Obviously."

"Obviously."

"Two. The Jesse Mayes solo project band."

That made me grin. Carefully. My tongue was still throbbing dully. "Nice. And I'll tell Raf you said that."

"Three. The Police."

"Interesting choice."

She eyed me, sidelong, as if waiting for an argument. "You don't want to piss off Sting, do you? That dude will out-Zen you to shit."

"I don't even know what that means."

"Number four. Queen."

"Wrong."

"What!?"

"Queen are legends. Excellent choice. Just not top five."

"Okay. Now I see why you guys fought. But guess what? You're driving, I've got beer, and you don't get a veto vote on my list. It's my top five. Queen. Number four." She threw back her beer, which was almost empty.

"Alright. Number five?"

"David Bowie."

"That's not a band."

"Whatever. Ziggy Stardust and the Spiders from Mars."

"You have some curious musical tastes for a woman who's only been around the last twenty-four years."

"Thank you." She took a self-congratulatory swig from her beer, emptying it, and excused herself to get a new one. "Your top five," she said as she returned, plopping into her seat. She tossed her feet up on the dash, making her mini skirt creep up, giving me an eyeful of those pale, smooth thighs, and a vivid idea of what I'd like to be doing with them… like wrapping them around my face.

"Okay." I cleared my throat, trying to focus. "The Doors. The Who. Cream. Zeppelin. Dylan. Done."

"Bob Dylan? 'That's not a band,'" she said, throwing my words back at me.

"Bob Dylan *and his band*."

"You have some curious musical tastes for a man who's only been around for the last… twenty-eight years?"

"Twenty-nine. Top five kinky things you want me to do to you that I haven't yet."

Katie laughed. "Ah, he finds a way to turn the good clean PG road game dirty."

"What? It's within the rules."

"I don't think you explained the rules to me."

"I told you. I name the category, you have to say the top five."

"Have to?"

"Yep. Or else the universe implodes or something. We once made Zane list the top five exports from Brazil before we'd let him take a piss. He'd had like twenty beers."

"Cruel! What were they?"

"The Brazilian exports? I have no fucking clue. I think Dylan did a Google search or something. We probably just made shit up in the end."

She laughed, then gave me a stern look. "Don't even try that on me or you'll regret it. If you keep me from the bathroom after *three* beers, I'll probably pee *on* you."

"Okay, but that's not really on my list. Unless it's on yours."

"What list?"

"Top five kinky things."

She twitched her nose at me. "Ew. No."

"Then you still have five things to name."

"Fine." She sipped her beer and got serious. "Okay. Kinky things. Um. Tie me up?"

"Really?"

"I don't know. It's kinky, right?"

"You can't just say kinky things. You have to say your top five."

"Okay. Not the tie up thing."

"I knew it. Liar."

"Take a shower with me. Is that kinky?"

"No. But I'll take it."

"Hey! It's kinky for some people."

"You've got four more. Blow my mind."

"Oh, God."

I grinned and didn't even try to pretend I wasn't enjoying the fuck out of this, as Katie sipped her beer and thought that over. Hard.

"Okay. Suck my toes?"

"Don't ask. Just tell."

"Alright. Spank me?"

"Stop asking."

"Um. Do me while you're wearing those hot leather pants."

Christ. I felt my pulse quicken in my throbbing tongue, in my dick, because she'd meant that one. She glanced over at me. I reminded myself that I was driving a very large bus and I'd feel really fucking bad if I killed everyone on it, and trained my eyes on the road. "Which ones?"

"The black ones with the low waist."

Damn. Now I had a visual.

"That's not very kinky," I said, as if my dick wasn't rock hard. I shifted in my seat, trying to accommodate the hard-on in my jeans.

"Again," she said, her gaze dropping briefly to my crotch. "Depends who you are."

"I'm me."

"Well, I'm me."

"Don't tell me you've never had a guy fuck you with his pants on."

Katie shrugged. "Josh was very... systematic. It was all clothes off, then the lights off, then get in bed under the covers. Then let the lovemaking commence."

Right. Josh.

Her only lover, before me.

"Okay, then. Leather pants it is."

"See? Kinky."

"You've got one more."

"Is this number one or number five?"

"Number one."

"Hmm."

She rolled the tip of her beer bottle over her lips, back and forth, as she considered. There was a dreamy, lusty look in her eyes as she gazed out at the road ahead, her eyebrows pinched. Katie was cute as all fuck when she was deep in thought.

Especially when she was thinking through whatever sexy shit she wanted me to do to her.

"Oh! I know." Her face lit up and she took a self-congratulatory swig of her beer. "Do me where all your groupies can see, so they get the message and fuck off." She smiled sweetly.

I raised an eyebrow. "You wanna make a sex tape, babe?"

"Oh! Forget the groupie thing. Let's make a sex tape!"

"Now I know you're drunk." I cast a sidelong glance at her; she was definitely looking a little glassy-eyed, a happy buzz curling the corners of her mouth.

"What? I'm serious. I mean, not so we can leak it on the interwebs. Gross. I mean, so we can watch it. How's that for kinky?" She sounded so self-satisfied, it was fucking adorable.

I wanted to throw her down on the floor of the bus and fuck that little smirk right off her face, make her lose herself in moans and screams. If only I could get rid of the assholes playing poker in the lounge.

Katie didn't like screaming when the guys were around to hear it, but I sure as fuck needed to make her scream. Soon.

Katie Bloom losing control; that was about the sexiest, kinkiest, most arousing thing I'd ever seen.

I cleared my throat. "Hot," I said. "If you meant it."

"I do mean it."

"No you don't."

"Why not?"

"Because you don't go from lights out every time you have sex to making a sex tape."

"Says who? I wasn't the one turning out the lights."

I swallowed that. And rearranged my throbbing dick, not bothering to be discreet about it.

"Stopping for lunch," I announced, to a bunch of cheers from the back.

"No fucking burgers," Raf called up.

"Mexican!" Mick shouted.

"No fucking Mexican!"

Katie leaned around her seat to join the debate. "No more fast food! I want a real meal with something green on my plate."

An argument erupted over what to have for lunch, but I wasn't listening. I didn't care what the fuck we ate.

As soon as the guys got off the bus, I was having Katie Bloom.

CHAPTER TWENTY-SEVEN

Katie

I WAS HANGING out behind the venue after the Austin show, leaning against the wall while Jesse signed autographs for a bunch of girls hanging out on the other side of the fence. It was a high, solid wood fence, but there was a big gate of chain link where the buses and trucks drove through, padlocked shut, and the girls were pressed up against it, squeezing pieces of paper and who knew what else through the holes for him to sign.

Jude was close by, as always, and I watched for a while as Jesse did his thing.

When he was done, Pepper and Raf went over to greet the girls and sign stuff for them too.

Jesse sauntered over to me, looking me up and down in my short skirt and halter top. He looked so fucking hot in his leather pants. Gorgeous, a sexy smile curling the corner of his mouth.

Devi's words kept coming back to me.

You're falling for him.

Maybe he's falling for you, too.

I'd realized a few days back that I'd been waiting for Jesse to start being a dick. Like when he did, I'd finally be getting a glimpse of his true colors, as if, if I paid close enough attention, he'd start showing signs of his overwhelming douchebaggery.

But he just never did.

Devi said the only thing that really mattered was that he was good to me. She was probably right about that. And he *was* good to me.

So why did I keep waiting for the other shoe to drop?

I reached for him and he picked me up, spun me around, and sat me on the edge of the hood of Jude's rental car. He spread my knees and stood between them, his back to the girls and the fence.

"What's going on behind those big blue-greens of yours?" he asked, wrapping his arms around my waist.

I draped my arms around his shoulders and played with his hair. "I was just thinking I've got a new top five for you."

"Oh yeah?"

"Yeah. Actually, I never signed that NDA… I could probably write an article instead. Sell it to a magazine. *Cosmo.* No, *Maxim.*" I cocked an eyebrow at him. "*Playboy*?"

He grinned. "And what would this article be called?"

"Top Five Things Groupies Say to Jesse Mayes Outside a Show."

He laughed. "I can think of a few."

"Uh-uh. Got it covered. You wanna hear?"

"Do I."

"Okay. Number five."

"A countdown. I like it already."

"Wait for it."

"I'm waiting."

I gathered my breath, laughed, making him grin, then drew a breath again, smacking his arm when he laughed. "Wait!" I gave it my breathiest, most girlie voice. "'Is Zane here?'"

Jesse laughed, loud. "Shit. That's bang on. I would've thought that one was higher than number five though."

"Nope."

"So what's my answer to that question?"

"Like you don't know."

"Just wanna see if you're paying attention."

"Well, you handle it quite well, actually, with grace and charm. Usually with some sort of casual deflection. My favorite was when you said, 'If you see him, tell him he owes me five bucks.'"

"He does owe me five bucks."

"Number four. 'How can I get backstage?'"

"Right."

"Though there are several variations on this one, including 'Where's the party after the show?' and 'I'll do anything to get backstage.'"

"Oh, my."

"Yep. But I've figured out that all of the above are just groupie code."

"Groupie code?"

"Uh-huh. For 'Please fuck me tonight.'"

"Wow."

"Like you didn't know. Sadly, for the groupies, you also deflect this question. Onto Jude. Who doles out the backstage passes as he sees fit, depending on his mood."

"Lucky Jude."

"Lucky road crew. What the groupies don't know is that Jesse Mayes, while horny as fuck after a show, does not fraternize with groupies backstage. However, some of his crew do."

"Consolation dick?"

I laughed and wrapped my legs around his hips as he pressed in closer. "Number three. 'I totally love you.' This one weirds me out a little. I think this comes from the ladies who would actually love it if you'd father their love child, even though they don't actually know you."

"I do have an incredible amount of children scattered across the globe."

"Gross." I gave him my most unimpressed look. "Number two. 'Will you sign my…' insert naked body part here."

"That is a popular one."

"I've actually come to respect this one. I've noticed that the girls who ask this question have come prepared, marker in hand, and have pretty much accepted the fact that you're *not* going to fuck them, so they take the opportunity to have you rub the tip of a felt marker on their flesh, usually their breasts or their butt crack, while they bend over provocatively, as a three-second substitute."

"The ultimate quickie?"

"It's all very ejaculatory, if you think about it."

"Sounds like you have." He ran his finger over my cleavage. "Come to think of it, you've never asked for a Jesse Mayes original…"

"Number one," I said, swatting his hand away.

"Can't wait to hear this one."

I tossed my hair and batted my eyelashes. "'Can I get a kiss?' Or a hug, etcetera. You get the idea."

"I do." His hands were on my thighs now and he was working my skirt up around my hips. "And how do I handle that one?"

I glanced over his shoulder but Pepper was entertaining the shit out of those groupies with his crazy stories. "Well, I have to say, you give out the rather chaste kiss on the cheek for a horny rock star."

Jesse unzipped his leather pants, freeing his gorgeous cock, hard and ready. I swallowed, my heart beating in my throat with the thrill of what I was pretty sure he was about to do. "Wouldn't want my girlfriend to get jealous," he murmured. He dragged me closer to him, to the very edge of the car, pulled the crotch of my panties aside, and filled me in one long, slow thrust.

"Fuck, you're wet," he whispered into my ear, wrapping me in his arms.

"Oh, God…"

Jesse was fucking me, on a car, in full view of a bunch of his groupies. Not that those girls could tell what we were doing, exactly… at least I didn't *think* they could.

Probably just looked like he was giving me a very… um… intimate hug?

"Look at us," he whispered in my ear, "doing two things from your list at once…"

Holy shit. We totally were.

He started to move in a slow rhythm. He wasn't just fucking me, he was pushing my boundaries. And I was starting to love having my boundaries pushed by this man.

Taking risks had never felt so good.

It's like he was slowly chipping away at my doubts and replacing them with pleasure… joy… uninhibited ecstasy…

"Do you think they can see?" I whispered, breathless.

"Don't care," he said, kissing my neck. Then he licked his way up to my ear. "The more they see me loving you… the more they buy the music."

And just like that…. total buzzkill.

Libido kill.

Mojo kill.

Everything felt unreal. Suspended. Slow-motion. I still felt him, still wanted him, still wrapped myself around him, but it was like he'd punched me right in the heart.

I closed my eyes.

But I let him finish fucking me.

Because I loved sex with Jesse Mayes. And apparently, Jesse Mayes loved sex with me.

He loved me helping him sell his music.

He just didn't love *me*.

CHAPTER TWENTY-EIGHT

Katie

I ROLLED over on my back and stretched out on the cool mattress, letting the air conditioning breeze over my naked body. When my nipples peaked, I drew the sheet up around my ribs.

Jesse lay next to me, partly propped up on some pillows, his back to me as he read the morning paper. We were in a hotel. A really nice hotel. I snuggled closer to the warmth radiating off his body, burrowing myself into the curve of his back. I saw his cheek curve as he smiled.

"Morning, sunshine."

"Mmm," I mumbled. "I love that smell."

"What smell?"

"Newsprint and newspaper ink. It reminds me of my dad." I opened one eye and looked up to find him looking down over his shoulder at me. "Is that weird?"

He just grinned and went back to his paper. "You want breakfast?"

"Totally."

"Good. The burnt bacon is waiting."

I sat up a little and looked across the room. A room service cart had been set up in front of the enormous window, the white tablecloth aglow in the morning sun. A couple of mimosas sparkled in champagne glasses, one of them garnished with a little plastic sword loaded with maraschino cherries.

I flopped back on the bed and sighed. "Jesse, I really like it here. Can we stay?"

He turned to me again, this time rolling right over to face me. "Here in bed?" He reached for me under the sheet and grasped my hip, pulling me against him.

"Mm-hmm... here in Texas."

He leaned in, breathing on my neck. "You like Texas, babe?"

"Um, yeah." I sighed as he started kissing me, sending little tingles of warmth through my body. "Pretty sure I fucking love Texas."

He kissed his way down my throat. "Yeah?"

"Mm-hmm. It's always sunny and dudes say y'all. What's not to like?"

"Mmm," he mumbled as he skimmed his lips over the swell of my breast. I wasn't sure if that was an agreement or not. He captured my nipple in his teeth, making me cry out from the little sting of pain, my body stiffening.

"What happened to my burnt bacon?" I protested as he lapped his tongue over the hard pink peak, over and again, soothing the pain.

I relaxed beneath him and he shifted against me, his hips pressing down onto mine, his hard length against my softness. I wriggled under the unexpected pressure, his cock grinding against my clit. "Ah—!" I managed before his mouth claimed mine in a deep kiss, his tongue plundering my mouth.

I wriggled beneath him again. Before I could arrange myself comfortably he reached down, fisted his cock and dragged the smooth head down, slipping against the slick heat of my pussy. I spread my legs to give him access.

He groaned and rubbed himself against me again in a long, torturous stroke.

I started rocking against him, panting softly against his mouth. His lips hovered against mine, kissing softly, slowly. He pressed the head of his cock to my opening and kept kissing me, so gently. All the while I panted on the bed beneath him, hungry for more, wanting his possessive thrust, which didn't come.

His dark eyes met mine as the head of his cock pushed into me. "Fuck, I love being in you," he whispered.

Slowly, so slowly, he slid deeper, filling me.

The more they see me loving you... the more they buy the music.

I groaned as Jesse's comment from last night came back. There was so much fucked up about that statement, I didn't even know where to start. I was pretty sure it was just one of those shitty things guys say without really hearing themselves say it and realizing how awful it sounds, that in the moment all his blood was thundering to his dick and he wasn't thinking clearly about what he was saying. I was definitely sure I'd said some ridiculous things in my life, and I was willing to let that one slide. But shit.

The more they see me loving you...

That part was kind of killing me. The mere implication that he loved me, when it wasn't true.

But I didn't want to ruin this. Any of it. Whatever this was that was happening between us.

I let my hips settle on the bed and just felt him, his heat, his weight, as he braced himself on his elbows above me and slowly swept his tongue into my mouth. I spread my knees as wide as I could to accommodate him as he sank gradually deeper, until he settled against me.

"I fucking want you, Katie," he said when he came up for air, his voice rough, his dick buried inside me.

And yeah, I was just gonna let last night slide. Because he also said things like *that*. A lot.

He pressed his forehead to mine and I squeezed my thighs around him. He kissed me again, slowly, and I kissed him back, frantically. I felt his cock pulse inside me and that was it. I lost it. I rocked against him, desperate for friction, throbbing with need.

"Please," I whispered, riding his cock from beneath, the inch or so I could maneuver, my hips pinned between his body and the bed. I squeezed him as hard as I could, sucked on his tongue when he thrust into my mouth again, grasped his ass with my fingers and tried like hell to urge him to fuck me. Hard.

Our mouths fused together in a deepening kiss and his breaths started to deepen, his chest moving against mine. My body undulated beneath his, urging him on.

Finally he lifted his hips, drawing back, dragging his swollen dick out of me, slowly.

Then he rammed himself back in.

I groaned and writhed beneath him, meeting his thrusts as he began fucking me, so fucking slowly. He raised himself above me, propped up on one arm, and planted the other hand on my hip, holding me still as he thrust into me, again and again. It was so slow and so fucking good and so deep, I was gonna come so hard just lying there beneath him, feeling him drag himself in and out. My pussy clamped down on him and I squeezed my thighs around his hips, holding him to me as I peaked.

I threw my head back and cried out. I think I swore a few times. For all I knew, I was speaking in tongues. My toes twitched. My nipples throbbed. The pleasure burst through me in a shower of stars.

He shoved in deep and I felt his cock pump inside me as he came. He groaned and clutched my breast. His head dropped, his silken curls just brushing my chest.

I reached up and cupped his face even as I heaved to catch my breath. He kissed the palm of my hand. He looked up, his gaze colliding with mine. I felt him jerk inside me and he moved his hips in a few more small thrusts, his eyes closing as he rode the aftershocks of pleasure.

Jesse in pleasure... it totally wrecked me.

"Ah... more," I managed to gasp as another wave crested in my clit, my whole body pulsing with lust. His eyes opened, meeting mine. He was still so swollen, filling me as I rode him, seeking another release. I probably could've gotten off on the look on his face alone.

Then he pinched my nipple lightly and my breath caught in my throat as the second climax tore me apart, hot and fast.

"Oh... fuck..." I heard myself groan as I melted into the bed, my body still humming with pleasure.

I didn't even realize I'd shut my eyes until I opened them to find Jesse staring at me, his dark eyes hazed with lust. His lips were swollen from kissing me, his hair all sexed up. His dick was still in me, gradually softening but still filling me. He licked his lips and ran his hand down from my breast to my pussy.

"Yeah... more," he whispered huskily as his thumb found my clit.

I panted at his touch, but this time I didn't close my eyes. I watched his face as he watched me, my body arching off the bed as pleasure crashed through me again.

I really could've stayed in bed all day, but Jesse insisted we get up to eat.

He lifted the lids off the dishes to reveal fresh fruit, bacon and pancakes with real Canadian maple syrup for me, bacon and an omelet for him. There was a jug of fresh-squeezed orange juice and a bottle of champagne to keep the mimosas flowing. And there was Jesse, sitting in his boxer briefs next to me.

Perfection.

"I was thinking," he said as we ate. "Every day, everything's always about me, you know? You never get anything that's just for Katie."

"So? It's your tour." And really, Katie got plenty. Between the room service and the shopping, the spa treatments and the fine restaurants and the clubbing, I wasn't exactly suffering here.

"Yeah. But I've canceled all my other shit so we can make today all about you."

"Really?" I had no idea what "all about you" meant, but I liked it already. I gestured over at the sex-rumpled bed and raised an eyebrow. "So that was all for me?"

"Nope. That was for me." He munched his bacon and grinned. "I'm a selfish bastard. But as of right now, it's Katie Day."

"Which means?"

"Which means you get a present."

"Cool," I said, my stomach doing a weird flip-flop thing. "Because I totally love presents." Especially if they're from Jesse in his underwear over post-sex breakfast, apparently.

He went to one of the closets and got out a long, flat gift-wrapped box, about the length of his arm. He brought it over to me and my heart thudded too hard as he put it in my lap. It was sorta heavy and made a little rattling noise.

"Open," he commanded.

I unwrapped it. Inside the box was a skateboard. A really fucking cool skateboard with cherries painted on it. I laughed. "What the fuck is this?" I looked up at Jesse, beaming. He was watching me, and licked his bottom lip like he was waiting for my reaction.

I smoothed my hand over the length of the board and turned it over.

"You like it?"

"It's awesome!" I dropped it on the carpet and started riding it around the room. "What made you think of this?"

He shrugged, playing it cool, but I could see the happy sparkle in his eyes as he topped up our mimosas. "The other day when we stopped for burgers on the road, there was that roller-skating place, remember?"

"Yeah. So?"

"So, you got all nostalgic and fairy-eyed and said you missed your wheels."

"I did not get fairy-eyed." I rolled my eyes, but he was right. I did miss my skateboard, hard. Besides Devi and my dog, it was the hardest thing to be without. I didn't bother bringing it on the road because I figured there'd be no place and no time to ride it. I was wrong about that. I'd even considered buying one a few cities back, but then I figured it would be too hard for Flynn to do his thing if I was on a board.

"How the hell is Flynn gonna follow me around on this?" I jerked to a dead stop. "Do *not* tell me you got him one." The mental image of my ultra-reserved, ex-military badass security guard tailing me on a skateboard was too fucking much. I threw my head back and laughed so hard tears welled in the corners of my eyes.

"You done?" Jesse asked after a moment, but he laughed too.

"Oh, shit." I wiped the tears away. "Okay. Shit. I'm better."

"No board for him," he said. "He'll just have to figure it out."

I hopped off and popped the board up into my hand. I couldn't find a brand logo anywhere on it. "It's gorgeous. Where did you get it? It's custom made?"

"Just found a guy who makes them," he said, like it was no big deal.

"You had a skateboard custom made for me in like two days?"

"No. But he had this one that he'd made and I talked him into selling it to me."

I couldn't stop grinning. "It's amazing, Jesse. Thank you." I leaned over and kissed him, my lips lingering longer than I meant them to. "Oh God," I said, my voice all lusty. "You taste like bacon and champagne."

"Mm-hmm," he murmured.

"Wouldn't have thought those would go so well together," I whispered, dropping the skateboard at my feet.

"Don't get any ideas," he said, but he kissed me again. "It's time to get dressed."

"Do I have to?" I climbed into his lap, straddling him on his chair. I was wearing one of his T-shirts and my skimpy white panties since I knew they made him horny. I jacked up the shirt a bit so he could see them as I settled against his cock, which was already rising to the occasion.

He groaned against my neck as I started grinding against him, rubbing up and down as he grew harder. I yanked his underwear down, freeing his dick.

He kissed my neck and reached under the T-shirt, grasping my breast. I buried my fingers in his hair and moaned as his other hand slid between my legs. He slipped his fingers inside my panties and stroked my wetness. Then he fisted the cotton and ripped it aside, and as I rubbed my way up his length he thrust into me.

No holding back this time, no making me wait.

I rode him fast and hard and he gripped my hips, slamming me down against him, forcing himself deeper with each thrust. We kissed so hard we bit each other. We grabbed so hard we bruised each other. My head spun with pleasure and I came in a sudden flurry, slamming down on him, holding him deep.

I shut my eyes and stars burst behind my eyelids. I gripped his hair and bit his neck to keep from screaming.

Jesse groaned and I felt his cock stiffen inside me. As he jerked into me, I sealed my mouth over his and kissed him, slow and deep.

When I felt him relax, I collapsed against him, burying my face in his neck, both of us panting and slippery with sweat. I couldn't think. I could barely breathe. I felt high, kind of floating and grounded by his warmth at once.

He was still inside me and all I wanted to do was fuck him again.

And again.

If only I could move.

He stirred a little, nuzzling my neck.

I sighed. "Get off you in a minute, I swear," I slurred against his salty skin. "Soon as I can feel my legs…"

He wrapped his arms around my hips to support me. Which was good, because otherwise I might've slipped off his lap right to the floor, since I couldn't feel my bones.

With Jesse, sex was always like this.

Crazy.

Molten.

Hot.

I may not have been very experienced in the sex department, but I was pretty sure I wasn't totally dense. The desire was definitely there between us, and it was real. I was sure of that much. He wanted me. Hungrily and often. Maybe that had more to do with his appetite than with me, but it had to at least have *something* to do with me.

And he bought me a skateboard. A super thoughtful gift, just to make me happy. That had to mean something.

Or did it?

Really, as far as I knew the guy made like a gazillion dollars, so maybe buying me a skateboard wasn't anything at all. Maybe he tossed such trinkets to every chick he knew, no big deal.

Fugh.

And there I went again. Just when I was sorta sure how something was between us, I twisted it all around into what it *wasn't*.

Because I still didn't actually know what it *was*.

And I sure as fuck wasn't gonna ask.

I peeled myself off him, maybe a little abruptly, and yanked the T-shirt down to cover myself as I stood up. "Time to get dressed," I announced, maybe a little too cheerily, but I didn't look him in the eye to see what he thought of my sudden departure. "Katie Day awaits."

And with that, I took my mimosa and stumbled to the bathroom on my rubbery, just-fucked legs, to enjoy my maraschino cherries in the shower.

Apparently Jesse also enjoyed cherries in the shower. If he got to eat them off my body.

When we finally dragged our asses out of the hotel room, the first thing I did with Katie Day was give Flynn the day off, with pay. Which left Jude to drive us around in his rented car, so Jesse could sit in the back seat with me.

Pretty much all I wanted to do was hang out with Jesse somewhere he wouldn't be recognized, which meant we ended up driving around a lot. We picked up food and a Frisbee and went to the park for a picnic and ended up there most of the day, though we still attracted some attention. I rode around on my new board for Jesse, at his request. Then we went to a cool skate shop that sold spray paints, bought a bunch of cans, and Jude found us a decently secluded yet not too sketchy bridge under which Jesse insisted I leave my mark.

I reminded him that it was illegal.

He reminded me that I used to do it all the time.

I reminded him that I was immature at that time.

"So be immature," he said. "It'll be fun."

I ended up painting his first name in huge, bubbly pink and purple letters. With flowers.

For dinner, he took me to an amazing restaurant where we had our own private room, and I insisted Jude join us. None of this separate tables bullshit.

Afterward, we went for a drive in the country, Jude at the wheel again, Jesse with me in the back.

It was another gorgeous late-summer day, a little too hot, which always made me feel like sex was in the air. I had no idea how people in this part of the world didn't just have sex all the time. You could barely wear any clothes, for one thing. I couldn't even stand any body hair and had taken to shaving it all off, which pretty much made me feel naked all the time no matter what I was wearing. Currently, I was wearing the lightest, tiniest sundress I could stand on my skin and the skimpiest panties I owned, and Jesse kept trying to slip his fingers inside them.

"Fucking love you bare," he breathed in my ear as I did my best to squirm away from him on the tiny backseat of whatever sports car we were in.

Jude was ignoring us anyway. He had the tunes cranked, loud. With Jude, it was always really heavy stuff, the kind of stuff I'd spent my teens listening to because my brother-in-law was super into it; the really good kind of heavy that always sounded best cranked in a car going high-speed down some random back road. Apparently, even better if it was some random back road in Texas.

Jude was driving way too fucking fast and my heart was racing, adrenalin surging through my veins. I still hadn't quite gotten used to Jesse's taste for high-powered cars or Jude's balls-out style of driving, but that didn't mean it all didn't turn me on, especially when Jesse was sitting next to me stroking me through my panties. By the time "Cowboys from Hell" kicked in, I gave in and let him have his way.

He got his whole hand inside my panties, his middle finger thrust up inside me, stroking me as his thumb slowly massaged my clit. I spread my thighs to accommodate his fist and melted into the feeling. There was just too much testosterone to resist. It was supercharging the air around me, crackling off the windshield, sweating up the leather seats, vibrating through my body with the heavy, driving grind of the song and the growling, feral vocals, and I was getting there, fast.

I was doing all I could not to cry out from the intensity of what Jesse was doing to me. Sweat rolled down my chest. I bit my lip and held onto his arm like somehow I could keep control of it.

I couldn't.

I kept shaking my head at him, willing him to stop before I went over, but he just leaned in and sucked on my earlobe.

"Come, Katie."

I heard his command, his hot breath in my ear, even over the music.

I locked on his eyes and the intensity there made me writhe against his hand. I struggled to focus on his mouth, but he licked his lip and it undid me.

I relaxed against the seat, willing my body to go limp as his hand worked. The orgasm shook me apart but I just tried not to move as my eyes rolled closed.

The song thumped in time with my heart.

Jesse licked my neck and withdrew his hand, straightening my panties. He lay his hand on my thigh. When I opened my eyes I could see my wetness on his fingers. I looked at him and he looked at me.

And for a moment, as my heartbeat throbbed through me and

the high of sexual release left me dizzy, I thought I might ask him. Like actually *ask* him.

What the fuck is going on here. Really.

But I didn't.

Instead I bit my tongue. Literally. Because better to suffer in confused silence for the rest of my life than hear those words I so dreaded from his gorgeous lips.

I just don't feel that way about you, babe.

The corner of his mouth curled in that sexy hint of a smile. "Yeah?" he asked, when I just stared at him, breathless and pleasure-buzzed.

"Yeah," I whispered.

Then he leaned in and kissed me, slow and deep, as we tore down the road and I tried to pretend that nothing else mattered in the world.

CHAPTER TWENTY-NINE

Katie

WHEN WE GOT BACK to our hotel that night I still felt dizzy, high on fresh air and Jesse Mayes.

I also felt confused.

Because did we just go on a date?

Sure, our time at the park might be considered the usual deal, the two of us engaging in PDA's for an audience.

But I was pretty damn sure, other than Jude and a few birds, we had no witnesses under that bridge.

By the time I emerged from the bathroom ready for bed though, I'd already convinced myself it *wasn't* a date. It was a hang out and it was sex, but really, didn't both people have to actually be interested in at least the *possibility* of some kind of future with the other person to consider it a date?

I heard Jesse on the phone with someone in the bedroom, and even though his voice wasn't raised I could tell he was upset. Angry, even.

"So you're not coming to the show? I told you, it's on the twenty-ninth."

I walked in and tried not to eavesdrop, but it was kind of hard not to notice that the voice coming through his cell was the voice of a woman. I couldn't tell what she was saying, but the twenty-ninth was in a week; we'd be in L.A.... and all I could think was, *Elle lives in L.A..*

He was upset because she wasn't coming to his show?

"Fine. I'll call you when I get in," he said, and he sounded distinctly unhappy. Then he hung up. I thought he'd turn to me, but it didn't happen. He just sat there on the edge of the bed looking lost, staring at the carpet.

For way too fucking long.

"Hey," I said softly.

He looked up and his face brightened when he saw me.

"Hey." He tossed his cell aside and reached for me, but I didn't go to him. It still felt weird to me, the idea that we'd maybe just been on a date, but maybe we hadn't, and I didn't even know. What I did know was that he was paying me for our time together, and he'd maybe just had an argument with his ex-girlfriend that had left him looking really fucking sad, and I'd never felt so jealous in my life.

Was he still in love with her?

What if he was still in love with her?

Was I about to have sex with a guy while he was actually in love with someone else?

Maybe.

But even so, what really mattered was that he *wasn't* in love with me. And I was definitely developing feelings for him.

Okay. Who the hell did I think I was kidding? Myself?

I turned my back to him so I could get my shit together without him staring at me.

The truth was I'd had feelings for Jesse Mayes since about the time he showed up at my apartment unannounced and made me bacon and eggs.

Or since he showed up at my place of work and asked me to come on tour.

Or since way before that.

I was trying to pinpoint the exact moment when my stomach had started doing the drunken butterfly dance in his presence, when he came up behind me and kissed my neck, and I blurted it out.

"Maybe we shouldn't have sex anymore."

He stopped kissing me.

"I mean, it just feels wrong, you know? Since you're paying me."

He let me go. "Okay. If that's what you want."

I was unprepared for his response. I'd expected some kind of argument, but he just walked back over to the bed. "No more sex." He turned to face me and stripped off his shirt, tossing it on the floor.

I narrowed my eyes at him. "That's not cool."

He undid his belt, slowly, exaggerating the movements as he pulled the buckle back and slid the leather end through. He undid the button of his jeans too. "Not forcing you to look."

I looked away, crossing my arms over my chest. Then he made a move toward me and my gaze snapped back to him before I could stop it.

He prowled up and took hold of my hands, lifting them over my head. He backed me up against the wall and pinned me there, but he really didn't have to hold me very hard. I was an incredibly willing captive, my body doing the exact opposite of what I meant it to.

"It just... feels... wrong..." I managed to repeat, as his lips brushed a hot trail of sparks up my neck.

"Mm-hmm." His tongue flicked my ear, sending a shiver down my back, straight to that magical erogenous zone at the base of my spine. "Like good wrong?"

I yanked a hand free, planted it in the middle of his hard chest and with a massive effort, pushed him away, the inch or so he would give. "No," I kinda lied. "Just wrong."

"Interesting..." he said against my neck, his lips moving over my skin, kissing and nibbling a trail to that sensitive spot where my neck met my shoulder. The man knew every button to push... and lick... and stroke. At the same time, his hand found its way up my thigh, beneath my skirt. "You seem to like wrong." His fingers pressed up into the damp heat of my panties, massaging my softness, making my knees nearly buckle.

"Jesse..." But the man was fast, and he knew what he wanted. He had my dress up and my panties askew in less time than it took me to draw my next breath, which was sharp and ended with a bitten lip, because his tongue was between my legs.

"Mmm, Katie," he groaned.

"*Ung*. God. Stop that." My newly-freed hands found the top of his head and my fingers delved into his hair, gripping him tight rather than pushing him away.

"Does this count as sex?" he asked between slow, hot licks.

"Oh, God... if you don't know the answer to that... we have a problem."

His hot breath tickled my thighs as he laughed, but I didn't look. I couldn't, *wouldn't* look at what he was doing, all over that sweet spot in that way he did that was about to make my head explode... among other things. "Ah... Jesse..."

"Mmm."

I lost the ability to form words and resorted to ragged panting. My body hadn't forgotten the attention it had received in the car; I was so worked up all it took was one mistaken glance at him between my legs and I came. The orgasm was sharp and hot and intense, and for a matter of minutes all I could do was roll my head from side to side as he licked me, his hands on my thighs holding me up. If he let go, I would've slid right down the wall into a heap on the floor.

"That's... *so*... unfair," I gasped when I could speak again.

"Just kissing you good night." He kissed my quivering flesh, sending aftershocks of pleasure through my core.

I worked my hands between my panties and his face and covered myself.

"Your oral fixation is just going to have to redirect. Can't you take up smoking again?"

He laughed. He got to his feet and kissed me, long and deep, his mouth wet with my arousal. "I prefer cherry pie," he said when he came up for air. He had his hands in my hair and he held me close, my face tipped up to his as he kissed me again.

The man was irresistible. And so fucking hard... I couldn't help it; my hands were all over him, rubbing up and down the hard length of him through his jeans. And his eyes darkened in that way they did, and I was hooked.

Jesse Mayes aroused, for me, was an aphrodisiac.

The world's most addictive drug.

The highest high.

"Katie," he whispered as I went down on my knees and unzipped him. I had the evidence of what that good night kiss had done to him in my hand, long and hard and thick, and the feel of him was intoxicating, all silk and heat and need.

I took him in my mouth, driven by his groans, and felt him lean into the wall above me, holding himself up. "Katie," he breathed, and when he came for me, he groaned and cupped my face in his hand.

I swallowed him down and stroked him until he shuddered from the intensity.

"I think we're gonna need to redirect your oral fixation," he said above me, panting. I looked up; he was leaning on his forearm on the wall, looking down at me. "Have you ever thought about taking up smoking?"

I laughed, and he pulled me to my feet and kissed me... like he never wanted to stop kissing me.

Sometime later, after a shower and a lot of sleepy groping, we ended up in bed in the dark. Jesse was inside me again. We were in this kind of delirious, over-tired but frantic daze, clutching at each other, moving in a slow, hungry rhythm, his body pinning me down, my thighs spread under his weight until they almost hurt, my legs wrapped around his waist, and all I wanted was *more*.

I could feel nothing, think nothing, but Jesse.

My heels dug into his muscled ass, my fingernails sinking into his flesh as he possessed me. I came, a slow, rolling boil this time, my body bucking beneath his with nowhere to go. He held me tight, breathing with me as he kissed me, his chest heaving in time with my own. He made me his with every possessive thrust, again and again and again, and my body didn't care if it wasn't real. I came again as he moved against me, sucking back my kisses and stealing my breath until I had to break away, panting.

I caught a glimpse of his eyes in the dark, shining, watching me, and then he pressed his forehead to mine, his cock throbbing deep inside me, his hips grinding against me as he came. I wrapped my arms around him, twisting my fingers in the whorls of his hair as he drove himself into me, holding him tight as he groaned.

"Fuck, Katie," he breathed as he settled against me.

It was four in the morning.

I was tangled up in Jesse, in his warmth, his limbs, neither one of us saying another thing. Eventually his breaths came slower and slower against my neck as he tumbled into sleep, his heartbeat thumping against mine.

He was still half on top of me. He was still inside me.

His arm tightened around my waist in sleep and my heartbeat surged.

I sighed a ragged sigh, sinking deeper into the bed, willing my pulse to slow, my breaths to calm, my body to relax into sleep.

I stroked the silken hair at his temple, brushing back a wayward curl, watching him sleep from beneath my half-mast eyelids. I couldn't look away, couldn't quite close them just yet.

And, yeah. In that moment, I knew it.

There was no point denying it to myself anymore.

I was in love with Jesse Mayes.

CHAPTER THIRTY

Katie

"THEY'RE NOT BACK YET?"

I stood in the doorway looking in at the empty hotel room. I hadn't seen Jesse since he took off that morning with Jude.

"I'll track them down," Flynn said behind me.

I walked into the room and dropped my bags on the bed. I'd been at the beach, then doing a little shopping to kill the time… but I was really hoping I'd get to see more of Jesse today.

It was my birthday, after all.

We'd been in L.A. for four days and something weird was going on.

On the surface everything was fine. Things had been pretty epic, actually, from about the moment Jesse and I started sleeping together. Then somewhere around Vegas things took a sharp turn. I kept hearing him on the phone with someone, a female some-one, semi-arguing. And his mood took a nose-dive. But he never mentioned it to me and I was way too scared to ask.

Because apparently, just when I thought things could hardly get any better between us—other than that pesky little problem of him not being in love with me—they got totally worse.

A lot worse.

The closer we got to L.A., the worse it got. Jesse got all broody and withdrawn. He took to spending more time alone with his guitar. He always had a smile for me and the sex was still phenomenal, but something was deeply wrong and I was about one more of those far-off, distracted looks in his eyes from becoming a total wreck.

In desperation, I'd even started hoping he might say something in his sleep to give me a hint at what was going on in his gorgeous head, but I hadn't heard anything beyond a bit of mumbling. And I'd had a lot of sleepless nights to eavesdrop.

"He's still in a meeting," Flynn reported, after texting Jude. "He'll meet you at the restaurant for dinner at eight. Still lots of time to make it to the show."

Shit. He was running late. On my birthday.

He'd already played two sold-out concerts in L.A. and tonight we were going to see Zane's side project band, Wet Blanket, play at a club. I'd been so looking forward to this night, because I was dying for more downtime with Jesse. He'd been busier than ever —at least, too busy for me—and even though we'd been "being seen" every night, as usual, at some club or restaurant or party, I didn't feel like I'd really seen *him* in over a week.

"Okay," I told Flynn, resigned. "I guess just knock on my door when you're ready to go." I tried to sound normal and not like my life was crumbling around me.

"We should head out at seven-thirty."

"Great."

Flynn left and I flopped onto the bed.

Fuck me.

What the fuck was going on?

L.A. had been amazing, other than this. For a surprise birthday present, Jesse had flown my sister and her family down when we first arrived. We'd had a ton of fun sightseeing and taking the kids to the beach, but they'd flown home last night; had to get back to work. They rarely went on holiday because of the coffee bar, so I was super grateful Jesse had managed to pull this together... but I also couldn't help wondering if he'd done it partly to keep me distracted.

I'd heard him on the phone again this morning, and he was definitely talking to a woman.

Elle hadn't shown up at his shows, so I still didn't know if that's what the argument was about. But I'd put money on the fact that he was talking to her, and whatever they were talking about, it wasn't good.

I just didn't know what I was supposed to do about it. Ignore it? Resign myself to the fact that I was losing him? Correction, had never had him in the first place. So if he wanted her back, or had some sort of unresolved shit to work through with her, who was I to say anything?

Or did I say something? Did I fight for him? Take a chance and tell him how I felt? Grab this situation by the balls and let the consequences be what they may?

At least then I would've tried.

Not like I was getting many more chances.

This was the last week of the tour. Which meant in one week Jesse and I were supposed to just... say goodbye?

I'd go home to Vancouver and he'd go... wherever Jesse Mayes went? All over the place, probably, writing and recording the next Dirty album and touring the world, and far the hell away from me. Soon enough I'd be out of sight, out of mind.

But not to worry. There'd be lineups of warm female bodies just waiting to take my place.

Fuck. Just *fuck*.

I rolled over and mashed my face into the pillow, trying really hard not to throw up.

Was that why he was pulling away? Was it going to be hard for him to say goodbye too?

Or was he so wrapped up with Elle he wasn't even thinking about it?

That thought was just too painful to consider.

When I heard him on the phone this morning, all I could think was, *He's talking to her. She's putting that brooding look on his face.*

And if he still had feelings for her, I really shouldn't be here at all. If that was the case, I didn't *want* to be here.

I just didn't know how to do this... this incredibly slow, agonizing letting go of someone I didn't want to let go of at all. I didn't want to say goodbye to what we had. Why would I? If this was a real relationship it would be perfect.

At least, before Elle came back into the picture.

Though maybe she'd never actually *left* the picture. If nothing else, they were still in a band together. Not like he wasn't ever going to see her again, like a *lot*.

And this *wasn't* a real relationship. It wasn't even a relationship. It was a business deal. With a time limit on it. A time limit that I, myself, had insisted on.

Like an idiot.

In my most desperate moments, like right now, I considered running away. Just quitting this fucked-up job, leaving the tour and going home. I knew I risked just getting more and more attached to Jesse the longer I stayed, but I couldn't bring myself to leave him. I didn't know how I'd survive being left by him, but I still couldn't leave.

Maybe I just needed more time to figure out how to tell him how I really felt.

Maybe I would never tell him at all.

I just didn't know yet.

I called my sister and made her put Max on the phone, just so I could hear my dog and know I still had a home and a family who would welcome me back at the end of this fucked-up-edness with open arms.

Then I called Devi to vent. As usual, she said all the right things. The things I knew were right as soon as I heard them. She said he was the world's biggest asshole if he hurt me. But she also said I didn't really know how he felt, so to stop torturing myself over the worst case scenario.

"How is he treating you?" she asked me, like she did every time we spoke.

"Good, I guess."

"What the hell does that mean?"

"I don't know. I mean, obviously we have wicked sexual chemistry. And he seems to like having me around."

"Of course he does. Because you're awesome." Leave it to a best friend to point that out. "What else?"

"He laughs at my jokes."

"Because your jokes are fucking funny."

And on and on we went, until I was feeling somewhat better about things, and super-confident that Devi definitely loved me. Which went a long way to cheering me up.

When we got off the phone it was six o'clock and I was still no closer to knowing how to proceed with Jesse. We were supposed to meet at six; at least, before he decided to keep doing whatever he was doing and meet me late.

On my birthday.

I dragged myself up from the fetal position and thought about that.

We'd had dinner plans. Birthday dinner plans. And now I was supposed to sit here by myself waiting until he said it was time to meet him, while he hung out with Elle... or whatever the fuck he was doing?

To hell with that.

I got dressed in the super-hot halter dress I'd picked out to wear tonight, got myself date-with-a-rock-star ready, and texted

Flynn to meet me in the lobby.

"Where is Jesse?" I crossed the lobby toward him; he was already waiting for me.

"In a meeting," he said.

"Where?"

"At the restaurant."

"What restaurant?" I stared at him. "*The* restaurant? Like the one where we're having dinner tonight?"

"Yes."

I digested that. I'd picked the restaurant myself based on Maggie's recommendation, and she'd worked her magic to get us a table on short notice. And now he was using it for his pre-dinner date with his ex or whoever?

"Is he with Elle?"

Flynn cocked his head a little, maybe surprised by the question, processing it. He didn't say anything for a really long time.

"I don't think so, Katie."

His tone said he knew so, but I didn't fully buy it. I didn't particularly buy anything Jesse's staff told me, because who was to say they didn't lie to cover for him on a daily basis? Surely they'd done it with his groupies, maybe they'd done it with other women he'd dated, and maybe they'd done it with me.

"Take me there," I said.

He hesitated. "We're not supposed to be there until eight."

"You can take me or I can take a cab, but either way, I'm going now."

Flynn drove. I sat in the backseat, a nervous wreck, trying to figure out what I'd say to Jesse if I found him with Elle. I kept picturing all the glamorous images I'd seen of her on magazine covers and wondering what she'd look like in person. Wondering how I'd keep my dignity when it became clear to all that she was now with Jesse, again, and I wasn't. Or, maybe she wasn't, but I definitely never had been.

Maybe this was for the best, in a warped way. Maybe this was what I needed. Something definitive to help me digest the fact that Jesse wasn't mine and was never going to be.

So he liked to fuck.

He liked having fun with me.

We got along well.

Those three facts did not equal a promise of future fidelity and happiness. Not when the guy in the situation had no interest in a future, or even having a girlfriend in general.

But how much longer could I pretend to Jesse that I was faking being in love, while the world got to see the truth, that I actually *was* in love? And when would it become obvious to him that I wasn't faking?

As we neared the restaurant, I started feeling nauseous. I hated confrontations, and I honestly didn't want one. I just had to see. I had to know. I couldn't stand this waiting anymore, and clearly he was never going to tell me what the hell had been making him all broody and withdrawn.

And I just couldn't stand to be made a fool of all over again.

That humiliating day at the altar had been more or less put to bed, but I didn't need to live through that shit again. Once was enough for a lifetime. Not that Jesse was leaving me at the altar; he hadn't told me he loved me or that he wanted a real relationship with me, much less proposed. But he was supposed to be with me, in the public eye, and if he was with another woman at the restaurant it might even be on the internet already.

I probably could've just gone online to find out who he was with. That thought almost made me laugh out loud. If it wasn't so fucking depressing.

As Flynn spoke with the valet, I went straight into the restaurant. I didn't wait my turn in line or pause to speak with the hostess. I spotted Jude up at the bar right away, and walked toward him. He started to get up but I didn't wait for him either. I knew where Jesse would be. Somewhere tucked away in the back, in Jude's line of sight.

I found him in a booth in the back corner of the restaurant. He was facing me and his companion had her back to me—and yes, it was a woman. Though it wasn't Elle. Elle was a platinum blonde; this woman had brown hair. It cascaded down her bare back in soft waves, over the low-slung back of her dress. My heart sank through my guts, because she was a knockout. I could tell that much without even seeing her face. Tall, slim and curvy, with mile-long legs.

I stopped dead. Because really, wasn't that about all I came to see? Did I need to see any more?

I hovered in the middle of the aisle, not sure what to do. On the one hand, Jesse would know I was coming. Flynn would've texted Jude, and Jude would've told Jesse. On the other hand, maybe I could slip out now and hop in a cab and just get the hell out of here without having to face him and his secret date. I started to seriously consider turning around and doing just that.

Which was when he looked up and saw me.

"*Katie.*" I barely heard it over the din of the restaurant but I saw his lips move as he said my name. He stood as I approached, and the brunette turned to me.

And yes, she was gorgeous. Like drop-dead gorgeous. She looked like a model. Actually, she looked like—

"Katie, this is my sister," Jesse said, reaching for my hand, "Jessa."

CHAPTER THIRTY-ONE

Katie

JESSE PULLED me in for a quick kiss, then said, "Jessa, this is Katie."

Jessa Mayes smiled and stood to greet me. "Katie! So nice to meet you. I've heard so many lovely things."

I wanted to say the same about her, but Jesse rarely said a word about her. All I knew was that he'd wanted to meet up with her in New York, but she'd bailed on him, and he'd hoped to see her again in L.A.…. Though when I didn't hear another word about it I'd just assumed it wasn't happening.

Which made me the biggest idiot in the world. Because all those tense phone calls… were with his sister.

Not with Elle.

Jesse had wanted to see his sister, really fucking badly, apparently, and here she was. And I was intruding.

"It's… um… nice to meet you, too," I stammered, blushing fiercely. "I'm sorry to barge in like this." I gave Jesse a pointed look that I hoped conveyed an incredibly frustrated, *You really could have told me.* "We were supposed to have dinner."

"We're just having a drink," Jessa said, pulling me into the booth with her. "You'll just have to join us. I'll head out soon and you can have your dinner."

"You could stay," Jesse said to her, sitting across from us. "You don't have to rush off." And there was something unnerving in his tone, some kind of vulnerability bordering on desperation, that I'd never heard from him before. "We weren't having dinner until eight or so."

"Actually," I put in, "why don't we just order now? Then Jessa can eat with us." Because clearly he really wanted her to stay.

After some mild protests on her part, Jessa finally agreed to stay, and over the course of dinner I discovered that Jessa Mayes was not only gorgeous, but sweet, smart, and charming. She might've been born with Jesse's dark hair, but she now had honey-blond highlights, which set off her slight California tan. She had Jesse's dark eyes and his full lips, and sometimes, his hearty laugh.

There wasn't a thing about her not to like.

Somehow, by the end of dinner I'd convinced her to come to the club with us afterward, to see Zane's band. I could tell Jesse was happy she was coming, though it felt like the entire evening the two of them were in some kind of unspoken argument right in front of me; about what, I had no idea. Every time I caught Jesse's eye, the corner of his mouth curled in a slight smile or he'd wink or squeeze my hand, reassuring me that everything was fine. But it didn't feel fine.

It felt far from fine.

I didn't know Jessa to be able to read her, but there was tension in the air. She smiled at me a lot and even seemed to be getting pumped for the show in the ride over to the club, but I didn't fully buy it.

It seemed to me that for such a beautiful woman, Jessa Mayes was missing a spark.

I doubted many people would notice it. She was *so* pretty that I was sure a lot of people, especially men, only got that far. But if you looked beyond that, it was there. A kind of flatness in her dark eyes. Something closed off or broken down, meant to keep you the hell out.

I was sure Jesse knew it was there. I was pretty sure, by the time we got to the club and Jude led us in through the back door, that it was the reason for Jesse's unease.

But I didn't want to pry and I didn't want to ruin this night. If they wanted to pretend everything was cool when it so obviously wasn't, I'd play along. The truth was, I didn't even care to be at the show; I would've much rather gone back to the hotel with Jesse so maybe he'd tell me what the fuck was going on over a beer.

Then we walked into the venue and I actually heard the band.

Judging by the frenzy of the crowd, Wet Blanket was deep into their set. I had no idea how the walls were still standing, because the whole club felt like it was about to blow apart at the seams. The band was rocking out, hard, just reaching the climax of The Kinks' "Lola," Zane's powerful voice belting out the twisted, sexy lyrics.

Okay. Maybe this was just what I needed.

I let out a deep breath, releasing a lot of the built-up tension from the day.

As Jessa followed Jude through the crowded hallway into the VIP area, she reached back and took my hand, lacing her fingers through mine. She flashed me a dazzling smile, so like her brother's it made me grin. I glanced back at Jesse and took his hand, the three of us forming a chain as a fleet of bouncers filtered us through the crowd.

The VIP area was a raised area at the back of the room like a stage of its own, closed off with velvet rope and a wall of well-built men. Inside were Raf, Letty, Pepper and their wives, Dylan and his friend Ash, and a bunch of other people I knew or at least recognized from Jesse's crew and various other events we'd been to along the tour. I knew almost everyone here.

It was a far cry from where I began at the beginning of the tour in my first VIP room with Jesse, where I knew hardly a soul.

I liked it. It kind of felt like coming home.

Dylan and Ash gave me a welcoming hug, but they really flipped their shit over Jessa. I got the feeling she didn't show her face often; everyone was pumped to see her and drinks were shoved our way. Jessa kept hold of my hand half the time and we ended up sharing a love seat vacated for us. Jesse squeezed in next to me. He looked happy, glad to be there with me, I think, but also really proud to be there with his sister. I felt like I had the seat of honor, sitting right there between them.

Happy birthday to me.

As I watched the band, I got goose bumps. Zane's stage presence was off the charts. His blond hair was shaved almost completely off at the sides, the top grown out like a really long mohawk that refused to stay up and fell over his eye. He wore loose, super low-slung jeans that showed off the V of his groin, and an incredibly small leather vest that was dead sexy. His lean, tight abs were on full display, his chest slick with sweat, his nipple piercing sparking as it caught in the light. He'd also grown a blond beard, and he looked pretty much like what I imagined the devil himself would look like, if the devil climbed on up out of hell to rock out, bent on corrupting the souls of a fuckload of women in the process.

He had every woman in the crowd, not to mention most of the men, dangling, hearts in throats and fists in the air, devouring his every move, every word. I'd never seen him rock out live. I'd only seen him on stage when he and Jesse played together at the VIP show in Vancouver, which was totally different. Unplugged.

Chill. And Zane was clearly trying not to upstage Jesse since it was his show.

This was full-on Zane, and I could see why he was Dirty's frontman. Jesse could own a stage. Zane owned the whole fucking place.

I'd pretty much died and gone to rock 'n' roll heaven.

All Wet Blanket played, all night long, were covers. Sizzling-hot, kick-ass covers, mostly of classic rock songs, which spoke to my heart and gave me a total lady boner. Though I wasn't the only woman in the crowd getting off on the show. When Zane announced they were down to their last few songs of the night, there was a backlash of screams. You'd think they'd just announced they were going to mass-murder the audience.

Then the band kicked into the hardest, hottest version of AC/DC's "Girls Got Rhythm" I'd ever heard, and all was forgiven. The entire club throbbed with it. The floor shook. I was pretty sure sweat was rolling down the walls. When they rocked out the final chords, I leaned over to Jesse and said, "If it weren't for our deal and the two hundred grand on the line, I'd say you've got competition, sweetie."

His eyes narrowed at that, but crinkled with amusement at the corners.

"Fucking Zane," he said.

At that moment, fucking Zane started talking into the mic.

"Recently one of my best friends fell in love." He looked straight to the back of the room, to the love seat where Jesse sat next to me, and pointed straight at him. "Welcome to the mother-fucking show, brother."

Jesse lifted his drink in salute. At this, there were a bunch of hoots and whistles, and a couple of women on the dance floor screamed, "I love you, Jesse!"

"When you see your friend that happy," Zane went on, "you

want to be happy for him. And you are. But when his girl's as awesome as his is, you also want to hate him just a bit." As the white light caught in Zane's ice-blue eyes, I was pretty sure he looked right at me. "Happy birthday, Katie. This one's for you."

I glanced at Jesse. He just shrugged; apparently he hadn't put Zane up to this. I felt the blush heating my cheeks, like everyone in the place was staring at me, though in reality, their attention was still on Zane. And maybe Jesse.

With the opening notes, and definitely the opening words, I recognized the song.

"Jessie's Girl."

I looked at Jesse. A huge grin split his face, his white teeth gleaming in the spotlight that was trained on him as he shook his head at Zane. I laughed and shrank back into the couch, out of the spotlight, hoping to disappear.

No such luck. By the time the chorus kicked in, Jessa had yanked me up off the seat and over to one of the knee-high tables, where she proceeded to pull me up and force me to dance. Which was to say that she started to dance, and I could either stand there like a party pooper and let her dance alone, or join her. I chose the latter.

We danced our asses off. Because why the hell not?

Zane Traynor was singing a song, for *me*, to a packed house. I was here with Jesse Fucking Mayes and his sister wanted to dance with me, on a table. It was my motherfucking birthday, I was turning twenty-five, and life was pretty fucking good.

I, Katie Bloom, was Jesse's girl.

More or less.

When the song was over I collapsed back onto the love seat with Jessa, laughing. More drinks were waiting for us. Jesse handed me a glass of bubbly and leaned in, his lips grazing my ear, sending a shiver of sparks down my spine. "Happy birthday,

Katie," he said, brushing my hair back over my shoulder and down my back.

And that's when I saw her.

Elle.

The one member of Dirty I hadn't yet met.

Jesse's gorgeous ex-girlfriend.

She was ensconced in a big leather booth at the other end of the VIP area, surrounded by a bunch of people, including Dylan and Ash. Maybe she'd just arrived. Maybe she'd been there the whole time. I had no idea.

She wasn't looking at me. Maybe she hadn't noticed me.

I was pretty sure by now she knew who I was. By now, everyone who knew Jesse knew who I was.

But table dancing aside, it was pretty packed in the club. If she hadn't noticed I was there, she was definitely about to, since my hand was attached to Jesse's, and my other hand was intermittently attached to his sister's.

Was she there during "Jessie's Girl"?

I wasn't sure why I cared. Why I was so nervous to come face-to-face with her. I had as much reason to be here as she did.

So why did I suddenly feel out of place?

"What's wrong?"

I looked up into beautiful molasses eyes, dark eyebrows that were furled together. And I had no desire to add to the stress of whatever Jesse was going through with his sister with my petty insecurities. So I said, "Nothing. Just going to find the ladies' room."

I was kind of hoping to drag Jessa with me as a gorgeous security blanket, but no luck. She was deep in conversation with Jude, so I went by myself, leaving Jesse with what I intended as a quick kiss. Instead, he delved his hand into my hair and held me to him, lip-locked, for a long, breathless moment before letting me go.

I got up a little dazed, straightened my halter dress, and weaved off in the direction of the exit signs at the back of the VIP area.

Moments later, I emerged from the cubicle in the ladies' room to find a number of women gathered at the sinks. Actually, they were gathered around a striking platinum blonde.

Elle was talking with one of her girlfriends in a hushed voice and fiddling with her long, white-blonde hair, which was teased up into a super-cool fauxhawk, the sides braided back, her slim, tan figure wrapped in an asymmetrical white mini-dress.

Her eye caught mine in the mirror.

I slipped up to the sink next to hers. Her girlfriends finished up and left; Elle stayed put, her eyes on me.

Shit. What was it with club bathrooms and confrontations?

I met her gaze in the mirror again as I dried my hands, thinking I'd say hello. But the look she gave me as she touched up her lipstick couldn't have been more unwelcoming.

"Jesse's girl," she said. But it wasn't with any trace of the affection or good-natured ribbing with which Zane had sung it.

"Hi," I said, because I couldn't think of anything else to say. I started to offer my hand to introduce myself properly.

"You won't last," she said. "They never do."

Then she continued applying her lipstick like I wasn't even there.

For a moment I just stood there, stunned, my hand frozen in the air. Humiliation, anger and hurt broiling up inside.

Then I dropped my hand. I found my voice. "You mean, because you didn't."

I looked at myself in the mirror and touched up my lip gloss the way I would have if she wasn't there, because no way was I about to go scurrying out of here with my tail between my legs just because Jesse's ex-girlfriend was a rude, jealous bitch.

I felt the cold prick of her stare, but I ignored it as I tucked my lip gloss away.

From the corner of my eye I saw her turn to leave. Then she paused and said, "At least when we were together, it was real."

Then she walked out, leaving me standing there alone.

CHAPTER THIRTY-TWO

Katie

I DIDN'T SEE Elle again until hours later, when the club was shutting down. The get-the-fuck-out lights were turned on and we'd gone out back to smoke up with the band and say our good-byes. I'd managed to avoid her completely in the club, but it wasn't as crowded outside and she was nearby, talking with Dylan.

Maybe some girls would've taken the opportunity to make out with Jesse and rub it in her face.

I wasn't one of those girls.

Instead I took the high road and just went on with my night, at Jesse's side, the way I would any other night. But her words had cut me deep.

At least when we were together, it was real.

And she was right. I felt like a fraud hanging out on his arm. Because I was living a total lie.

Not the lie I'd started living at the beginning of the tour, the one that said we were a couple when we weren't. This was a worse lie. It was a lie to Jesse. It was a lie to myself.

Because I was totally in love with the guy, just like the world thought I was, but pretending to both him and myself that I wasn't.

I went with him to put his sister in a cab, and after we said our goodbyes and she was gone, I told him, "She's so beautiful, Jesse."

I meant it as a legit compliment, but he didn't smile. He just looked all tense and distracted like he had most of the night and said, "Yeah."

While he was doing his final rounds I went over to thank Zane for the song. His ice-blue eyes lit up when he saw me coming. I didn't know what it was, exactly; his drop-dead gorgeous looks, his crazy-cool style, that charismatic smile? But the man had danger written all over him.

I let him scoop me up in his arms for a lingering hug, the kind I was sure he gave most women, his entire body flush against mine. He didn't even pretend to try to leave a respectable distance between his groin and mine the way most guys, and friends of Jesse's, would. "Katie," he said, and I could've sworn he smelled my hair.

Suddenly Maggie's advice to me at the beginning of the tour came back. *Really, the only useful thing I can tell you about Zane Traynor is keep your distance.*

I decided to ignore that warning, trusting Jesse's friendship with the man in my arms. Plus, the man had sung me a birthday song, I was pleasantly content with my champagne buzz, and since I wasn't *really* Jesse's girl I could hug whomever the fuck I wanted to.

"Zane," I said. "That was the best birthday present a girl could get."

Other than the one Jesse gave me when he flew my family out to surprise me, but I didn't feel like going there with Zane.

He got a big, shit-eating Viking grin on his face and tipped his head back, laughing that big, cocky laugh of his, showing me all his perfect white teeth. He still had one hand on my lower back, holding me to him, and his other hand was on my ass before I knew it. Then he kissed me on the cheek and said, "Anytime, Jesse's girl."

He let me go and I scrambled over to Jesse, who wrapped me in his arm and tucked me into his side, still talking to some guy. He hadn't even noticed the exchange between Zane and I, and I didn't particularly want him to.

I had no warm, gushy or conflicted feelings for Zane, and while he was gorgeous to look at, I wasn't attracted to him. I thought he was fucking cool, and as Jesse's friend and bandmate I would've liked to be able to call him a friend. But the truth was I didn't really know the guy, and the way he looked at me confused the shit out of me. I didn't think he actually wanted me. I was pretty sure he was just fucking with me to amuse his giant ego, which probably rivaled Jesse's for all-time Rock and Roll Hall of Fame giant egos.

It was a wonder the two of them ever fit on the same stage together.

We said our goodbyes, and while I got my goodbye hugs from pretty much everyone *except* Elle, Jesse had a few words with her, which I was glad to see did *not* end with a lingering groin-to-groin hug complete with ass squeeze.

But on the way back to the hotel, I decided to bring it up.

Jude was driving us but Jesse was with me in the backseat, and there was music on loud enough that I was pretty sure we wouldn't be overheard.

"Did you tell Elle about us?" I was leaning into Jesse's side and his arm was around me. When he didn't answer right away, I tipped my head back to look up at him.

He didn't look like he'd heard me. His gaze was unfocused, directed out the window. When I elbowed his ribs, lightly, his dark eyes snapped to mine.

"Huh? What about us?"

"I don't know. What did you tell her?"

"Nothing," he said. "She didn't ask. I didn't bring it up."

I turned away, but he caught my chin and turned my face back to his.

"She knows we're together. We're not exactly hiding it."

That was true. There were images of Jesse and I all over the place, and the only thing that made me feel okay rather than totally nauseous about that was the fact that Jesse and I looked very cozy in those pictures. That thought made me feel a little better, because fuck Elle if she was gonna be like that.

But then I just felt bad.

As soon as we got to the hotel I went straight into the shower. I needed a few minutes alone to blast myself with steamy water and clear my head. It had been such a crazy day.

First, thinking Jesse was meeting someone, probably Elle, behind my back. Ordering Flynn to take me to crash his date, which I should really apologize to both of them for. Then meeting Jesse's beautiful but obviously troubled sister, and seeing him bent out of shape all night about something. I'd never felt that kind of tension coming off him. The only tension I was used to feeling in Jesse's presence was of the sexual variety, which was a lot more fun.

Then there was the kick-ass show, which made me both excited to see Dirty play together someday, and depressed as hell that this tour was almost over and I may never actually get the chance to do that... because I could not see myself standing in line to buy a ticket to a Dirty concert sometime next year when they went on their next tour, and standing in the crowd watching them up on stage, out of my reach, like any other fan. The thought almost brought me to tears.

And then there was the run-in with Elle, which made me feel sick to my stomach. And the booze I'd drank to try to numb out that feeling. And the overly-familiar hug from Zane, which had been unexpected, a little flattering and not too out of place in the moment, but now felt kinda shitty. I was wondering if I should tell Jesse about it when the door to the shower opened and he appeared, naked, and stepped into my steam.

"We never had that shower you mentioned," he said, his arms wrapping around my waist as he pressed up against my backside.

"What shower?"

"You know, the one on your list. Top five kinky things."

"Oh," I breathed as he kissed my neck. "That."

And with that, all the woes of the evening melted down the drain. It was far too distracting showering with a naked, wet Jesse to even remember all the things I thought I was upset about only moments ago. Especially when he started washing me with a soapy washcloth and nibbling my ear, then whispered a heartfelt, "Thank you."

"For what?"

"Jessa likes you," he said, turning me to face him. "I haven't seen her that happy…" Something dark passed over his features, troubling me all over again. "Well, in a long time."

"You mean she never table danced with your other girlfriends?"

A slight smile quirked his lips. "That would be a no."

Half an hour later we were all steamed up but clean, dry, and I was ready to collapse into bed. Jesse followed, leaving on the lamp by the bed as he climbed in under the sheet with me. He stretched out next to me and I wrapped my arm lazily around his waist. He was so warm, his skin soft. He trailed his fingers through my hair, his arm flung around me on the pillow.

We hadn't even gotten it on in the shower, which only fueled the uneasy feeling that had been building all night.

"So…" I asked, rather bravely, since the blood coursing through my veins was still at least fifty percent champagne, "how come you don't do the girlfriend thing?"

After a moment, Jesse sighed. "The answer to that will make me sound like an ass."

"So be an ass." I smiled to encourage him and elbowed him gently. "Come on. Tell me."

"The truth, Katie Bloom," he said while playing with my hair, "is that in my experience the women I date usually want something from me I'm not prepared to give. So I just don't go there."

"But you did with Elle."

"I did with Elle."

"May I ask why?"

He considered that for a moment before he answered. "I felt a lot of pressure to be what she wanted." His eyes met mine and he stopped playing with my hair. "Man, that does make me sound like an ass."

"Kind of," I said. He frowned a little and I grinned. At least he looked mildly amused, which was miles better than the strained look he'd had on his face most of the night.

"I knew when we got together it couldn't just be a hook up," he said. "There was too much at stake. The band, our working relationship. A longtime friendship. I didn't want to fuck any of that up."

"Very sensible." It killed me a little to hear him talk about her. Even though they were no longer together, they had been together, and according to Elle, what they had was real. But I wanted to know. I wanted to know what it took to have a man like Jesse Mayes.

For real.

"So why did you take the risk?"

He sighed again. "She wanted us to. And after a while I thought maybe it would be worth it to give it a try."

"Lucky her," I teased. "It *is* every woman's dream to have the man she wants 'give it a try' with her."

Jesse gave me a dirty look and smacked my bare ass cheek under the sheet, sending a sting of excitement straight to my clit. "Smart-ass," he growled. Then he squeezed my tingling cheek, and I *almost* forgot what we were talking about.

"The truth is," he went on, kneading my ass as he spoke, "I spent the last decade listening to the world hypothesize about what a scorching couple Elle and I would make. Sometimes it seemed like everyone thought we should be together. Including Elle. I thought maybe there was something I was missing, and once we were together I'd find out what it was. But that never happened, and after a while I accepted the fact that we weren't right for each other. But it takes a while to navigate breaking up from someone you care about whose life is so intertwined with yours. I never wanted to hurt her, but I knew I couldn't stay with her."

Well. That would explain the way Elle treated me tonight. It wasn't so much that she didn't like me. She didn't even know me.

It was that Jesse had broken her heart.

"People call me a heartbreaker," he said, as if reading my mind. "I don't enjoy breaking hearts."

I got that. I felt it. And I believed him.

In light of what he'd just told me, it even made total sense why he didn't want a girlfriend.

What better way to avoid breaking hearts than to never let anyone love you in the first place?

Problem was, I did love him, already and completely. And right in the middle of it I was trying to figure out how I was supposed to let him go. I knew this was all coming to an end, soon, and despite the pain that had started creeping in around the edges, making it harder and harder to breathe every time I looked at him, I'd never wanted to kiss him more than I did right now.

So I did.

I put my hand on his cheek, leaned in, and sealed my lips to his. I kissed him, gently, slowly. He kissed me back, his body gradually tensing, his breaths getting heavier as he curled up off the bed to envelop me. He rolled me over, driving me into the mattress with his weight, and I let him. I wanted to be smothered by him. By the feel of his body, hot and strong against me, his smell, his taste as he kissed me until I could barely find breath.

He pulled away and I caught some air. His eyes were hooded with lust, and that sparkle was back in their dark depths. He leaned in to kiss my throat and I sighed. In that moment I would've let him do pretty much anything he wanted, no matter how much my heart would hurt later. I didn't care. We still had a week. I'd take what I could get.

"How about some good old missionary sex," he murmured in my ear. "I hear it's your favorite position."

I laughed as he nuzzled into my neck, but whispered back, "I'm not sure it is anymore."

"No?" He lifted up to look in my eyes, intrigued.

"Well... it's got competition, anyway." It was true. As much as I loved Jesse on top of me, pinning me down as he fucked me until I saw stars, I'd come to appreciate various other positions. Especially...

"Show me," he said, his teeth dragging over his lip.

I put my hands on his shoulders and pushed him back; he went easily, letting me take the lead. In seconds I had him on his back, pinned beneath me, straddled by my thighs. "I'd say this position has its advantages." I reached between my legs and grabbed his hard cock, giving him a long, tight stroke.

He groaned and dropped his head back into the pillows. "Such as?"

"Mmm... killer view," I murmured, leaning down to kiss him. I watched his gorgeous eyes roll closed as I lowered myself onto his cock, taking him inside me in one long, slow thrust.

I was still watching him moments later when his mouth dropped open. His eyes opened, locking on me. I rode him, so slowly at first that it was sweet torture, and gradually faster, harder. I was still watching him when his breath caught, his hands gripping my hips and squeezing me, hard, as he came inside me.

I leaned in and kissed him again, melting against him. Then he flipped us over and went down on me, his unhurried tongue bringing me slowly to orgasm. I was still watching him when I came, my hands buried in his dark hair, with the words running through my head that I wouldn't let leave my lips.

I love you.

I so fucking love you.

He was still watching me, too.

And if this wasn't real, if none of this was real, it was going to shred me to pieces.

"You have the same tattoo," I whispered, not even sure if Jesse was still awake.

I was curled against him in the dark, my heart still beating faster than normal. I hadn't yet fully come down from the thrill of getting fucked up against the wall, my legs wrapped around Jesse's hips, gravity driving me down on his cock... because apparently, when I'd come on his tongue it turned him into a horny beast in need of another round.

He stirred, his fingers coiling in my hair, breath fanning on my neck. "Hmm?"

"Your tattoo." I skimmed my fingers over the figure on his

wrist. "Jessa has the same one, on her ankle. It's a lot smaller, but I saw it at the club."

"Mmm," he murmured. "Got them when Mom died."

My fingers stilled. Then I traced the long lines of the wings that I was pretty sure belonged to a kick-ass, rock 'n' roll angel. *Shit*. I didn't even know what to say.

There was so much about him, about his life, that I didn't know. So much I still wanted to learn.

"Why didn't you just tell me you were going to meet up with her?"

I waited for the warm plume of his breath on my throat but it didn't come. Finally, he let it go on a silent sigh. "She asked me not to tell anyone."

I tightened my grip on his waist. "I don't mean to pry. But… is everything okay? You seemed upset at dinner."

"Our mom died nine years ago this week," he said. "It's always a hard time for Jessa."

Oh, man. I had no idea.

I noticed, though, that he didn't say it was a hard time for *him*.

"I'm so sorry," I whispered. He didn't say anything, so I ventured on. "Your mom sounds like a really strong woman. She raised you alone, right?" I looked at him but I could barely make out his face. He seemed to be staring straight up at the dark void of the ceiling. "Dolly mentioned it."

He didn't respond. I started to wonder if he'd heard me, even though it was dead quiet in the room. I didn't really know if he was here with me, or somewhere else.

"Yeah," he finally said, rubbing his hand over his face. "Without Dolly I don't know where we'd be. When Mom got really sick Jessa pretty much lived with her."

"Do you want to talk about it?" I offered. "About your mom?" Maybe this wasn't the kind of conversational territory a fake girlfriend ventured into, but fuck it.

I was more than just his fake girlfriend or his employee, even if he didn't see it. I, Katie Bloom, was the girl who loved him.

Hell, maybe I was one of many girls who loved him, for all I knew. But I did love him. And maybe it was a bad idea to keep digging for reasons to love him even more, but it wasn't wrong to be compassionate when he was hurting. I couldn't stand to just pretend that he wasn't.

"Not much to tell," he said. "After our dad left, she was always working to try to give us a better life than the one she got. She loved us but we never really knew her. She never let anyone get close after what happened with my dad."

"Sounds like she had a hard life," I said softly.

"Sometimes I think she kept us at a distance because she couldn't stand getting hurt again. She never figured out how to trust anyone again or find someone else she could love."

The way he spoke about her... the words so sad, yet his tone so detached. And after what he'd said about breaking hearts, it made me wonder...

"You're not like her, you know." I leaned up on my elbow to look at his face, though I could still barely see him. "You're not like your mom. Afraid to let anyone in. If that's what you're afraid of; turning into her. You're not her."

Even though I couldn't see his eyes I felt the subtle shift as he looked away. "I'm not afraid of turning into my mom, Katie." He sighed again, and I could feel his pain crackling in that tight breath. "I'm afraid of Jessa turning into our dad. He killed himself when I was nine."

CHAPTER THIRTY-THREE

Jesse

I WAS out of bed on the razor's edge of dawn. It was a cool morning so I put on a hoodie and went for a run alone. Jude wouldn't like it, but I needed some time to think. I'd been doing too much of that lately, probably, but it was harder than fuck to climb up out of this place once I was all down in it.

I hated feeling powerless, but every time I spoke with my sister, that's exactly how I felt.

My conversation with Jessa last night kept rolling through my head; pretty much the same as every other conversation we'd had in the past nine years.

Before the tour, I'd managed to get some time with her while I was in L.A., and she'd seemed better than she had in a long time. More like her old self.

Then just when things seemed to be going well, like always, she withdrew.

Disappeared.

And as always, I'd skirted around the issue when I saw her last night, afraid if I confronted her about it directly she'd bail and disappear even longer.

I was pretty much running out of shit to say to her. I hated

sounding like a nagging broken record. Brody was probably right.
Maybe I should talk to a therapist or something and they could
help me figure out how to get through to her. Because what I'd
been doing for the past nine years wasn't fucking working.

She still refused to commit to anything.

She still refused to stay in one place longer than a month.

She still refused to come home.

The only thing I was totally sure of was that I had no idea how
to talk to her, about any of it. She just kept pretending that everything was fine, and when I pressed, she pulled away.

It was fucking impossible.

I was still going over it in the shower and afterward, over
breakfast with Katie. At least she seemed to be doing better than
she was yesterday when she showed up at the restaurant, but she
still looked tired and on edge, like she hadn't gotten a good sleep
in a week. Which would make two of us.

She was her usual sweet self, but kind of preoccupied, texting
with Devi. She tried to bring up what we talked about last night,
asking if there was anything she could do to help, but by now I
was so wrung out over all of it I just downplayed the whole thing.

"It's probably not as bad as I made it sound," I said. "I've just
always felt responsible for her, you know?"

"But you don't think she's happy." She studied me with her
keen blue-greens, her brows pinched together and her pink mouth
in a thoughtful pout.

I shrugged and stuffed my mouth with eggs, and when she
tried to press the issue, to gently get me to open up, I mumbled
something about my imagination and started pretending to read
the paper. Like a dick.

She gave me a long, unsure look, then went back to her
phone.

"Shit. Have you seen this?"

She handed the phone to me. Her browser was open to an

article on some trashy entertainment news website, "news" being a loose term.

There were two images side-by-side at the top of the page, one of Elle and I at the show last night, and one of Katie and I, also from last night. The headline above the images read *Bizarre Love Triangle*. A larger photo below the first two showed Katie and—

I looked up at her and her eyes went huge. "It's *not* what it looks like."

What it looked like was Katie and her ex-fiancé tongue battling. They were pressed together and he was gripping her by her arms. Their mouths were locked together, eyes closed, but I recognized the red lace dress she'd worn to the VIP party in Vancouver and I knew the image was from that night. It was taken from a high angle in the corner of the otherwise empty hallway where I found them, obviously from a security cam. Which meant that either the douche himself or one of his staff had given the image to the media.

"I know it's not," I told her.

"*He* kissed *me*," she insisted. "I pulled away like a millisecond after that was taken."

I scrolled down through the brief, insubstantial article, which was more images than actual reporting, never mind that most of it was total bullshit. I didn't even bother reading all of it. The piece pitted Katie and Elle against one another in some non-existent tug-of-war over me, and included more photos of each of them at the club last night, including one of Katie in Zane's arms, his hand planted on her ass. I knew I had Zane to thank for that shitty move, and I would, but it didn't make Katie look like a saint. Especially when juxtaposed with the other images.

While I was shown outside the restaurant with my sister, Katie was shown at various clubs the last few nights, partying with my band and even Jack, her brother-in-law. In every picture she was in the arms of another guy. I happened to know all the guys and know the hugs were innocent, but the article made Katie look like some trashy party girl.

The only image that didn't paint Katie as the town slut was one of her with her brother-in-law and her niece and nephew out walking in the city during their visit. But her sister was conveniently cropped out of the photo, which was right next to another one of Katie and Jack looking cozy as they did shots together in a bar.

When I looked up again, tears were shining in Katie's eyes. I understood why it would upset her, because this was all new to her. There had been plenty of tabloid stories about Elle and I during our relationship; there still were, even though we weren't together and I'd barely seen her since the last tour ended. We were together, we weren't, we were cheating, we were fighting, we were making up. It was all bullshit meant to sell magazines or web clicks for advertisers. But Katie was new at this, and this was probably the first time she'd seen a nasty article putting a vindictive spin on her actions.

"Don't sweat it, babe." I handed the phone back to her. "They'll be onto something else tomorrow. Don't let it get to you. You know it's all bullshit."

She scrolled through the article again. "What the fuck," she whispered. She turned the phone to me, flashing the image of herself with her family. "My niece and nephew? They're just little kids. And some creeper put their picture on the internet? With pictures of their auntie looking like the slutbag from hell?"

"That's what they do."

She went scrolling through the article, pausing to shake her head at each image. "Fuck. What the *fuck*. I can't believe I did all this shit."

"Come on, Katie. You didn't do anything—"

"Yeah, obviously I did." She flashed me the image of her doing shots with her brother-in-law, her hand on his back.

"Well, when you're not expecting anyone to take your picture—"

"But I should have, right? I should've known better by now. A *lot* better." She tossed the phone down on the table. "Jack is like my brother. I've known him since I was seven." She put her face in her hands.

"Babe, it's cool. You're just taking it hard because it's been an emotional twenty-four hours."

She peered up at me, her eyes pink-rimmed, but at least no tears were falling. "Try five weeks," she whispered.

Ouch. That fucking hurt, but I didn't know what to say. I was so emotionally tapped out from dealing with Jessa. And the tour. And whatever the fuck was happening with Katie that had my guts in a vice when she looked at me that way.

"This is totally my fault," she said. "Owen and Sadie are in the press and it's my fault. This pretty much says I'm fucking their dad. Owen is *four*. Sadie's six." She stood. "Which is fucking worse, because she might see this and ask questions." She started pacing. "Oh my God. I have to call them. What if my sister's seen this? Of course she has. Devi sent it to me. She probably copied my sister." She grabbed up the phone and started tapping around. "*Fuck*."

Okay. She was freaking out.

I went over to her. "Katie. Look at me. This isn't as big a deal as you think. Really. This shit happens all the time. You need to grow a thicker skin is all. You'll get used to it." She didn't seem to be listening, still fussing with her phone, but I kept going. "It hurts at first, right? But you'll see, you get used to it. It'll just roll off. Don't let it bring you down."

She looked up at me, blinking, like she'd just realized I was still here. "I don't want to get used to this, Jesse."

"I know. I get that. But... what are you doing?"

She was tapping furiously on her phone. "I'm sending Devi on a diplomatic mission to my sister's place to tell her, in person, that I didn't fuck her husband."

"You really think your sister is going to think that? From a stupid tabloid article?"

"No," she said. "But it couldn't hurt to—oh, for fuck's sake."

"What?"

She sighed. "Devi's saying the same thing you are."

I followed her to the bedroom where she started throwing her things in her suitcase, which made my guts clench in a really fucking awful way.

"What're you doing?"

"Was it Elle?" she asked, voice shuddering as she fought back tears. "Did Elle tell them all those things about me?"

"None of that shit was even true, Katie," I said in my best soothing voice. I was shit at soothing women, case in point, my sister, who I had no fucking clue how to get through to. I just started pulling things back out of the suitcase.

"No, it wasn't true, was it?" she said, taking her clothes from my hands and stuffing them back in. "Except for one thing. You know, that thing about our relationship being fake. Oh, and that other thing about you hiring me." She pulled off the flip-flops she was wearing and crammed them into the suitcase too. "Someone must have told them about that."

Damn. The article said all that? Maybe I should've actually read it.

Katie started tossing pillows and looking behind furniture.

"It wasn't Elle," I said.

"She knows about us. Someone must've told her. She said our relationship was fake."

I watched her search beneath the table we ate our breakfast on. "Katie—"

"It *is* fake," she said. "It *is* fucking fake and none of this is worth it. None of it is worth *this*." She jabbed at the screen of her phone, then turned it to me, showing the photo of Zane's hand on her ass.

"Did something happen last night? With Zane? Did you talk to Elle? What am I missing here?"

She got down on her hands and knees and started crawling around, looking under the beds.

"If someone told her about us, I don't know who it was... What the fuck are you doing?"

"Where the hell is my sketchbook?" she cried, digging under the sheets.

"It's over here." I plucked it from the desk where she'd left it and handed it to her. I had no fucking idea why I did that, since the next thing she did was pack it, and that was the last thing I wanted her to do. But I couldn't handle seeing her lose her shit.

She went into the bathroom and started grabbing up all her cherry-vanilla-cream-smelling lotions and whatever and I just about lost it.

"Katie. Calm the fuck down." I followed her back to the bed where she smushed all her toiletries in with her clothes and jammed the suitcase shut. I'd never seen her so irrational. This was the girl who usually sealed all her little bottles of shampoo and whatever in separate Ziploc bags in case they leaked.

"Look," I said, but she wouldn't even look at me as she zipped up the suitcase. "Since I took off on your birthday to deal with Jessa and made you worry, everything's been fucked up. Things haven't been right between us."

"Things were never *right* between us, Jesse."

"I rattled your trust in me, and for that, I'm sorry."

"It's not that. It's not *you*." She looked at me with the saddest eyes I'd ever seen. "I'm truly sorry for whatever is going on with your sister, Jesse. She's so lovely. And what the two of you have been through makes my heart hurt." She rubbed her nose, still fighting back tears. I almost wished she'd just go ahead and cry; maybe then she'd sit down and stop trying to get the hell out of here. "It's not that I don't care. Really. The problem is I won't have anything left to give, to deal with anything, if I go down this road. Did you know I haven't been drawing all this week? I'm not even eating much."

"I didn't know—"

"I feel like I'm totally losing myself, Jesse. Just like I did when I was with Josh. I tried to be what he wanted and I ended up totally forgetting who I am."

"That's not what's happening," I said, though I had no idea if that was true. I'd been so consumed with worrying about Jessa the last while I hadn't even noticed if Katie wasn't eating or feeling right about things. "You're just using this as an excuse to run away," I said, though I didn't know if that was true either.

"*This* is my family," she said, finally turning to face me. "I would never use them for anything. These are *children*, being photographed by some creep with a telephoto lens while we didn't even know they were there. This is the people I love being affected by what I'm doing."

"That's what happens when you're in the spotlight, Katie. Sometimes it bleeds over onto people you care about. That's the life."

"Then it's not a life for me." She yanked her suitcase off the bed and put it on the floor at her feet. "I can't hack it, Jesse. You said if I couldn't hack it, you'd let me go."

"That was before."

"Before what?"

She stared up at me and I knew I had a chance, right now. She was giving me that chance. To say something meaningful. *Before I got to know you. Before I started to care.*

Before I figured out that I couldn't stand to lose you.

I didn't say any of those things. I didn't say anything. I just stood there, the words all clogged up in my throat.

She swallowed and nodded, seeming to file my silence away as further evidence of my stone-cold heart. "I can't be famous for fucking a rock star," she said, calmly, "and all those other guys too."

"You didn't fuck any of them, and I know that."

"But no one else does. This is out there. My *family* is out there. And who knows what it will be next."

"This hurt you. I know. But we can talk about it."

"I can't," she said, much quieter, and she wouldn't even look me in the eye as she said it. "I can't be your fake girlfriend anymore. It's just… kind of killing me."

"I don't want you to be my fake girlfriend," I managed to say, even quieter. I wasn't even sure she heard me. I wasn't even sure what I was saying, but I didn't fucking want her to go.

"I just need to figure out what the fuck I'm doing with my life and I can't do it like this." She turned and put on the shoes that were sitting beside the door.

I didn't even want to ask her what "like this" meant. My heart was freefalling into my guts.

"Katie, I don't care what the fuck you're doing. Just do it here." She looked over at me. "I can take care of you," I added lamely. I knew it was lame as soon as it was out of my mouth.

She shook her head. "I don't want to be taken care of, Jesse. I want something of my own. I can't just be the girl who's famous for being photographed making out with the famous guy. Don't you get that?"

"Then don't be that."

"Fine." She gathered up her little pink sweater and her purse.

Shit. Not what I meant.

"I'll make arrangements with Jude," she said. "Flynn can take me to the airport. Jude or Maggie or someone can help me get a flight. You don't need to worry about it. I'll be okay."

"Fuck that." I grabbed her hand to stop her as she reached for her suitcase. "What do you want? You want to draw? You want to bake? Whatever it is…"

But she was shaking her head again. Her blue-green eyes settled on me, and I knew I'd lost her. "I just want someone who cares about me," she said, so quietly.

My chest felt tight; it was getting harder to breathe by the second. Did she really not get it?

"*I* care about you."

"No, Jesse," she said. "You care about record sales."

I let her hand fall from mine. And maybe it wasn't fucking fair of me to be hurt by that, but those words cut me to the bone. "Is that what you think?"

"That was the deal, right? Six weeks to help your record sales and sell tickets? Well, the tour is sold out and you've said yourself that the album has outdone everyone's expectations. Your six weeks are almost up anyway. I'll pay you back what I owe you for the last week." She picked up her suitcase and stood there, looking small and so fucking unsure. "I'm so sorry," she said. "This isn't your fault. I should never have agreed to this. I can't just follow you around while you work and follow your dream—"

"Katie—"

"No. It's not who I am. I'm not a groupie. I'm not your wife. I'm not even your girlfriend. This is just a job. And I quit."

She headed for the door and I just stood there like an asshole. The asshole who'd gotten the bright idea to hire her in the first place. The asshole who'd promised her this was only a business deal.

And now a business deal was all I was ever going to get.

"Katie—"

"Look." She turned on me, practically pleading. "I know I've been a coward before but please understand, I just can't do this again."

"Do what again?"

She sighed and her shoulders sagged, like everything was just too fucking heavy. "What I did with Josh. I didn't know how to say goodbye. I didn't know how to end it, even though it was over. And look at it. It's still dragging around behind me wherever I go." She stepped closer. "So I'm saying goodbye."

She kissed me on the cheek. Then she looked at me, her big blue-greens bright with unshed tears.

"Goodbye, Jesse Mayes."

CHAPTER THIRTY-FOUR

Jesse

"I CAN'T DO IT, man. I've gotta fly back and make this right."

I was so fucking tired I was practically slurring. It was an ungodly early hour and I was standing in my hotel room in San Francisco in my underwear gripping my phone like a lifeline. It was seventeen hours since Katie walked out and I was falling apart. I'd barely eaten. I hadn't even slept.

At the other end of the line I heard a very tired Brody sigh. "Not today, brother," he said. "There's not enough time."

"I can fly up there and make it back for the show. There's gotta be a way."

"And then what? Even if we could make the flights work, what are you gonna do? Talk to her for an hour, turn around and fly back out to do another show? Risk getting held up at Customs and fucking over your fans? What's the point of that?"

I paced the length of the hotel room feeling like a fucking caged lion, all the things I should've said to Katie while she was here broiling in my head.

"The point is I need to see her. Right fucking now."

"We'll take care of Katie on our end. Flynn got her back safe, and he won't let her out of his sight. You do what you've gotta do out there, finish the tour, then you come home."

I held a sharp breath.

"Flynn's got this, brother. No worries."

I sat on the bed and punched my thigh. Hard. I'd never been so pissed off at myself as I was for letting Katie get on that plane.

"You care about her, give her everything you've got. Not just a slice of time between your other commitments."

"I don't know, man."

"It's only three more shows," Brody said. "Finish the tour. Then you can have all the time you need with her back home."

"Fuck, Brody. It can't be like this. Family first, remember?"

"I do remember."

"So?" I said.

"You telling me she's family?"

I didn't answer that.

"If she is, then give her all you've got. That's all I'm gonna say."

"This is me giving my all. It's taking everything I've got not to go after her right fucking now and leave you all without a fucking show tonight. Family fucking first. You know that, Brody. I told you that from the start. That if it ever came down to it, if Jessa needed me in the middle of the night, any fucking day of the week, if she called me and needed that, I was gone."

Brody was silent for a long while. So long I checked my phone to make sure the call hadn't dropped.

"Tell me," he finally said. "How many times over the years has that happened, Jessa calling you up and asking you to drop everything to come help her out?"

Brody knew the answer to that. The answer was zero.

Jessa had never once asked for my help.

I sighed, hard. "Katie thinks Elle knows, about the deal. That she put it out there."

"Elle didn't leak shit. She's not gonna say shit to anyone about you or Katie."

"I know. I told Katie that."

"Anyway, it was me."

I pressed my fingers into my eyes. I heard it; I knew what I heard. Couldn't fucking believe it. "You did what?"

"I talked to the media."

"The fuck you did."

"You want to sell music? You want to stay at the top? The fans love your music, brother, but they're fucking insatiable for this love triangle shit. Last night that live version of 'New Girl' you recorded in New York was hovering at the edge of the charts. Today it's the most downloaded song on the planet. You can thank me when you're in a better fucking mood."

"Thank you for what? Making Katie look like a whore in the press? You think that's what I want the world to think? The fans? Katie's family? Did you think about how she was gonna feel to have that out there? That I fucking paid her to be my girlfriend?"

"No one's saying that. And if they did, who would believe it?"

"Why wouldn't they?"

"Let's see, man. Because no one's going to believe that Jesse Mayes had to pay a woman to do anything. And because no one's going to buy, for a split second, that that girl isn't right where she wants to be."

"Right. Because she's sitting here right now, on my dick."

Brody got quiet in a way I knew I wasn't gonna like. "You're such an asshole, man."

"Fuck you, Brody. I don't need this shit right now."

"Anyone can see you're in love with her."

Christ.

I put my head in my hand and rubbed my eyes until I saw stars.

"Okay," he said. "Anyone but you."

"I'm hanging up."

"You told me to be ruthless," he reminded me. "Ruthless. You told me that. And yes, you told me family first. You also stood here in my living room three months ago and told me anything to make this album, this tour, a success. Any fucking thing, Jesse."

"You should have come to me."

"Did you say that to me or not?"

"I said it."

"And you meant it." It wasn't even a question.

"Yeah. I fucking meant it. You know I fucking meant it. You still should've talked to me before you went to the media."

"Maybe I would have if you hadn't pulled a disappearing act at the time I needed to talk to you. And I didn't go to them. They came to me. They asked about these rumors they got wind of that Katie was hired to work for you. They were hot to spin this whole love triangle thing and I said yes. That's all. They think she was hired as your assistant. Big fucking deal. They invented the rest."

"And now she's gone."

"She's not gone, brother. She's home. She'll be here when you get back."

"She better fucking be."

"She will."

"You're an asshole yourself, you know?"

Brody was silent.

It was rare that Brody and I argued. I remembered how Katie had described her friend Devi as her in-case-of-emergency phone call. For me, that call was Brody. The friend who'd been my rock since day one, who'd kept the crazy at bay, kept me from capsizing as I weathered the wildest, most fucked-up storms of my life.

The only person who really knew, who *really* knew, what this album meant to me.

And why.

"You know," he said, "Jude wouldn't even tell me where you went the other night in L.A.."

Fuck me.

My heart fell about two feet. Brody knew. Or at the very least, he suspected that I met up with Jessa in L.A. and didn't tell him.

"She asked me not to tell anyone, man."

"Right," he said. "Family first."

"For fuck's sake, Brody. You want me to choose between you and my sister?"

"Not asking you to choose, brother. Never asked you to choose."

Jesus. How did we get onto this? We never talked about this.

Ever.

"Right," Brody said when I didn't respond. "So maybe this is a good time to remind you why you're doing this tour in the first place. This album was your idea. Remember who you're doing it for." Then he hung up.

I stared at the phone in my hand. It was the first time in fifteen years of friendship and business partnership that Brody had ever hung up on me.

And he was right, of course. Brody was rarely wrong.

I punched the bed, because it was a better idea than punching the fucking wall, which I really wanted to do.

Then I texted Katie.

Be home in 5 days. Can we talk?

It was barely five in the morning, so I didn't expect a response. I was lucky Brody picked up, but then again, Brody would take my call any time of any night.

Fuck.

I couldn't even be pissed off at the guy. Not when he was the only one who knew what was at stake here, and the only one who cared about it as much as I did. Which was why I'd called him.

Because I also knew he was the only one who'd be able to talk me into finishing the tour.

Yeah. Just *fuck*.

I scrubbed my hand over my face. I knew I had to finish what I'd started, but I couldn't wait to be done with this fucking tour. I was already done with pretending I didn't feel for Katie what I felt.

Done pretending I didn't want her like I did.

I stared at the phone in my hand. She hadn't responded to my text.

I texted her again anyway, hoping like hell it wasn't far too little, far too late.

Miss you like hell.

It was true. I did miss her.

More than that.

I never wanted to be apart from her again.

CHAPTER THIRTY-FIVE

Katie

I'D BEEN BACK in Vancouver for almost thirty-six hours. I'd barely slept and had eaten little more than iced cherry-vanilla lattes with copious amounts of cherries—which, according to my sister, did not count as food.

Devi had met me at Nudge, where soon enough I'd be in rotation again to keep the cash rolling in. I kept telling her I was giving Jesse his money back, and she kept telling me not to be an idiot, that I'd earned every penny. I wasn't so sure. But we'd kind of given up on arguing about it. Somewhere around the hundredth time I asked her what I should do and she told me, for the hundredth time, "Talk to him," we called it a stalemate. For now.

Even I could see I was beyond reason, for the moment. I just needed to wallow a bit. And Devi could respect a good wallow. As long as it was brief.

We sat at the far end of the bar, where I hoped no one would recognize me. I had my hair pulled back and my sunglasses on just like that chick in "The Boys of Summer," a rocking cover of which was currently playing over the sound system, though I was pretty sure I didn't actually have the love of the hero in my personal story of—unrequited—summer love. I was just trying to be invisible.

Somehow it had never even occurred to me, until now, that if I was uncomfortable with the negative attention I got as Jesse Mayes' girlfriend, the attention I'd get as his ex-girlfriend could only be worse. I was trying to prepare for that eventuality, but the news had not yet dropped that I'd left the tour or that the great Canadian love story was over. Apparently Jesse's people weren't talking, and I was hardly going to be the one to break the news.

Devi kept saying I didn't need to worry about it, that she'd handle it, that we could even hire a PR person to deal with it. I couldn't even begin to wrap my head around that. I just kept replaying the last few months of my life in excruciating detail. Every thrilling, amazing, crazy-ass moment of it. Even the ones that had led some paparazzo to believe I was some kind of whore.

And all the things I'd said to Jesse when I walked out on him... those were pretty much on repeat.

I felt dazed, horrified, and emotionally wrung out.

But I was also getting mad. As fuck.

Because it hadn't exactly escaped my notice that that whole slam piece had little to stand on other than the fact that I'd kissed another guy while I was supposed to be Jesse's girl, as evidenced by the incriminating photo *someone* had leaked. Never mind that Josh was kissing *me*. According to that photo, I was guilty as sin.

And I had a pretty good idea who'd turned *that* over to the media.

"So do I go talk to him or what?" I asked Devi for at least the dozenth time.

"Hell yes, you go talk to him."

"Not *him*. I mean Josh."

Devi gave an exasperated sigh, for the dozenth time. "Fuck that. Why would you waste another second on that creep?"

"I don't know. Closure or something? Tell him to F off once and for all?"

"For what? Nothing you can say will ever get through to him. You've just got to accept that. The guy is an entitled prick and he always will be. You'd do much better leaving him in your rearview, like permanently, babe."

"I know, but—"

"Hell, no!" Devi spun around on her stool and called across the bar to my sister, who was making an espresso at the other end. "Turn this panty-peeling vagina heroin *off*."

"Dirty Like Me" had just come on, the original Dirty version. Normally I would've laughed my ass off at Devi's description of the song, which was bang on, but at the moment I was far closer to tears than laughter. I waved Becca away from the iPod dock anyway. "No. Just leave it on."

Because I *loved* this song.

It was pretty much the best of what Dirty was. Their most famous song. Their biggest hit, ever.

It was probably the last thing I needed to hear right now, but I loved it. Couldn't help loving it.

And everything I was feeling right now, this song pretty much said it all. I could barely breathe while I listened to it, each word, each grinding chord from Jesse's guitar chafing at my heart.

It wasn't a love song, exactly, or a breakup song, or a make out song, but some kind of blood and gut and soul-fueled synthesis of all three. A kind of musical hate fuck wrapped in the sweetest love letter.

Flaying flesh and bone to reveal the raw underbelly of lust, need, and marrow-deep desire for acceptance. That's what one reviewer had wrote about it, and the words had stuck with me.

Another called it *The anthem of the done-wrong.*

And they were both right. Because deep beneath that underbelly of lust, need, and desire was an anguish so soul-splitting it set my hairs on end.

As I listened to the song, it felt like my heart was gaping open, raw and aching, for everyone to see. Like a wound that had never been allowed to heal because each time it started, I picked at it, just enough to make it bleed... all over again.

I only realized I was crying when the tears dripped off my cheeks, my eyes so flooded I couldn't see Devi right in front of me. "Oh, hon," she said, just beyond the tear-blur. "We've got to turn this off."

"No," I managed, as I wiped the tears away. Thank God for the sunglasses. "Just let it play."

I was kind of in shock, it had been so long since I'd cried.

Over two years.

And now, the tears I'd been holding back since that awful day standing at the altar, alone, were finally pouring out. I'd never cried over it. Not that day, not any day since.

Not once.

And if I thought it hurt when Josh left me, that was nothing compared to this.

This was heartbreak in slow motion.

Why did I think I could just walk away? Like that would make it better? Like I could somehow magically avoid getting hurt, when my heart was already involved?

No. This was way too deep for that. Jesse was way too deep.

When I was with him, I wanted things I didn't think I would ever want again until he rocked his way right into my life, my bed, my heart. The man was in my head, in my blood, and under my skin.

"You were so right, Dev. I've been living my life like I can't be loved. I'm totally in love with Jesse, but I'm afraid he can't possibly love me back because I'm fundamentally unlovable or something."

Even I heard how fucked up that sounded. Because I never even gave Jesse a chance to love me. I just assumed it wasn't possible.

"Are you ever going to return his calls?" Devi asked for like the zillionth time as she glanced at my cell on the bar between us. It was vibrating and playing The Black Keys' "Girl Is On My Mind," thanks to my best friend reprogramming it while I dumped all my woes at her feet last night; her way of reminding me that Jesse probably actually *did* miss me, like his texts said, and I was being a dumbass.

"I'm telling you, Dev," I said as I ignored the phone and devoured about the dozenth maraschino straight from the jar, "from this moment forth, you run my life. *Friends* style, just like Monica did for Rachel when she realized she made bad decisions."

"First of all," Devi said, seizing the jar of cherries and sliding it out of my reach, "those things stay in your system for like seven years, just like gum and licorice."

"Urban legend. If that were true, I'd weigh like a thousand pounds, nine-tenths of it cherry gut."

"Ew." Devi wrinkled up her perfect little nose but I just shrugged. I'd spent the last five weeks on a tour bus with a bunch of men—gross humor didn't even faze me anymore. "Second, your life is not a sitcom, babe. I think that storyline lasted like half an episode. Why? Because no one's actually supposed to run your life but you. It's called free will and you're the only one who has to lie in the bed you made, so buck up and get your shit together."

"Fugh. Fine." I slurped my whipped cream and shoved my glass toward Becca. "More whip!"

My sister scowled at me but went to get the whipped cream canister.

"And *third*…" Devi said with a weird inflection in her voice. I turned to see the perfectly threaded arch of her eyebrow raise in a way that made me follow her gaze toward the door. "You can't hide forever, babe."

My heart lurched into my throat.

There was a man standing in the doorway kind of blocking out the sun, moment-of-destiny style, and while it wasn't Jesse Mayes it was a gorgeous brown-haired dude in a leather moto jacket and jeans, a cool tat on the back of his hand as he took off his sunglasses. His eyes were locked on me, because clearly he was here for only one reason.

To make me lie in that bed I'd made.

Brody headed over and I looked from Devi to my sister, who were both watching me. Becca had just topped up my glass with whip. I sighed. "I'll take it to go."

I turned to Brody in defeat. I knew he was one of Jesse's best friends, but since he was also his manager, I figured he was here to square up the business end of this deal. I'd already been paid for my weird-ass services, in full, and it was only fair that I return at least some of that money. Not to mention I'd broken my verbal contract with Jesse, so maybe there were more complicated ramifications to that.

"Am I gonna need a lawyer for this?"

"Don't think so, Katie." His eyes crinkled in a warm, friendly way. "How about I just give you a ride."

I studied him. I didn't know him well, but I was pretty sure even if Jesse was disappointed in how I ran out on him, he wouldn't send someone to totally screw me over.

"Where?"

He moved to the door and opened it for me. "Wherever you're going."

I gave Brody the address of where I'd just decided to go, then sat back in the passenger seat of his big-ass black truck and waited for him to lecture me, or grill me, or whatever the hell he'd come here to do.

He didn't say a thing. He just drove, westbound, headed for the tree-lined streets and gated mansions of Shaughnessy.

"I'm sorry for leaving the tour," I finally blurted when I couldn't take the silence any longer. "I really am. It was a mistake."

Brody looked at me sidelong, his deep blue eyes assessing me. All that look told me was that I wouldn't want to be on the wrong side of a business negotiation with the man. It was the look of a man who had the patience, the persistence and the low tolerance level for other people's bullshit that, in most situations, probably got him exactly what he set out to get.

"I mean... I think it was a mistake. It *was*. I'm pretty sure."

"Uh-huh."

"I just... I don't know. I couldn't handle it."

"Uh-huh."

"You know, all the bullshit stuff in the media. Creepy dudes with telephoto lenses taking pictures of me with my family. People taking pictures of me in clubs with their cell phones and putting them online. Watching me. Judging me. Saying all kinds of shit that wasn't even true." I glanced at him guiltily. "And some that was. But, you know, it was pretty shitty to have to read about it."

"Is that the truth? Or is that what you're telling yourself to give yourself a way out?"

Ouch. "Shit. Are you always like this?"

He laughed. "Yep. According to your boyfriend, I'm a real asshole."

The smile fell from my face. "He's not my boyfriend."

"That so?"

I looked out the window. I took a breath, then took a fortifying sip of my coffee. I focused on the blue ridge of the mountains in the distance, erupting above the downtown skyline. Even though I was smack-dab in a world of hurt, it felt good to be home. I loved Vancouver. I grew up here. Everyone I loved lived here.

Even Jesse lived here, somewhere.

I watched the city roll by and thought, *I don't even know where he lives.*

I glanced over at Brody, whose eyes were on the road.

"You knew them before they were famous, right? How did they handle it? Was it so easy for them to adapt to fame?"

"Easy?" he said. "Hell, no. We lost Seth at the end of the first tour."

Seth. I knew that was the name of Dirty's original rhythm guitarist; he played on the first album, *Love Struck*—the one that rocketed Dirty to fame.

"He couldn't handle it?"

"Well, it's fair to say Seth was already headed off the rails before the band made it big." He glanced over at me. "Drugs. But Zane almost went that way, too. In his case it was booze. He went to rehab though and stuck it out. Hasn't drank a drop in six years, but I can't say that's been easy on him, living the life he lives."

"I had no idea." My Google searches had centered so much on Jesse that I'd neglected to stalk the other band members for gossip. Definite oversight. Surely there must've been a lot of it over the years, and Brody was right—none of that could've been easy on them. Not if they were good people, like I knew Jesse was.

"They've all had their struggles with fame," Brody went on. "Maybe not as serious as all that, but... I can't say it's been easy on Jesse. Being on the road so much, away from family."

"Family. You mean his sister?"

Brody got quiet. For a long, long moment I wondered if I'd said something out of line.

"Jesse mentioned…" I said, but I didn't know quite where to go with that. Brody looked at me again, but whatever he was thinking behind those deep blue eyes, he wasn't sharing. "He mentioned he's worried about her. And I got the feeling it's been that way a while."

Finally, Brody said, "Jesse's had a lot of loss in his life, Katie. Both of his parents gone when he was young, never got to see what he'd make of himself. That still hurts, I'm sure, but Jesse's not one to talk about his pain. He writes music, gets it out that way. Which is maybe why writing with his sister is so important to him. It's a bonding thing. A chance to get to know her better."

I stared at him. "Jesse writes music with his sister?"

Brody glanced over at me. "She's a fantastic lyricist. She co-wrote most of the songs on *Sunday Morning*."

Okay. Totally new information. "How long have they been writing together?"

"Used to do it all the time when we were kids. But this is the first time she's written with him since *Love Struck*."

My jaw dropped a little. "She wrote with Dirty?"

"Fucking right. That album still outsells all of their other albums combined. It's a fan favorite. Jesse's favorite too." Brody looked over at me. "Or it was, until this one. Jesse's always said the songs she co-wrote are the best Dirty ever recorded. Got that same feeling on this new album."

"I had no idea."

"I guess there's a lot you don't know. Maybe you should stick around, find out some more."

I ignored that, because I wasn't about to be swayed to stick around for anything, by anyone, other than Jesse himself, and he wasn't here telling me these things. "Why didn't she keep writing with Dirty?"

Brody shrugged. "Wanted to go off and do her own thing, not tour the world on her brother's fame. Wanted something of her own."

Something of her own.

Shit.

That was the same thing I told Jesse I wanted when I left him in L.A..

I'd promised to call him when I landed to let him know I got home safe, but I didn't. I'd been avoiding him, ignoring his calls. And I could picture perfectly the look on his face during all those phone calls with his sister, that look I now knew to be deep worry.

Was I making him feel that way now?

God. To think I'd kicked him right where it hurt… It was kind of unforgivable. I didn't even think I could blame him if he couldn't forgive me for it.

"I know it wasn't cool of me to leave him like I did," I said quietly.

"He cares about you, Katie," was all Brody said in return.

"He wanted me to help him sell music. That's all," I said, feeling kind of desperate to still believe it, because then maybe I wasn't such a total ass. "I did that. As much as I felt I could."

Brody looked at me like I was dead crazy. "That's all you think this was?"

I didn't know. I just didn't know anymore.

But if Jesse wanted anything more from me than that, why hadn't he told me so?

So far, he hadn't even told me he wanted me to be his girlfriend for real. Or stick around two seconds longer than the end of the tour.

"Then why did he hire me in the first place, Brody? He said he needed me because 'together, we sell.' He said he needed help staying in the minds of the fans, that this album had to be a success or the record company wouldn't let him do another solo album."

"That's true, but Jesse doesn't need more money or more fame, Katie. He just wants to keep bringing Jessa's lyrics to the world. That's what this album was about."

Shit. I didn't fucking know.

I mean, it's not like he told me.

I had no idea all of this was for his sister. To try to help her?

"So he wants this album to be a success… so he can make more music with her?"

"He's hoping it will convince her to come home and write with him again full-time." Brody glanced over at me. "He's afraid if we can't get her back for the music, we'll never get her back."

I noticed this time he said *we*.

"Do you think she'll come back?"

"No," he said, and my heart kind of fell at his bluntness, at the thought that Jesse wasn't going to get what he'd hoped for. "It's not like we don't all hope… but the girl's been gone a long time. She changed when Dirty left on their first tour. Jesse's always blamed himself for that."

"But couldn't you guys just pay for her to come home? Maybe she could take a break from modeling or something?"

"Jessa Mayes doesn't need money from big brother," Brody said. "And she wouldn't take it anyway. She doesn't even accept royalties for the songs. It all just goes into a trust account."

"Why?"

"She says she wants to make her own way. Incredibly stubborn on that point." He gave me a meaningful look.

"I get it," I said. "But I'm not Jesse's sister. I'm not family. I'm not even his girlfriend."

"Maybe that's how it started five weeks ago," he said, "but things can change, Katie."

Yeah. Things could really fucking change.

We were getting closer to the very familiar mega-mansion where I knew I'd find Josh. Even though I hadn't been there in over two years, I knew there was no way he would ever miss Sunday brunch at his parents' house. And I'd been so sure, when I got into Brody's truck, that I had to talk to him. To face him once and for all, to tell him I was over him and that he needed to let me go. No more showing up uninvited in my life. No giving photos of us to the media. No more *us*.

I'd thought it would be the bravest thing I could do to face him, but I was wrong.

It would be truly brave to take a chance on loving someone again—and give him a chance to love me back.

"Um… can we turn around? There's somewhere I need to go."

Brody looked at me, curiosity piqued. "Yeah?"

I took a deep breath and nodded.

Finally, I knew what Jesse wanted. And if there was anything I could do to help him get it, I had to do it.

Because that's what love was, right?

"Yeah," I said. "Do you think you can take me to the airport?"

CHAPTER THIRTY-SIX

Katie

I WAS PRETTY EXCITED.

For the first time in over a week, maybe *weeks*, I felt like I was doing the right thing. I was taking control of my life. I was honoring Katie and what Katie needed. Thanks to Brody, I now knew what Jesse wanted, though I still had no idea what he wanted with *me*. That just didn't matter anymore. Because it was time for me to grab my life by the balls.

I was going to show Jesse Mayes how much I loved him.

And if he got what he set out to get when he first asked me to come on tour, and he still wanted me by his side, I would know he loved me back.

I just had to get Jessa to come home.

I didn't know how I was going to do it, but since Jesse *was* a guy, and Brody said he didn't like to talk about his pain, I figured I could safely assume that he'd probably never actually *told* his sister how worried he was about her. And Jessa and I seemed to have rapport. I mean, we table danced for fuck's sake. Some good old-fashioned girl talk could probably go a long way.

My gusto lasted all the way to L.A. and most of the way

through my perfectly enjoyable dinner with Jesse's sister. The dinner I was about to ruin, though that part was kind of inevitable.

Somewhere in the middle of dessert, it sputtered to an awkward death over the raspberry sorbet, during my clumsy explanation about why I was here. When I eventually ran out of words, Jessa Mayes just stared at me.

And stared some more.

"You mean, you flew here *today*? Just to see me?"

She sat across from me, tall and poised, her broad shoulders at an angle, one eyebrow cocked in a disbelieving look. She was just as beautiful as I remembered, but that thing I'd noticed the last time we met was more pronounced today; that flatness in her eyes, that lack of a spark.

I tried again, awkwardly, to explain what Jesse had told me. All except the suicide part.

It had all seemed so earnest when he'd said it, and so clear when I'd gone over it in my head. But coming out of my mouth, it just sounded wrong.

"I just thought maybe I could help. You know, to explain…"

"And you flew here? Today?" Jessa seemed stuck on that one detail more than any other.

And I just kept trying to steer her back to the point. "Well, he's worried about you. I don't know if he's come right out and told you that, or if he ever would. But he is worried. And I think he has reasons for that. If that's not overstepping for me to say so."

Jessa set down her spoon, like she'd lost what was left of her appetite. "I didn't know he felt that way."

"He does."

"I'm sorry for that." She waved down the waiter. "I think we're done here," she told him, and I got a sick, desperate feeling in my gut.

The waiter cleared away our dishes, but I held fast to my wine glass. I took a swig, then took a leap.

"Why do you feel dirty?"

Jessa was touching up her plum-red lipstick in a gold compact. She paused and gazed at me across the candles. "Pardon me?"

It was hard to imagine the woman seated across from me feeling that way; the way the lyrics sounded. But...

"'Dirty Like Me.' You wrote it, right?"

Jessa looked surprised. She sat back in her chair, closing her compact with a snap and stuffing the makeup back in her purse. She held my gaze, but I could feel the wall going up. I was losing her, fast.

"I did," she said. "The lyrics, anyway. Jesse and Seth wrote the music."

"So why do you feel dirty? That's what the song's about, right?"

Jessa glanced around the room, then returned her gaze to me. "Is that what it's about?" she said. I really couldn't get a lock on her. Was she upset? Indifferent?

"I think so. That... and, I think, feeling beautiful. And power-ful. And scared. And small. To tell you the truth, I just thought it was a raunchy rock song. But the first time I really listened to the words, it fucking gutted me."

She looked like she could almost smile at that, but she didn't. "Most people just think it's sexy."

"Sure. If by sexy you mean devastating, annihilating, soul-fucking-obliterating..."

The waiter came with the bill, and Jessa took it before I could react. "It's on me. I'll have to get going once they run my card. I've got a shoot early tomorrow."

"Jessa—"

"I'm sorry, Katie. I really am. I appreciate that you flew all the way here to talk to me, and that you did it out of love for my brother."

"I—"

"I can see what this means to you. And now, thanks to your kind words, I can see what it means to him. And I'll talk to him, I promise. He needs to know it means a lot to me, what he's trying to do. But it won't change anything."

When we stood outside, moments later, I tried again.

"Jessa—"

"It's alright, Katie. There's nothing more anyone can say to change the fact. Not you. Not my brother. I love him. I love you for trying." With that, she took me gently by the shoulders, leaned in and pressed a kiss to my cheek that left me cold. Then she held me out at arm's length and said, "I'm not coming back."

It was possibly the most depressing conversation I'd ever had. I just couldn't figure out why.

As much as I'd wanted to bring her home, I realized that I'd also wanted to help. But I was so set on this being the way I got to Jesse that I had no idea if I'd helped or harmed. I had a sinking feeling in my gut, and for a moment, standing there on the curb watching Jessa walk away, I had a small taste of what Jesse must be feeling.

He was right. There was something desperately wrong with his sister.

I could see it. No, I could *feel* it.

I just had no idea what it was.

The valet pulled up with the car and Flynn got my door; Brody had insisted I have security in L.A.. "Any more stops, Katie?" he asked, once we were settled.

Right about now, I felt utterly defeated.

So what the hell was one more blow?

"That depends," I said. "Can you get me to Elle?"

Apparently, he could.

He encouraged me to call ahead, and when I told him I didn't have her number, he suggested I get it from Jesse. When I made it clear that wasn't going to happen, he drove me to a tree-lined street in the Hollywood Hills where soaring gates stood at the end of every drive and I saw not a single person.

Flynn parked on the street and got out, walked up to the end of the nearest drive, to the security box, and pressed the ringer. I saw him speaking, but couldn't hear what was said. He then strolled back to the car and opened my door for me. "Go on in."

I stepped out of the car just as the gate opened. I scooted up the drive, hearing the gate shut behind me, wondering if Elle was watching me on a security cam somewhere. I glanced back to see Flynn lounging against the car, ankles crossed, lighting a cigarette and watching me go.

No doubt he'd be on his phone the second I was out of eyesight, reporting to Jude or Jesse or both.

The house appeared through the trees, this beautiful Spanish-looking stucco thing with rounded corners and a huge double door of dark wood. A luxury SUV with tinted windows and a Ramones bumper sticker was parked in the drive. Before I could knock, the front door cracked, then swung open about two feet and stopped.

Elle stood there in the opening, staring at me.

First thing I noticed: she was shorter than she seemed at the club. She was probably wearing heels then. Now she was barefoot and just an inch or two taller than me.

She wore white skinny jeans with a floral pattern embroidered up the sides, and a small cream-colored crochet halter over her tan torso, a gold string bikini top beneath. Her long white-blonde hair was pulled back from her face in several chunky braids, the braids and her loose hair all side-swept into a messy ponytail that hung over one shoulder. Without a trace of makeup she was beautiful, her clear steel eyes regarding me. And she wore glasses. Small rectangular frames, thin and a gunmetal color that went with her eyes.

I was glad I'd worn my sexiest jeans and a flattering ruffled strapless top; I'd dressed for dinner with a supermodel, which, as it turned out, was also the way to dress to face one's fake boyfriend's ex-girlfriend.

Elle tipped her head to the side, throwing a glance at the empty drive behind me, then fixed her gaze on me again. "Where's Jesse?"

"On the road," I said. Then I took a breath and said what I'd come to say. "It wasn't real."

"Excuse me?"

"Our relationship. You were right. It wasn't real. But… then I think maybe it was. Kind of." I hesitated. "Now… I don't know. I don't know what it is."

Elle crossed her tanned arms. "I see."

I had no idea what I was reading in those steel-gray eyes. "I just thought you should know the truth. And that's the truth of it."

Elle stared at me. "I know Jesse, hon," she said. "I've seen him with a lot of women. Saw him waking up next to me. Saw him with you, too. If what you had was real, I'd know it. If it wasn't real, I'd know it. Either way, you don't need to come to my house to tell me."

"I just thought you should hear it from someone, face-to-face, instead of the way you did," I told her. "I've seen the things they've been saying in the media, and you should know that it's not true. You weren't replaced overnight. There was no overlap, and you deserve to know that. I never meant for you to be publicly embarrassed over the whole thing."

Elle stared at me some more, then did the last thing I expected. She laughed. A short, humorless sort of laugh. "Honey," she said, "if I can't handle a little public embarrassment, I'm in the wrong game."

"Oh." Well that had to be true. And maybe that should've occurred to me before now. But it still didn't mean she deserved what she'd got. The media had been merciless, like vultures picking over the scraps of the breakup, sniffing for dirt. Rubbing all those shots of Jesse and me making out in her face. It hadn't seemed that way to me at the time, because I liked seeing pictures of myself with Jesse. I just hadn't thought about how it would feel for *her* to see them.

She studied me, then uncrossed her arms and drew the door open a little farther. "You want some chili?"

"Um. What?"

"Just made some." She stepped back, swinging the door wide, inviting me in.

Even though I'd already had dinner, I was tempted. I stepped over the threshold, and after Elle shut the door, I followed her deeper into the house. Once my eyes adjusted, the art on the walls snagged my attention. There was tribal art everywhere, pieces she'd obviously collected all over the globe.

We passed a room lined with guitars and big plush pillows on the floor. She had a massive black-and-white painting of Jimi Hendrix on one wall in the living room, which had a vinyl collection to rival my own. I recognized many of the spines and it was safe to say she had incredible taste in music; Bob Marley was playing over a surround sound system.

She also had two incredibly hot men in her kitchen.

Could this chick be any cooler?

Dylan was sitting on a bar stool at the island and Ash, wearing a frilly apron, was pulling a pan of something that smelled amazing out of the oven when we walked in.

"Katie!" Dylan stood and pulled me into a rib-crushing hug, which I was grateful for. It was a relief to see a friendly face. Not that Elle had been unfriendly, exactly, but at least now I knew she wasn't planning to hack me up and put me in her freezer. Not with witnesses.

"Where's that bony fucker of a boyfriend of yours?" Ash greeted me, giving me a hug as well. Which was funny, since bony wasn't a word I'd use to describe Jesse Mayes. Though Dylan did overshadow him by several inches and probably fifty pounds.

"He's playing in Portland tonight." I glanced at Elle. She was cutting into the pan Ash had pulled from the oven.

"You want some jalapeno corn bread?" she asked me.

"It's Elle's grandma's patented recipe," Ash said. "And we've got margaritas."

"I'll pass on the margaritas, thanks." I took a stool next to Dylan. "I'm still sweating off the last batch you served me. And I just had dinner, actually. But I'd love to taste the corn bread."

I hung out with the three of them while they ate chili and talked about some side project Dylan was working on. Apparently he was going to be an underwear model. Which made a lot of sense. I'd seen the man in a kilt.

When they were done with the chili, the guys refilled their margaritas and made themselves scarce. Maybe Elle told them to go; I didn't know. But when we were alone in the kitchen, she said, "He ended it." She looked at me with a cool, level gaze. "Knowing Jesse, he probably let you believe our breakup was mutual, out of respect for me. It wasn't mutual. He knew we weren't right, he ended it. I didn't see it, not then. I get it now. Took a while for me to get to that place. I'm there now. That's all you need to know."

I digested that.

I appreciated her honesty. And that she thought enough of me to tell me. Not to mention the courage it took to admit that, aloud, to me.

But when I looked into her steely eyes, I remembered our confrontation in the washroom, only days ago, and I had to wonder if she *was* being honest. Fully honest. If she'd really gotten to that place... or was still getting there.

"Okay," I said. There didn't seem to be anything more to say, though it felt like there was something left undone. I just didn't know quite what it was.

I could tell, as I'd sat here in Elle's home enjoying her hospitality, that she wasn't keen to have me here. And I couldn't blame her for that. Even so, she was a perfect hostess, which just reminded me that she was a seasoned pro at all of this, and I was still so fresh. So unsure. For all I knew she felt like the enemy had landed, unannounced, in her kitchen, but she played it like it was second nature to her to treat Jesse's new girlfriend with nothing but respect.

Surely she'd been through it all with him. The fame, the media, the women. And Katie Bloom wasn't about to make her sweat.

I could probably learn a thing or two from this woman. Though I kinda doubted she'd be letting me in on the secrets behind her steel-gray eyes anytime soon.

I didn't want to outwear my tenuous welcome, so it was probably time I get a move on. Before I did, I excused myself to use the guest washroom, where I checked my phone, which had buzzed while I was eating my corn bread.

It was Jesse.

What r u doing?

Clearly, he'd heard from Flynn.

I'd texted Jesse to let him know I was in L.A., but not why I was here. Other than that, I hadn't been in communication with him, since it was harder to obsess over everything I'd done wrong and what I was going to do to make it right when I was obsessing over what I should say in reply to his texts. I couldn't even think about getting him on the phone. But it seemed unfair to leave him hanging in this instance.

Eating corn bread, I replied. Then I added, *In Elle's kitchen.*

I waited, a good four minutes, for his response. During that time, I pictured him pacing, running his hands through his thick, dark hair, maybe rubbing the back of his neck, eyebrows drawn together in thought.

God... I *so* missed him. Brooding and all.

My phone buzzed.

When r u flying home?

Tomorrow, I think, I texted. *If your ex-girlfriend lets me out of here alive.* And then, just in case that joke didn't land, I added a winky face.

What r u doing, Katie?

I answered, *Just something I need to do.*

Then do it and come home to me.

Jesus.

The man had me reeling.

Those were not the words of a man who didn't care. I was pretty sure of that.

See you when you get there, I texted. Because I'd probably reach Vancouver before he did.

When I emerged from the bathroom, Elle was waiting in the kitchen. "I should get going," I said, and as she walked me to her front door, Jesse's words repeated in my head.

... come home to me.

Words that made me feel warm, and nervous at the same time. Because Jessa's words were in there too.

I'm not coming home.

I turned to Elle, determined to make the most of this moment and not fuck it up. Because who knew if I would ever get another?

I didn't exactly expect another dinner invite anytime soon. It was fair to say that Jesse's ex and I were never going to be BFFs.

But that didn't mean we couldn't be civil.

"Look," I said to her. "I know you're a celebrity and all the attention, good and bad, is part of the deal. I mean, so they tell me. I'm just figuring it out myself. I can't possibly know what it's like to be you. But I do know what it's like to be left, and I know how it feels when it happens in public, and how hard it is to process when everyone's watching and saying cruel things that aren't even true. I know I didn't replace you overnight, no matter what they say. I know that you're family to Jesse, and that means he loves you. Other than that, I don't believe a thing they say. Unless I hear it from you. And whatever they say about us, about me, I hope you won't believe it either."

"Okay," she said. And that was all.

She opened the door and I hovered on the threshold. I smiled a little, but she didn't. I just hoped I hadn't made things worse by coming here, but just like after my dinner with Jessa, I wasn't sure.

"I know it's over between Jesse and me, Katie," she said, her steel eyes on mine. "But the heart needs time to heal. You know him. I'm sure you can imagine the kind of time that might take."

Um, yeah. I could imagine.

It was pretty much all I'd been imagining for weeks now.

And I could do the math.

It had been four and a half months since the end of their relationship. Before that, Jesse said there had been several months of a "prolonged breakup." My breakup with Josh had taken two years of my life, and I couldn't even imagine how I would feel if during that time his new girl had shown up at my door to eat my corn bread and wave a white flag.

I had a lot of respect for Jesse's ex-girlfriend just now.

"Thank you for the corn bread."

"You're welcome," she said. "Don't ask for the recipe."

Then she smiled at me, slightly, for the first time, and I got a glimpse of the girl behind the rock star. The girl Jesse Mayes loved like family.

And it killed me a little.

Because if this girl was family, and so many others were all but forgotten... where did that leave me?

CHAPTER THIRTY-SEVEN

Jesse

KATIE WAS SITTING on the front steps when I pulled into my driveway. When I saw her there, the tightness in my chest released. As I parked the Ferrari, I felt like I could draw my first full breath in days.

"Jesus Christ, Katie," I said, getting out of the car. "Did you know we were looking for you?"

I'd spent the last three hours driving between Nudge and Devi's office and Katie's apartment and any other fucking place they told me I might find her, around and fucking around—never mind that I was supposed to be at sound check like an hour ago—because she'd pulled a Houdini on Flynn at the airport when they landed and I was going out of my mind. If she was avoiding me this fucking hard, it didn't exactly bode well for me ever getting to talk to her again.

Thank fuck Jude had finally found her, at her parents' place.

"I'm sorry," she said, getting to her feet. She looked from me to Jude, who'd just stepped out of the house behind her. Her eyes went wide and I realized we were probably scaring her, more than she'd scared us.

I flicked my chin at Jude. "Why don't you head to the venue, man. Give Brody a hand and tell him I'll be there. Raf can cover for me 'til then."

"Sure, brother. See you, sweetheart."

"Bye."

I waited for the Bentley to pull out of the drive as I collected myself, blew out a breath between my teeth, and turned to Katie. Man, she was a fucking sight for sore eyes in her ripped jeans and little white top, her dark hair blowing loose around her shoulders.

"Hey," she said softly. "Did I just get Flynn in trouble?"

"Don't worry about Flynn. He can take care of himself."

Her eyebrows pinched together. "And I can't?"

"That's not what I meant. Shit." I raked my hand through my hair. It had been a long fucking day, a long fucking week, without her.

I walked up the steps, but she didn't meet me or rush into my arms. She just stood there, leaving a space between us. It was only a foot, but it felt like the whole fucking world.

"I got all your messages," she said. "I could've come back sooner, but Brody said it was okay to stay in L.A. a couple of days, and I felt like I really needed some time to think about everything. You know, on my own."

"Yeah," I said. Turns out I did, too. Even though I wanted her back by my side and in my bed, the time apart had given me crystal fucking clarity. It had also scared the shit out of me. What if she decided she really didn't want this? Didn't want me?

"It was my first chance to be truly alone in six weeks and—"

"Me too," I said. "Kind of hated it."

She hugged herself against the breeze coming off the water behind the house, and the corner of her pink mouth twitched in the hint of a smile. I'd missed that look. I'd missed her sweet face. I'd missed every fucking thing about her. Even the way she was always "tidying up" my things so neither of us could find them, and the way she ate food off my plate without asking if I was going to finish it, and the way she always seemed to be losing a shoe. Even the way she sang "Bohemian Rhapsody" in the shower really, really badly.

Hell, maybe especially that.

"Come inside," I said.

She followed me into the house, which was a rental. Just a place I slept when I wasn't on tour or wherever. I wouldn't exactly call it a home.

A home had people in it.

Though it smelled pretty homey at the moment, thanks to the giant tray of cookies on the kitchen counter.

I raised an eyebrow at Katie.

"Did some baking with my mom," she said, a little pink in her cheeks. "Helps me chill out."

I led her to the living room at the back of the house, which overlooked False Creek. Katie drifted around the room, taking in the floor-to-ceiling windows and the epic view.

"You want a drink?"

"No, thanks." My heart dropped, because I knew what was coming. "I don't think I'll stay long."

"Katie—"

"I think I just need some time to process things. In my own bed."

Wasn't that what she'd just had?

"I mean, I've barely even gotten to see my dog, and my place is kind of a mess..."

"Katie, I'm so fucking sorry for what happened in L.A.. Those pictures of you with your niece and nephew. I know that freaked you the fuck out. And I'm sorry it happened."

"It's okay," she said, stepping a little closer. I wanted to reach out and grab her, pull her to me and never let her go. But she was hovering there in the middle of the room like some frightened doe. I was scared she'd run away if I moved too fast.

"It's not okay."

"No," she agreed. "But it's not your fault, either."

"It sure as fuck isn't your fault."

"Well, if it's anyone's fault, it's the paparazzi guy who stalked me, took the photos and sold them, and the media agency that put them out there. But that's life, right?"

But it wasn't *her* life. Not until she met me.

"Katie. I know it upset you. I know that. And I understand why—"

"It wasn't just what happened with my niece and nephew," she said, coming closer. "You were right. I used that as an excuse. I used them, and I feel like the worst coward in the world."

"Katie, you don't have to—"

"Please. I need to say this. It wasn't the thing about me being paid to come on tour with you. It wasn't even the thing about our relationship not being real. It wasn't all the pictures of me with your friends either, and being called a 'party girl' like they were slut-shaming me."

"You're not a slut," I said. "I've known sluts. Zane is a slut." It was my attempt to lighten the mood.

No dice.

She looked at me and tears gleamed in her eyes. She looked so small, just kind of floating there in the middle of the room, and fragile in a way I'd never seen her look, and I really didn't fucking like it. I took a step closer, meaning to take her in my arms.

"It was the photo of me and Josh."

I stopped just short of touching her.

"I just saw the look on my face in that photo," she said, "and I remembered how it felt when he kissed me. And there it was, staring me in the face, and worse, it was out there for all the world to see."

"What was?"

"It's hard to explain. I was so confused, Jesse. When he kissed me, I shouldn't have felt anything but anger, or disgust or annoyance. And I did feel those things." She looked at me, and it cracked my heart a little, the uncertainty and the disappointment on her face. "I felt *confused*. It was like everything we'd had was in that kiss. All the questions and memories and the good times and all the shit, five years of our lives, all rolled up in one kiss, and I felt sad. And sorry for him. And flattered, which is truly pathetic. And kind of glad." She sniffled. "Glad that he wanted me again."

"Babe, you have history. And he broke your heart."

"I didn't want him to break my heart."

"No one wants a broken heart, sweetheart."

"I mean, I wished that I'd never given him that power. I know I pretend I'm over it, but I think I still hate him because it makes it easier to pretend he didn't hurt me. That he wasn't ever someone who amazed me and thrilled me and put a smile on my face. That he wasn't ever the man of my dreams. Or at least, the man I thought was the man of my dreams."

I knew I had to tell her then. Tell her the truth about Josh. But I hesitated. I could stand the kick in the stomach of jealousy when she talked about him like that, but I couldn't take her suffering thinking he was such a good guy.

"Babe, Josh was the one who gave that image to the press."

She nodded. "I know."

Damn. Didn't expect that. Why she wasn't more pissed off about it, I wasn't sure. But maybe it was a good sign. A sign that she was finally putting it to rest. "Then you know that he wanted you to see it. He wanted me to see it. He wanted you to feel everything you're feeling right now."

It was true. The guy was still trying to fuck with her. And I could send Jude to take care of that. That part wasn't a problem.

The problem was how it was making Katie feel, which was like shit, apparently.

I moved closer, until we were inches apart. I wanted to touch her so fucking bad.

I didn't know if she wanted me to touch her.

"When things like this happen," I told her, "it's often the people around you that you need to look at. It's not always the paparazzi. It's people who have access, and a motive beyond just making a quick buck." I smoothed her hair out of her eye and let my fingers trail down her cheek. "Most of the time the things they say about you, the ones that really hurt, are the ones that are true."

She peered up at me, looking defeated. "So what do you do about it?"

"You keep good people around you and you live your life. And you don't apologize to anyone for being who you are."

"That's it?"

"That's all that really matters."

She looked at me and nodded. "You're good at it," she said softly.

It didn't feel like a compliment.

She turned and walked away. She went to the windows overlooking the patio and the water below. Beyond, the downtown skyline glimmered in the lowering sun as dusk neared.

I could see her face reflected, faintly, in the glass, shimmering with the motion of the water beyond. I tried to read the look in her eyes but I couldn't, so I moved to stand behind her. I inhaled her sweet scent, deep. I put my hands on her shoulders and felt her take a deep breath.

"The thing is…" she said, "…I thought I loved Josh. I did love him, Jesse, at least some of the time we were together. And when he cut me loose, in public, it was really painful. I guess I didn't want to be a part of putting someone else through that. That's why I went to see Elle."

With every word she said, I only admired her more. She was so fucking strong and she didn't even know it. I turned her to face me. I wrapped her in my arms and lowered my head until my forehead touched hers. "You're a sweetheart, Katie Bloom."

She took a breath, maybe in surprise, maybe to say something, but I kissed her before she could. Long and deep, until my toes fucking curled. When she drew away and bit her lip, I said, "Been waiting to do that all day." Which was an understatement. Kissing her was all I'd wanted to do since she walked out in L.A..

I admired her for sticking to her principles, for fighting for who she was, even though it hurt like hell watching her walk out the door.

"Jesse." She pulled back a bit, but held onto my arms. "I'm sorry for how I left. I just needed some room to breathe, to figure out how I feel." She shook her head and let me go, taking a step away. "No, that's not true." She crossed her arms over her stomach. "I know how I feel. I know exactly how I feel. I just... I couldn't stand it any longer not knowing how *you* feel."

Right.

I pretty much got that by now, and I knew what I wanted to say. But the words didn't come fast enough and she turned away.

"You know what your friends say about you? 'Jesse's not one to talk about his pain.'"

I tried to smile. "Yeah." I rubbed at the back of my neck the way I did when I was nervous. I didn't do it much, but this girl had my guts in knots. "I guess I'm kind of an asshole that way."

"You're *not* an asshole, Jesse. Don't make jokes."

"I'm not joking. You wouldn't be the first woman to run for the hills when I wouldn't open up, Katie. I guess I'm shit at opening up."

She came closer, looking up into my face like she was searching for clues. *Shit.* Was I really that hard to read? "But you write all those songs about the most intimate things. What's the difference?"

"The difference is I write the music. Jessa and Zane and Raf write the words."

"But you sing them."

"Yeah. I sing them." I wrapped her in my arms and pulled her close. "I'm good at that." I kissed her lightly and she softened against me. Then I took a steadying breath. "Please tell me you'll come to the show tonight," I whispered.

"Jesse…"

"Katie." I held her tight so she wouldn't pull away. Then I took another breath and dug deep for the words. "I want you there with me. I hated playing those last three shows without you. It felt… wrong."

She blinked at me, her cheeks flushed, but slowly shook her head. "I told you. I can't just follow you around while you work. It's not enough for me." She stared into my eyes. "I just need you to understand. To not hate me for needing more than all the amazing things you've given me. For understanding why it's not enough."

"I do understand."

I did, to the marrow of my bones.

She wanted more, but she wasn't asking for it, either. Maybe she was afraid I'd never give it? Which was insane, because I'd give this girl the fucking world.

"It's just not who I am, Jesse. It will kill me inside, bit by bit, and I'll end up resenting you, and myself. I just…" She took a deep, fortifying breath. "I changed who I was, for Josh, and then he left me."

So that was it? She thought I was gonna use her up and spit her out, dump her by the roadside?

No fucking way.

I leaned in and whispered in her ear, "So what if you weren't just following me around?"

I couldn't hold back my grin. I was fucking dying to lay this on her. It was pretty much the business proposal I should've offered her from day one, if only I'd known about her talent.

"What do you mean?"

"I mean, what if you were working?"

"Your paid escort again? No thanks." She smiled a little and poked my chest. "Don't get me wrong. The job has its perks. But I won't respect either of us in the morning, ever again."

I laughed and Katie grinned. God, I loved that grin.

I lifted her off her feet and kissed her again. When I set her down, looking adorably flushed, I said, "What if I told you the band wants you to do our art work?"

She gave me the most twisted, skeptical look I'd ever seen on her face and blinked her blue-greens at me. Several times. "Dirty?" she said in a small voice.

"Yeah, Dirty."

"What do you mean? *Why*?"

"Why?" I shook her a little by her sweet hips. "Because your work is fucking awesome."

She stared at me.

"It would mean a big contract. Enough to keep you going, and keep you busy. We need it all. Album covers, website graphics, clothing, stage backdrops, you name it. We're talking about a total reworking of our image for our next album, which we're about to record, and the new tour. It's our tenth anniversary tour. It will mean a ton of exposure."

Katie looked dumbstruck. Awestruck. Completely *what the fuck* struck.

"But... are you sure? This is what the band wants? I mean... they're not just agreeing to this because they think I'm your girl?"

"Yes, it's what they want. We had a conference call about it while you were on the plane."

She blinked at me again. "And Elle too?"

"Yes, cherry pie. Elle too. Last I checked, she was in the band."

She shook her head, like she couldn't fucking believe it. "But... they haven't even seen my work."

"Actually," I said, "they have."

CHAPTER THIRTY-EIGHT

Katie

JESSE WOULDN'T TELL me where the fuck we were going. By the time we got there I was bouncing around in the passenger seat like a dog.

He parked us in front of a long, white two-story building in a commercial neighborhood, just a few blocks from Devi's office. The building was free-standing and took up half the block.

He let us in with a key and disabled the alarm.

Inside was a big, open room with a small kitchen built into one corner. There was a set of stairs to a loft above and a big skylight streaming light down in the center. It was clean and empty—except for my paintings, the ones I stored in Becca's basement, leaning against one wall. A few of them were propped up on easels too.

All my *unfinished* paintings. Because I never finished anything anymore.

I hadn't finished a single painting in the last two years.

I walked over and started flipping through the canvases that were leaning against the wall. They were all in here; everyone I loved, or had ever loved. My parents, my sister, my brother-in-law and the kids. Devi. Some of my other friends. The paintings, while portraits, were experiments in texture, color and emotion. No two paintings had quite the same style, but the aesthetic was always my own, something I'd been exploring before I pretty much gave up on it.

And Josh was here, too.

Even when he dumped me, I didn't have the heart to throw him out.

It really didn't matter what I painted anyway, or who, since no one ever saw it. But it mattered to me. In fact, it should've mattered *more* to me. I could see that now.

Maybe that was what Jesse was trying to show me.

There were tears in my eyes when I turned to him. "What is this?"

"It's yours, if you want it."

"What do you mean?" I was in shock again.

My whole life had suddenly become a *what the fuck* situation.

"You went to see my sister," he said. "I went to see yours."

Shit. He knew about my dinner with Jessa?

I didn't know how to feel. So many emotions fought for dominance. Embarrassment. Sorrow. Joy. More than anything, though, I was humbled. No one had ever done something like this for me before.

"We used to use it as a rehearsal space for the band, but we have a new one."

"You own this place?"

"Yeah. It's a great neighborhood."

No shit. It was an *expensive* neighborhood. "I can't let you pay for this."

"Then consider me an investor." He walked over to me and looked down at my unfinished work. "I think your work is incredible, Katie. And I think it should be seen." He turned to look at me, in all seriousness. "I think *you* should be seen. I've always felt that way." He ran his knuckle lightly along my jaw and I fought the urge to melt into a puddle right at his feet.

"Jesse…"

"You can finally have that art show you wanted to have. With your newfound infamy," he added with a little grin, "you're sure to get a crowd. And Brody is connected up the ass, babe. He can bring in real art buyers with money. We can even get someone handling PR. Your work can be famous, but every little detail of your private life doesn't have to be."

"Why? Why are you doing this?"

"Because I believe in you. And I believe in your talent." He glanced around the room. "It's a good space. And I know you like the neighborhood."

"Which is how I know how much this costs."

He ignored that. "It's close to Nudge, and Devi's office is three blocks away. You can go for coffee."

"I noticed."

He walked over to the painting I'd started the day Devi told me I'd been chosen to be in his music video. The day my life took a sharp turn. I'd gone to Becca's basement to paint and think it over, and clear my head. But I hadn't been able to clear it. Not of him. Not of the man who'd made an unforgettable impression on me from the first moment I saw his face.

"When did you paint this?" he asked.

It was a painting of Jesse, of how I'd first seen him when we met. Beautiful and abstract, something ungettable, unknowable. Or so I'd thought.

I swallowed hard. "The day I met you," I whispered. I couldn't find my voice. I felt like I was floating away, like this was all some incredible dream.

"You said you didn't know who I was when we met."

"I didn't."

He stared at me, those unreadable molasses eyes sliding over my face. I trembled, though it wasn't cold in the studio, and hugged myself.

"Katie…" he said.

We were interrupted by a knock. He went to the door and let my sister in, and Devi was right behind her. Becca smiled at me, and Jesse headed up to the loft.

What the hell was going on?

I hugged my sister and held on tight. "Katie," she whispered, "it's okay."

"I don't know, I don't know…" I just kept saying it, over and over, while she held me.

When we drew apart, she held my face in her hands, like it was small and precious to her, the way she had when we were young.

"Take the studio," she said. "There's no guilt in quitting the coffee bar. We'll survive without you, I promise."

"What about what happened? The paparazzi? It can get a lot worse than that."

"We'll be alright, Katie."

"But what are you going to do if they get harassed at school? It's hard on kids, being the center of attention, having people talk about them, say things that aren't even true."

"Well, their father's always threatening to homeschool them anyway. Or move us all to Costa Rica."

"You aren't seriously going to leave Nudge."

"I'll do whatever's right for my family. And that includes you." She put her hands on my arms and squeezed. "We'll be alright, Katie. Do this for yourself." She pulled me in for another hug. "From what I can see, he really cares about you. This is a real opportunity. Do it for your art." She glanced off toward the stairwell, where Jesse had vanished. "And for your heart."

My sister smoothed my hair off my cheek, and I loved her so much in that moment.

Then it was Devi's turn. I clung to her as she hugged me, feeling safe in the arms of the person who knew me better than anyone on the planet. When we came apart, she looked me in the eye, strong and steady, and told me the truth.

"It's time to move forward, sweetie."

After I let Becca and Devi out, I locked the door and walked around the room.

It really was the perfect space for an art studio. I could imagine all my supplies organized into the shelves along the walls. There was enough room for several easels, and to store all my work, and then some.

Hell, I could do art shows *here*.

I went upstairs, emerging from the spiral staircase into the partial loft that overlooked the studio below. Jesse was there, standing in front of the paneled windows that merged with the skylight above, fiddling with his phone. Two things struck me at once: the fact that he'd probably heard every word that had been spoken below, and the view.

"If you want to be independent, Katie, you need to have something to build your dream on," he said, stashing away his phone. "Something that's your own. This is yours. No strings attached."

"It's just that I had that before," I said, moving closer to him. "I *thought* I had that before, but there were strings. I just didn't see them until it was too late."

"No strings," he said. "I'll sell the property to you, dirt cheap. Whatever it takes so you can make it your own. You have mad talent, and it kills me to think you don't know it."

I didn't know what to say. "I mean... I think my work can be better. But that's the thing about art. It grows and evolves." I was growing, too. I had a lot of ideas for the work I wanted to do. "And I'm so out of practice... but I've kind of been dying to get back into it."

And with a place to do it, and funds to support me while I worked... it really was my dream come true.

"Don't you have a show to get to?" I asked as he came closer.

"I'll get there," he said, unconcerned. "And if this doesn't work for you, we can do it any other way."

We? I looked up at him and took a deep breath.

"It works," I said.

He nodded and rubbed the back of his neck. "And you know, with the money you just made on the tour, you can make a go of this. With or without me." He looked at me and I knew he was waiting for me to say something.

He was giving me a chance to take the money, and now the studio, and run.

As if I could ever do that.

"I'll do the contract work for Dirty. But I can't take that other money, Jesse. I'm giving it back."

"It's yours. You earned it."

"While I was having sex with you. It just feels..."

"Dirty?" His mouth curled in a small grin.

"Yeah."

"Katie, I didn't pay you to have sex with me."

"I know, but—"

"I didn't pay you to love me, either."

I stared at him, at the plain truth there on his face, wanting to refute it.

I couldn't.

"Jessa told me what you did. What you said to her in L.A.." He stepped closer, until all I could see was him. I looked up at his face. He was searching my eyes. "Why did you go see her?"

I swallowed. "Same reason I went to see Elle, I guess. I don't like someone you care about being in pain."

He didn't say anything. I still didn't always know how to read his eyes, and it killed me that I had no idea what he was thinking.

"I'm sorry if I stuck my nose in where it didn't belong. It just seemed to me that she needed to hear all those things you said to me, you know, about how much you worried for her, and—"

"Katie. I'm trying to tell you. I love you, too."

I stood there, stunned, just kind of gaping at him for a long moment. "But... I failed."

"What the hell do you mean?"

"I tried to get her to come home. She wouldn't."

"Katie. It's been years. If she won't do it for anyone else, she won't do it for you." He pulled me closer and cupped my face in his hands. "I'm fucking blown away that you tried." He kissed me softly on the lips. "What you tried to do for her," he said softly. "For me. That means everything to me." He took hold of my hands. "It's only ever been me and Jessa, you know? Us and Mom, and when she died... a lot of people stepped up. Dolly. The guys. I know Jude and Brody would kill for me. Literally. For Jessa, too. And the band, they're family to me. You know that. But I'm telling you, Katie, I've never loved anyone, ever, like I love you."

I felt the tingle in my nose, the tears pricking my eyes. Was he going to make me cry?

"I love you. I fucking love you and I should've told you that a long time ago," he said. "You're always on my mind. You're in everything I do. I could barely even get through the end of the tour without you there. It just didn't seem to matter anymore without you. Even the music wasn't the same, and the music is in my fucking soul. I just missed you, so fucking much."

"I missed you too," I managed, still in shock.

"I know I can't make you stay with me," he said. "But I can beg you not to go."

He got down on one knee in front of me and that was it; I pinched the bridge of my nose and took a shaky breath.

"Jesse. Don't you dare start begging me or I'm going to cry. And I fucking hate crying."

"Okay. Then I'll just ask. Katie Bloom, will you marry me?"

He'd taken something out of his pocket so smoothly I didn't even notice until he flipped open the small velvety box. A ring box.

Inside was a plain silver band with one tiny skull etched into it.

"I know it's not much," he said. "It was my mom's. The only thing besides us that my dad left her. And you didn't seem very keen on diamonds. But if you want something else, I'll buy you anything you want."

I looked at it, at him, my vision swimming, and drew a shaky breath.

"It's perfect."

Jesse's eyes shone up at me and he bit his lip a little. Jesus, was he going to cry now?

"You need to know," he said. "If you say yes, I'm never going to leave you. You don't have to marry me tomorrow. We can get married whenever you want. I just need to know you're mine, forever."

Then I did start to cry.

"I love you, Katie. I know you've been through shit. I know it still hurts, and it's a giant leap of faith for you to trust me. But if I'm what you want—"

"Yes! Yes, Jesse. You're what I want. You're everything I want."

"Then I'm marrying you," he told me, and he slipped the ring on my finger. It was too big. He slipped it on and off several fingers; the only one it fit was my thumb.

I laughed and wiped tears from my eyes.

"We'll get it sized," he said, and kissed the base of my thumb where it met my palm.

I cupped his face. "I don't want it sized. It's part of you. Part of your family. I'll wear it right where it fits, with pride."

"You're my family now, Katie," he said, all choked up.

"Then get up off your knees and kiss me." I tried to draw him to me, but he wrapped his arms around me and pulled me down to him instead.

We rolled on the floor and I laughed, the tears streaming down my face, tears of ridiculous ecstasy and relief. I wrapped my arms around his neck and kissed him with everything I had in my heart. When he kissed me back, the truth of it burned deep, straight to my soul; it was the first time he'd kissed me when it wasn't a ruse —or at least, when I *knew* it wasn't a ruse.

It was just Jesse. Kissing the woman he was going to marry.

He drew back and scowled at me. "Were you about to break up with me?"

"No," I said, and kissed his nose. "Couldn't break up with you. We were never together."

"That's true." He narrowed his eyes at me. "I guess I should ask you out on a date, then."

"You should."

"Come to the show tonight," he said, "and I'll take you for dinner afterward. Just the two of us."

"Okay," I said. "But only because I love you, Jesse Mayes."

He drew me out onto the roof of the studio, where across the water I could see the arena where Jesse would rock a sold-out crowd tonight. Where his new fiancée would be cheering him on from backstage.

"We may be famous," he murmured, "but there are still places where no one will find us…"

He kissed me while the sun set over the water, gold and amber and scarlet reflecting off the glass towers of downtown.

"I will always love you, Katie Bloom," he whispered in my ear.

It was the best thing anyone had ever said to me.

And it was enough to build a dream on.

EPILOGUE

Jessa

Two months later…

THE COURIER CAUGHT me just as I was leaving my apartment in New York.

I was on my way to London for a job; the cab was already waiting at the curb. I signed for the package while the doorman and the driver loaded my things into the trunk. Once I was settled into the backseat and we were on our way to JFK, I tried to relax.

It had been a rough morning.

Dirty had started writing music for the new album, and it wasn't bad enough my brother had laid an epic guilt trip on me about not being there, several times over, to the point that I'd started avoiding his calls again. I knew he meant well; he always did. But hearing that careful concern in his voice drove me up the wall. He'd been tiptoeing around me ever since Katie came to see me in L.A.. I'd talked to him about her visit, like I'd told her I would; it went well, a lot better than I feared it might, acknowledging the fact that he was worried about me. He'd never really said so out loud, and usually I just pretended it wasn't happening.

We'd been doing this dance for years.

Talking about it didn't really change anything, though. He still didn't understand. I still didn't want him to.

We still kept doing our little dance.

To make matters worse, his equally well-meaning fiancée had been sending me photos.

It started with snapshots from the band's jam sessions. Zane rocking out on the mic. Katie pretending to play Dylan's drum kit. My brother wrapped around his guitar, surrounded by scraps of paper as he worked on new songs.

She had also sent me photos of her and Jesse, hanging out with her dog or her niece and nephew at the beach. Sometimes other people were in the photos, too.

Sometimes I caught a glimpse of Brody and it hurt so bad I couldn't breathe.

Last night, I could've sworn my heart stopped beating.

Katie had sent me a text with a photo taken inside Brody's house. I recognized the party room; I hadn't been back there in six years but it was exactly the same. Some of the guys were hanging out on the couch. It was a sweet picture, and I could see why she'd sent it. It was Jesse, Zane, Jude and Brody, the four of them looking exactly like they had so many times when we were kids, relaxed and happy in one another's company, laughing at some shared joke.

Brody looked so fucking handsome it hurt. With his dark blue eyes and the deep laugh lines at the corners, his brown hair a little messed up and that smile on his face. I hadn't laid eyes on him in years. Not until Katie's photos started coming in. I really didn't need to see him at all, but it wasn't Katie's fault.

She didn't know.

I knew better, but somehow I'd let myself slip. Instead of deleting the photo like I should have, I kept it. I must've looked at it a hundred times last night, studying the haunting lines of his face.

God, he looked so happy.

And messed up as I was, I couldn't even begin to process how I felt about that.

I'd attempted to process it with several cocktails, and when that didn't work, I'd gone to a party with some friends, and woken up this morning in an apartment in Williamsburg with some hipster I could hardly remember hooking up with last night. I'd slipped out before he woke up, and on my way home, he'd texted me.

Not my one-night stand. Brody.

It was a shock to my hungover system. Not that he never messaged me, but it had been a long time. Seeing his name and number in my messaging app, I felt dirty and twisted and alone. I thought about deleting it; deleting him. Completely blocking him from ever contacting me again.

As if I could wipe what happened off the face of the Earth.

Thinking about you.

That was all he said. But Brody always managed to say just the thing to blow my life wide open.

I stared out the cab window, not really seeing a thing but his smiling face in that photo. I closed my eyes and he was there, awaiting me in the dark. I couldn't seem to erase him from my thoughts, but I knew I couldn't let myself backslide like this.

I started to get my phone out of my purse to delete the text and the photo, when the corner of the courier package caught my eye.

I'd almost forgotten about it.

I dug it out from under my purse. It was a smallish envelope, one of those stiff ones that documents came in. I noted the sender's name and address with a small smile. It was from Katie, but the address was my brother's. Had they moved in together?

She'd said they were moving in together next month, but I knew my brother was anxious to move her out of her "slum"—his word—and into his place. Katie had been taking her time packing her things and making the arrangements, and didn't seem to want to rush things. I knew all of this because Katie had been really sweet about keeping in touch with me, via email and text, even when I didn't always write her back.

Guilt gnawed at my stomach and I made a little vow to make more of an effort there. I also made a mental note to send them a housewarming gift, something cool and thoughtful from London.

I slit the courier envelope open, just hoping it wasn't photos… and because I was my own worst enemy, kind of hoping it was.

A small white envelope slipped out, embossed with a simple music note pattern.

My breath caught as I picked it up.

At a glance, it was obvious what it was. It said *Jessa Mayes* on it, in what I assumed was Katie's careful, pretty handwriting, a little heart drawn next to my name. I reminded myself to breathe and told myself to get a grip even as my heart thudded in my chest. I'd known this was happening for a while now. Katie and Jesse had called me together on Skype to tell me about the engagement.

But now it was getting real.

I turned the envelope over; it was sealed with a small silver sticker in the shape of an electric guitar. I smiled again, tears pricking my eyes, overcome with joy and a terrible, heartrending dread all at once. My fingers shook a little as I opened the envelope and pulled out the card inside.

This was all happening so fast.

And not that I didn't wish my brother every happiness and a long, loving marriage to an amazing girl like Katie, but in reality I hadn't expected him to find the right girl so suddenly. In theory, I'd had six years to prepare for this eventuality.

In reality, I wasn't prepared at all.

I opened the little card, which requested my presence at the wedding of Katherine Anne Bloom and Jesse Anderson Mayes, and I shuddered with the force of withholding my tears.

God, I was so incredibly happy for them.

And so shit-scared for me.

Katie had already told me she wanted me to be one of her bridesmaids. And chickenshit that I was, I'd told her I'd think about it.

I sniffled a little, struggling to keep my shit together, and gazed out the window. It had started to drizzle just a little. I had a long flight ahead of me, and a lot of time alone in London after the shoot. I'd never spent much time in England and I'd thought it might be fun to have some downtime to take in the sights.

Now all I saw before me was a dangerous amount of time alone with my thoughts, filled with the potential for bad decisions.

I had no idea how to process my feelings about any of this, and whenever I struggled to process my feelings... life got messy. Ugly.

Dirty.

I tried to look at things objectively.

On the one hand, I was about to gain a kick-ass sister-in-law. And if I was really lucky, a couple of adorable nieces and nephews. What's not to be thrilled about there?

On the other hand... attending my brother's wedding would mean confronting things I'd never wanted to think about again.

But it was inevitable, wasn't it? Jesse was never going to live his life alone.

He wasn't like me.

Which meant I'd just have to deal with this, somehow. There was no way I was going to skip out on my brother's wedding. Not even I could justify that.

I took a deep breath and tucked the card back into the envelope. It seemed they'd finally gotten their wish.

Like it or not... it was time for me to go home.

THANK YOU FOR READING!

Need more of Jesse and Katie's happily ever after?
Get the free *Dirty Like Me* bonus epilogue at
jainediamond.com/bonus-content

And don't miss *Dirty Like Us*,
the prequel book featuring Zane & Maggie's (secret) story!

Turn to the end of this book to read an excerpt from
Brody and Jessa's story, the next book in the Dirty series…

Dirty Like Brody

It's never too late for a second chance at true love.

ACKNOWLEDGMENTS

First of all, I'd like to thank all the bloggers who were so kind and welcoming to me when I released my first book, *DEEP*. You were both enthusiastic and brave, taking a chance on a new author, without knowing a thing about me or my work. It's book-loving ladies like you who help make this whole thing possible, and I cherish your ongoing support. A special thank you to Jennifer and Mindy at Hines & Bigham's Literary Tryst for being the very first bloggers to review, and love, *Dirty Like Me*. "I think I could read this book over and over!" Praise every author dreams of.

I'd like to acknowledge all the bands who made the music I grew up on and those I've seen play live over the years—from classic rock to heavy metal, there are just too many to name. But I could not write a rock 'n' roll book without saying a special thank you to The Police, my first ever favorite band; the genius of your lyrics inspired me at a very young age and helped spark my passion for writing.

Thank you to Guin, Chris and Marjorie, my amazingly accommodating beta readers, for reading this book so quickly and at such short notice. Thank you, Guin, for loving Jesse! Thank you, Chris, for loving Max! ;) Thank you, Marjorie, for telling me that reading my books has inspired you to turn off the TV and get back into reading... That has to be about the most awesome thing an author can hear. I love you. Thank you for always making time for me and my books.

Ah, Mr. Diamond. What can I say? You rock, and I'm pretty sure you know it. You hear it pretty much every day, but here are a few things just so you know I haven't forgotten. Thank you for pushing me (with love) to be better, in every way. Thank you for reading the first three chapters of this book, loving it, and demanding more. Thank you for wanting to hang with Katie and Jesse. (If only, right? We'd go to Nudge Coffee and share a mocha.) Thank you for introducing this rock 'n' roll girl to electronic music years ago; it was only natural that the music in our home influence the vibe in this book. Thank you for advising me on what Jesse and Jude would drive. Thank you for popping your head into the room as I'm writing this and asking, "If I make nachos, will you have some?" Um, yes. Thank you for being the best baby daddy ever to our little girl, and keeping our shit together so I can write. I heart you big time. We'll go to Hawaii again, I promise.

To my readers: THANK YOU for reading this book! I'm so honored that you chose to read this love story; my intent as a romance author is to spread love. As an independent author, I could not do what I do without you. If you've enjoyed Jesse and Katie's story, please consider leaving a review and telling your friends about this book; your support means the world to me.

With love and gratitude
from the beautiful west coast of Canada,
Jaine

PLAYLIST

Find links to the full playlist on Spotify and Apple Music here:
jainediamond.com/dirty-like-me

New — No Doubt
Sweet Emotion — Aerosmith
Start Me Up — The Rolling Stones
You Shook Me All Night Long — AC/DC
Rude Boy — Rihanna
99 Problems — Hugo
Your Touch — The Black Keys
R U Mine? — Arctic Monkeys
Black Dog — Led Zeppelin
Somebody Told Me — The Killers
I've Been Thinking — Handsome Boy Modeling School
Are You Gonna Be My Girl — Jet
Hello, I Love You — The Doors
Let Me Blow Ya Mind (feat. Gwen Stefani) — Eve
Rock n Roll — GRiZ
Suga Suga — Baby Bash
Magic Man — Heart

Electric Feel — MGMT
Can't Feel My Face — The Weeknd
Foxy Lady — The Jimi Hendrix Experience
Layla — Derek & The Dominos
Riptide — Vance Joy
Dream Weaver — Gary Wright
Next To You — The Police
Crazy Little Thing Called Love — Queen
Cowboys from Hell — Pantera
Shiver — Coldplay
Gold — Chet Faker
Lola — The Kinks
Girls Got Rhythm — AC/DC
Jessie's Girl — Rick Springfield
Gimme Sympathy — Metric
Don't Let Me Down (feat. Daya) — The Chainsmokers
The Boys of Summer — The Ataris
Girl Is on My Mind — The Black Keys
Waiting in Vain — Bob Marley & The Wailers
Let Love Rule — Lenny Kravitz
Adventure of a Lifetime — Coldplay

EXCERPT FROM DIRTY LIKE BRODY

Dirty Like Brody

*An angsty childhood-friends-to-lovers romance
featuring a broody, overprotective hero,
a heroine tortured by the mistakes of her past,
and a long overdue second chance.*

PROLOGUE

Jessa

I will never forget the first time he spoke to me.

I remember everything, right down to the music that was playing on the Discman I had tucked into the back of my jeans. (It was my brother's new Chris Cornell album, and the song was "Can't Change Me.") When the bullies started taunting me I turned it up, but I still heard what they said.

I was eight years old, and the last girl on the playground

anyone would ever guess would grow up to become a fashion model. Every day I came to school in clothes that were worn and usually a couple sizes too big for me, hand-me-downs, either from my brother or from Zane. When I wore their baggy clothes, the other kids didn't spend so much time telling me how skinny I was.

But they said other things.

I was sitting alone in the playground after school when it happened, up on top of a climbing dome; my brother and his friends called it "Thunderdome" because they'd made a game of dangling like monkeys from the bars inside and kicking the crap out of each other. The bullies were standing at the bottom of Thunderdome, so I couldn't even run away. They were big bullies. Fifth grade bullies, and while my brother, who was in seventh, would've intervened, he wasn't there.

"How come you got shit stains all over your jeans?" the dumb-looking one asked me, leaning on Thunderdome and looking bored. "Doesn't your mom do laundry?"

"You got a shit leak in those saggy diapers, dork?" the even dumber-looking one asked, and they both snorted.

"Yeah, she's so full of shit her eyes are brown."

"What's wrong, baby dork? You gonna cry?"

No. I wasn't going to cry. My brother had a lot of friends and while they were never *that* mean to me, twelve-year-old boys could be relentless. I knew how to hold my own. I'd cry later, at home, when no one could see me.

Besides... the new boy was coming over, and I definitely wasn't crying in front of him.

He was in seventh grade, but the rumor was that he was thirteen or even fourteen and had flunked a grade or two. Obviously, he was super cool. He wore an actual leather jacket, black with silver zippers, like rock stars wore. He smoked outside the school, hung out alone at the edge of the school grounds, and spent more time in the principal's office than the principal. I never knew what he did to get in trouble, but whatever it was, he did it a lot.

The other kids in my class thought he was scary. I just thought he was sad.

Ever since Dad died, I knew sad when I saw it.

The bullies saw him coming and they started getting squirrelly. I thought they'd run but he was there too fast, closing the distance with his leisurely, long-legged stride.

"You guys're so interested in shit, there's some over here I can show you, yeah?" He stood with his hands in his pockets, his posture relaxed, as the bullies started going pale.

I slipped my headphones off.

"Naw, I don't wanna—"

"Sure you do, it's right over here." He toed the ground at his feet with his sneaker. The grass was still damp from a bit of rain in the afternoon and mud squished out.

The bullies started shaking and sniveling, babbling apologies and excuses. There was a brief, almost wordless negotiation, at the end of which they ended up on their knees in front of him.

He hadn't moved. His hands were still in his pockets.

"Just have a little taste and tell me if it's fresh," he told them, in a tone that brooked no argument, squishing his foot in the muck again.

Then he looked up, his brown hair flopping over one eye, and winked at me.

I stared from my perch atop Thunderdome with unabashed, eight-year-old awe as the bullies bent forward, shuddering.

He was going to make them eat shit!

For me!

I was ninety-nine-point-nine percent sure it was just wet mud, but those bullies were scared enough to believe it. And ate it, they did.

He then told them to apologize to me, which they also did,

eyes downcast and shaking, spluttering mud. One of them was crying, snuffling through his snot and tears. Then he told them to beat it and they ran away, blubbering and tripping over their own feet.

I stared down at my savior as his unkempt hair fluttered in the breeze. He wore a Foo Fighters T-shirt under his leather jacket and his jeans were ripped, like mine. "You can go home now, you know," he said, like maybe I was slow.

I just sat there, picking dried mud from my jeans.

"Aren't your parents waiting?"

I didn't answer. I knew better than to answer questions like that.

When other kids found out what happened to Dad they either made fun of me or worse, they felt sorry for me. And Jesse said not to tell anyone Mom was sick again. He said if they knew how sick she was, they might take us away from her.

So I said, "I'm waiting for my brother."

He glanced around at the empty playground. "Who's your brother? And why isn't he here kicking those little shits up the ass?"

"Jesse," I said. "My brother is Jesse. He's in detention with Zane."

He took a step closer, teetering on the edge of the sandbox. "Yeah? How come?"

"They... um... got in an argument with Ms. Nielsen because she said I can't come to school in dirty clothes. They do that a lot," I mumbled, wishing maybe I hadn't said all that, except he looked kind of impressed about the detention thing.

He looked at my jeans; I'd gotten them muddy when I sat in a ditch to listen to music before school. I could pretend it didn't hurt me if he said something mean about it, but that didn't mean I wanted to hear it.

Why didn't he just go away?

"Well, you can come down. Those little shits aren't coming back."

I picked at the hole in the knee of my jeans, where my kneecap was poking through.

He leaned over, resting his elbows on Thunderdome. "What're you doing up there?"

"Playing Thunderdome."

I knew how stupid it sounded when no one else was there. It wasn't like I didn't have *any* friends to play with when my brother wasn't around, but they all had parents who picked them up after school. Anyway, I thought it might impress him. Thunderdome was outlawed by the teachers and we only played it after school.

He stepped into the sandbox. "How do you play?"

"It's quicksand!" I squealed. "You can't step in it!"

"Oh. Shit." He jumped up on the dome. "Almost lost a shoe." He looked up at me and his hair fell over his eye again. Blue; his eyes were a deep, dark blue. He climbed to the top of the dome and sat across from me.

Maybe he wasn't making fun of me; he just didn't know the rules of Thunderdome.

"It's okay," I told him. "You're safe up here with me. I'm the princess."

It was true; my brother and his friends always let me be the princess so I'd stay out of the way while they played, and sometimes they let me decide on the winner in case of a tie. But I figured it sounded more important if I left that out.

He pulled out a cigarette and lit it with a shiny flip-top lighter that had been scraped and dented all to hell, and started smoking. His hands were scraped too, his knuckles split and scabbed over. His fingernails were too short, chewed all down into the nail bed, his cuticles all ragged and blood-encrusted. They were a mess. But his face...

He was so... pretty.

"What happened to your hands?"

He didn't answer. Just smoked his cigarette and looked out across the school grounds, his arms wrapped around his knees, watching as parents picked their kids up in the distance, along the road in front of the school.

"A princess, huh?"

"*The* princess."

"So who's the prince, then?"

"Don't need one."

He looked at me. "Then who's gonna save you if you fall in the quicksand?"

"I will."

"What if you can't?"

"Then you can," I said. "If you want to. But you might get stuck in there, too."

He stared at me for a minute. Then he smiled, slowly, and it was like the sun coming out from behind the clouds.

"Then I guess we'll sink together." He took a couple of drags of his cigarette, his eyes squinting through the smoke. "You got a name, princess?"

"Jessa Mayes."

"Jessa Mayes," he repeated. "Don't ever let those little shits talk to you that way, yeah? Next time they try, you make a fist, like this." He showed me, clenching his fist until his split knuckles looked like they might burst. "And you hit 'em, right here, in the nose, as hard as you can. You do it hard enough, they'll go down. Then you run away. You do that once, they're not gonna bother you again."

I shook my head. "I'm not supposed to hit people. My brother says sticks and stones—"

"Yeah?" He flicked the ash off his cigarette and spat on the sand below. "Well, your brother's a pussy who doesn't know shit."

I gaped at him.

No one talked about Jesse like that. The other kids all thought he walked on water because he could play guitar.

"I can't make a fifth-grader eat crap." My face was getting hot and I looked down at the sand. "Maybe you can. I can't."

When I glanced up again, he was taking something off his jacket. He held it out to me. "Take it," he said.

I took it from his outstretched hand and examined it. It was a little silver pin shaped like a motorcycle. It said *Sinners MC* on a banner that wrapped around the tires. There was a woman on the motorcycle but she wasn't riding it, exactly. She was facing the wrong way and reclined back, her back arched, shoving her boobs out.

I was eight.

I had no idea what *Sinners MC* meant, so it never occurred to me to wonder why he had a pin that belonged to an outlaw motorcycle club.

"You wear that," he said, glancing over my shoulder, "no one's gonna mess with you." He was looking in the direction of the school, his eyes narrowing as he dragged on his cigarette.

"Smoking on school grounds *again* Mr. Mason?"

I turned to find a teacher stalking toward us, one of those shit-eating bullies in tow, red-faced, looking anywhere but at us. "What will your parents have to say about this?"

"Can't wait to find out," he muttered. His blue eyes met mine as he tossed his cigarette aside. Then he smiled at me again.

I smiled back.

He leapt to the ground, jumping over the quicksand and landing in the grass.

"See you around, princess."

I watched him shove his hands in the pockets of his jeans and walk away. But it wasn't true; I didn't see him around. He never even came back to school after that day.

Not for two whole years.

Those bullies never bothered me again, though. None of them did. And I was pretty sure it wasn't because of some pin. It was because of *him*.

Because he'd made two fifth-graders eat shit for being mean to me, and no one wanted to eat shit.

The next year, when a new girl in my class asked me about my motorcycle pin, she didn't believe me when I told her where I'd gotten it. As if I'd made up the whole thing about the badass boy in the leather jacket who saved me from a couple of bullies— then mysteriously vanished from school, never to return—just to impress her.

But I knew he was real.

I had his pin, and I had his picture. In the seventh grade class photo in the school yearbook he was standing right next to my brother, staring down the lens of the camera like he was ready to take on the world... and make it eat shit.

His name was Brody Mason.

He was the love of my life.

If only I'd figured that out a lot sooner than I did.

ABOUT THE AUTHOR

Jaine Diamond is a Top 50 Amazon US and a Top 5 international bestselling author. She writes contemporary romance featuring badass, swoon-worthy heroes endowed with massive hearts, strong heroines armed with sweetness and sass, and explosive, page-turning chemistry.

She lives on the beautiful west coast of Canada with her real-life romantic hero and daughter, where she reads, writes and makes extensive playlists for her books while binge drinking tea.

For the most up-to-date list of Jaine's **published books and reading order** please go to: jainediamond.com/books

Get the **Diamond Club Newsletter** at jainediamond.com for new release info, insider updates, giveaways and bonus content.

Join the private **readers' group** to connect with Jaine and other readers: facebook.com/groups/jainediamondsVIPs

goodreads.com/jainediamond
bookbub.com/authors/jaine-diamond
instagram.com/jainediamond
tiktok.com/@jainediamond
facebook.com/JaineDiamond

Made in the USA
Las Vegas, NV
30 March 2024